To Olga Kosakievicz

Simone de Beauvoir was born in Paris in 1908. She took a degree in philosophy at the Sorbonne in 1929, and was placed second to Jean-Paul Sartre, with whom her name was to be inextricably linked for the next fifty years. De Beauvoir taught in Marseilles and Rouen during the 1930s and in Paris during the war. After Liberation she emerged as one of the leading figures of the Existentialist movement and, with Sartre, Camus and many others, was to set the course of Left Bank intellectual life for many decades thereafter.

Simone de Beauvoir's first novel, *She Came to Stay*, was published in 1943. The book explored a woman's quest for moral and intellectual self-determination, a theme which was to run throughout all her work. Author of six novels, de Beauvoir won the prestigious Prix Goncourt in 1954 for *The Mandarins*. *The Second Sex*, her classic account of the status and nature of women, was published in 1949; hugely influential, it confirmed de Beauvoir's role as a pioneer in the development of post-war feminism. Her other writings include her four-volume autobiography, *Memoirs of a Dutiful Daughter*, *The Prime of Life*, *Force of Circumstance* and *All Said and Done*, and a moving account of her relationship with her dying mother, *A Very Easy Death*.

In her later years de Beauvoir was actively involved in many socialist and feminist causes, and in 1975 was awarded the Jerusalem Prize for 'writers who have promoted the concept of individual liberty'. She died in 1986.

By the same author

SIMONE DE BEAUVOIR

She Came to Stay

Translated by Yvonne Moyse
and Roger Senhouse

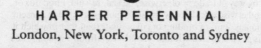

HARPER PERENNIAL
London, New York, Toronto and Sydney

Harper Perennial
An imprint of HarperCollinsPubpublisher
1 London Bridge Street
London SE1 9GF

www.heperperennial.co.uk

This edition published by Harper Perennial 2006

Previously published in paperback by Flamingo 1984 and by Fontana 1975

This translation first published jointly by Seeker & Warburg
and Lindsay Drummond 1949

First published in France by Editions Gallimard under the title *L 'Invitee* 1943

A catalogue record for this book
is available from the British Library

ISBN-13 978-0-00-720464-9
ISBN-10 0-00-720464-7

Printed by CPI Group (UK) Ltd, Croydon CR0 4YY

MIX
Paper from
responsible sources
FSC C007454

PART ONE

Chapter One

Françoise raised her eyes. Gerbert's fingers were flicking about over the keyboard of his typewriter, and he was glaring at his copy of the manuscript; he looked exhausted. Françoise herself was sleepy; but there was something intimate about her own weariness, something cosy. The black rings under Gerbert's eyes worried her, his face was haggard and tense; he almost looked his full twenty years.

'Don't you think we ought to stop?' she asked.

'No, I'm all right,' said Gerbert.

'Anyway, I've only one more scene to revise,' said Françoise.

She turned over a page. Two o'clock had struck a short time ago. Usually, at this hour, there was not a living soul left in the theatre: tonight there was life in it. The typewriter was clicking, the lamp threw a rosy glow over the papers ... 'And I am here, my heart is beating. Tonight the theatre has a heart and it is beating.'

'I like working at night,' she said.

'Yes,' said Gerbert, 'it's quiet.'

He yawned. The ashtray was filled with the stub-ends of Virginian cigarettes; two glasses and an empty bottle stood on a small table. Françoise looked at the walls of her little office: the rosy atmosphere was radiant with human warmth and light. Outside was the theatre, deprived of all human life and in darkness, with its deserted corridors circling a great hollow shell. Françoise put down her fountain pen.

'Wouldn't you like another drink?' she asked.

'I wouldn't say no,' said Gerbert.

'I'll go and get another bottle from Pierre's dressing-room.'

She went out of the office. It was not that she had any particular desire for whisky; it was the dark corridors which were the attraction. When she was not there, the smell of dust, the half-light, and their forlorn solitude did not exist for anyone; they did not exist at all. And now she was there. The red of the carpet gleamed through the darkness like a timid night-light. She exercised that power: her presence snatched things

1

from their unconsciousness; she gave them their colour, their smell. She went down one floor and pushed open the door into the auditorium. It was as if she had been entrusted with a mission: she had to bring to life this forsaken theatre now in semi-darkness. The safety-curtain was down; the walls smelt of fresh paint; the red plush seats were aligned in their rows, motionless but expectant. A moment ago they had been aware of nothing, but now she was there and their arms were outstretched. They were watching the stage hidden behind the safety-curtain: they were calling for Pierre, for the footlights and for an enraptured audience. She would have had to remain there for ever in order to perpetuate this solitude and this expectancy. But she would have had to be elsewhere as well: in the props-room, in the dressing-rooms, in the foyer; she would have had to be everywhere at the same time. She went across the proscenium and stepped up on to the stage. She opened the door to the green-room. She went on down into the yard where old stage sets lay mouldering. She alone evoked the significance of these abandoned places, of these slumbering things. She was there and they belonged to her. The world belonged to her.

She went through the small iron stage-door and out into the middle of the formal garden. The houses all round the square were sleeping. The theatre was sleeping, except for a rosy glow from a single window. She sat down on a bench. The sky was glossy black above the chestnut trees: she might well have been in the heart of some small provincial town. At this moment she did not in the least regret that Pierre was not beside her: there were some joys she could not know when he was with her; all the joys of solitude. They had been lost to her for eight years, and at times she almost felt a pang of regret on their account.

She leaned back against the hard wood of the bench. A quick step echoed on the asphalt of the pavement; a motor lorry rumbled along the avenue. There was nothing but this passing sound, the sky, the quivering foliage of the trees, and the one rose-coloured window in a black façade. There was no Françoise any longer; no one existed any longer, anywhere.

Françoise jumped to her feet. It was strange to become a woman once more, a woman who must hurry because pressing work awaits her, with the present moment but one in her life like all the others. She put her hand on the door-knob, then turned back with a qualm of conscience. This was desertion, an act of treason. The night would once more swallow the small provincial square; the rose-coloured window would gleam in vain; it would no longer shine for anyone. The sweetness of this hour would be lost for ever; so much sweetness lost to all the earth. She crossed the yard and climbed the green wood steps. She had long since given up this kind of regret. Only her own life was real. She went into Pierre's dressing-room and took the bottle of whisky from the cupboard. Then she hastened back upstairs to her office.

'Here you are, this will put new strength into us,' she said. 'How do you want it? Neat, or with water?'

'Neat,' said Gerbert.

'D'you think you'll be able to get home?'

'Oh, I'm learning to hold my whisky,' said Gerbert with dignity.

'You're learning . . . ,' said Françoise.

'When I'm rich and run my own house, I'll always keep a bottle of Vat 69 in my cupboard,' said Gerbert.

'That will be the end of your career,' said Françoise. She looked at him with a kind of tenderness. He had pulled his pipe out of his pocket and was filling it with great deliberation. It was his first pipe. Every evening, when they had finished their bottle of Beaujolais, he put it on the table and looked at it with childish pride; he smoked it over his glass of cognac or marc. And then they went out into the streets, a little dazed after the day's work, the wine and the brandy. Gerbert strode along, his lock of black hair over his face and his hands in his pockets. Now that was all over. She would often be seeing him again, but only with Pierre or with all the others, and once more they would be like two strangers.

'And what about you! You hold your whisky well for a woman,' said Gerbert, quite impartially. He looked hard at Françoise. 'But you've been overworking today, you ought to get a little sleep. Then I'll wake you up, if you like.'

'No. I'd rather finish it off,' said Françoise.

'Aren't you hungry? Wouldn't you like me to go out and get you some sandwiches?'

'No, thanks,' said Françoise. She smiled at him. He had been so considerate, so attentive. Whenever she felt discouraged

3

she had only to look into his laughing eyes to regain her confidence. She would like to have found words in which to thank him.

'It's almost a pity that we've finished,' she said. 'I've become so used to working with you.'

'But it will be even greater fun when we go into production,' said Gerbert. His eyes glistened; the whisky had given a flush to his cheeks. 'It's so good to think that in three days everything will be starting all over again. How I love the opening of the season.'

'Yes, it will be fun,' said Françoise. She pulled her papers towards her. He was apparently not at all sorry to see the end of their ten days together; that was only natural. She was not sorry either; surely she had no right to expect Gerbert alone to be sorry.

'Every time I walk through this dead theatre I get the shivers,' said Gerbert. 'It's dismal. This time I really thought it was going to stay closed the whole year.'

'We've had a narrow escape,' said Françoise.

'Let's hope that this lasts,' said Gerbert.

'Oh, it will last,' said Françoise.

She had never believed in the possibility of war. War was like tuberculosis or a railway accident: something that could never happen to *me*. Things like that happened only to other people.

'Are *you* able to imagine some really terrible misfortune befalling you personally?'

Gerbert screwed up his face: 'Nothing easier,' he said.

'Well, I can't,' said Françoise. There was no point in even thinking about it. Dangers from which it was possible to protect oneself had to be envisaged, but war did not come within the compass of man. If one day war did break out, nothing else would matter any more, not even living or dying.

'But that won't happen,' murmured Françoise. She bent over her manuscript; the typewriter was clicking, and the room smelt of Virginian tobacco, ink, and the night. On the other side of the window-panes, the small, secluded square was asleep under the black sky; and, some way away, a train was moving through an empty landscape . . . And I am there. I am there, but for me this square exists and that moving train . . . all Paris, and all the world in the rosy shadows of this little office , , , and in this very instant all the long years of

4

happiness. I am here, at the heart of my life . . .

'It's a pity that we have to sleep,' said Françoise.

'It's even more of a pity we can't know that we are asleep,' said Gerbert. 'The moment we begin to be aware that we are sleeping, we wake up. We gain nothing by it.'

'But don't you think it's marvellous to stay awake while everyone else is asleep?' Françoise laid down her fountain pen and listened attentively. Not a sound could be heard; the square was in darkness, the theatre in darkness. 'I'd like to think that the whole world is asleep, that at this moment you and I are the only living souls on earth.'

'Oh no, that would give me the creeps.' He tossed back the long lock of black hair that kept falling into his eyes. 'It's like when I think about the moon; all those icy mountains and crevasses and nobody about on them. The first person to go up there will have to have a nerve.'

'I wouldn't refuse if anyone were to suggest going,' said Françoise. She looked at Gerbert. Usually, they sat side by side, and she was happy to feel him near her even though they did not speak. Tonight, she felt that she wanted to talk with him. 'It seems queer to think of what things are like when one isn't there,' she said.

'Yes, it does seem queer,' said Gerbert.

'It's like trying to imagine you're dead; you can't quite manage it, you always feel that you are somewhere in a corner, looking on.'

'It's maddening to think of all the goings-on one never will see,' said Gerbert.

'It used to break my heart to think that I'd never know anything but one small section of the world. Don't you feel like that?'

'Perhaps,' said Gerbert.

Françoise smiled. From time to time, conversation with Gerbert reached a dead-end; but it was difficult to extract a definite opinion from him.

'I feel calmer now, because I'm convinced that wherever I may go, the rest of the world will move with me. That's what keeps me from having any regrets.'

'Regrets for what?' said Gerbert.

'Having to live only in my own skin when the world is so vast.'

Gerbert looked at Françoise.

5

'Yes, specially since you live such a well-regulated life.'

He was always so discreet; this vague question amounted to a kind of impudence for him. Did he think Françoise's life too well regulated? Was he passing judgement on it? I wonder what he thinks of me . . . this office, the theatre, my room, books, papers, work . . . Such a well-regulated life.

'I came to the conclusion that I must be resigned to making a choice,' she said.

'I don't like having to make a choice,' said Gerbert.

'At first it was hard for me; but now I have no regrets, because I feel that things that don't exist for me, simply do not exist at all.'

'How do you mean?' said Gerbert.

Françoise hesitated. She felt very strongly about this; the corridors, the auditorium, the stage, none of these things had vanished when she had again shut the door on them, but they existed only behind the door, at a distance. At a distance the train was moving through the silent countryside which encompassed, in the depths of the night, the warm life of her little office.

'It's like a lunar landscape,' said Françoise. 'It's unreal. It's nothing but make-believe. Don't you feel that?'

'No,' said Gerbert. 'I don't think I do.'

'And doesn't it irk you never to be able to see more than one thing at a time?'

Gerbert thought for a moment.

'What worries me is other people,' he said. 'I've a horror when someone talks to me about some chap I don't know, especially when they speak well of him: some chap outside, living in his own sphere, who doesn't even know that I exist.'

It was rare for him to speak about himself at such length. Was he, too, aware of the touching though transitory intimacy of the last few hours? The two of them were living within this circle of rosy light; for both of them, the same light, the same night. Françoise looked at his fine green eyes beneath their curling lashes, at his expectant mouth – 'If I had wanted to . . .' Perhaps it was still not too late. But what could she want?

'Yes, it's insulting,' she said.

'As soon as I get to know the chap, I feel better about it,' said Gerbert.

'It's almost impossible to believe that other people are conscious beings, aware of their own inward feelings, as we

6

ourselves are aware of our own,' said Françoise. 'To me, it's terrifying when we grasp that. We get the impression of no longer being anything but a figment of someone else's mind. But that hardly ever happens, and never completely.'

'That's right,' said Gerbert eagerly, 'perhaps that's why I find it so unpleasant to listen to people talking to me about myself, even in a pleasant way. I feel they're gaining some sort of an advantage over me.'

'Personally, I don't care what people think of me,' said Françoise.

Gerbert began to laugh. 'Well, it can't be said that you've too much vanity,' he said.

'And their thoughts seem to me exactly like their words and their faces: things that are in my own world. It amazes Elisabeth that I'm not ambitious; but that's precisely why. I don't want to try to cut out a special place for myself in the world. I feel that I am already in it.' She smiled at Gerbert. 'And you're not ambitious either, are you?'

'No,' said Gerbert. 'Why should I be?' He thought a moment. 'All the same, I'd like to be a really good actor some day.'

'I feel the same; I'd like to write a really good book some day. We like to do our work well; but not for any honour or glory.'

'No,' said Gerbert.

A milk-cart rattled by underneath the windows. Soon the night would be growing pale. The train was already beyond Châteauroux and approaching Vierzon. Gerbert yawned and his eyes became red-rimmed like a child's full of sleep.

'You ought to get some sleep,' said Françoise.

Gerbert rubbed his eyes. 'We've got to show this to Labrousse in its final form,' he said stubbornly. He took hold of the bottle and poured himself out a stiff peg of whisky. 'Besides, I'm not sleepy. I'm thirsty!' He drank and put down his glass. He thought for a moment. 'Perhaps I'm sleepy after all.'

'Thirsty or sleepy, make up your mind,' said Françoise gaily.

'I never really know what I want,' said Gerbert.

'Well, look,' said Françoise, 'this is what you are going to do. Lie down on the couch and sleep. I'll finish looking over this last scene. Then you can type it out while I go to meet Pierre at the station.'

7

'And you?' said Gerbert.

'When I've finished I'll get some sleep too. The couch is wide, you won't be in my way. Take a cushion and pull the cover over you.'

'All right,' said Gerbert.

Françoise stretched herself and took up her fountain pen. A few minutes later she turned round in her chair. Gerbert was lying on his back, his eyes closed, his breath coming in regular intervals from between his lips. He was already asleep.

He was good-looking. She gazed at him for a while, then turned back to her work. Out there, in the moving train, Pierre was also asleep, his head resting against the leather upholstery, his face innocent . . . He'll jump out of the train, and draw up his slight frame to its full height; then he'll run along the platform; he'll take my arm . . .

'There,' said Françoise. She glanced at the manuscript with satisfaction. 'Let's hope he likes this. I think it will please him.' She pushed back her chair. A rosy mist was suffusing the sky. She took off her shoes and slipped under the cover beside Gerbert. He groaned and his head rolled over on the cushion till it rested on Françoise's shoulder.

'Poor Gerbert, he was so sleepy,' she thought. She pulled up the cover a little, and lay there motionless, her eyes open. She was sleepy, too, but she wanted to stay awake a little longer. She looked at Gerbert's smooth eyelids, at his lashes as long as a girl's; he was asleep, relaxed and impersonal. She could feel against her neck the caress of his soft black hair.

'That's all I shall ever have of him,' she thought.

There must be women who had stroked his hair, as sleek as that of a Chinese girl's; pressed their lips against his childish eyelids; clasped this long, slender body in their arms. Some day he would say to one of them: 'I love you.'

Françoise felt her heart thumping. There was still time. She could put her cheek against his cheek and speak out loud the words which were coming to her lips.

She shut her eyes. She could not say: 'I love you.' She could not think it. She loved Pierre. There was no room in her life for another love.

Yet, there would be joys like these, she thought with slight anguish. His head felt heavy on her shoulder. What was precious was not the pressure of this weight, but Gerbert's tenderness, his trust, his gay abandon, and the love she bestowed upon him. But Gerbert was sleeping, and the love and tenderness were only dream things. Perhaps, when he held her in his arms, she would still be able to cling to the dream; but how could she let herself dream of a love she did not wish really to live?

She looked at Gerbert. She was free in her words, in her acts. Pierre left her free; but acts and words would be only lies, as the weight of that head on her shoulder was already a lie. Gerbert did not love her; she could not really wish that he might love her.

The sky was turning to pink outside the window. In her heart Françoise was conscious of a sadness, as bitter and rosy as the dawn. And yet she had no regrets: she had not even a right to that melancholy which was beginning to numb her drowsy body. This was renunciation, final, and without recompense.

Chapter Two

From the back of a Moorish café, seated on rough woollen cushions, Xavière and Françoise were watching the Arab dancing girl.

'I wish I could dance like that,' said Xavière. A light tremor passed over her shoulders and ran through her body. Françoise smiled at her, and was sorry that their day together was coming to an end. Xavière had been delightful.

'In the red-light district of Fez, Labrousse and I saw them dance naked,' said Françoise. 'But that was a little too much like an anatomical exhibition.'

'You've seen so many things,' said Xavière with a touch of bitterness.

'So will you, one day,' said Françoise.

'I doubt it,' said Xavière.

'You won't remain in Rouen all your life,' said Françoise.

'What else can I do?' said Xavière sadly. She looked at her fingers with close attention. They were red, peasant's fingers, in strange contrast to her delicate wrists. 'I could perhaps try to be a prostitute, but I'm not experienced enough yet.'

'That's a hard profession, you know,' said Françoise with a laugh.

'I must learn not to be afraid of people,' said Xavière thoughtfully. She nodded her head. 'But I'm improving. When a man brushes against me in the street, I no longer let out a scream.'

'And you go into cafés by yourself. That's also an improvement,' said Françoise.

Xavière gave her a shamefaced look. 'Yes, but I haven't told you everything. At that little dance-hall where I was last night, a sailor asked me to dance and I refused. I gulped down my calvados and rushed out of the place like a coward.' She made a wry face. 'Calvados is terrible stuff.'

'It must have been fine rot-gut,' said Françoise. 'I do think you could have danced with your sailor. I did all sorts of things like that when I was younger, and no harm ever came out of them.

'The next time I shall accept,' said Xavière.

'Aren't you afraid that your aunt will wake up some night? I should think that might very well happen.'

'She wouldn't dare to come into my room,' said Xavière, with defiance. She smiled and began to hunt through her bag. 'I've made a little sketch for you.'

It was of a woman, who had a slight resemblance to Françoise, standing at a bar with her elbows resting on the counter. Her cheeks were green and her dress was yellow. Beneath the drawing Xavière had written in large, purple lettering: 'The Road to Ruin.'

'You must sign it for me,' said Françoise.

Xavière looked at Françoise, looked at the sketch, and then pushed it away. 'It's too difficult,' she said.

The dancing girl moved towards the middle of the room; her hips began to undulate, and her stomach to ripple to the rhythm of the tambourine.

'It seems almost as if a demon were trying to tear itself from her body,' said Xavière. She leaned forward, entranced. Françoise had certainly had an inspiration in bringing her here; never before had Xavière spoken at such length about herself, and she had a charming way of telling a story. Françoise sank back against the cushions; she, too, had been affected by the shoddy glamour of the place, but what especially delighted her was to have annexed this insignificant, pathetic little being into her own life: for, like Gerbert, like Inès, like Canzetti, Xavière now belonged to her. Nothing ever gave Françoise such intense joy as this kind of possession.

Xavière was absorbed in the dancing girl. She could not see her own face, its beauty heightened by the state of her excitement. Her fingers stroked the contours of the cup which she was holding lightly in her hand, but Françoise alone was aware of the contours of that hand. Xavière's gestures, her face, her very life depended on Françoise for their existence. Xavière, here and now at this moment, the essence of Xavière, was no more than the flavour of the coffee, than the piercing music or the dance, no more than indeterminate well-being; but to Françoise, her childhood, her days of stagnation, her distastes, were a romantic story as real as the delicate contour of her cheeks. And that story ended here in this café, among the vari-coloured hangings, and at this very instant in Françoise's life, as she sat looking at Xavière and studying her.

'It's seven o'clock already,' said Françoise. It bored her to have to spend the evening with Elisabeth, but it was unavoidable. 'Are you going out with Inès tonight?'

'I suppose so,' said Xavière gloomily.

'How much longer do you think you'll be staying in Paris?'

'I'm leaving tomorrow.' A flash of rage appeared in Xavière's eyes. 'Tomorrow, all this will still be going on here and I shall be in Rouen.'

'Why don't you take a secretarial course as I suggested? I could find you a job.'

Xavière shrugged her shoulders despondently. 'I couldn't do it,' she said.

'Of course you could. It's not difficult,' said Françoise.

'My aunt even tried to teach me how to knit,' said Xavière, 'but my last sock was a disaster.' She turned to Françoise with a discouraged and faintly provocative look. 'She's quite right. No one will ever manage to make anything of me.'

'Definitely not a good housewife,' said Françoise cheerfully. 'But one can live without that.'

'It's not because of the sock,' said Xavière hopelessly. 'Yet that was an indication.'

'You lose heart too easily. But still, you would like to leave Rouen, wouldn't you? You have no attachments there to anyone or anything.'

'I hate the people and the place,' said Xavière. 'I loathe that filthy city and the people in the streets with their leering glances.'

'That can't go on,' said Françoise.

'It will go on,' said Xavière. She jumped up suddenly. 'I'm going now.'

'Wait, I'll go with you,' said Françoise.

'No, don't bother. I've already taken up your entire afternoon.'

'You've taken up nothing,' said Françoise. 'How strange you are!' She looked in slight bewilderment at Xavière's sullen face. What a disconcerting little person she was: with that beret hiding her fair hair, her head looked almost like a small boy's; but the face was a young girl's, the same face that had held an appeal for Françoise six months earlier. The silence was prolonged.

'I'm sorry,' said Xavière. 'I've a terrible headache.' With a pained look, she touched her temples. 'It must be the smoke.

I've a pain here, and here.'

Her face was puffy under her eyes and her skin blotchy. The heavy smell of incense and tobacco made the air almost unbreathable. Françoise motioned to the waiter.

'That's too bad. If you were not so tired, I'd take you dancing tonight,' she said.

'I thought you had to see a friend,' said Xavière.

'She'd come with us. She's Labrousse's sister, the girl with the red hair and a short bob whom you saw at the hundredth performance of *Philoctetes*.'

'I don't remember,' said Xavière. Her face lighted up. 'I only remember you. You were wearing a long tight black skirt, a lamé blouse and a silver net on your hair. You were so beautiful!'

Françoise smiled. She was not beautiful, yet she was quite pleased with her face. Whenever she caught a glimpse of it in a looking-glass, she always felt a pleasant surprise. For most of the time, she was not even aware that she had a face.

'You were wearing a lovely blue dress with a pleated skirt,' she said. 'And you were tipsy.'

'I brought that dress with me. I'll wear it tonight,' said Xavière.

'Do you think it wise if you have a headache?'

'My headache's gone,' said Xavière. 'It was just a dizzy spell.' Her eyes were shining, and her skin had regained its beautiful pearly lustre.

'That's good,' said Françoise. She pushed open the door. 'But won't Inès be angry, if she's counting on you?'

'Well, let her be angry,' said Xavière, pouting disdainfully. Françoise hailed a taxi.

'I'll drop you at her place, and I'll meet you at the Dôme at nine-thirty. Just walk straight up to the boulevard Montparnasse.'

'Yes, I know,' said Xavière.

In the taxi Françoise sat close beside Xavière and slipped an arm through hers.

'I'm glad we still have a few hours ahead of us.'

'I'm glad too,' said Xavière softly.

The taxi stopped at the corner of the rue de Rennes. Xavière got out, and Françoise drove on to the theatre.

Pierre was in his dressing-room, wearing a dressing-gown and munching a ham sandwich.

'Did the rehearsal go off well?'

'We worked very hard,' said Pierre. He pointed to the manuscript lying on the desk. 'That's good,' he said, 'really good.'

'Do you mean it? Oh, I'm so glad! I was a little upset at having to cut out Lucilius, but I think it was necessary.'

'Yes, it was,' said Pierre. 'That changed the whole run of the act.' He bit into a sandwich. 'Haven't you had dinner? Would you like a sandwich?'

'Of course I'd like a sandwich,' said Françoise. She took one and looked at Pierre reproachfully. 'You don't eat enough. You're looking very pale.'

'I don't want to put on weight,' said Pierre.

'Caesar wasn't skinny,' said Françoise. She smiled. 'You might ring through to the concierge and ask her to get us a bottle of Château Margaux.'

'That's not such a bad idea,' said Pierre. He picked up the receiver, and Françoise curled up on the couch. This was where Pierre slept when he did not spend the night with her. She was very fond of this small dressing-room.

'There, you shall have your wine.'

'I'm so happy,' said Françoise. 'I thought I'd never get to the end of that third act.'

'You've done some excellent work,' said Pierre. He leaned over and kissed her. Françoise threw her arms around his neck. 'It's you,' she said. 'Do you remember what you said to me at Delos? That you wanted to introduce something absolutely new to the theatre? Well, this time you've done it.'

'Do you really think so?' said Pierre.

'Don't you?'

'Well, I've just a dawning suspicion.'

Françoise began to laugh. 'You know you have. You look positively smug, Pierre! If only we don't have to worry too much over money, what a wonderful year we'll have!'

'As soon as we're a little better off I shall buy you another coat,' said Pierre.

'Oh, I'm quite accustomed to this one.'

'That's only too obvious,' said Pierre. He sat down in an armchair near Françoise.

'Did you have a good time with your little friend?'

'She's very nice. It's a pity for her to rot away in Rouen.'

'Did she tell you any stories?'

'Endless stories. I'll tell you them some day.'

'Well then, you're happy; you didn't waste your day.'

'I love stories,' said Françoise.

There was a knock and the door opened. With a majestic air the concierge carried in a tray with two glasses and a bottle of wine.

'Thank you very much,' said Françoise. She filled the glasses.

'Please,' said Pierre to the concierge, 'I'm not in to anyone.'

'Very good, Monsieur Labrousse,' said the woman. She went away.

Françoise picked up her glass and started on a second sandwich.

'I'm going to bring Xavière along with us tonight,' she said. 'We'll go dancing. I think that will be fun. I hope she'll neutralize Elisabeth a little.'

'She must be in the seventh heaven,' said Pierre.

'Poor child, it's painful to see her. She's so utterly miserable at having to return to Rouen.'

'Is there no way out of it?' said Pierre.

'Hardly,' said Françoise. 'She's so spineless. She would never have the strength of mind to train for a profession. And the only prospect her uncle can think of for her is a devoted husband and a lot of children.'

'You ought to take her in hand,' said Pierre.

'How can I? I only see her once a month.'

'Why don't you bring her to Paris?' said Pierre. 'You could keep an eye on her and make her work. Let her learn to type and we can easily find a job for her somewhere.'

'Her family would never consent to that,' said Françoise.

'Well, let her do it without their permission. Isn't she of age?'

'No,' said Françoise. 'But that isn't the main point. I don't think that the police would be set on her trail.'

Pierre smiled.

'What is the main point?'

Françoise hesitated; actually she had never suspected that there was a debatable point.

'In other words, your idea would be for her to live in Paris at our expense until she sorts herself out?'

'Why not?' said Pierre. 'Offer it to her as a loan.'

'Oh, of course,' said Françoise. This trick he had of conjuring up a thousand unsuspected possibilities in only a few words always took her by surprise. Where others saw only an

15

impenetrable jungle, Pierre saw a virgin future which was his to shape as he chose. That was the secret of his strength.

'We've had so much luck in our life,' said Pierre, 'we ought to let others benefit from it whenever we can.'

Françoise, perplexed, stared at the bottom of her glass.

'In a way I feel very tempted,' she said. 'But I would really have to look after her. I hardly have the time.'

'Little busy bee,' said Pierre affectionately.

Françoise coloured. 'You know I haven't much leisure,' she said.

'Yes, I know,' said Pierre. 'But it's odd, the way you draw back as soon as you're confronted by something new.'

'The only something new which interests me is our future together,' said Françoise. 'I can't help it. That's what makes me happy. You've only yourself to blame for it.'

'Oh, I don't blame you,' said Pierre. 'On the contrary, I think you are far more honest than I am. There's nothing in your life that rings false.'

'That's because you attach no importance to your life as such. It's your work that counts,' said Françoise.

'That's true,' said Pierre. He began to gnaw one of his nails, and he looked ill at ease. 'With the exception of my relationship with you, everything about me is frivolous and wasteful.' He kept worrying his finger. He would not be satisfied until he had made it bleed. 'But as soon as I've got rid of Canzetti, all that will be finished.'

'That's what you say,' said Françoise.

'I shall prove it,' said Pierre.

'You are lucky. Your affaires are always easily terminated.'

'It's because, basically, no one of these dear little creatures has ever been really in love with me,' said Pierre.

'I don't think Canzetti is a self-seeking girl,' said Françoise.

'No, it's not so much to get herself parts. Only she thinks I'm a great man and she has a notion that genius will rise from her sex-appeal to her brain.'

'There's something in that,' said Françoise laughing.

'I no longer enjoy these affaires,' said Pierre. 'It's not as if I were a great sensualist, I don't even have that excuse!' He looked at Françoise confusedly. 'The truth is that I enjoy the early stages. You don't understand that?'

'Perhaps,' said Françoise. 'But I would not be interested in an affaire which had no continuity.'

'No?'

'No,' she said. 'It is something stronger than myself. I'm the faithful sort.'

'It's impossible to talk about faithfulness and unfaithfulness where we are concerned,' said Pierre. He drew Françoise to him. 'You and I are simply one. That's the truth, you know. Neither of us can be described without the other.'

'That's thanks to you,' said Françoise. She took Pierre's face between her hands, and began to kiss his cheeks, on which she could smell the fumes of tobacco somehow blended with the childish and unexpected smell of pastry. 'We are simply one,' she murmured.

Nothing that happened was completely real until she had told Pierre about it; it remained poised, motionless and uncertain, in a kind of limbo. When, in the past, she had been shy with Pierre, there were a number of things that she had brushed aside in this way: uncomfortable thoughts and ill-considered gestures. If they were not mentioned, it was almost as if they had not existed at all, and this allowed a shameful subterranean vegetation to grow up under the surface of true existence where she felt utterly alone and in danger of suffocation. Little by little she had resolved everything: she no longer knew aloneness, but she had rid herself of those chaotic subterranean tendrils. Every moment of her life that she entrusted to him, Pierre gave back to her clear, polished, completed, and they became moments of their shared life. She knew that she served the same purpose for him. There was nothing concealed, nothing modest about him: he was crafty only when he needed a shave or when his shirt was dirty; then he would pretend to have a cold and stubbornly keep his muffler wrapped around his neck, which gave him the appearance of a precocious old man.

'I must be leaving you in a moment,' she said regretfully. 'Are you going to sleep here or come to my place?'

'I'll come over to you,' said Pierre. 'I want to be with you again just as soon as I can.'

Elisabeth was already at the Dôme. She was smoking a cigarette, and staring fixedly into space. 'Something's gone wrong,' thought Françoise. She was very carefully made-up, yet her face had a puffy, tired look. She caught sight of Françoise and a fleeting smile seemed to release her from her thoughts.

17

'Hullo, I'm so glad to see you,' she said enthusiastically.

'So am I,' said Françoise. 'Tell me, I hope it won't annoy you, but I've asked the Pagès girl to come along with us. She's dying to go to a dance-hall. We can talk while she dances. She's no bother.'

'It's ages since I've heard any jazz,' said Elisabeth. 'That would be fun.'

'Isn't she here yet?' said Françoise. 'That's strange.' She turned towards Elisabeth. 'Well, what about your trip?' she said gaily. 'Are you definitely leaving tomorrow?'

'You think it's as simple as that,' said Elisabeth, laughing unpleasantly. 'To do that, apparently, would hurt Suzanne, and Suzanne has already gone through so much because of what happened in September.'

So that was it. Françoise gave Elisabeth a look of indignant pity: Claude's behaviour towards her was really disgusting.

'As if you hadn't suffered too.'

'Yet, but I happen to be a strong, clear-minded individual,' said Elisabeth sarcastically. 'I'm a woman who never makes a scene.'

'Yes, but Claude is no longer in love with Suzanne,' said Françoise. 'She's old and frumpy.'

'He's no longer in love with her,' said Elisabeth. 'But Suzanne is a superstition. He's convinced that, without her behind him, he'll never succeed in anything.'

Silence ensued. Elisabeth was absorbed in watching the smoke from her cigarette. She gave no outward sign of it, but what blackness there must be in her heart! She had been expecting so much from this trip, and perhaps this long period together might finally persuade Claude to break with his wife. Françoise had grown sceptical, for Elisabeth had been waiting two years for the decisive hour. She felt Elisabeth's disappointment with a painful tightening of her heart.

'I must say Suzanne is clever,' said Elisabeth. She looked at Françoise. 'She's now trying to get one of Claude's plays produced with Nanteuil. That's something else that's keeping him in Paris.'

'Nanteuil!' Françoise repeated lazily. 'What a strange idea!' She looked toward the door a little uneasily. Why hadn't Xavière come?

'It's idiotic.' Elisabeth steadied her voice. 'Besides, it's obvious; as far as I can see only Pierre could put on *Partage*,

He would be magnificent as Achab.'

'It's a good part,' said Françoise.

'Do you think he might be interested?' said Elisabeth. There was an anxious appeal in her voice.

'*Partage* is a very interesting play,' said Françoise. 'Only it's not at all the sort of thing Pierre is looking for. Listen,' she added hastily, 'why doesn't Claude take his script to Berger? Would you like Pierre to write to Berger?'

Elisabeth gulped painfully. 'You have no notion of how important it would be to Claude if Pierre were to accept his play. He's got so little self-confidence. Only Pierre could get him out of that state of mind.'

Françoise looked away. Battier's play was dreadful, there was no possible question of accepting it; but she knew how much Elisabeth had staked on this last chance, and, confronted with her drawn face, she really felt pained herself. She was fully aware how much her life and her example had influenced Elisabeth's life.

'Frankly, that can't be done,' she said.

'But *Luce et Armanda* was quite a success,' said Elisabeth.

'That's why – after *Julius Caesar* Pierre wants to try to launch an unknown playwright.'

Françoise stopped almost in the middle of a sentence. With relief she saw Xavière coming towards them. Her hair was carefully arranged and a light film of make-up toned down her cheekbones and made her large sensual nose look more refined.

'I think you've met already,' said Françoise. She smiled at Xavière. 'You're terribly late. I feel sure you haven't had dinner. Would you like something to eat?'

'No, thanks, I'm not at all hungry,' said Xavière. She sat down, hanging her head so that she seemed ill at ease. 'I got lost,' she said.

Elisabeth stared at her. She was sizing her up.

'You got lost? Did you have far to come?'

Xavière turned a distressed face to Françoise.

'I don't know what happened to me. I walked straight up the boulevard, but it seemed endless. I came to an avenue that was pitch black. I must have passed the Dôme without seeing it.'

Elisabeth began to laugh. 'That took some doing,' she said. Xavière scowled at her.

'Well, here you are at last, that's the main thing,' said

Françoise. 'What about going to the Prairie? It's no longer what it was when we were younger, but it's not bad.'

'Just as you like,' said Elisabeth.

They left the café. Along the boulevard Montparnasse a strong wind was sweeping up the leaves of the plane-trees. Françoise derived a certain pleasure in crackling them underfoot, it gave her a faint suggestion of dried nuts and warm wine.

'It's at least a year since I've been to the Prairie,' she said. No one answered. Xavière, shivering, clutched her coat collar; Elisabeth was carrying her scarf in her hand; she seemed neither to feel the cold nor to see anything.

'What a crowd there is already,' said Françoise. All the stools at the bar were taken. She chose one of the more secluded tables.

'I'll have a whisky,' said Elisabeth.

'Two whiskies,' said Françoise. 'And you?'

'The same as you,' said Xavière.

'Three whiskies,' said Françoise. This smell of alcohol and smoke took her back to her girlhood. She had always enjoyed the jazz-bands, the yellow lights and the swarming crowds in night clubs. How easy it was to live a full life in a world that held both the ruins at Delphi and the bare Provençal hill-sides, as well as this congeries of humanity! She smiled at Xavière.

'Look at that snub-nosed blonde at the bar. She lives in my hotel. She wanders about the corridors for hours on end in a pale-blue nightgown. I think she's trying to hook the Negro who lives above me.'

'She's not pretty,' said Xavière. Her eyes opened wide. 'There's a dark-haired woman next to her who is very attractive. She's really beautiful!'

'I'd better tell you that her boy-friend is a wrestler; they stroll round our neighbourhood clinging to each other's little fingers.'

'Oh!' said Xavière reproachfully.

'I'm not responsible,' said Françoise.

Xavière rose to her feet: two young men had come up to their table and were smiling engagingly.

'I'm sorry, I don't dance,' said Françoise.

Elisabeth hesitated and she too rose.

'At this moment she hates me,' thought Françoise. At the

next table a rather tired blonde and a very young man were affectionately holding hands: the youth was talking ardently in a low voice, the woman smiling cautiously, without letting a single wrinkle furrow her once pretty face; the little professional from the hotel was dancing with a sailor, clinging tightly against him, her eyes half-closed; the attractive brunette, seated on her bar stool, was munching banana slices, with an expression of boredom. Françoise smiled proudly. Each one of these men, each one of these women present here tonight was completely absorbed in living a moment of his or her insignificant individual existence. Xavière was dancing. Elisabeth was shaken by convulsions of anger and despair. 'And I – here I am at the very heart of the dance-hall – impersonal and free. I am watching all these lives and all these faces. If I were to turn away from them, they would disintegrate at once like a deserted landscape.'

Elisabeth returned and sat down.

'You know,' said Françoise, 'I am sorry that it can't be managed.'

'I understand perfectly well . . .' Her face fell. She was incapable of remaining angry for any length of time, especially in the presence of others.

'Aren't things going well with you and Claude at the moment?' asked Françoise.

Elisabeth shook her head. Her face gave an ugly twitch, and Françoise thought she was going to burst into tears. But she controlled herself.

'Claude is working up for a crisis. He says that he can't work as long as his play has not been accepted, that he doesn't feel really free. When he's in one of those states he's terrible.'

'Surely, you can't be held responsible?' said Françoise.

'But the blame always falls on me,' said Elisabeth. Again her lips trembled. 'Because I'm a strong-minded woman. It doesn't occur to him that a strong-minded woman can suffer just as much as any other,' she said in a tone of passionate self-pity.

She burst into sobs.

'My poor Elisabeth!' said Françoise, taking her hand.

Through her tears Elisabeth's face regained a kind of child-like quality.

'It's ridiculous,' she said, dabbing her eyes. 'It can't go on

21

like this, with Suzanne always between us.'

'What do you want him to do?' said Françoise. 'Divorce her?'

'He'll never divorce her,' Elisabeth began to sob again in a kind of fury. 'Is he in love with me? As far as I'm concerned, I don't even know if I'm in love with him.' She looked at Françoise and her eyes were wild. 'For two years I've been fighting for this love. I've been killing myself in the process. I've sacrificed everything. And now I don't even know if we're in love with each other.'

'Of course you're in love with him,' said Françoise, her courage failing. 'At the moment you're angry with him, so you don't know what you feel, but that doesn't mean anything.' It was absolutely essential for her to reassure Elisabeth. What a terrible discovery she would make if one day she were to decide to be sincere from start to finish! She must have feared this herself, for her flashes of lucidity always stopped in time.

'I don't know any longer,' said Elisabeth.

Françoise pressed her hand tighter. She was really moved. 'Claude is weak, that's all. But he has shown you a thousand times over that he loves you.' She looked up. Xavière was standing beside the table, observing the scene with a curious smile on her face.

'Sit down,' said Françoise, embarrassed.

'No, I'm going to dance again,' said Xavière. Her expression was contemptuous, and almost spiteful. This malicious reaction gave Françoise an unpleasant shock.

Elisabeth had recovered. She was powdering her face.

'I must be patient,' she said. She steadied her voice. 'It's a question of influence. I've always played too fair with Claude, and I don't make demands on him.'

'Have you ever told him plainly that you couldn't stand the situation?'

'No,' said Elisabeth. 'I must wait.' She had resumed her hard, cautious expression.

Was she in love with Claude? She had thrown herself at his head simply because she, too, wanted to have a great love; the admiration she had showered on him was just another way of protecting herself against Pierre. Yet because of him she endured suffering in which both Françoise and Pierre were powerless to help her.

'What a mess,' thought Françoise with a pang.

Elisabeth had left the table. She was dancing, her eyes swollen, her mouth set. Something like envy flashed through Françoise. Elisabeth's feelings might well be false, her objective false, and false her whole life, but her present suffering was violent and real. Françoise looked at Xavière while she was dancing, her head thrown back, her face ecstatic. Her life had not yet begun; for her everything was possible and this enchanted evening held the promise of a thousand unknown enchantments. For this young girl, and for this heavy-hearted woman, the moment had a sharp and unforgettable quality. 'And I,' thought Françoise, 'just a spectator. But this jazz, and the taste of this whisky, and these orange-coloured lights, these are not mere stage effects, there must be some way of finding a proper use for them! But what?'

In Elisabeth's fierce, tense soul, the music was gently transformed into hope; Xavière transmuted it into passionate expectation; and Françoise alone found nothing in herself that harmonized with the plaintive sound of the saxophone. She searched for a desire, a regret; but behind her and before her there stretched a radiant and cloudless happiness. Pierre – that name was incapable of awakening pain. Gerbert – she was no longer concerned about Gerbert. No longer was she conscious of risk, or hope, or fear; only of this happiness over which she did not even have control. Misunderstanding with Pierre was impossible; no act would ever be irreparable. If one day she tried to inflict suffering upon herself, he would understand so well, that happiness would once more close over her. She lit a cigarette. No, she could find nothing beyond this abstract regret of having nothing to regret. Her throat was becoming dry; her heart was beating a little more quickly than usual, but she could not even believe that she was honestly tired of happiness. This uneasiness brought her no pitiful revelation. It was only a ripple on the surface, a short and, in a way, foreseeable modulation that would be resolved in peace. No longer did she get caught up in the forcefulness of a passing moment: she knew that no one of these moments was of intrinsic value. 'Imprisoned in happiness,' she murmured to herself. But she was conscious of a smile somewhere deep down within her.

Françoise cast a discouraged look at the empty glasses and the over-full ashtray: it was four o'clock, Elisabeth had long since left, but Xavière had never left off dancing. Françoise did not dance, and to pass the time she had drunk and smoked too much. Her head was heavy and she was beginning to feel all over her body the lassitude of sleepiness.

'I think it's time to go,' she said.

'Already!' said Xavière. She looked at Françoise with disappointment. 'Are you tired?'

'A little,' said Françoise. She hesitated. 'You can stay on without me,' she said. 'You've been to a dance-hall alone before.'

'If you leave, I'll go with you,' said Xavière.

'I don't want to oblige you to go home,' said Françoise.

Xavière shrugged her shoulders with an air that accepted the inevitable. 'Oh, I may just as well go home,' she said.

'No, that would be a pity,' said Françoise. She smiled. 'Let's stay a bit longer.' Xavière's face brightened. 'This place is so nice, isn't it?' She smiled at a young man who was bowing to her and then followed him to the middle of the dance floor.

Françoise lit another cigarette. After all, nothing obliged her to resume her work the very next day. It was slightly absurd to spend hour after hour here without dancing, without speaking to a soul, but if one set one's mind to it there was fascination to be found in this kind of self-absorption. It was years since she had sat thus, lost in alcohol fumes and tobacco smoke, pursuing little dreams and thoughts that led nowhere.

Xavière came back and sat down beside Françoise.

'Why don't you dance?'

'I dance very badly,' said Françoise.

'But aren't you bored?' asked Xavière in a plaintive tone.

'Not at all. I love to look on. I'm fascinated just listening to the music and watching the people.'

She smiled. She owed to Xavière both this hour and this evening. Why exclude from her life this offering of refreshing richness, a young, completely fresh companion, with her demands, her reticent smiles and unexpected reactions?

'I can see that it can't be very amusing for you,' said Xavière. Her face looked quite dejected; she, too, now seemed a little tired.

'But I assure you that I am quite happy,' said Françoise. She gently patted Xavière's wrist. 'I enjoy being with you.'

Xavière smiled without conviction. Françoise looked at her affectionately. She no longer understood very clearly the resistance she had put up against Pierre. It was just this very faint scent of risk and mystery that intrigued her.

'Do you know what I was thinking last night?' she asked abruptly. 'That you will never do anything as long as you stay in Rouen. There's only one way out of it and that's to come and live in Paris.'

'Live in Paris?' said Xavière in astonishment. 'I'd love to, unfortunately!'

'I'm in earnest,' said Françoise. She hesitated; she was afraid Xavière might think her tactless. 'I'll tell you what you could do: you could stay in Paris, at my hotel, if you like. I would lend you what money you need and you would train for a career, a typist perhaps. Or, better still, I have a friend who runs a beauty-parlour and she would employ you as soon as you have your certificate.'

Xavière's face darkened.

'My uncle would never consent to that,' she said.

'You can do without his consent. You aren't afraid of him, are you?'

'No,' said Xavière. She stared at her sharply pointed nails. Her pale complexion, her long fair hair a little in disorder from dancing, gave her the woebegone look of a jellyfish washed up on dry sand.

'Well?' said Françoise.

'Excuse me,' said Xavière. She rose to rejoin one of the young men who was making signs to her and her features were alive again. Françoise's glance followed her in utter amazement. Xavière had strange abrupt changes of mood. It was a little disconcerting that she had not even taken the trouble to think over Françoise's suggestion. And yet, this plan was eminently sensible. With some impatience she waited for Xavière to come back.

'Well,' she said, 'what do you think of my plan?'

'What plan?' said Xavière. She seemed honestly at a loss.

'To come and live in Paris,' said Françoise.

'Oh, to live in Paris,' said Xavière.

'But this is serious,' said Françoise. 'You seem to imagine that I'm romancing.'

Xavière shrugged her shoulders. 'But it can't be done,' she said.

'It can – if you want to do it,' said Françoise. 'What's standing in your way?'

'It's impossible,' said Xavière with annoyance. She looked round about her. 'This place is getting sinister, don't you think? All these people have eyes in the middle of their face. They are taking root here because they haven't even the strength to drag themselves elsewhere.'

'Well, let's go,' said Françoise. She crossed the room and opened the door. A faint grey dawn was visible in the sky. 'We could walk a little,' she said.

'We could,' said Xavière. She pulled her coat tight around her neck and began to walk very quickly. Why had she refused to take Françoise's offer seriously? It was irritating to feel this small, hostile, stubborn mind beside her.

'I must convince her,' thought Françoise. Up to the present, the discussion with Pierre and the vague dreams of the evening, the very opening of this conversation, had been only a game. Suddenly, everything had become real. Xavière's resistance was real and Françoise wanted to break it down. It was outrageous; she had felt so strongly that she was dominating Xavière, possessing her even in her past and in the still unknown meanderings of her future. And yet there was this obstinate will against which her own will was breaking.

Xavière walked faster and faster, scowling as if in pain. It was impossible to talk. Françoise followed her silently for a while, then lost her patience.

'You're sure you don't mind walking?' she said.

'Not at all,' said Xavière. Her face contorted tragically. 'I hate the cold.'

'You should have said so,' said Françoise. 'We'll go into the first bistro we find open.'

'No, let's walk if you'd like to,' said Xavière in gallant self-sacrifice.

'I'm not particularly keen on walking any farther,' said Françoise. 'But I would very much like a cup of hot coffee.'

They slackened their pace a little. Near the Gare Montparnasse, at the corner of the rue d'Odessa, people were grouped at the counter of the Café Biard. Françoise went in and sat down in a corner at the far end of the room.

'Two coffees,' she ordered.

At one of the tables a woman was asleep, with her body slumped forward: there were suitcases and bundles on the floor. At another table three Breton peasants were drinking calvados.

26

Françoise looked at Xavière. 'I don't understand you,' she said.

Xavière looked at her uneasily. 'Do I aggravate you?'

'I'm disappointed,' said Françoise. 'I thought you would be brave enough to accept my offer.'

Xavière hesitated. She looked around her with an agonized expression. 'I don't want to do facial massage,' she said plaintively.

Françoise laughed.

'There's nothing to force you to do that. I might well be able to find you a job as a mannequin, for instance. Or you could certainly learn to type.'

'I don't want to be a typist or a mannequin,' said Xaviere vehemently.

Françoise was taken aback.

'My idea was that it would be only a beginning. Once you are trained and in a job you would have time to look about you. What exactly would interest you? Studying, drawing, acting?'

'I don't know,' said Xavière. 'Nothing in particular. Is it absolutely necessary for me to do something?' she asked a little haughtily.

'A few hours of boring work wouldn't seem to me too much to pay for your independence,' said Françoise.

Xavière wrinkled her face in disgust.

'I hate these compromises. If one can't have the sort of life one wants, one might as well be dead.'

'The fact is that you will never kill yourself,' said Françoise a little sharply. 'So it would be just as well to try to live a suitable life.'

She swallowed a little coffee. This was really early morning coffee, acrid and sweet like the coffee you drink on a station platform after a night of travel, or in country inns while waiting for the first bus. Its dank flavour softened Françoise's heart.

'What do you think life should be like?' she asked amiably.

'Like it was when I was a child,' said Xavière.

'Having things come to you without your having to look for them? As when your father took you for a ride on his big horse?'

'There were a great many other moments,' said Xavière. 'When he took me hunting at six o'clock in the morning and

27

the grass was covered with fresh cobwebs. Everything seemed important.'

'But you'll find similar happiness in Paris,' said Françoise. 'Just think, music, plays, dance-halls.'

'And I would have to be like your friend, counting the number of drinks I've had and looking at my watch all the time, so that I can get to work the next morning.'

Françoise felt hurt, for she had been looking at the time.

'She almost seems annoyed with me. But why?' she thought. This clearly unpredictable Xavière interested her.

'Yet you are prepared to accept a far drearier life than hers,' she said, 'and one which is ten times less free. As a matter of fact, it's obvious: you're afraid. Perhaps not afraid of your family, but afraid of breaking with your own little ways, afraid of freedom.'

Xavière bent her head without replying.

'What's the matter?' said Françoise softly. 'You are so completely obstinate. You don't seem to put any trust in me.'

'But I do,' said Xavière coldly.

'What is the matter?' repeated Françoise.

'It drives me mad to think of my life,' said Xavière.

'But that's not all,' said Françoise. 'You have been queer the whole evening.' She smiled. 'Were you annoyed at having Elisabeth with us? You don't seem to care very much for her.'

'Why?' said Xavière. She added stiffly: 'She must surely be a very interesting person.'

'You were shocked to see her crying in public, weren't you?' said Françoise. 'Admit it. I shock you too. You thought me disgracefully sentimental.'

Xavière stared, wide-eyed. She had the frank blue eyes of a child.

'It seemed odd to me,' she said ingenuously.

She remained on the defensive. It was useless to press the matter. Françoise stifled a little yawn. 'I'm going home,' she said. 'Are you going to Inès's place?'

'Yes, I'm going to try to pick up my things and get out without waking her,' said Xavière. 'Otherwise she'll tell me off.'

'I thought you were fond of Inès?'

'Yes, I am fond of her,' said Xavière. 'But she's the sort of person in front of whom one can't even drink a glass of milk without having a guilty conscience.'

Was the bitterness of her voice aimed at Inès or Françoise?

28

In any case it was wise not to insist.

'Well, let's go,' said Françoise. She put her hand on Xavière's shoulder. 'I'm sorry you didn't have a pleasant evening.'

Xavière's face suddenly fell and all the hardness disappeared. She looked at Françoise with despair.

'But I've had a lovely time,' she said. She looked down and said quickly: 'But you can't have had a very good time dragging me around like a poodle.'

Françoise smiled. 'So that's it,' she thought. 'She really thought that I was taking her out simply from pity.' She looked affectionately at this touchy little person.

'On the contrary, I was very happy to have you with me, otherwise I wouldn't have asked you,' said Françoise. 'Why did you think that?'

Xavière gave her a look of loving trust.

'You have such a full life,' she said. 'So many friends, so much to do, I felt thoroughly insignificant.'

'That's foolish,' said Françoise. It was astonishing to think that Xavière could have been jealous of Elisabeth. 'Then when I spoke to you about coming to Paris, you thought I wanted to offer you charity?'

'I did – a bit,' said Xavière humbly.

'And you hated me for it,' said Françoise.

'I didn't hate you for it; I hated myself.'

'That's the same thing,' said Françoise. Her hand moved from Xavière's shoulder and slipped down her arm. 'But I'm fond of you,' she said. 'I would be extremely happy to have you near me.'

Xavière turned overjoyed and incredulous eyes towards her.

'Didn't we have a good time together this afternoon?' said Françoise.

'Yes,' said Xavière embarrassed.

'We could have lots of times like that! Doesn't that tempt you?'

Xavière squeezed Françoise's hand.

'Oh, how I'd like to,' she said enthusiastically.

'If you agree it's as good as done,' said Françoise. 'I'll get Inès to send you a letter saying that she's found you a job. And the day you make up your mind, all you'll have to do is write to me "I'm coming," and you will come.' She patted the warm hand that lay trustingly in hers. 'You'll see, you'll have a beautiful rich little life.'

'Oh, I do want to come,' said Xavière. She sank with all her weight against Françoise's shoulder; for some time they remained motionless, leaning against each other. Xavière's hair brushed against Françoise's cheek. Their fingers remained intertwined.

'It makes me sad to leave you,' said Françoise.

'So it does me,' said Xavière softly.

'My dear little Xavière,' murmured Françoise. Xavière looked at her, with eyes shining, parted lips; mollified, yielding; she had abandoned herself completely. Henceforth Françoise would lead her through life.

'I shall make her happy,' she decided with conviction.

Chapter Three

A ray of light shone from under Xavière's door. Françoise
heard a faint jingling and a rustle of garments, and then she
knocked. There was a prolonged silence.

'Who is it?'

'It is I, Françoise. It's almost time to leave.'

Ever since Xavière had arrived at the Hotel Bayard, Françoise had learned never to knock at her door unexpectedly,
and never to arrive early for an appointment. All the same,
her arrival always created mysterious agitation on the other
side of the door.

'Would you mind waiting for me a minute? I'll come up
to your room in a moment.'

'All right, I'll wait for you,' said Françoise.

She went upstairs. Xavière liked formality. She never opened
her door to Françoise until she had made elaborate prepara-
tions to receive her. To be taken by surprise in her everyday
privacy would have seemed to her obscene.

'I only hope everything goes well tonight,' thought Françoise. 'We'll never be ready in three days.' She sat down on
the sofa and picked up one of the manuscripts which were
piled on the night table. Pierre had asked her to read the plays
sent in to him and it was work that she usually found entertaining. *Marsyas, or The Doubtful Metamorphosis.* Françoise
looked despondently at the titles. Things had not gone at all
well that afternoon; everyone was worn out. Pierre's nerves
had been on edge and he had not slept for a week. With
anything less than a hundred performances to a full house,
expenses would not be covered.

She threw down the manuscript and rose to her feet. She
had plenty of time to make up her face again, but she was too
agitated. She lit a cigarette, and a smile came to her lips.
Actually she enjoyed nothing better than this last-minute
excitement. She knew perfectly well that everything would be
ready when the time came. Pierre could do wonders in three
days. That question of mercury lights would be settled. And if
only Tedesco could make up his mind to fall into line with

31

the rest of the company . . .

'May I come in?' asked a timid voice.

'Come in,' said Françoise.

Xavière was wearing a heavy coat and her ugly little beret. On her childlike face was a faint, contrite smile.

'Have I kept you waiting?'

'No, it's all right. We're not late,' said Françoise hastily. She had to avoid letting Xavière think she might have been in the wrong; otherwise, she would become spiteful and sullen. 'I'm not even ready myself.'

She powdered her nose a little, by force of habit, and turned quickly away from the looking-glass. Whatever face she wore tonight did not really matter: it did not exist for herself and she had a vague hope that it would be invisible to everyone else. She picked up her key and gloves and closed the door.

'You went to a concert, didn't you?' she asked. 'Was it good?'

'No, I haven't been out,' said Xavière. 'It was too cold and I didn't feel like going.'

Françoise took her arm.

'What have you done all day? Tell me about it.'

'There's nothing to tell,' said Xavière plaintively.

'That's the answer you always give me,' said Françoise. 'But I've told you all the same that it gives me pleasure to imagine your life in detail.' Smiling, she looked at her closely. 'You've washed your hair.'

'Yes,' said Xavière.

'You've set it beautifully. One of these days I'll ask you to do mine. And what else? Did you read? Did you sleep? What sort of lunch did you have?'

'I didn't do anything at all,' said Xavière.

Françoise insisted no further. It was impossible to achieve any fixed degree of intimacy with Xavière. The trifling occupations of a day seemed to her as indecent a subject of conversation as her bodily functions, and since she hardly ever left her room she rarely had anything to recount. Françoise had been disappointed by her lack of curiosity. Tempting movies, concerts, outings had been suggested to her to no purpose; she remained obstinately in her room. Françoise had been stirred by a moment of romantic excitement that morning in a Montparnasse café when she thought she had acquired a rare treasure. Xavière's presence had brought her nothing fresh.

'I had a full day myself,' said Françoise gaily. 'This morning I gave the wig-maker a bit of my mind; he'd only delivered half the wigs. And then I went hunting for props. It's difficult to find just what I want; it's a real treasure hunt. But you can't imagine what fun it is rummaging among curious old theatre props. I must take you with me some day.'

'I would like to come very much,' said Xavière.

'This afternoon there was a long rehearsal and I spent a lot of time giving the finishing touches to the costumes.' She laughed. 'One of the actors, who is very stout, had padded his buttocks instead of his stomach. You should have seen his figure!'

Xavière gently squeezed Françoise's hand.

'You mustn't tire yourself out. You'll make yourself ill!'

Françoise looked at the anxious face with sudden affection. At times Xavière's reserve melted; she was no more than a fond ingenuous little girl, and one almost wanted to cover her pearly cheeks with kisses.

'Now there won't be anything else for a long time,' said Françoise. 'You know, I wouldn't lead this sort of life all the time; but when it lasts only a few days and we hope to be successful, it's worth while giving everything in one's power.'

'You are so energetic,' said Xavière.

Françoise smiled at her.

'I think it will be interesting tonight. Labrousse always has his finest inspirations at the last minute.'

Xavière said nothing. She always appeared embarrassed when Françoise spoke of Pierre, although she made a show of admiring him greatly.

'It won't bore you to go to this rehearsal?' said Françoise.

'I'll enjoy it very much,' said Xavière. She hesitated. 'Obviously I'd prefer to see you under different circumstances.'

'So would I,' said Françoise without warmth. She hated these veiled reproaches which Xavière let fall from time to time. Unquestionably she had not given her much of her time, but surely she could not be expected to sacrifice to her the few hours she had for her own work!

They found themselves in front of the theatre. Françoise looked up affectionately at the old building with rococo festoons ornamenting its façade. It had a friendly, demure look that warmed the heart. In a few days, it would assume its gala appearance, it would be ablaze with all its lights: tonight, it was bathed in shadow. Françoise walked towards the stage-door.

'It's strange to think that you come here every day, much as you might go to an office,' said Xavière. 'The inside of a theatre has always seemed so mysterious to me.'

'I remember before I knew Labrousse,' said Françoise, 'how Elisabeth used to put on the solemn air of an initiate when she led me along the corridors. I felt very proud of myself.' She smiled; the mystery had faded. But this yard, cluttered with old stage sets, had lost none of its poetry by becoming an everyday sight. The little wooden staircase, the same colour as a garden bench, led up to the green-room. Françoise paused for a moment to listen to the murmur coming from the stage. As always, when she was going to see Pierre, her heart began to beat faster.

'Don't make any noise. We're going to cross the stage-floor,' she said.

She took Xavière by the hand and they tiptoed along behind the scenery. In a garden of green and purple shrubs, Tedesco was pacing up and down like a soul in torment. Tonight, his voice sounded curiously choked.

'Sit down here. I'll be back in a moment,' said Françoise.

There were a great many people in the theatre. As usual, the actors and the small-part players were grouped together in the back stalls, while Pierre alone was in the front row. Françoise shook hands with Elisabeth, who was sitting beside a little actor from whom she had scarcely been separated for a moment during the last few days.

'I'll come and see you in a moment,' she said. She smiled at Pierre without speaking. He sat all hunched up, his head muffled in a big red scarf. He looked anything but satisfied.

'Those clumps of shrubbery are a failure!' thought Françoise. 'They will have to be changed.' She looked uneasily at Pierre and he made a gesture of utter helplessness. Tedesco had never been so poor. Was it possible they had been mistaken in him up till now?

Tedesco's voice broke completely. He put his hand up to his forehead.

'I'm sorry. I don't know what's the matter with me,' he said. 'I think I'd better rest a while. I'm sure I'll be better after a quarter of an hour's rest.'

There was a deathly silence.

34

'All right,' said Pierre. 'Meanwhile, we'll adjust the lighting. And will somebody get Vuillemin and Gerbert? I want someone to rearrange this scenery.' He lowered his voice. 'How are you? You don't look well.'

'I'm all right,' said Françoise. 'You don't look too good, either. Stop rehearsals at midnight tonight. We are all worn out; you can't keep up this pace till Friday.'

'I know,' said Pierre. He looked around. 'Did you bring Xavière with you?'

'Yes, I'll have to spend a little time with her.' Françoise hesitated. 'Do you know what I've been thinking? All three of us could go and have a drink together when we leave. Would you mind that?'

Pierre laughed.

'I haven't told you yet. This morning when I was coming up the stairs I met her on her way down. She scurried off like a scared rabbit and locked herself in the lavatory.'

'I know,' said Françoise. 'You terrify her. That's why I'm asking you to see her just for this once. If you are really friendly towards her, it will simplify matters.'

'I'd be only too glad to,' said Pierre. 'I find her rather amusing. Oh, there you are. Where's Gerbert?'

'I've looked everywhere for him,' said Vuillemin, coming up almost out of breath. 'I've no idea where he's gone.'

'I said goodbye to him at seven-thirty in the props-room. He told me he was going to try to get some sleep,' said Françoise. She raised her voice: 'Régis, would you please go and look back-stage and see if you can find Gerbert?'

'It's appalling, that barricade you've gone and landed me with over there,' said Pierre. 'I've told you a thousand times that I do not want any painted scenery. I want a built-up set.'

'And another thing, the colour won't do,' said Françoise. 'Those bushes could be very pretty, but at present it's got a dirty rusty look.'

'That's easily done,' said Vuillemin.

Gerbert ran across the stage and jumped down into the auditorium. His suède jacket was open over a check shirt. He was covered with dust.

'I'm sorry,' said Gerbert. 'I fell sound asleep.' He ran his hand through his uncombed hair. His face was livid and there were deep rings under his eyes. While Pierre was speaking to him, Françoise affectionately scanned his pinched face. He looked like a poor sick monkey.

'You make him do too much,' said Françoise, when Vuillemin and Gerbert had gone off.

'He's the only one I can rely on,' said Pierre. 'Vuillemin will make a mess of things again if he isn't watched.'

'I know, but he isn't as strong as we are,' said Françoise. She got up. 'I'll see you later.'

'We're going to try out the lighting,' shouted Pierre. 'Give me night; only blue back-stage floods.'

Françoise went over and sat down beside Xavière.

'Still, I'm not quite old enough,' she thought. There was no denying it, she had a maternal feeling towards Gerbert – maternal, with a faintly incestuous touch. She would have liked to put that weary head against her shoulder.

'Do you find it interesting?' she said to Xavière.

'I don't understand what's supposed to be happening,' said Xavière.

'It's night. Brutus has gone down into his garden to meditate. He has received messages asking him to revolt against Caesar. He hates tyranny, but he loves Caesar. He's perplexed.'

'Then this fellow in the brown jacket is Brutus?' said Xavière.

'When he wears his beautiful white toga and make-up he looks much more like Brutus.'

'I never imagined him like that,' said Xavière sadly. Her eyes shone. 'Oh, how beautiful the lighting is!'

'Do you think so? That makes me very happy,' said Françoise. 'We worked like slaves to get just that impression of early morning.'

'Early morning?' said Xavière. 'It's so chill. This light makes me think of . . .' she hesitated and then added in one breath, 'of a light like the beginning of the world, before the sun and the moon and the stars were created.'

'Good evening, Mademoiselle,' said a harsh voice. Canzetti was smiling with timid coquetry. Two thick black curls framed her charming gypsy face. Her lips and cheeks were very heavily made up.

'Does my hair look all right now?'

'I think it's very becoming,' said Françoise.

'I took your advice,' said Canzetti gently, pursing her lips.

There was a short blast of a whistle and Pierre's voice shouted. 'We'll take the scene again from the beginning, with the lighting, and we'll go right through. Is everyone here?'

'Everyone's here,' said Gerbert.

'Goodbye, Mademoiselle, and thank you,' said Canzetti.

'She's nice, isn't she?' said Françoise.

'Yes,' said Xavière. She added petulantly: 'I loath that type of face and I think she looks dirty.'

Françoise laughed.

'Then you don't think she's at all nice.'

Xavière scowled and made a wry face.

'I'd tear my nails out one by one rather than speak the way she spoke to you. A worm couldn't be as low.'

'She used to teach at a school near Bourges,' said Françoise. 'She gave up everything to try her luck in the theatre. She's starving to death here in Paris.' Françoise looked with amusement at Xavière's inscrutable face. Xavière hated anyone who was at all close to Françoise. Her timidity towards Pierre was mingled with hatred.

A moment before, Tedesco had begun once more to pace the stage. Out of a religious silence, he began to speak. He seemed to have recovered himself.

'That still isn't it,' thought Françoise in distress. Only another three days, and in the auditorium there would be the same gloom, on the stage the same lighting, and the same words would move through space. But instead of this silence they would come into contact with a world of sounds. The seats would creak, restless fingers would rustle programmes, old men would cough persistently. Through layer upon layer of indifference, the subtle phrases would have to blaze a trail to a blasé and intractable audience; all these people, preoccupied with their digestion, their throats, their lovely clothes, their household squabbles; bored critics, malicious friends – it was a challenge to try to interest them in Brutus's perplexity. They had to be taken by surprise, taken out of themselves. Tedesco's restrained, lifeless acting was inadequate.

Pierre's head was bent: Françoise regretted she had not gone back and sat down beside him. What was he thinking? This was the first time that he had put into effect his aesthetic principles so systematically, and on such a large scale. He himself had trained all these actors. Françoise had adapted the play according to his instructions. Even the stage designer had followed his orders. If he succeeded he would have asserted decisively his conception of art and the theatre. Françoise's clenched hands became moist.

'There's been no stint either in work or money,' she thought, with a lump in her throat. 'If we fail, it will be a long, long time before we're in any position to start over again.'

'Wait,' said Pierre suddenly. He went up on to the stage. Tedesco froze.

'What you're doing is all very well,' said Pierre. 'It's quite correct. But, don't you see, you're acting the words, but you're not acting the situation enough. I want you to keep the same nuances – but at a different level.'

Pierre leaned against the wall and bowed his head. Françoise relaxed. Pierre just did not know how to talk to actors. It embarrassed him to have to bring himself down to their level. Yet when he demonstrated a part he was remarkable.

> *... 'I know no personal cause, to spurn at him,*
> *But for the general' ...*

Françoise watched the miracle with inexhaustible wonder. Physically, Pierre in no way looked the part. He was stocky, his features were irregular, and yet, when he raised his head, it was Brutus himself who turned a tortured face to the heavens.

Gerbert leaned toward Françoise. He had sat down behind her without her having noticed him.

'The angrier he gets the more amazing he is,' he said. 'At this very moment he's seething.'

'With good reason,' said Françoise. 'Do you think Tedesco will ever make anything of his part?'

'He's on to it,' said Gerbert. 'He's only to make a start and the rest will follow.'

'You see,' Pierre was saying, 'that's the pitch you have to get and then you can be as restrained as you like. I will feel the emotion. If the emotion isn't there, it's no damn good.'

Tedesco leaned against the wall, and bowed his head.

> *'It must be by his death: and for my part,*
> *I know no personal cause, to spurn at him,*
> *But for the general.'*

Françoise gave Gerbert a triumphant smile. It seemed so simple, and yet she knew that nothing was more difficult than to awaken in an actor this sudden enlightenment. She looked

38

at the back of Pierre's head. She would never grow tired of watching him work. Of all her lucky breaks, the one she valued the most was that which gave her the opportunity of collaborating with Pierre. The weariness they shared and their efforts united them more surely than an embrace. There was not one moment of all these harassing rehearsals that was not an act of love.

The conspirators' scene had gone off without a flaw; Françoise got up from her stall.

'I'm just going to say something to Elisabeth,' she said to Gerbert. 'If I'm needed I'll be in my office. I haven't the energy to stay any longer. Pierre hasn't finished with Portia.' She hesitated. It was not very nice to leave Xavière, but she had not seen Elisabeth for ages; it was verging on rudeness.

'Gerbert, I'm leaving my friend Xavière in your hands,' she said. 'You might take her back-stage while the scenery's being changed. She doesn't know what a theatre is like.'

Xavière said nothing: ever since the beginning of the rehearsal there had been a look of resentment in her eyes.

Françoise put her hand on Elisabeth's shoulder.

'Come and smoke a cigarette,' she said.

'I'd love to. It's tyrannical not to allow people to smoke. I'll have to speak to Pierre about it,' said Elisabeth with mock indignation.

Françoise stopped in the doorway. A few days earlier, the room had been repainted a light yellow which gave it a welcome rustic look. A faint smell of turpentine still hung in the air.

'I hope we never leave this old theatre,' said Françoise, as they climbed the stairs.

'I wonder if there's anything left to drink,' she said, pushing open the door of her office. She opened a cupboard half-filled with books and looked at the bottles lined up on the top shelf. 'There's a little whisky here. Would you like that?'

'Splendid,' said Elisabeth.

Françoise handed her a glass. There was such warmth in her heart that she felt a burst of affection for Elisabeth. She had the same feeling of comradeship and ease as when, in the past, they had come out of a difficult and interesting class and strolled arm in arm in the lycée yard.

Elisabeth lit a cigarette and crossed her legs.

'What was the matter with Tedesco? Guimiot insists that he

is taking drugs. Do you think that's true?'

'I've no idea,' said Françoise, and she blissfully swallowed a long pull of whisky.

'That little Xavière is not at all pretty,' said Elisabeth. 'What are you doing about her? Was everything put right with her family?'

'I know nothing about that,' said Françoise. 'Her uncle may show up any one of these days and kick up a row.'

'Do be careful,' said Elisabeth, with an air of importance. 'You may run into trouble.'

'Careful of what?' said Françoise.

'Have you found her any work?'

'No. She's got to get used to things first.'

'What's her particular bent?'

'I don't think she'll ever be capable of much work.'

Elisabeth thoughtfully exhaled a puff of smoke.

'What does Pierre say about it?'

'They haven't seen much of each other. He rather likes her.'

This cross-examination was beginning to irritate her. It almost seemed as if Elisabeth were arraigning her. She cut her short.

'Tell me, is there any news about you?' she said.

Elisabeth gave a short laugh.

'Guimiot? During the rehearsal last Tuesday, he came over to talk to me. Don't you think he's handsome?'

'Very handsome. That's just why we took him on. I don't know him at all. Is he nice?'

'He certainly knows how to make love,' said Elisabeth in a detached tone.

'You didn't lose much time,' said Françoise a little taken aback. Whenever Elisabeth took a liking to a man she began to talk about sleeping with him. But actually, she had remained faithful to Claude for the last two years.

'You know my principles,' said Elisabeth gaily. 'I'm not the sort of woman who is taken. I'm a woman who does the taking. That very first evening, I asked him to spend the night with me. He was flabbergasted.'

'Does Claude know?' said Françoise.

Elisabeth very deliberately tapped the ash from her cigarette. Whenever she was embarrassed her movements and her voice became hard and resolute.

'Not yet, I'm waiting for just the right moment.' She

40

hesitated. 'It's all very complicated.'

'Your relations with Claude? It's a long time since you've spoken to me about him.'

'Nothing's changed,' said Elisabeth. The corners of her mouth drooped. 'Only I have changed.'

'Did you get nowhere when you had it out with him a month ago?'

'He keeps on telling me the same old thing: that it's me who has the better part of the bargain. I'm fed up with that old story. I almost said to him: "It's much too good for me, thank you; I would be satisfied with the other."'

'You must have been too conciliatory again,' said Françoise.

'Yes, I think so,' Elisabeth gazed fixedly into space; an unpleasant thought was passing through her mind. 'He thinks he can make me swallow anything,' she said. 'He'll get a big surprise.'

Françoise studied her with some interest. At this moment she was not consciously striking an attitude.

'Do you want to break off with him?' said Françoise.

Something relaxed in Elisabeth's face. She became matter of fact.

'Claude is far too attractive a person for me ever to let him go out of my life,' she said. 'But I would like to be less in love with him.'

She wrinkled the corners of her eyes and smiled at Françoise with a hint of mutual understanding, which passed between them only very rarely.

'We've poked enough fun at women who let themselves be victimized. And say what you like, it's not in my line to be a victim.'

Françoise returned her smile. She would have liked to advise her, but it was a difficult thing to do. What was necessary, was for Elisabeth not to be in love with Claude.

'Putting an end to it in your own mind only won't get you very far,' she said. 'I wonder if you shouldn't compel him outright to make a choice.'

'This isn't the moment,' said Elisabeth sharply. 'No, I think that when I've won back my inner independence, I'll have made great progress. But to do that, it's essential for me to succeed in dissociating the man from the lover in Claude.'

'Will you stop sleeping with him?'

'I don't know. But what I do know is that I shall sleep with other men.' She added with a shade of defiance: 'Sexual faithfulness is perfectly ridiculous. It leads to pure slavery. I don't understand how you can tolerate it.'

'I swear to you that I don't feel that I'm a slave,' said Françoise.

Elisabeth could not help confiding in someone; after which she invariably became aggressive.

'It's odd,' said Elisabeth slowly, and as if she had been following a train of thought with surprised sincerity. 'The way you were at twenty, I would never have thought you would be a one-man woman. Especially as Pierre has affaires.'

'You've already told me that, but I am certainly not going to put myself out,' said Françoise.

'Nonsense. You're not going to tell me that it's never happened to you to feel a desire for a man,' said Elisabeth. 'You're talking like all the people who won't admit they have prejudices. They pretend they are subject to them as a matter of personal choice. But that's just so much nonsense.'

'Pure sensuality does not interest me,' said Françoise. 'And besides, does pure sensuality even have a meaning?'

'Why not? It's very pleasant,' said Elisabeth with a sneering little laugh.

Françoise rose.

'I think we might go down. The sets must have been changed by now.'

'You know, that young Guimiot is really charming,' said Elisabeth as she walked out of the room. 'He deserves more than a small part. He could be a worthwhile recruit for you. I'll have to speak to Pierre about it.'

'Do speak to him,' said Françoise. She gave Elisabeth a quick smile. 'I'll see you later.'

The curtain was still down. Someone on the stage was hammering. Heavy footsteps shook the flooring. Françoise walked over to Xavière who was talking to Inès. Inès blushed furiously and got up.

'Don't let me disturb you,' said Françoise.

'I was just going,' said Inès. She shook hands with Xavière. 'When am I going to see you?'

Xavière made a vague gesture.

'I don't know. I'll ring you up.'

'We might have dinner together tomorrow, between rehearsals.'

42

Inès remained standing in front of Xavière looking unhappy. Françoise had often wondered how the notion of becoming an actress could have entered that thick Norman skull: she had slaved for four years without making any appreciable progress: out of pity, Pierre had given her one line to speak.

'Tomorrow . . .' said Xavière. 'I'd rather ring you up.'

'You'll come through all right, you know,' said Françoise encouragingly. 'When you're not excited your diction is good.'

Inès smiled faintly and walked away.

'Will you never ring her up?' asked Françoise.

'Never,' said Xavière irritably. 'Just because I slept at her place three times, there's no reason why I should have to see her all my life.'

'Didn't Gerbert show you round?'

'He suggested it,' said Xavière.

'It didn't interest you?'

'He seemed so embarrassed,' said Xavière. 'It was painful.' She looked at Françoise with unveiled bitterness. 'I loathe foisting myself on people,' she said vehemently.

Françoise felt herself in the wrong. She had been tactless in leaving Xavière in Gerbert's hands, but Xavière's tone surprised her. Could Gerbert really have been off-hand with Xavière? That certainly wasn't his way.

'She takes everything so seriously,' she thought with annoyance.

She had decided once and for all not to let Xavière's childish fits of surliness poison her life.

'How was Portia?' said Françoise.

'The big dark girl? Monsieur Labrousse made her repeat the same sentence twenty times. She kept getting it all wrong.' Xavière's face glowed with scorn. 'Is it really possible for anyone as stupid as that to be an actress?'

'There are all kinds,' said Françoise.

Xavière was bursting with rage: that was obvious. Without a doubt she felt that Françoise was not giving her sufficient attention. She would get over it. Françoise looked at the curtain impatiently. The change of scenery was taking far too long. At least five minutes would have to be saved.

The curtain went up. Pierre was reclining on Caesar's couch and Françoise's heart began to beat faster. She knew Pierre's every intonation, his every gesture. She anticipated them so exactly that she felt as if they sprang from her own will. And yet, it was outside her, on the stage, that they materialized. It was agonizing. She would feel herself responsible for the slightest failure and she couldn't raise a finger to prevent it.

'It's true that we are really one,' she thought with a burst of love. Pierre was speaking, his hand was raised, but his gestures, his tones, were as much a part of Françoise's life as of his. Or rather, there was but one life and at its core but one entity, which could be termed neither he nor I, but we.

Pierre was on the stage, she was in the audience, and yet for both of them it was the same play being performed in the same theatre. Their life was the same. They did not always see it from the same angle, for through their individual desires, moods, or pleasures, each discovered a different aspect. But it was, for all that, the same life. Neither time nor distance could divide them. There were, of course, streets, ideas, faces, that came into existence first for Pierre, and others first for Françoise; but they faithfully pieced together these scattered experiences into a single whole, in which 'yours' and 'mine' became indistinguishable. Neither one nor the other ever withheld the slightest fragment. That would have been the worst, the only possible betrayal.

'Tomorrow afternoon at two o'clock, we'll rehearse the third act without costumes,' said Pierre. 'And tomorrow morning we'll go through the whole thing, in sequence and in costume.'

'I'm going to beat it,' said Gerbert. 'Will you need me tomorrow morning?'

Françoise hesitated. With Gerbert the worst drudgery became almost fun; the morning without him would be arid, but his pathetic tired face was heart-breaking to behold.

'No, there isn't much left to do,' she said.

'Is that really true?' said Gerbert.

'Absolutely true. You can go and sleep like a log.'

Elisabeth walked up to Pierre.

'You know, this Julius Caesar of yours is really extraordinary,' she said. Her face had an intent expression. 'It's so different and at the same time so realistic. The silence at that moment when you raise your hand – the quality of that silence – it's magnificent.'

'That's sweet of you,' said Pierre.

'I assure you it will be a success,' she said emphatically. She looked Xavière up and down with amusement.

'This young lady doesn't seem to care very much for the theatre. So blasée already?'

'I had no idea the theatre was like this,' said Xavière in a disdainful tone.

'What did you think it was like?' said Pierre.

'They all look like shop assistants. They look so intent.'

'It's thrilling,' said Elisabeth. 'All this groping, all this seemingly confused effort which finally bursts forth as a thing of beauty.'

'Personally, I find it disgusting,' said Xavière. Anger had swept away her timidity. She threw a black look at Elisabeth. 'An effort is not a pretty thing to see. And when the effort miscarries, well then,' she sneered, 'it's ludicrous.'

'It's the same in every art,' said Elisabeth curtly. 'Beautiful things are not easily created. The more precious they are, the more work they require. You'll see.'

'The things I call precious,' said Xavière, 'are those that fall like manna from heaven.' She pouted. 'If they have to be bought, they're merchandise just like anything else. That doesn't interest me.'

'What a little romantic!' said Elisabeth with a cold laugh.

'I know what she means,' said Pierre. 'All our seethings and bubblings can scarcely appear very appetizing.'

Elisabeth turned an almost belligerent face towards him.

'Well! That's news! Do you now believe in inspiration?'

'No, but it's true that our work isn't beautiful. On the whole, it's a disgusting mess.'

'I didn't say this work was beautiful,' said Elisabeth abruptly. 'I know that beauty lies only in the completed work, but I find it thrilling to watch the transition from the formless to the pure and completed state.'

Françoise looked at Pierre imploringly. It was painful to argue with Elisabeth. If she couldn't have the last word, she felt she had lost prestige in the sight of the onlookers. To compel their esteem, their love, she fought them with vicious dishonesty. This might go on for hours.

'Yes,' said Pierre looking vague, 'but only a specialist can appreciate that.'

There was a silence.

'I think it would be wise to go,' said Françoise.

Elisabeth looked at her watch.

'Heavens! I'll miss the last métro,' she said with dismay.

45

'I'm going to dash away. I'll see you tomorrow.'

'We'll take you home,' said Françoise feebly.

'No, no, you'll only delay me,' said Elisabeth. She seized her gloves and bag, cast a wavering smile into space and disappeared.

'We could go somewhere and have a drink,' said Françoise.

'If you two aren't too tired,' said Pierre.

'I don't feel the least bit sleepy,' said Xavière.

Françoise locked the door and they left the theatre. Pierre hailed a taxi.

'Where shall we go?' he said.

'To the Pôle Nord. It's quiet there,' said Françoise.

Pierre told the driver the address. Françoise turned on the light and powdered her nose. She wondered if she had been well advised in suggesting that they go out together. Xavière was sullen and the silence was already becoming awkward.

'Go in. Don't wait for me,' said Pierre, looking for change to pay the taxi.

Françoise pushed open the leather door.

'Is that table in the corner all right?' she said.

'Yes. This place looks very nice,' said Xavière. She took off her coat.

'Excuse me for one moment. I feel a little untidy and I don't like making up my face in public.'

'What shall I order for you?' said Françoise.

'Something strong,' said Xavière.

Françoise's eyes followed her.

'She said that deliberately because I powdered my face in the taxi,' she thought. When Xavière adopted this attitude of discreet superiority, it was because she was frothing with rage.

'Where has your little friend gone?' said Pierre.

'She's titivating. She's in a queer mood tonight.'

'She really is rather charming,' said Pierre. 'What are you having?'

'An aquavit,' said Françoise. 'Order two.'

'Two aquavits,' said Pierre. 'But give us the real aquavit. And one whisky.'

'You're so thoughtful,' said Françoise. The last time she had been brought some cheap brandy. That had been two months ago but Pierre had not forgotten. He never forgot anything connected with her.

'Why is she in a bad mood?' said Pierre.

'She thinks I didn't see enough of her. It's annoying, all the time I waste with her and still she isn't satisfied.'

'You've got to be fair,' said Pierre. 'You don't see much of her.'

'If I were to give her any more time, I wouldn't have a minute to myself,' said Françoise vehemently.

'I understand,' said Pierre. 'But you can't expect her to be so particularly satisfied with you. She has only you and she's very fond of you. That can't be much fun.'

'I don't say it is,' said Françoise. Perhaps she was a little off-hand with Xavière. She found the idea unpleasant. She didn't want to have the slightest reason for blaming herself. 'Here she is,' she said.

She looked at her with surprise. The blue dress fitted revealingly over a slender, rounded body, and the delicate youthful face was framed by sleek hair. The supple, feminine Xavière was something Françoise had not seen since their first meeting.

'I ordered an aquavit for you,' said Françoise.

'What is it?' said Xavière.

'Taste it,' said Pierre, pushing a glass toward her.

Xavière cautiously put her lips to the transparent spirit.

'It's terrible,' she said smiling.

'Would you like something else?'

'No, brandy is always terrible,' she said soberly, 'but one has to drink it.' She leaned her head back, half-closed her eyes and lifted the glass to her mouth.

'It burns all the way down my throat,' she said. She ran her fingers along her slender neck. Her hand slipped slowly along her body. 'And it burns here. And here. It is odd. I feel as if I were being lighted up from inside.'

'Is this the first time you've been to a rehearsal?' said Pierre.

'Yes,' said Xavière.

'And you were disappointed?'

'A little.'

'Do you really believe what you said to Elisabeth?' asked Françoise, 'or did you say it because she annoyed you?'

'She did annoy me,' said Pierre. He pulled a tobacco-pouch out of his pocket and began to fill his pipe. 'In point of fact, to a pure and uninitiated soul, the solemn way in which we seek to create the exact reproduction of something that doesn't exist must seem positively obscene.'

'There's no choice, since we really do want to make it exist,' said Françoise.

'If at least we succeeded the first time, and enjoyed it! But no, we have to grumble and sweat. All that drudgery to produce a ghost . . .' He smiled at Xavière. 'You think it's ridiculous obstinacy?'

'I never like to take trouble over anything,' said Xavière demurely.

Françoise was a little surprised that Pierre took these childish whims so seriously.

'You are questioning the validity of art as a whole, if you take that line,' she said.

'Yes, why not?' said Pierre. 'Don't you see that at this moment the world is in turmoil? We may have war within the next six months.' He caught his left hand between his teeth. 'And here I am trying to reproduce the colour of dawn.'

'What do you want to do?' said Françoise. She felt very upset. Pierre it was who had convinced her that the greatest thing in the world was to create beauty. Their whole life together had been built on this belief. He had no right to change his opinion without warning her.

'Why, I want *Julius Caesar* to be a success,' said Pierre. 'But I feel the size of a bee's knee.'

When had he begun to think that? Did it really worry him or was it one of those brief flashes of illumination which gave him a moment's pleasure and then disappeared without leaving a trace? Françoise dared not continue the conversation. Xavière did not seem bored, but she was looking down.

'Suppose Elisabeth were to hear you,' said Françoise.

'Yes, art is like Claude. It mustn't be touched, otherwise . . .'

'It will collapse immediately,' said Françoise. 'She seems almost to have a premonition.' She turned to Xavière. 'Claude, you know, is the chap who was with her at the Flore the other evening.'

'That horrible dark fellow!' said Xavière.

'He's not so ugly,' said Françoise.

'He's pseudo-handsome,' said Pierre.

'And a pseudo-genius,' said Françoise.

Xavière's look brightened.

'What would she do if you were to tell her that he is stupid and ugly,' she said winningly.

'She wouldn't believe it,' said Françoise. She thought a

moment. 'I think she would break with us and she would hate Battier.'

'You haven't a very high opinion of Elisabeth,' said Pierre cheerfully.

'Not very high,' said Xavière a little embarrassed. She seemed determined to be pleasant to Pierre. Perhaps in order to show Françoise that her ill humour was directed at her alone. Perhaps, too, she was flattered that he took her side.

'What exactly do you dislike about her?' asked Pierre.

Xavière hesitated.

'She's so artificial. Her scarf, her voice, the way she taps her cigarette on the table, it's all done deliberately.' She shrugged her shoulders. 'And it's done badly. I'm sure she doesn't like tobacco. She doesn't even know how to smoke.'

'She's been practising since the age of eighteen,' said Pierre.

Xavière smiled furtively. Her smile indicated a secret under-standing with herself.

'I don't dislike people who act a part in front of other people,' she said. 'The ridiculous thing about that woman is that, even when she's alone, she has to walk with a firm step and make deliberate movements with her mouth.'

Her voice was so hard that Françoise felt hurt.

'I think you like to dress up yourself,' said Pierre. 'I wonder what your face is like without the fringe and those rolls that hide half of it. And your handwriting is disguised, isn't it?'

'I've always disguised my handwriting,' said Xavière proudly. 'For a long time I wrote in a round hand, like this.' She traced letters in the air with the point of her finger. 'Now I use a pointed hand. It's more refined.'

'The worst thing about Elisabeth,' said Pierre, 'is that even her feelings are false. Fundamentally, she doesn't give a damn about painting. She's a communist and she admits she doesn't give a damn about the proletariat!'

'Lying doesn't bother me,' said Xavière. 'What I think is monstrous is making up one's mind in that way, as if to order. To think that every day at a set hour she begins to paint without having any desire to paint. She goes to meet her man whether she has any desire to see him or not . . .' Her upper lip curled in a contemptuous sneer. 'How can anyone submit to living according to plan, with time-tables and homework, as if they were still at a boarding school? I'd rather be a failure!'

She had achieved her aim: Françoise had been struck by

the indictment. Usually, Xavière's insinuations left her cold; but tonight, it was a different matter. The attention Pierre was paying to Xavière's opinions lent them weight.

'You make appointments and then don't keep them,' said Françoise. 'It's all very well when you do that to Inès, but you might also ruin some real friendships by going through life like that.'

'If I like people, I'll always want to keep appointments,' said Xavière.

'That's not bound to happen every time,' said Françoise.

'Well, that's just too bad,' said Xavière. She pouted disdainfully. 'I've always ended up by quarrelling with everyone.'

'How could anyone quarrel with Inès?' said Pierre. 'She's like a sheep.'

'Oh, don't be too sure of that,' said Xavière.

'Really?' said Pierre. His eyes wrinkled gaily. He was curiosity itself. 'With that big, innocent face do you mean to tell me she's liable to bite you? What has she done to you?'

'She hasn't done anything,' said Xavière reticently.

'Oh, please tell me,' said Pierre in his most coaxing voice. 'I'd be delighted to know what's hidden in the depths of those still waters.'

'Oh nothing. Inès is a dunce,' said Xavière. 'The point is, I don't like anyone to feel they hold any proprietary rights over me.' She smiled and Françoise's uneasiness crystallized. When alone with Françoise, Xavière, despite herself, permitted loathing, pleasure, affection, to be visible on a defenceless face, a child's face. Now she felt herself a woman in front of a man and her features displayed precisely the shade of confidence or reserve she wanted to express.

'Her affection must be an encumbrance,' said Pierre with a look of concurrence and innocence which trapped Xavière.

'That's right,' said Xavière brightening. 'Once I put off an appointment at the last minute – the evening we went to the Prairie. She pulled a face a yard long . . .'

Françoise laughed.

'Yes,' said Xavière excitedly. 'I was rude, but she dared to make some uncalled-for remarks,' she blushed and added, 'about something that was none of her concern.'

So that was it. Inès must have questioned Xavière about her relations with Françoise, and perhaps, with her calm Norman heavy-handedness, had joked about it. Beneath all Xavière's

50

vagaries there was without question a whole world of obstinate and secret thoughts. It was a somewhat disquieting idea.

Pierre laughed.

'I know someone, that young Eloy girl, who always answers when a friend breaks a date: "It so happens that I'm no longer free!" But not everyone has that amount of tact.'

Xavière frowned.

'In any case, not Inès,' she said. She must have been vaguely aware of the sarcasm, because her face had frozen.

'It's very complicated, you know,' said Pierre seriously. 'I can readily understand that you find it distasteful to follow the rules, but it's also impossible to live only for the moment.'

'Why?' said Xavière. 'Why do people always have to drag so much dead weight about with them?'

'Look,' said Pierre, 'time isn't made up of a heap of little separate bits into which you can shut yourself up in turn. When you think you're living purely in the present, you're involving your future whether you like it or not.'

'I don't understand,' said Xavière. Her tone was not friendly.

'I'll try to explain,' said Pierre. When he became interested in a person, he was capable of carrying on a discussion for hours with angelic sincerity and patience. It was one form of his generosity. Françoise rarely took the trouble to explain what she thought.

'Let's assume you've decided to go to a concert,' said Pierre. 'Just as you're about to set out, the idea of walking or taking the métro there strikes you as unbearable. So you convince yourself that you are free as regards your previous decision, and you stay at home. That's all very well, but when ten minutes later you find yourself sitting in an arm-chair, bored stiff, you are no longer in the least free. You're simply suffering the consequences of your own act.'

Xavière laughed dryly.

'Concerts! That's another of your beautiful inventions. As if anyone could want to hear music at fixed hours! – It's utterly ridiculous.' She added in a tone of almost bitter hatred: 'Has Françoise told you that I was supposed to go to a concert this afternoon?'

'No, but I do know that as a rule you can never bring yourself to leave your room. It's a shame to live like a hermit in Paris.'

'Well, this evening isn't going to make me want to change

my mind,' she said scornfully.

Pierre's face darkened.

'You'll miss scores of precious opportunities if you carry on like that,' he said.

'Always being afraid of losing something! To me there's nothing more sordid. If it's lost, it's lost, that's all there is to it!'

'Is your life really a series of heroic renunciations?' said Pierre with a sarcastic smile.

'Do you mean I'm a coward? If you knew how little I care!' said Xavière smugly, with a slight curl of her upper lip.

There was a silence. Pierre and Xavière both assumed poker-faces.

'I think we'd better go home to bed,' said Françoise.

What was most aggravating was that she herself could not overlook Xavière's ill humour as easily as during the rehearsal. Xavière had suddenly begun to count, though no one understood exactly why.

'Do you see that woman facing us?' said Françoise. 'Listen to her a moment. She's been telling her boy-friend all the particular secrets of her soul for quite a long time.'

She was a young woman with heavy eyelids. She was staring, as if hypnotized, at her companion. 'I've never been able to follow the rules of flirting,' she was saying. 'I can't bear being touched; it's morbid.'

In another corner, a young woman with green and blue feathers in her hair was looking uncertainly at a man's huge hand that had just pounced on hers.

'This is a great meeting-place for young couples,' said Pierre.

Once more a long silence ensued. Xavière had raised her arm to her lips and was gently blowing the fine down on her skin. Françoise felt she ought to think of something to say, but everything sounded false even as she was putting it into words.

'Have I ever told you anything about Gerbert?' said Françoise to Xavière.

'A little,' said Xavière. 'You've told me he's very nice.'

'He had a queer childhood,' said Françoise. 'He comes from a completely poverty-stricken working-class family. His mother went mad when he was a baby, his father was out of work, and the boy earned a few sous a day selling newspapers. One fine day a pal of his took him along to a film-studio to look for a job as an extra, and it happened that both were taken on.

He couldn't have been more than ten years old at the time. He was very likeable and he attracted attention. He was given minor parts and, later on, more important ones. He began to make good money, which his father squandered royally.' Françoise gazed apathetically at a tremendous white cake, decorated with fruit and arabesques of icing, which reposed upon a nearby tray; just looking at it was enough to make anyone feel sick. No one was listening to her story.

'People began to take an interest in him. Péclard more or less adopted him; he's still living with him. He's had as many as six adoptive fathers at one time. They dragged him out to cafés and night clubs; the women used to stroke his head. Pierre was one of these fathers; he helped him with his work and his reading.' She smiled and her smile was lost in space. Pierre, huddled into himself, was smoking his pipe. Xavière looked barely polite. Françoise felt ridiculous, but she kept talking with stubborn animation.

'That boy had a very funny education. He was an expert on surrealism without ever having read a line of Racine. It was touching, because to fill in the gaps he used to go to the public libraries to pore over atlases and books on mathematics like a real little self-educator, but he kept it all a secret. And then he had a very hard time of it. He was growing up; people could no longer find amusement in him as if he were a little performing monkey. About the same time as he lost his job in the movies, his adoptive fathers dropped him, one after the other. Péclard dressed and fed him when he thought of it, but that was all. It was then that Pierre took him in hand and persuaded him to take up the theatre. Now he's made a good start. He still lacks experience, but he's talented and has a great stage-sense. He'll get somewhere.'

'How old is he?' asked Xavière.

'He looks sixteen, but he's twenty.'

Pierre smiled faintly.

'I must say, you do know how to spin out a conversation,' he said.

'I'm very glad you've told me his story,' said Xavière eagerly. 'It's extremely amusing to picture that little boy and all those self-important men who condescendingly kicked him around, and so felt strong and generous, and patronizing.'

'You can easily see me doing that, can't you?' said Pierre, pulling a wry face.

'You? Why? No more than the others,' said Xavière, in all innocence. She looked at Françoise with marked affection. 'I always thoroughly enjoy your way of telling stories.'

She was offering Françoise a transference of her allegiance. The woman with the green and blue feathers was saying in a flat voice: '. . . I only rushed through it, but for a small town it's very picturesque.' She had decided to leave her bare arm on the table and as it lay there, forgotten, ignored, the man's hand was stroking a piece of flesh that no longer belonged to anyone.

'It's extraordinary, the impression it makes on you to touch your eyelashes,' said Xavière. 'You touch yourself without touching yourself. It's as if you touched yourself from some way away.'

She spoke to herself and no one answered her.

'Have you noticed how pretty those green and gilt latticed windows are?' said Françoise.

'In the dining-room at Lubersac,' said Xavière, 'there were leaded windows, too. But they weren't as wishy-washy as these, they had beautiful rich colours. When I looked out at the park through the yellow panes, there might have been a thunderstorm over the landscape; through the green and blue it appeared like paradise, with trees of precious stones and lawns of brocade; and when through the red, I thought I was in the bowels of the earth.'

Pierre made a perceptible effort to be amiable. 'Which did you prefer?' he asked.

'The yellow, of course,' said Xavière. She stared into space, as if in suspense. 'It's terrible the way one loses things as one grows older.'

'But you can't remember everything?' he said.

'Why not? I never forget anything,' said Xavière scornfully. 'For instance, I remember very clearly how beautiful colours used to transport me in the past; now . . .' she said with a disillusioned smile, 'I only find them pleasing.'

'Yes, of course! That always happens when you grow older,' said Pierre in a kind voice. 'But there are other things to be gained. Now you understand books and pictures and plays which would have been meaningless to you in your childhood.'

'But I don't give a damn about understanding just with my mind,' said Xavière with unexpected violence and with a kind of sneer. 'I'm not an intellectual.'

'Why do you have to be so disagreeable?' said Pierre abruptly.

Xavière stared, wide-eyed.

'I'm not being disagreeable.'

'You know very well that you are. You hate me on the slightest pretext. Though I think I can guess why.'

'What do you think?' asked Xavière.

Her cheeks were flushed with anger. Her face was extremely attractive, with such subtly variable shadings that it seemed not to be composed of flesh, but rather of ecstasy, of bitterness, of sorrow, to which the eye became magically sensitive. Yet, despite this ethereal transparency, the outlines of her nose and mouth were extremely sensual.

'You thought I wanted to criticize your way of life,' said Pierre, 'that's not so. I was arguing with you as I would argue with Françoise, or with myself. And for the simple reason that your point of view interested me.'

'Of course you chose the most malicious interpretation at once,' said Xavière. 'I'm not a sensitive child. If you think I'm weak and capricious and I don't know what else, you can surely tell me.'

'Not at all, I'm very envious of your capacity to feel things so strongly,' said Pierre. 'I understand your putting a higher value on that than on anything else.'

If he had taken it into his head to win his way back into Xavière's good graces, this was only the beginning.

'Yes,' said Xavière with a certain gloom; her eyes flashed. 'I'm horrified that you should think that of me. It's not true. I don't get annoyed like a child.'

'Still, don't you see,' said Pierre in a conciliatory tone, 'you put an end to the conversation, and from that moment on you were no longer in the least friendly.'

'I wasn't aware of it,' said Xavière.

'Try to remember; you're sure to become aware of it.'

Xavière hesitated.

'It wasn't for the reason you thought.'

'What was the reason?'

Xavière made a brusque gesture.

'No, it's stupid, it's of no importance. What good does it do always to hark back to the past? It's over and done with now.'

Pierre sat up and faced Xavière squarely, he would spend the whole night here rather than give in. To Françoise, such

55

persistence sometimes seemed tactless, but Pierre was not afraid of being tactless. He had consideration for other people's feelings only in small things. What exactly did he want of Xavière? polite rencontres on the hotel staircase? an affaire? love? friendship?

'It's of no importance if we expect never to see each other again,' said Pierre. 'But that would be a pity: don't you think we could establish pleasant relations?' He had infused a kind of wheedling timidity into his voice. He had such absolute control over his face and his slightest inflections, that it was a little disconcerting.

Xavière gave him a wary and yet almost affectionate look. 'Yes, I think so,' she said.

'Then let's get this straight,' said Pierre. 'What did you hold against me?' His smile already held an implication of secret understanding.

Xavière was playing with a strand of hair. Watching the slow and steady movement of her fingers, she said:

'It suddenly occurred to me that you were trying to be nice to me because of Françoise, and I disliked that.' She flung back the golden strand. 'I have never asked anyone to be nice to me.'

'Why did you think that?' said Pierre. He was chewing the stem of his pipe.

'I don't know,' said Xavière.

'You thought that I'd been too hasty in putting myself on terms of intimacy with you? And that made you angry with me and with yourself? Isn't that so? Therefore, out of some sort of surliness, you decided that my cordiality was only a pretence.'

Xavière said nothing.

'Was that it?' asked Pierre with a twinkle.

'Yes, in a way,' said Xavière with a flattered and embarrassed smile. Again she took hold of a few hairs and began to run her fingers up and down them, squinting at them with a stupid expression. Had she given it so much thought? Certainly Françoise, out of laziness, had over-simplified Xavière; she even wondered, a little uneasily, how she could possibly have treated Xavière like an insignificant little girl for the last few weeks; but wasn't Pierre deriving some pleasure out of making her complicated? In any case, they did not both view her in the same light. Slight as it was, this variance was apparent to Françoise.

'If I hadn't wanted to see you, it would have been very simple to go straight back to the hotel,' said Pierre.

'You might have wanted to see me out of curiosity,' said Xavière. 'That would be natural; you and Françoise have a way of pooling everything.'

A whole world of secret resentment was discernible in this short off-hand sentence.

'You thought we had mutually agreed to lecture you?' said Pierre. 'But that had nothing to do with the case.'

'You were like two grown-ups giving a child a good talking-to,' said Xavière, who seemed now to be sulking only on principle.

'But I didn't say anything,' said Françoise.

Xavière assumed a knowing look. Pierre stared at her, smiling earnestly.

'You'll understand, after you've seen us together enough times, that you need have no fear of considering us as two distinct individuals. I could no more prevent Françoise from being friendly towards you, than she could force me to be friendly towards you if I didn't feel so inclined.' He turned to Françoise. 'Isn't that so?'

'Certainly,' said Françoise with a warmth that apparently did not ring false. She felt a little sick at heart; 'we are but one': that's all very nice, but Pierre was demanding his independence. Of course, in a sense they were two, that she knew very well.

'You both have so many ideas in common,' said Xavière. 'I'm never sure which of you is speaking or to whom to reply.'

'Does it seem preposterous that I, personally, should have a feeling of affection for you?' said Pierre.

Xavière looked at him in some hesitation.

'There's no reason why you should; I've nothing interesting to say, and you . . . you have so many ideas about everything.'

'You mean that I'm so old,' said Pierre. 'You're the one who drew the malicious conclusions. You think I fancy myself.'

'How could you think that!' said Xavière.

Pierre's voice became grave, faintly betraying the professional actor.

'Had I taken you for a charming inconsequential little person, I would have been more polite to you; I would wish for something other than mere politeness between us, because it so happens that I think very highly of you.'

'You are wrong,' said Xavière without conviction.

'And it's on purely personal grounds that I hope to win your friendship. Would you like to make a pact of personal friendship with me?'

'Gladly,' said Xavière. She opened wide her innocent eyes. She smiled a charming smile of assent, an almost amorous smile. Françoise looked at this unknown face, filled with reticence and promise, and she saw again that other face, innocent and childish, leaning on her shoulder one grey dawn. She had been unable to retain it; it had become obliterated; it was lost, perhaps, for ever. And suddenly, with regret, with resentment, she felt how much she might have loved her.

'Shake hands on it,' said Pierre. He put his open hand on the table. He had pleasing hands, dry and delicate. Xavière did not hold out her hand.

'I don't like that gesture,' she said coldly. 'It seems adolescent to me.'

Pierre withdrew his hand. When he was thwarted, his upper lip jutted forward, making him look unnatural and a little ill-bred. Silence ensued.

'Are you coming to the dress rehearsal?' asked Pierre.

'Of course, I'm looking forward to seeing you as a ghost,' said Xavière eagerly.

The room was almost empty. Only a few half-drunken Scandinavians were left at the bar. The men were flushed, the women bedraggled, and everyone was kissing everyone else roundly.

'I think we ought to go,' said Françoise.

Pierre turned to her anxiously.

'That's true, you've got to get up early tomorrow. Aren't you tired?'

'No more than I should be.'

'We'll take a taxi.'

'Another taxi?' said Françoise.

'Well, that can't be helped. You must get some sleep.'

They went out and Pierre stopped a taxi. He sat on the tip-up seat opposite Françoise and Xavière.

'You look sleepy, too,' he said amiably.

'Yes, I am sleepy,' said Xavière. 'I'm going to make myself some tea.'

'Tea!' said Françoise. 'You would do better if you went to

bed. It's three o'clock.'

'I detest going to bed when I'm dead tired,' said Xavière, with an apologetic look.

'You prefer to wait until you're wide awake?' said Pierre in an amused tone.

'The very thought of being subject to natural needs disgusts me,' said Xavière haughtily.

They got out of the taxi and went upstairs.

'Good night,' said Xavière. She opened her door without holding out her hand.

Pierre and Françoise went on up another flight. Pierre's dressing-room at the theatre was topsy-turvy these days and he had been sleeping in Françoise's room every night.

'I thought you were going to get angry again when she refused to put her hand in yours,' said Françoise.

Pierre sat down on the edge of the bed.

'I thought she was going to put on her shy act again and it irritated me,' he said. 'But on second thoughts, it sprang from a good motive. She didn't want an agreement, which she took dead seriously, to be treated like a game.'

'That would be just like her, certainly,' said Françoise. She had a curiously murky taste in her mouth that she could not get rid of.

'What a proud little devil she is!' said Pierre. 'She was well disposed towards me at first, but as soon as I dared to express a shadow of criticism, she hated me.'

'You explained things beautifully to her,' said Françoise. 'Was that out of politeness?'

'Oh, there was a lot on her mind tonight,' said Pierre. He did not go on, he appeared absorbed. What exactly was going on in his mind? She looked at his face questioningly. It was a face that had become too familiar and no longer told her anything. She had only to reach out her hand to touch him, but this very proximity made him invisible; it was impossible to think about him. There was not even any name with which to describe him. Françoise called him Pierre or Labrousse only when she was speaking about him to others; when she was with him, or even when she was alone, she never used his name. He was as intimate and as unknowable to her as she was to herself: had he been a stranger, she would at least have been able to form some opinion of him.

'What do you want of her, when all's said and done?' she asked.

'To tell the truth, I'm beginning to wonder,' said Pierre. 'She's no Canzetti, I can't expect just to have an affaire with her. To have a serious liaison with her, I would have to commit myself up to the hilt. And I've neither the time nor the inclination for that.'

'Why not the inclination?' asked Françoise. This fleeting uneasiness that had just come over her was absurd; they told one another everything, they kept nothing hidden from each other.

'It's complicated,' said Pierre, 'the very thought of it tires me. Besides, there's something childish about her that I find a little nauseating. She still smells of mother's milk. All I want is for her not to hate me, but to be able to talk to her once in a while.'

'I think you can count on that,' said Françoise.

Pierre looked at her hesitatingly.

'You weren't offended when I suggested to her that she and I should have a personal relationship?'

'Of course not,' said Françcoise. 'Why should I be?'

'I don't know, you seemed to be a little put out. You're fond of her, you might want to be the only one in her life.'

'You know perfectly well that she's rather an encumbrance,' said Françoise.

'I know that you're never jealous of me,' said Pierre, smiling. 'All the same, if you ever do feel like that, you must tell me. This confounded mania of mine for making a conquest . . . there's another case of making myself feel as small as an insect; and it means so little to me.'

'Of course I would tell you,' said Françoise. She hesitated, perhaps she ought to attribute her uneasiness of this evening to jealousy; she had not liked Pierre taking Xavière seriously; she had been worried by the smiles Xavière gave Pierre. It was a passing depression, caused largely by fatigue. If she spoke of it to Pierre, it would become a disquieting and gripping reality instead of a fleeting mood. Thenceforth, he would have to bear it in mind even when she herself attached no importance to it. No, there was nothing to it, she was not jealous.

'You may even fall in love with her, if you wish,' she said.

'There's no question of that,' said Pierre. He shrugged his shoulders. 'I'm not even sure that she doesn't hate me now even more than before.'

He slipped into bed. Françoise lay down beside him and kissed him.

'Sleep tight,' she said fondly.

'Sleep tight,' said Pierre, kissing her.

Françoise turned over towards the wall. In the room below theirs, Xavière would be drinking tea; she had probably lit a cigarette; she was free to choose the hour when she would get into bed, all alone in her bed, far removed from any alien presence; she was mentally and emotionally free. And without doubt, at this moment, she was revelling in this freedom, was using it to blame Françoise. She would be imagining Françoise, dead-tired, lying beside Pierre, and she would be delighting in her proud contempt.

Françoise stiffened, but she could no longer simply close her eyes and blot out Xavière. Xavière had been growing steadily all through the evening, she had been weighing on her mind as heavily as the huge cake at the Pôle Nord. Her demands, her jealousies, her scorn, these could no longer be ignored, for Pierre had entered into them to give them value. Françoise tried with all her strength to thrust into the background this precious and encumbering Xavière who was gradually beginning to take shape, and it was almost hostility that she felt within her. But there was nothing to be done, no way of going back. Xavière did exist.

Chapter Four

Elisabeth opened the door of her wardrobe in a state of despair. Of course, she could keep on her grey suit; it did well enough for any occasion and it was for that very reason that she had bought it. But just for once in a while, she would have liked to change her dress to go out in the evening: a different dress, a different woman. Tonight, Elisabeth was feeling languid, unpredictable and sensuous. 'A blouse for every occasion! – they make me sick with their millionaire's conception of economy.'

At the back of the wardrobe there was an old black satin dress that Françoise had admired two years ago: it was not so badly out of date. Elisabeth made up her face again and then put on the dress. She looked at herself in the looking-glass a little dubiously. She was not sure what to think; in any case, her hair style was wrong now. With a sweep of the brush she tousled its tidiness. 'Your beautiful burnished gold hair.' She might have had a different life; but she regretted nothing, she had freely chosen to sacrifice her life to art. Her nails were ugly, an artist's nails. However short she cut them, they were always smeared with a little cobalt or indigo; fortunately they made nail polish very thick nowadays.

Elisabeth sat down at her dressing-table and began to spread a creamy red lacquer over her nails.

'I would have been really elegant,' she thought, 'more elegant than Françoise. She always looks unfinished.'

The telephone rang. Elisabeth carefully put the tiny wet brush back in its bottle and got up.

'Is that you, Elisabeth?'

'Yes.'

'This is Claude. How are you? Well, everything is all right for tonight. Can I come back with you afterwards?'

'Not here,' said Elisabeth quickly. She gave a little laugh. 'I'd like a change of atmosphere.' This time she would really have it out with him, to the finish – not here, or it would only start all over again, as it had last month.

'As you wish. But where then? At the Topsy, or the Maisonnette?'

'No, just let's go to the Pôle Nord, it's the best place for talking.'

'All right. Half past twelve at the Pôle Nord. See you later.'

'So long.'

He was looking forward to an idyllic evening. But Françoise was right. If she really wanted to do any good, he must be made aware of it. Elisabeth sat down again and resumed her painstaking labour. The Pôle Nord was perfect. The leather upholstery would deaden a voice raised in anger and the subdued lighting would be merciful to a ravaged countenance. All those promises Claude had made her! and everything remained obstinately the same; one moment of weakness was enough for him to feel reassured. The blood rushed to Elisabeth's face. What a disgrace! For an instant, he had hesitated, his hand on the door-knob; she had driven him away with unforgivable words. All he had to do was to go; but without a word, he had come towards her. The memory smarted so that she closed her eyes. Again her mouth felt his mouth, so feverish that her lips parted despite herself; she felt on her breasts those gentle, urgent hands. Her breast swelled and she sighed as she had sighed in the intoxication of defeat. If only the door were to open now, if he were to come in . . . Elisabeth quickly put her hand to her mouth and bit her wrist.

'I'm not to be had like that,' she said aloud. 'I'm not a bitch.' She had not hurt herself, but she noticed with satisfaction the small white marks her teeth had made on her skin; she also noticed that the wet polish had smeared on three of her nails; there was a kind of bloody deposit sticking round the edges.

'What an ass!' she murmured. Eight-thirty. Pierre would be dressed already. Suzanne would be putting on her mink cape over an impeccable dress, her nails would be glistening. On a sudden impulse, Elisabeth reached out for the nail-polish remover. There was a crystalline tinkle, and there on the floor lay little splinters of glass, sprinkled over a yellow puddle that reeked of pear-drops.

Tears rose to Elisabeth's eyes; not for anything in the world would she go to the dress rehearsal with these butcher's fingers: it would be better to go straight to bed. To attempt to be elegant on no money was a bad bet. She slipped on her coat and ran down the stairs.

'Hôtel Bayard, rue Cels,' she told the taxi-driver.

When she got to Françoise's she could repair the damage. She took out her compact – too much rouge on her cheeks, and her lipstick too heavy and badly applied. No, do not touch a thing in the taxi or everything will be ruined – taxis give one an excellent opportunity to relax – taxis and lifts – a brief respite for over-busy women – other women are lying on couches with fine linen tied around their heads, as in the Elizabeth Arden advertisements, with gentle hands massaging their faces – white hands, white linen in white rooms – they will have smooth, relaxed faces and Claude will say with his masculine naïveté: 'Jeanne Harbley is really extraordinary.' Like Pierre, we used to call them tissue-paper women – competition on that basis is impossible.

She got out of the taxi. For an instant she stood motionless in front of the hotel. It was most aggravating: she could never approach any place where Françoise's life was spent without a throb in her heart. The wall was grey and peeling a little. It was a shabby hotel like a great many others; yet she certainly had enough money to rent a pleasant studio for herself. She opened the door.

'May I go up to Mademoiselle Miquel's room?'

The porter handed her the key. She climbed the staircase on which there lingered a faint smell of cabbage. She was in the very heart of Françoise's life; but, for Françoise, the smell of cabbage and the creaking of the stairs held no mystery. Françoise passed through this setting without noticing what Elisabeth's feverish curiosity distorted.

'I must try to imagine that I'm coming home, just part of the daily routine,' Elisabeth said to herself as she turned the key in the lock. She remained standing in the doorway. It was an ugly room, papered in grey with a pattern of huge flowers. Clothes were strewn over all the chairs, piles of books and papers on the desk. Elisabeth closed her eyes: she was Françoise, she was returning from the theatre, she was thinking about tomorrow's rehearsal. She opened her eyes. Above the wash-basin was a notice:

Guests are kindly requested:
Not to make any noise after ten p.m.
Not to wash any clothes in the basin.

Elisabeth looked at the couch, at the mirror-wardrobe, at

the bust of Napoleon on the mantelpiece beside a bottle of eau-de-Cologne, at some brushes and several pairs of stockings. She closed her eyes once more, and then opened them again. It was impossible to make this room her own: it was only too unalterably evident that it remained an alien room.

Elisabeth went over to the looking-glass in which the face of Françoise had so often been reflected and she saw her own face. Her cheeks were fiery. The least she could have done was to have kept on her grey suit; there was no doubt that she looked very well in it. Now she could do nothing about this unusual reflection, yet it was the permanent picture of her that people would take away with them tonight. She snatched up a bottle of nail-polish remover and a bottle of lacquer, and sat down at the desk.

A volume of Shakespeare's plays lay open at the page Françoise had been reading when she had suddenly pushed back her chair. She had thrown her dressing-gown on the bed and it still bore, in its disordered folds, the impress of her careless gesture; the sleeves were puffed out as if they still enclosed phantom arms. These discarded objects gave a more unbearable picture of Françoise than would her real presence. When Françoise was near her, Elisabeth felt a kind of peace: Françoise never gave away her real, true face but at least, when her smile was friendly, her true face did not exist at all. Here, in this room, Françoise's true face had left its mark and this mark was inscrutable. When Françoise sat down at this desk, alone with herself, what remained of the woman Pierre loved? What became of her happiness, her quiet pride, her austerity?

Elisabeth pulled towards her some sheets of paper which were covered with notes, rough drafts, ink-stained sketches. Thus scratched out and badly written, Françoise's thoughts lost their definiteness; but the writing itself and the erasures made by Françoise's hand still bore witness to Françoise's indestructible existence. Elisabeth pushed away the papers in sudden fury. This was ridiculous. She could neither become Françoise, nor could she destroy her.

'Time, just give me time,' she thought passionately. 'I, too, will become someone.'

A great many motors were parked in the square. With an artist's trained eye, Elisabeth looked at the yellow façade of the theatre gleaming through the bare branches: those ink-black lines standing out against the luminous background were beautiful. A real theatre, like the Châtelet and the Gaieté Lyrique which we used to think so marvellous! All the same, it was tremendous to think that the great actor, the great producer, now the talk of Paris, was none other than Pierre. It was to see him that this surging perfumed crowd was thronging into the foyer – we weren't ordinary children – we swore that we would be famous – I always had faith in him. But this is it, she thought, dazzled. This is it, really it; tonight the dress rehearsal at the Tréteaux, Pierre Labrousse in *Julius Caesar*.

Elisabeth tried to form the sentence as if she were just an ordinary Parisian and then to say quickly to herself : 'He's my brother,' but it was difficult to carry off. It was maddening, for all around you there were hundreds of such potential pleasures, on which you could never quite succeed in laying your hands.

'What's become of you?' said Luvinsky. 'You're never about these days.'

'I'm working,' said Elisabeth. 'You must come and see my canvases.'

She loved dress rehearsals. Perhaps it was childish, but she derived tremendous pleasure from shaking hands with all these writers and actors; she had always needed a congenial environment really to find and be herself – 'When I'm painting, I don't feel that I'm a painter; its thankless and discouraging.' Here she was, a young artist on the threshold of success, Pierre's own sister. She smiled at Moreau who looked at her admiringly, he had always been a little in love with her. In the days when she used to spend a great deal of time at the Dôme with Françoise, in the company of the beginners with no future and the old failures, she would have looked with wide-eyed envy at that vigorous, gracious young woman who was talking casually to a newly-arrived group.

'How are you?' said Battier. He looked very handsome in his dark lounge suit. 'The doors here are well guarded at least,' he added peevishly.

'How are you?' said Elisabeth, shaking hands with Suzanne. 'Did you have any trouble getting in?'

'That doorman scrutinizes all the guests as if they were criminals,' said Suzanne. 'He kept on turning over our card in his fingers for at least five minutes.'

She looked handsome, all in black, exactly right; but, to be frank, she looked distinctly old now, one could hardly suppose that Claude still had physical relations with her.

'They have to be careful,' said Elisabeth. 'Look at that fellow with his nose glued to the window, there are dozens like him in the square, trying to scrounge invitations: we call them "swallows", gate-crashers.'

'An amusing name,' said Suzanne. She smiled politely and turned to Battier. 'We ought to go in now, don't you think?'

Elisabeth followed them in; for a moment or so, she stood motionless at the back of the auditorium. Claude was helping Suzanne to slip off her mink cape; then he sat down beside her; she leaned towards him and laid her hand on his arm. A sharp stabbing pain suddenly shot through Elisabeth. She recalled that December evening when she had walked through the streets drunk with joy and triumph because Claude had said to her: 'You're the one I really love.' On her way home to bed she had bought a huge bunch of roses. He loved her, but that had changed nothing. His heart was hidden; that hand on his sleeve could be seen by every eye in the theatre, and everyone took it for granted that this was its natural place. A formal bond, a real bond, that was perhaps the sole reality of which one could be actually certain; but for whom does it really exist, this love that exists between us? At this moment, even she did not believe in it, nothing remained of it anywhere in the whole of existence.

'I've had enough,' she thought; once more she was going to suffer all through the evening, she foresaw the whole gamut: shivers, fever, moist hands, buzzing head. The very thought of it made her feel sick.

'Good evening,' she said to Françoise. 'How beautiful you look.'

She was really beautiful tonight. She had a large comb in her hair and her dress was ablaze with vivid embroidery; she attracted a great many glances without seeming to be aware of them. It was a joy to feel that this brilliant and calm young woman was her friend.

'You look lovely, too,' said Françoise. 'That dress looks so well on you.'

'It's old,' said Elisabeth.

She sat down on the right of Françoise. On her left sat Xavière, insignificant in her little blue dress. Elisabeth rucked

67

up the material of her skirt between her fingers. It had always been her principle to own few but expensive things.

'If I had money I would certainly be able to dress well,' she thought. She looked with a little less distress at the back of Suzanne's well-arranged hair. Suzanne belonged to the tribe of victims. She accepted anything from Claude – but we belong to a different species, we are strong and free and live our own lives. It was from pure generosity that Elisabeth did not reject the tortures of love, yet she did not need Claude; she was not an old woman – I shall say to him gently but firmly: 'You see, Claude, I have thought it over. I think we ought to change the basis of our relationship.'

'Have you seen Marchand and Saltrel?' asked Françoise. 'They're in the third row on the left. Saltrel is already coughing; he's getting ready to spring. Castier is waiting for the curtain to go up before taking out his spittoon. You know he always carries it with him; it's an exquisite little box.'

Elisabeth glanced at the critics, but she was in no mood to be amused by them. Françoise was obviously preoccupied about the success of the play; that was to be expected, there could be no help from her.

The lights went down and three metallic raps rang out across the silence. Elisabeth felt herself growing completely limp. 'If only I could be carried away by the acting,' she thought, 'but I know the play by heart – the scenery is pretty and so are the costumes – I'm sure I could do at least as well, but Pierre is like all relatives – no one ever takes members of their own family seriously – he ought to see my paintings without knowing they're by me. I have no social mask – it's such a nuisance to have to bluff all the time. If Pierre didn't always treat me like an inconsequential little sister, Claude might have looked upon me as an important, dangerous person.'

The familiar voice startled Elisabeth.

Stand you directly in Antonius' way . . . Calphurnia!

Pierre really had an amazing presence as Julius Caesar. His acting inspired a thousand thoughts.

'He's the greatest actor of the day,' said Elisabeth to herself.

Guimiot rushed on to the stage and she looked at him a little apprehensively: twice during rehearsals he had knocked over the bust of Caesar. He dashed across the open space and ran round the bust without touching it; he held a whip in his hand; he was almost naked, with only a strip of silk around his loins.

'He's remarkably well-built,' thought Elisabeth without being able to summon up any special feelings about him – it was delightful to sleep with him, but really that was forgotten as soon as over – it was light as thistledown – Claude . . .

'I'm overwrought,' she thought. 'I can't concentrate.'

She forced herself to look at the stage. 'Canzetti looks pretty with that heavy fringe on her forehead – Guimiot says that Pierre doesn't have much to do with her any longer, and that she's now after Tedesco – I don't really know – they never tell me anything.' She studied Françoise. Her face had not changed since the curtain had risen; her eyes were riveted on Pierre. How severe her profile was! One would have to see her in a moment of affection or of love, but she would be capable even then of preserving that Olympian air – she was lucky to be able to lose herself in the immediate present in this way – all these people were lucky. Elisabeth felt lost in the midst of this docile audience that allowed itself to be glutted with images and words. Nothing held her attention, the play did not exist; these were only minutes that were slowly ebbing away. The day had been spent in the expectation of these hours, and now they were crumbling away, becoming, in their turn, another period of expectancy. And Elisabeth knew that when Claude stood before her she would still be waiting; she would await the promise, the threat, that would tinge tomorrow's waiting with hope or horror. It was a journey without end, leading to an indefinite future, eternally shifting just as she was reaching the present. As long as Suzanne was Claude's wife the present would be intolerable.

The applause crackled. Françoise stood up, her cheeks were a little flushed.

'Tedesco never fumbled a line, everything went off perfectly,' she said excitedly. 'I'm going to see Pierre. If you wouldn't mind, it might be better for you to go round during the next interval. The crush is terrible at the moment.'

Elisabeth stood up as well.

'We could go into the foyer,' she said to Xavière. 'We shall hear people's comments. It's quite amusing.'

Xavière followed her obediently. 'What on earth can I say

to her?' Elisabeth wondered: she did not find her congenial.

'Cigarette?'

'Thank you,' said Xavière.

Elisabeth held up a match.

'Do you like the play?'

'I like it,' said Xavière.

How vigorously Pierre had defended her the other day! He was always inclined to be generous about strangers; but this time he really hadn't shown very good taste.

'Would you like to go on the stage yourself?' Elisabeth asked.

She was trying to discover the crucial question, the question that would draw from Xavière a reply by which she could once and for all be classified.

'I've never thought about it,' said Xavière.

Surely she spoke to Françoise in a different tone and with a different look! But Françoise's friends never showed their true selves to Elisabeth.

'What interests you in life?' Elisabeth asked abruptly.

'Everything interests me,' said Xavière politely.

Elisabeth wondered if Françoise had spoken to Xavière about her. How was she spoken of behind her back?

'You have no preferences?'

'I don't think so,' said Xavière.

With a preoccupied look, she was puffing at her cigarette. She had kept her secret well; all Françoise's secrets were well kept. At the other end of the foyer, Claude was smiling at Suzanne. His features reflected his servile affection.

'The same smile that he gives me,' thought Elisabeth, and a savage hatred entered her heart. Without any gentleness, she would speak to him without a trace of gentleness. She would lean her head back against the cushions and she would break into ruthless laughter.

The second intermission bell sounded. Elisabeth caught a glimpse of her red hair and her bitter mouth as she passed a looking-glass: there was something bitter and smouldering in her. She had made up her mind, tonight would be decisive. At times Suzanne drove him mad and at others she filled him with maudlin pity: he never could decide to separate from her once and for all. The auditorium grew dark. A picture flashed through Elisabeth's mind – a revolver – a dagger – a phial with a death's head on it – to kill someone . . . Claude? Suzanne?

Myself? – it didn't matter. This dark murderous desire violently took possession of her heart. She sighed – she was no longer young enough for insane violence – that would be too easy. No – what she had to do was to keep him at a distance for a time; yes – to keep at a distance his lips, his breath, his hands. She desired them so intensely – she was being smothered with desire. There, in front of her, on the stage, Caesar was being assassinated. 'Pierre is staggering across the Senate, and it is I, I who am really being assassinated,' she thought in despair. This empty excitement in front of cardboard scenery was nothing but an insult to her, since it was she who was sweating out her agony, in her flesh, in her blood, and with no possibility of resurrection.

Although Elisabeth had sauntered slowly along the boulevard Montparnasse, it was only twenty-five minutes past twelve when she walked into the Pôle Nord. She could never succeed in being deliberately late, and yet she felt certain that Claude would not be punctual, for Suzanne would purposely be keeping him with her, counting each minute as a tiny victory. Elisabeth lit a cigarette. She was not specially anxious for Claude to be there, but the thought that he was elsewhere was intolerable.

She felt her heart contract. Each time it was the same: when she saw him in flesh and blood in front of her, she was seized with anguish. There he was: he held Elisabeth's happiness in the palm of his hand and he was coming towards her casually; with no suspicion that each one of his gestures was a threat.

'I'm so glad to see you,' said Claude. 'At last, a real evening to ourselves!' He smiled eagerly. 'What are you drinking? Aquavit? I know that stuff; it's filthy. Give me a gin fizz.'

'You may be glad, but you stint your pleasures,' said Elisabeth, 'it's one o'clock already.'

'Seven minutes to one, darling.'

'Seven minutes to one, if you prefer,' she said with a slight shrug.

'You know very well it's not my fault,' said Claude,

'Of course,' said Elisabeth.

Claude's face darkened.

'Please, my pet, don't look so cross. Suzanne left me with a face like a thunder-cloud. If you start sulking too, it will be the end of everything. I was so looking forward to seeing your warm smile again.'

'I don't smile all the time,' said Elisabeth, hurt. Claude's lack of understanding was at times stupefying.

'That's a pity. It's so becoming to you,' said Claude. He lit a cigarette and looked about him benignly. 'This place isn't bad. It's a bit gloomy though, don't you think?'

'So you said the other day. On one of the rare occasions when I do see you, I'm not anxious to have a crowd all round us.'

'Don't be cross,' said Claude. He put his hand on Elisabeth's hand, but he looked annoyed. A second later she drew her hand away. This was a bad start: an important heart-to-heart explanation ought not to begin with petty squabbling.

'On the whole, it was a success,' said Claude. 'But I wasn't really carried away for an instant. I think Labrousse doesn't know precisely what he's after. He's wavering between complete stylization and pure and simple realism.'

'It's just that touch of stylization that he's after,' said Elisabeth.

'But there isn't any special touch about it,' said Claude in cutting tones. 'It's a series of contradictions. Caesar's assassination looked like a funereal ballet, and as for Brutus's watch in his tent – well, it was like going back to the days of the *Théâtre libre.*'

Claude was being too clever. Elisabeth did not let him settle questions as arbitrarily as that. She was pleased because her reply came readily to her lips.

'That depends on the situation,' she said quickly. 'An assassination has got to be stylized, or else it degenerates into melodrama, and by contrast, a supernatural scene has to be played as realistically as possible. That's only too obvious.'

'That's just what I'm saying. There's no unity. Labrousse's aesthetic is simply a kind of opportunism.'

'Not at all,' said Elisabeth. 'Of course, he takes the text into account. You're amazing; you used to accuse him of making the setting an end in itself. Do make up your mind.'

'But it is he who can't make up his mind,' said Claude. 'I'd very much like to see him carry out his famous plan of writing a play himself. Then we might know where we stand.'

'He'll certainly do that,' said Elisabeth. 'Probably next year.'

'I'd be curious to see it. You know I have a great admiration for Labrousse, but I don't understand him.'

'But it's so easy,' said Elisabeth.

'I'd be very grateful if you'd explain it to me,' said Claude.

Elisabeth was silent for a while, tapping her cigarette on the table. Pierre's aesthetic was no mystery to her. From it she took the inspiration for her painting, but words failed her. She saw once again the Tintoretto that Pierre loved so much; he had explained things to her about the attitudes of the figures, just what, she could not remember. She thought of Dürer's woodcuts, of a marionette show, of the Russian ballet, of the old silent movies; the idea was there, familiar and obvious, and this was terribly annoying.

'Obviously, it's not so simple that you can pin a label on it. Realism, impressionism, naturalism, if that's what you want,' she said.

'Why are you being so gratuitously unkind?' said Claude. 'I'm not used to technical terms.'

'I beg your pardon, but it was you who started talking about stylization and opportunism. But don't make excuses; your fear of being mistaken for a professor is superbly comic.'

More than anything, Claude dreaded sounding in the least academic, and, in all fairness, no one could look less like a professor than he.

'I can promise that I have nothing to fear on that count,' he said dryly. 'It's you who always deliberately introduce a kind of Germanic ponderosity into our discussions.'

'Ponderosity . . .' said Elisabeth. 'Yes, I know, every time I disagree with you, you accuse me of being pedantic. You're amazing. You can't bear to be contradicted. What you mean by intellectual companionship is the devout acceptance of all your opinions. Ask Suzanne for that, not me! I have the misforunte to have a brain and to presume to use it.'

'There you go! Can't keep your temper!' said Claude.

Elisabeth controlled herself This was hateful; he always found a way of putting her in the wrong.

'I may be bad tempered,' she said with crushing calm, 'but you can't hear yourself talk. You sound as if you were delivering a lecture.'

'Let's not squabble again,' said Claude in a conciliatory tone.

She looked at him resentfully. He had clearly made up his mind to be nice to her tonight; he felt affectionate, charming and generous, but she would show him. She coughed a little to clear her throat.

'Frankly, Claude, have you found this month's experiment a happy one?' she said.

'What experiment?' he said.

The blood rushed to Elisabeth's face, and her voice trembled a little.

'If we have kept on seeing one another after our heart-to-heart a month ago, it was only by way of an experiment. Have you forgotten?'

'Oh, of course . . .' said Claude.

He had not taken seriously the idea of a complete break; she had, of course, ruined everything by sleeping with him that very night. For a moment she was put out of countenance.

'Well, I think I've reached the conclusion that the present situation is impossible,' she said.

'Impossible? Why so suddenly impossible? What's happened now?'

'That's just it, nothing,' said Elisabeth.

'Well, then, explain your meaning. I don't understand.'

She hesitated. Of course, he had never mentioned that he would one day leave his wife; he had never made any promises; in a sense, he was unassailable.

'Are you really happy like this?' said Elisabeth. 'I put our love on a higher plane. What intimacy have we? We see one another in restaurants, in bars, and in bed. Those are just meetings. I want to share your life.'

'Darling, you're raving,' said Claude. 'No intimacy between us? Why, I haven't a single thought that I don't share with you. You understand me so wonderfully.'

'Yes, I have the best part of you,' said Elisabeth, sharply. 'Actually, you see, we should have kept to what, two years ago, you called an ideological friendship. My mistake was to love you.'

'But since I love you . . .'

'Yes,' she said. It was most irritating; she was unable to pin down any definite grounds for complaint against him without their seeming nothing but petty grievances.

'Well?' said Claude.

'Well, nothing,' said Elisabeth. She had put a world of misery into these words, but Claude did not choose to take notice of it. He looked round the room with a beaming smile; he felt

74

relieved and was already preparing to change the subject when she hurriedly added: 'Fundamentally you're a very simple soul. You were never really aware that I wasn't happy.'

'You take pleasure in tormenting yourself,' said Claude.

'Perhaps that's because I'm too much in love with you,' said Elisabeth dreamily. 'I wanted to give you more than you were prepared to accept. And, if one is sincere, to give is a way of insisting on some return. I suppose it's all my fault.'

'We aren't going to question our love every time we meet,' said Claude. 'This sort of conversation seems absolutely pointless to me.'

Elisabeth looked at him angrily. He could not even sense this pathetic lucidity that now made her so piteous. What was the good of it all? Suddenly, she felt herself growing cynical and hard.

'Never fear. We shall never question our love again,' she said. 'That's just what I wanted to tell you. From now on, our relations will be on an entirely different basis.'

'What basis? What basis are they on now?' Claude looked very annoyed.

'Henceforth, I only want to have a peaceful friendship with you,' she said. 'I'm also tired of all these complications. Only, I didn't think I could stop loving you.'

'You've stopped loving me?' Claude sounded incredulous.

'Does that really seem so extraordinary to you?' said Elisabeth. 'Please understand me. I'll always be very fond of you, but I shan't expect anything from you, and as far as I am concerned, I shall take back my freedom. Isn't it better that way?'

'You're raving,' said Claude.

Elisabeth turned scarlet with anger.

'But you're insane! I tell you that I'm no longer in love with you! A feeling can change. And you – you weren't even conscious of the fact that I had changed.'

Claude gave her a puzzled look.

'Since when have you stopped loving me? A few minutes ago, you said that you loved me too much.'

'I used to love you too much.' She hesitated. 'I'm not sure just how it all happened, but it's true, things are not as they used to be. For instance . . .' she added quickly in a slightly choked voice, 'before I could never have slept with anyone but you.'

'You've been sleeping with someone?'

'Does that upset you?'

'Who is it?' said Claude inquisitively.

'It doesn't matter. You don't believe me.'

'If it's true, you might have been loyal enough to tell me,' he said.

'That's exactly what I'm doing,' said Elisabeth. 'I am informing you. Surely you didn't expect me to consult you beforehand?'

'Who is it?' repeated Claude.

His expression had changed, and Elisabeth was suddenly afraid. If he was suffering, she would suffer too.

'Guimiot,' she said in a wavering voice. 'You know, the naked messenger in the first act.'

It was done; it was irreparable; it would be useless to deny it; Claude would not believe her denials – she didn't even have time to think – she must go blindly ahead. In the shadows, something horrible was threatening her.

'Your taste isn't bad,' said Claude. 'When did you meet him?'

'About ten days ago. He fell madly in love with me.'

Claude's face became inscrutable. He had often showed suspicion and jealousy, but he had never admitted to it. He would far rather have been hacked to pieces than utter a word of censure, but that was of no reassurance to her.

'After all, that's one solution,' he said. 'I've always thought it a pity than an artist should limit himself to one woman.'

'You'll soon make up for lost time,' said Elisabeth. 'Why, that Chanaux girl is just waiting to fall into your arms.'

'The Chanaux girl . . .' Claude grinned. 'I prefer Jeanne Harbley.'

'There's something to be said for that,' said Elisabeth.

She clutched her handkerchief in her moist hands; now she could see the danger and it was too late. There was no way of retreat. She had thought only of Suzanne. There were all the other women, young and beautiful women, who would love Claude and who would know how to make him love them.

'You don't think I stand a chance?' said Claude.

'She certainly doesn't dislike you,' said Elisabeth.

This was insane. Here she was trying to brazen it out and each word she uttered sucked her deeper into the slough of

'Don't let's stay here,' said Elisabeth nervously. 'It's horrible to feel them staring at our backs.'

'They're not paying any attention to us,' said Claude.

'It's odious . . . all these people,' said Elisabeth. Her voice broke. Tears rose to her eyes. She would not be able to hold them back much longer. 'Let's go to my studio,' she said.

'Just as you like,' said Claude. He called the waiter and Elisabeth put on her coat in front of the looking-glass. Her face was distraught. In the depths of the glass she caught sight of the others. Xavière was talking. She was gesticulating, and Françoise and Pierre were looking at her as if fascinated. That really was too inconsiderate. They could waste their time on any idiot, but they were blind and deaf to Elisabeth. Had they been willing to admit her with Claude into their intimate life, had they accepted *Partage*? It was their fault. Anger shook Elisabeth from head to foot; she was choking. They were happy, they were laughing. Would they be everlastingly happy, with such overwhelming perfection? Would not they, too, some day drop into the depths of this sordid hell? To wait in fear and trembling, to call vainly for help, to implore, to stand alone in the midst of regrets, anguish and an endless disgust of self. So sure of themselves, so proud, so invulnerable. By keeping careful watch, could not some way be found to hurt them?

Elisabeth stepped into Claude's car without a word. They did not exchange a single sentence until they reached her door.

'I don't think we have anything left to say to each other,' said Claude when he had stopped the car.

'We can't part like this,' said Elisabeth. 'Come up for a minute.'

'What for?' said Claude.

'Come up. We haven't really thrashed it out,' said Elisabeth.

'You don't love me any more, you think hateful thoughts about me. There's nothing to discuss.' said Claude.

This was blackmail, pure and simple, but it was impossible to let him go – when would he come back?

'You mean a great deal to me, Claude,' said Elisabeth. These words brought tears to her eyes. He followed her. She climbed the stairs crying spasmodically, with no effort at self-control; she staggered a little, but he did not take her arm. When they had entered the studio, Claude began to pace up and down in a black mood,

'You're quite free not to love me any more,' he said, 'but there was something else besides love between us, and that, you should try to salvage.' He glanced at the couch. 'Did you sleep here, with that fellow?'

Elisabeth had let herself drop into an arm-chair.

'I didn't think you would be angry with me for it, Claude,' she said. 'I don't want to lose you over a thing like that.'

'I'm not jealous of a second-rate little actor,' said Claude. 'I'm angry with you for not having told me anything. You should have spoken to me sooner. And, besides, tonight, you said things to me that make even friendship between us impossible.'

Jealous, he was just plain jealous: she had wounded his male pride and he wanted to torture her. She was well aware of that, but it made matters no better, his steely voice was exacerbating.

'I don't want to lose you,' she repeated. She began to sob undisguisedly.

It was stupid to abide by the rules, to play the game loyally; you got no thanks for that. You thought that one day all the hidden suffering and all the inner sensitivities and struggles would come to the surface, and that he would be overwhelmed with admiration and remorse. But no, this was just so much wasted effort.

'You know that I'm at the end of my tether,' said Claude. 'I'm going through a spiritual and intellectual crisis that's exhausting me. You were all I had to lean on, and this is the moment you have chosen!'

'Claude, you're unfair,' she said weakly. Her sobs increased; it was an emotion which carried her away with so much violence, that dignity and shame became mere futile words, and she found herself saying anything. 'I was too much in love with you, Claude,' she said. 'It's because I was too much in love with you that I wanted to free myself from you.' She hid her face in her hands. This passionate confession ought to call Claude to her side. Let him take her in his arms; let everything be blotted out! Never again would she utter a complaint.

She looked up, he was leaning against the wall, the corners of his mouth were trembling nervously.

'Say something to me,' she said. He was looking viciously at the couch, it was easy to guess what he saw there; she should never have brought him here, the picture was too vivid.

'Will you stop crying?' he said. 'If you treated yourself to that little pansy, it was because you wanted to. You no doubt got what you wanted.'

Elisabeth stopped, almost choking in the effort; she felt as if she had received a direct blow on her chest. She could not bear coarseness, she was physically incapable of it.

'I forbid you to speak to me like that,' she said with violence.

'I'll speak to you in whatever way I choose,' said Claude, raising his voice. 'I find it amazing that you now take the line that you're the victim.'

'Don't shout,' said Elisabeth. She was trembling, it seemed to her that she was listening to her grandfather, when the veins on his forehead became swollen and purple. 'I won't allow you to shout.'

Claude directed a kick at the chimney-piece.

'Do you want me to hold your hand?' he said.

'Stop screaming,' said Elisabeth, in an even more hollow voice. Her teeth were beginning to chatter, she was on the verge of hysteria.

'I'm not screaming. I'm going,' said Claude. Before she could move, he was outside the door. She dashed to the landing.

'Claude,' she called. 'Claude.'

He did not look back. She saw him disappear and the street door slammed. She went back into the studio and began to undress; she was no longer trembling. Her head felt as if it were swollen with water and the night, it became enormous, and so heavy that it pulled her towards the abyss – sleep, or death, or madness – a bottomless pit into which she would disappear for ever. She collapsed on her bed.

When Elisabeth opened her eyes again, the room was flooded with light; she had a taste of salt water in her mouth; she did not move. Pain, still somewhat deadened by fever and sleep, throbbed in her burning eyelids and in her pulsing temples. If only she could fall asleep again till tomorrow – not to have to make any decisions – not to have to think. How long could she remain plunged in this merciful torpor? Make believe I'm dead – make believe I'm floating – but already it was an effort to narrow her eyes and see nothing at all. She rolled herself up tighter in the warm sheets. Once again, she was slipping towards oblivion when the bell rang shrilly.

She jumped out of bed and her heart began to race. Was

it Claude already? What would she say? She glanced in the looking-glass. She did not look too haggard, but there was no time to choose her expression. For one second, she was tempted not to open the door – he would think she was dead or had disappeared – he would be frightened. She listened intently. There was not a breath to be heard on the other side of the door. Perhaps he had already turned round, slowly; perhaps he was going down the stairs – she would be left alone – awake and alone. She jumped to the door and opened it. It was Guimiot.

'Am I disturbing you?' he said, smiling.

'No, come in,' said Elisabeth. She looked at him somewhat horror-stricken.

'What time is it?'

'It's noon, I think. Were you asleep?'

'Yes,' said Elisabeth. She straightened the sheets and plumped up the bed; in spite of everything, it was better to have someone there. 'Give me a cigarette,' she said, 'and sit down.'

She was irritated by his way of walking in and out between the furniture like a cat, he liked to show off his body; his movements were supple and smooth, his gestures graceful and overdone.

'I was only passing by. I don't want to be in your way,' he said. He also overdid his smile, a thin smile that made his eyes wrinkle. 'It's a pity that you couldn't come last night. We drank champagne until five o'clock this morning. My friends told me that I was a sensation. What did Monsieur Labrousse think?'

'It was very good,' said Elisabeth.

'It seems that Roseland wants to meet me. He thinks I have a very interesting head. He is expecting to put on a new play soon.'

'Do you think it's your head he's after?' said Elisabeth. Roseland made no secret of his habits.

Guimiot gently pressed one moist lip against the other. His lips, his liquid blue eyes, his whole face made one think of a damp spring day.

'Isn't my head interesting?' he said coquettishly. A pansy grafted on to a gigolo, that was Guimiot.

'Isn't there a scrap to eat here?'

'Go and look in the kitchen,' said Elisabeth – 'Bed, breakfast and what have you,' she thought harshly – he always managed to cadge something, a meal, a tie, a little money borrowed but never returned. Today, she did not find him amusing.

'Do you want some boiled eggs?' shouted Guimiot.

'No, I don't want anything,' she answered. The sound of running water, and the clatter of pots and dishes came from the kitchen – she did not even have the courage to throw him out – when he left she would have to think.

'I've found a little wine,' said Guimiot. He put a plate, a glass and a napkin on one corner of the table. 'There's no bread, but I'll make the eggs soft-boiled. Soft-boiled eggs can be eaten without bread, can't they?'

He sat himself on the table and began to swing his legs.

'My friends told me that it's a pity I have such a small part. Do you think that Monsieur Labrousse might at least let me be an understudy?'

'I mentioned it to Françoise Miquel,' said Elisabeth – her cigarette tasted acrid and her head ached – it was just like a hangover.

'What did Mademoiselle Miquel say?'

'That she would have to see.'

'People always say they'll have to see,' said Guimiot sententiously. 'Life is very difficult.' He leapt toward the kitchen door. 'I think I hear the kettle singing.'

'He ran after me because I was Labrousse's sister,' thought Elisabeth – that was nothing new – she'd been well aware of it for ten days. But now she put her thoughts into words. She added: 'I don't care.' With unfriendly eyes she watched him put the pot on the table and open an egg with finicky gestures.

'There was a stout lady, rather old and very smart, who wanted to drive me home last night.'

'Fair, with a pile of little curls?'

'Yes. I refused to go because of my friends. She seemed to know Monsieur Labrousse.'

'That's our aunt,' said Elisabeth. 'Where did you and your friends have supper?'

'At the Topsy, and then we wandered round Montparnasse. At the bar of the Dôme we met the young stage-manager who was completely squiffy.'

'Gerbert? Whom was he with?'

'There were Tedesco and the Canzetti girl and Sazelat and

somebody else. I think Canzetti went home with Tedesco.'
He opened a second egg.

'Is the young stage-manager interested in men?'

'Not that I know of,' said Elisabeth. 'If he made any
advances to you it was because he was plastered.'

'He didn't make any advances to me,' said Guimiot, looking
shocked. 'It was my friends who thought he was so handsome.'
He smiled at Elisabeth with sudden intimacy. 'Why don't you
eat?'

'I'm not hungry,' said Elisabeth – this couldn't last much
longer – soon she would begin to suffer; she could feel it
beginning.

'That's pretty, that thing you're wearing,' said Guimiot, his
feminine hands running lightly over her silk pyjamas. The
hand became gently insistent.

'No, leave me alone,' said Elisabeth wearily.

'Why? Don't you love me any more?' said Guimiot. His
tone carried the suggestion of some lewd complicity, but
Elisabeth had ceased to offer any resistance. He kissed the
nape of her neck, he kissed her behind her ear; strange little
kisses; it almost seemed as if he were grazing. This would
always retard the moment when she would have to think.

'How cold you are!' he said almost accusingly. His hand
had slipped underneath the silk and he was watching her
through half-closed eyes. Elisabeth surrendered her mouth and
closed her eyes; she could no longer bear that look, that
professional look. She felt suddenly that these deft fingers
which were scattering a shower of downy caresses over her
body were the fingers of an expert, endowed with a skill as
precise as those of a masseur, a hairdresser, or a dentist.
Guimiot was conscientiously doing his job as a male. How
could she tolerate these services rendered, ironic as they were?

She made a movement to free herself. But she was so heavy,
so weak, that before she could pull herself together she felt
Guimiot's naked body against hers. The ease with which he
had stripped, this too, was one of the tricks of the trade. His
was a sinuous and gentle body that too easily embraced hers.
Claude's clumsy kisses, his crushing embrace . . . She opened
her eyes. Guimiot's mouth was curved and his eyes were
screwed up with pleasure. At this moment, he was thinking
only of himself, with the greed of a profiteer. She closed her
eyes again. A scorching humiliation swept over her. She was

84

anxious for it to end.

With an insinuating movement Guimiot put his cheek on Elisabeth's shoulder. She pressed her head against the pillow. But she knew that she would not be able to sleep any more. Now things must take their course, there was no help for it. That was that: one could no longer avoid suffering.

Chapter Five

'Three coffees, and bring them in cups,' said Pierre.

'You're pig-headed,' said Gerbert. 'The other day, with Vuillemin, we measured it out; the glasses hold exactly the same amount.'

'After a meal, coffee should be drunk from a cup,' said Pierre with finality.

'He maintains that the taste is different,' said Françoise.

'He's a dangerous dreamer!' said Gerbert. He thought for a minute. 'Strictly speaking, we might agree that it cools less rapidly in cups.'

'Why does it cool less rapidly?' said Françoise.

'Surface of evaporation is reduced,' said Pierre sententiously.

'Now you're well off the rails,' said Gerbert. 'What happens is that china retains the heat better.'

They were always full of fun when they debated a physical phenomenon. It was usually something they had made up on the spur of the moment.

'It cools all the same,' said Françoise.

'Do you hear what she says?' said Pierre.

Gerbert put a finger to his lips with mock discretion; Pierre nodded his head knowingly: this was the usual mimicry to express their impertinent complicity, but today, there was no conviction in this ritual. The luncheon had dragged out cheerlessly; Gerbert seemed spiritless, they had discussed the Italian demands at great length: it was unusual for their conversation to be swamped in such generalities.

'Did you read Soudet's criticism this morning?' said Françoise.

'He's got a nerve. He asserts that to translate a text word for word is to falsify it.'

'Those old drivellers!' said Gerbert. 'They won't dare admit that Shakespeare bores them stiff.'

'That's nothing, we've got vocal criticism on our side,' said Françoise, 'that's the most important thing.'

'Five curtain calls last night, I counted them,' said Gerbert.

'I'm delighted,' said Françoise. 'I felt sure we could put it across without making the slightest compromise.' She turned gaily to Pierre. 'It's quite obvious now that you're not merely a theorist, an ivory tower experimenter, a coterie aesthete. The porter at the hotel told me he cried when you were assassinated.'

'I've always thought he was a poet,' said Pierre. He smiled, as if somewhat embarrassed, and Françoise's enthusiasm subsided. Four days earlier, when they had left the theatre at the close of the dress rehearsal, Pierre had been feverishly happy and they had spent an intoxicating night with Xavière! But the very next day, this feeling of triumph had left him. That was just like him: he would have been devastated by a failure, but success never seemed to him to be any more than an insignificant step forward towards still more difficult tasks that he immediately set himself. He never fell into the weakness of vanity, but neither did he experience the serene joy of work well done. He looked at Gerbert questioningly.

'What is the Péclard clique saying?'

'That you're right off the mark,' said Gerbert. 'You know they're all for the return to the natural and all that tripe. All the same, they would like to know just what you've got up your sleeve.'

Françoise was quite sure she was not mistaken, there was a certain restraint in Gerbert's cordiality.

'They'll be on the look-out next year when you produce your own play,' said Françoise. She added gaily: 'Now, after the success of *Julius Caesar*, we can count on the support of the public. It's grand to think about.'

'It would be a good thing if you were to publish your book at the same time,' said Gerbert.

'You'll no longer be just a sensation, you'll be really famous,' said Françoise.

A little smile played on Pierre's lips.

'If the brutes don't gobble us up,' he said.

The words fell on Françoise like a cold douche.

'Do you think we'll fight for Djibouti?'

Pierre shrugged his shoulders.

'I think we were a little hasty in our rejoicings at the time of Munich. A great many things can happen between now and next year.'

There was a short silence.

'Put your play on in March,' said Gerbert.

'That's a bad time,' said Françoise, 'and besides, it won't be ready.'

'It's not a question of producing my play at all costs,' said Pierre. 'It's rather one of finding out just how much sense there is in producing plays at all.'

Françoise looked at him uneasily. A week earlier when they were at the Pôle Nord with Xavière, and he had referred to himself as an obstinate mule, she had chosen to interpret it as a momentary whim; but it seemed that a real anxiety was beginning to possess him.

'You told me in September that, even if war came, we should have to go on living.'

'Certainly, but how?' Pierre vaguely contemplated his fingers. 'Writing, producing . . . that's not after all an end in itself.'

He was really perplexed and Françoise almost felt a grudge against him, but she must go on quietly trusting in him.

'If that's the way you look at it, what is an end in itself?' she said.

'That's exactly the reason why nothing is simple,' said Pierre. His face had taken on a clouded and almost stupid expression: the way he looked in the morning when, with his eyes still pink with sleep, he desperately began searching for his socks all over the room.

'It's half-past two, I'll beat it,' said Gerbert.

He was never the first to leave as a rule; he liked nothing so much as the moments he spent with Pierre.

'Xavière is going to be late again,' said Françoise. 'It's most aggravating. Your aunt is so particular that we should be there for the first glass of port sharp at three o'clock.'

'She's going to be bored stiff there,' said Pierre. 'We should have arranged to meet her afterwards.'

'She wants to see what a private view is like,' said Françoise. 'I don't know what her idea of it can be.'

'You'll have a good laugh!' said Gerbert.

'It's one of aunt's protégés,' said Françoise, 'we simply can't get out of it. As it is, I cut the last cocktail party, and that didn't go down too well.'

Gerbert got up and nodded to Pierre.

'I'll see you tonight.'

'So long,' said Françoise warmly. She watched him walk off in his big overcoat which flapped over his ankles; it was one of

Péclard's old casts-off. 'That was all rather forced,' she said.

'He's a charming young fellow, but we don't have a great deal to say to each other,' said Pierre.

'He's never been like that before; I thought he seemed very depressed. Perhaps it's because we let him down on Friday night; but it was perfectly plausible that we should want to go home to bed right away when we were so exhausted.'

'At least so long as nobody else ran into us,' said Pierre.

'Let's say that we buried ourselves at the Pôle Nord, and then jumped straight into a taxi. There's only Elisabeth, but I've warned her.' Françoise ran her hand across the back of her head and smoothed her hair. 'That would be a bore,' she said. 'Not so much the fact itself, but the lie, that would hurt him terribly.'

Gerbert had retained from his adolescence a rather timid touchiness and, above all, he dreaded feeling that he was in the way. Pierre was the only person in the world who really counted in his life; he was quite willing to be under some sort of obligation to him, but only if he felt that it was not from a sense of duty that Pierre took an interest in him.

'No, there's not a chance,' said Pierre. 'Besides, yesterday evening he was still gay and friendly.'

'Perhaps he's worried,' said Françoise. It saddened her that Gerbert should be sad and that she could do nothing for him. She liked to know that he was happy: his steady and pleasant life delighted her. He worked with discernment and success. He had a few friends whose varied talents fascinated him: Mollier who played the banjo so well, Barrisson who spoke in flawless slang, Castier who had no trouble in holding six Pernods. Many an evening in the Montparnasse cafés he practised bearing up under Pernod with them: he had more success with the banjo. The rest of the time he deliberately shunned company. He went to the movies; he read; he wandered about Paris, cherishing modest and persistent little dreams.

'Why doesn't that girl come?' said Pierre.

'Perhaps she's still asleep,' said Françoise.

'Of course not, yesterday evening when she dropped into my dressing-room she said quite clearly that she'd have herself called,' said Pierre. 'Perhaps she's ill, but then she would have telephoned.'

'Not she, she's got a holy fear of the telephone, she thinks it's an instrument of evil,' said Françoise. 'But I do think it's likely she's forgotten the time.'

'She never forgets the time except out of spite,' said Pierre, 'and I don't see why she should have a sudden change of mood.'

'She does occasionally, for no known reason.'

'There's always a reason,' said Pierre, a little irritably. 'Only you don't try to understand them.'

Françoise found his tone unpleasant; it was in no way her fault.

'Let's go and fetch her,' said Pierre.

'She'll think that's indiscreet,' said Françoise. Perhaps she did treat Xavière rather like a piece of machinery, but at least she handled the delicate mechanism with the greatest care. It was very annoying to have to offend Aunt Christine; but, on the other hand, Xavière would take it greatly amiss if they were to go to her room to fetch her.

'But it's she who's in the wrong,' said Pierre. Françoise rose. After all, Xavière might be ill. Since her discussion with Pierre a week earlier, she had not had the slightest change of mood: the evening the three had spent together, the Friday after the dress rehearsal, had passed in cloudless merriment.

The hotel was quite close and it took them only a moment to get there. Three o'clock. There was not a minute more to be lost. As Françoise disappeared up the stairs the proprietress called her.

'Mademoiselle Miquel, are you going to see Mademoiselle Pagès?'

'Yes, why?' said Françoise a little arrogantly. This plaintive old lady was fairly accommodating, but her inquisitiveness was sometimes misplaced.

'I would like to have a word with you about her.' The old woman stood hesitatingly on the threshold of the little drawing-room, but Françoise did not follow her in. 'Mademoiselle Pagès complained a little while ago that the basin in her room was stopped up. I pointed out to her that she had been throwing tea-leaves, lumps of cotton-wool and slops into it.' She added: 'Her room is in such a mess! There are cigarette ends and fruit-pips in every corner, and the bedspread is singed all over.'

'If you have any complaints to make about Mademoiselle

Pagès, please speak to her,' said Françoise.

'I have done so,' said the proprietress, 'and she told me that she wouldn't stay here one day more. I think she's packing her bags. You'll appreciate that I have no trouble in letting my rooms. I have enquiries every day and I'd be only too happy to let a tenant like that go. The way she keeps the lights burning all night long, you have no idea how much it costs me.' She added, ingratiatingly: 'Only because she's a friend of yours, I wouldn't want to inconvenience her. I wanted to tell you, that if she changes her mind I won't raise any objections.'

Ever since Françoise had lived there, she had been treated with unusual consideration. She showered the good woman with complimentary tickets and the old lady was flattered by it: and, most important of all, she paid her rent very regularly.

'I'll tell her,' said Françoise. 'Thank you.' With decisive steps, she went on up the stairs.

'We can't let that little wretch become a damned nuisance,' said Pierre. 'There are other hotels in Montparnasse.'

'But I'm very comfortable in this one,' said Françoise. It was well heated and well located: Françoise liked its mixed clientèle and the ugly-flowered wallpaper.

'Shall we knock?' said Françoise hesitantly. Pierre knocked. The door was opened with unexpected promptitude and Xavière stood there, bedraggled and almost scarlet in the face; she had pulled up the sleeves of her blouse and her skirt was covered with dust.

'Oh, it's you!' she said with a look of complete surprise.

It was useless to try to anticipate Xavière's greeting, one was always wrong. Françoise and Pierre stood rooted to the spot.

'What are you doing here?' said Pierre.

Xavière's throat swelled.

'I'm moving,' she said in a tragic voice. The scene was stupefying. Françoise thought vaguely of Aunt Christine whose lips must have already begun to tighten, but everything seemed trivial in comparison with the cataclysm that had ravaged this room as well as Xavière's face. Three suitcases lay gaping in the middle of the room; the cupboards had disgorged on to the floor piles of crumpled clothing, papers, and toilet articles.

'And do you expect to be finished soon?' asked Pierre who was looking sternly at this havoc-stricken sanctuary.

91

'I'll never get finished!' said Xavière. She sank into an armchair and pressed her fingers against her forehead. 'That old hag . . .'

'She spoke to me just now,' said Françoise. 'She told me that you could stay on for tonight, if that suits you.'

'Oh!' said Xavière. A look of hope flashed into her eyes and died immediately. 'No, I ought to leave at once.'

Françoise felt sorry for her.

'But you aren't going to find a room this evening.'

'Oh, surely not,' said Xavière. She bent her head and sat prostrated for some time. Françoise and Pierre stood as if spellbound, staring at her golden head.

'Well, leave all that,' said Françoise with a sudden return to consciousness. 'Tomorrow we'll go and look together.'

'Leave this?' said Xavière. 'But I couldn't live in this rubbish heap for even an hour.'

'I'll help you to tidy it up tonight,' said Françoise. Xavière gave her a look of plaintive gratitude. 'Listen to me. You are going to get dressed and wait for us at the Dôme. We'll dash off to the private view and we'll be back in an hour and a half.'

Xavière jumped to her feet and clutched her hair.

'Oh, I would so like to go! I'll be ready in ten minutes. I just have to tidy myself up a bit.'

'Aunt has already begun to fume,' said Françoise.

Pierre shrugged his shoulders.

'In any case, we've missed the port,' he said angrily. 'Now, there's no longer any point in getting there before five o'clock.'

'As you wish,' said Françoise. 'But the blame will fall on me again.'

'Well, after all, you don't give a damn,' said Pierre.

'You'll smile at her winningly,' said Xavière.

'All right,' said Françoise. 'You'll have to think of a good excuse for us.'

'I'll try,' grumbled Pierre.

'Then we'll wait for you in my room,' said Françoise.

They went upstairs.

'It's an afternoon wasted,' said Pierre. 'There won't be enough time left to go anywhere after we leave the exhibition.'

'I told you she couldn't learn how to live,' said Françoise. She walked over to the looking-glass: with this upswept coiffure it was impossible to keep the back of one's neck looking neat. 'If only she doesn't insist on moving.'

'You haven't got to move with her,' said Pierre. He seemed furious. He had always been so cheerful with Françoise that she had almost reached the point of forgetting that he was not good-tempered, that his fits of anger were legendary at the theatre. If he took this affair as a personal offence, the afternoon was going to be grim.

'But I will; you know that. She won't insist, but she'll sink into black despair.'

Françoise glanced over the room.

'My nice little hotel. Fortunately, I can rely on her inertia.'

Pierre walked over to the pile of manuscripts stacked on the table.

'You know,' he said. 'I think I'll hang on to *Monsieur le Vent*. This fellow interests me, he ought to be encouraged. I'll ask him to have dinner with us one of these evenings so that you can form some opinion of him.'

'I also want to look at *Hyacinthe*,' said Françoise. 'I think it's promising.'

'Show it to me,' said Pierre. He began to look through the manuscript and Françoise leaned over his shoulder to read with him. She was not in a good mood: alone with Pierre, she would have got the private view over and done with very quickly, but with Xavière about, everything tended to become burdensome, it made one feel that one was walking through life with clods of clay on the soles of one's shoes. Pierre should never have decided to wait for her; even he looked as though he had got out of the wrong side of the bed. Nearly half an hour passed before Xavière knocked. Then they hurried downstairs.

'Where do you want to go?' said Françoise.

'I don't mind,' said Xavière.

'Since we've only an hour,' said Pierre, 'let's go to the Dôme.'

'How cold it is,' said Xavière, tightening her scarf round her face.

'It's only a few steps from here,' said Françoise.

'We haven't got the same conception of distance,' said Xavière whose face was screwed up.

'Or of time,' said Pierre dryly.

Françoise was beginning to read Xavière very well. Xavière knew that she was in the wrong. She thought they were angry with her and she was taking the lead; and besides, her attempts at moving had worn her out. Françoise wanted to take her arm: wherever they had gone on Friday night, they had walked arm in arm, and kept in step.

'No,' said Xavière, 'it's much faster on one's own.'

Pierre's face darkened again, Françoise was afraid he was going to lose his temper. They sat down at the back of the café.

'You know,' said Françoise, 'this private view won't be at all interesting. Aunt's protégés never have an ounce of talent, she's never been known to fail in that respect.'

'I don't care a hang about that,' said Xavière. 'It's the reception I'm interested in. Pictures always bore me stiff.'

'That's because you've never seen any,' said Françoise. 'If you were to come with me to exhibitions, or even go to the Louvre . . .'

'That wouldn't make any difference,' said Xavière. She made a wry face. 'A picture is so arid, it's completely flat.'

'If you were to get to know a little about it, I'm sure you would enjoy it,' said Françoise.

'You mean I would understand why I ought to enjoy it,' said Xavière. 'I'd never be satisfied with that. The day when I no longer feel anything, I'm not going to look for excuses to feel.'

'What you call feeling is really a way of understanding,' said Françoise. 'You like music, well then . . . !'

Xavière stopped her short.

'You know, when people speak about good and bad music, it goes right over my head,' she said with aggressive modesty. 'I don't understand the first thing about it. I like the notes for themselves; the sound alone is enough for me.' She looked Françoise in the eye. 'The pleasures of the mind are repulsive to me.'

When Xavière was being obstinate it was useless to argue. Françoise looked reproachfully at Pierre; after all, it was he who had wanted to wait for Xavière, he could at least join in the conversation, instead of entrenching himself behind a sardonic smile.

'I warn you that the reception, as you call it, is not a bit amusing,' said Françoise. 'Just a lot of people exchanging polite remarks.'

'Oh, still there'll be a crowd, and excitement,' said Xavière in a tone of passionate insistence.

'Do you feel a need for excitement now?'

'Of course I need it!' said Xavière, and a wild untamed

look glinted in her eyes. 'Shut up in that room from morning till night, why, I'll go mad! I can't stand it there any more, you can have no idea how happy I'll be to leave that place.'

'Who prevents you from going out?' asked Pierre.

'You say that there isn't any fun in going dancing with women, but Begramian or Gerbert would be only too glad to take you, and they dance very well,' said Françoise.

Xavière shook her head.

'Once you decide to have a good time to order, it's always pitiful.'

'You want everything to fall into your lap like manna from heaven,' said Françoise, 'you don't deign to lift your little finger, and then you proceed to take it out on everyone. Obviously . . .'

'There must be some countries in the world,' said Xavière, as if in a dream, 'warm countries – Greece or Sicily – where it surely isn't necessary to lift a finger.' She scowled. 'Here you have to grab with both hands – and to get what?'

'You have to do the same out there,' said Françoise.

Xavière's eyes began to sparkle.

'Where is that red island that's completely surrounded by boiling water?' she said hungrily.

'Santorin, one of the isles of Greece,' said Françoise. 'But that isn't exactly what I told you. Only the cliffs are red, and the sea boils only between two small black islets thrown up by volcanic eruptions. Oh, I remember,' she said, warming to her subject, 'a lake of sulphurous water in the midst of the lava. It was all yellow and edged by a peninsula as black as anthracite and on the other side of this black strip the sea was a dazzling blue.'

Xavière looked at her with rapt attention.

'When I think of all you've seen,' she said in a voice filled with resentment.

'You consider that it's quite undeserved,' said Pierre.

Xavière looked him up and down. She pointed to the dirty leather banquettes, the grubby tables.

'To think, after seeing all that, that you can come and sit here.'

'What good would it do to pine away with regrets?' asked Françoise.

'Of course, you don't want to have any regrets,' said Xavière. 'You are so anxious to be happy.' She looked away into space. 'But I wasn't born resigned.'

Françoise was cut to the quick. Surely she couldn't contemptuously push aside the acceptance of this happiness that seemed to her so clearly to be asserting itself. Right or wrong, she no longer regarded Xavière's words as outbursts: they held a complete set of values that ran counter to hers. However much she refused to acknowledge this fact, its existence was awkward.

'This life of ours is no resignation,' she said sharply. 'We love Paris, and these streets, and these cafés.'

'How can anyone love sordid places, and hideous things, and all these wretched people?' Xavière's voice emphasized her epithets with disgust.

'The point is that the whole world interests us,' said Françoise. 'You happen to be a little aesthete. You want unadulterated beauty; but that's a very narrow point of view.'

'Am I supposed to be interested in that saucer because it presumes to exist?' asked Xavière, and she looked at the saucer with annoyance. 'It's quite enough that it's there.' With intentional naïveté she added: 'I should have thought that when one is an artist, it is just because one likes beautiful things.'

'That depends on what you call beautiful things,' said Pierre. Xavière stared at him.

'Heavens! you're listening,' she said, wide-eyed but gently. 'I thought you were lost in deep thought.'

'I'm paying close attention.'

'You're not in a very good mood,' said Xavière, still smiling.

'I'm in an excellent mood,' said Pierre. 'I think we're spending a most delightful afternoon. We're about to start off for the private view, and when we're through with that, we'll have just enough time to eat a sandwich. That works out perfectly.'

'You think it's all my fault,' said Xavière, showing more of her teeth.

'I certainly don't think it's mine,' said Pierre.

It was simply for the purpose of behaving disagreeably towards Xavière that he had insisted on meeting her again as soon as possible. 'He might have given me a thought,' Françoise reflected with bitterness; she was beginning to find the situation intolerable.

'That's true. When for once in a while you've got some free time,' said Xavière, whose grin became more perceptible, 'what a tragedy it is, if a little of it is wasted!'

This reproach surprised Françoise. Had she once more mis-read Xavière? Only four days had passed since Friday and at the theatre, yesterday evening, Pierre had greeted Xavière most amiably. She would already have to be very fond of him to feel that she had been neglected.

Xavière turned to Françoise.

'I imagined the life of writers and artists to be something quite different,' she said in a sophisticated tone. 'I had no idea it was regulated like that – by the ring of a bell.'

'You would have preferred them to wander about in the storm with their hair streaming in the wind?' said Françoise, who felt herself grow utterly fatuous under Pierre's mocking look.

'No. Baudelaire didn't let his hair stream in the wind,' said Xavière. She continued more naturally: 'What it amounts to is that, except for him and Rimbaud, artists are just like civil servants.'

'Because we do a little work regularly every day?' Françoise asked.

Xavière pouted coyly.

'And then you count the number of hours you sleep, you eat two meals a day, you pay visits, and you never go for a walk one without the other. It couldn't possibly be otherwise . . .'

'But do you consider that unbearable?' asked Françoise with a forced smile. This was not a flattering picture of themselves which Xavière was showing them.

'It seems queer to sit down every day at one's desk and write line after line of sentences,' said Xavière. 'I admit that people should write, of course,' she added quickly. 'There's something voluptuous about words. But only when the spirit moves you.'

'It's possible to have a desire for a piece of work as a whole,' said Françoise. She felt a little inclined to justify herself in Xavière's eyes.

'I admire the exalted level of your conversation,' said Pierre. His malicious smile was aimed at Françoise as well as at Xavière, and Françoise was disconcerted; was he able to judge her objectively, like a stranger, she who could never bring herself to keep the slightest thing from him? This was disloyalty.

Xavière never batted an eyelash. 'It becomes home-work,' she said and she laughed indulgently. 'But then that's the way you always do things, you turn everything into a duty.'

'What do you mean?' said Françoise. 'I can assure you that

I don't feel myself so particularly handicapped.'

Yes, she would have it out with Xavière, once and for all, and she in her turn would tell her just what she thought of her; it was all very well to let her assume all these little superiorities, but Xavière was overdoing it.

'Your relations with people, for example.' Xavière counted on her fingers. 'Elisabeth, your aunt, Gerbert, and so many others. I'd rather live alone in the world and keep my freedom.'

'You don't understand that to have a more or less regular way of life does not constitute slavery,' said Françoise with irritation. 'It's quite of our own free will that we try not to hurt Elisabeth, for example.'

'You give them rights over you,' said Xavière disdainfully.

'Absolutely none,' said Françoise. 'With Aunt, it's a kind of cynical bargain because she gives us money. Elisabeth takes what she's given, and we see Gerbert because we like to do so.'

'Oh, he certainly feels he has rights over you,' said Xavière in tones of assurance.

'No one in the world is less aware that he has rights than Gerbert,' said Pierre calmly.

'Do you think so?' said Xavière. 'I happen to know otherwise.'

'What can you possibly know?' asked Françoise, intrigued. 'You haven't exchanged three words with him.'

Xavière hesitated.

'It's one of those intuitions whose secret is known to superior persons,' said Pierre.

'Well, since you want to know,' said Xavière with a transport of anger, 'he looked like an offended little princeling when I told him last night that I went out with you on Friday.'

'You told him!' said Pierre.

'We warned you to say nothing,' said Françoise.

'Oh, it slipped out,' said Xavière nonchalantly. 'I'm not accustomed to all this diplomacy.'

Françoise exchanged a look of consternation with Pierre. Xavière had clearly done it deliberately, out of mean jealousy. She was not in the least absent-minded and she had stayed in the foyer only a very short while.

'There you are,' said Françoise. 'We ought never to have lied to him.'

'Well, who would have thought it?' said Pierre.

He began to nibble one of his nails, he seemed deeply

concerned. This was a blow to Gerbert's blind confidence in Pierre from which he might never recover. Françoise felt a lump in her throat when she thought of this anchorless little soul who was wandering about Paris at this very moment.

'We've got to do something,' she said nervously.

'I'll have a talk with him this evening,' said Pierre, 'but what is there to explain? Having chucked him isn't so bad, but the lie seems so gratuitous.'

'It always seems gratuitous when it's discovered,' said Françoise.

Pierre looked severely at Xavière.

'What exactly did you say to him?'

'He was telling me how they all got drunk on Friday, with Tedesco and Canzetti, and what fun it was. I said that I regretted very much not having met them, but that we had stayed shut up in the Pôle Nord and hadn't seen anything,' said Xavière sullenly.

She was all the more reprehensible, since it was she who had insisted on staying at the Pôle Nord all night.

'Are you sure that's all you said?' asked Pierre.

'Of course, that's all,' said Xavière ungraciously.

'Well, perhaps it can still be straightened out,' said Pierre, looking at Françoise. 'I'll say that it had been our firm intention to go home, but that at the last minute Xavière appeared to be so upset that we resigned ourselves to sitting up all night.'

Xavière pursed her lips.

'Either he'll believe you or he won't,' said Françoise.

'I'll see to it he believes it,' said Pierre, 'at least, we have the advantage of never having lied to him before.'

'It's true that you're a bit of a St John Chrysostom,' said Françoise. 'You ought to try to see him right away.'

'And Aunt? Well, so much the worse for Aunt!'

'We'll call on her at six o'clock,' said Françoise nervously. 'Oh no, we've got to drop in, otherwise she'll never forgive us.'

Pierre got up. 'I'll ring him up,' he said.

He went off. Françoise lit a cigarette to keep her composure. Inside, she was trembling with rage; it was hateful to think of Gerbert being unhappy, and unhappy through some fault of theirs.

Xavière tugged at her hair in silence. 'After all, it won't kill the little fellow,' she said with barely restrained insolence.

'I'd like to see you in his shoes,' said Françoise bitterly.

Xavière was taken aback. 'I didn't know it was so serious,' she said.

'You were warned,' said Françoise.

Silence became prolonged. A little terror-stricken, Françoise thought over this living catastrophe that had surreptitiously invaded her life. It was Pierre who, by his respect, by his esteem, had broken down the dikes within which Françoise had confined her. Now that she was let loose, how far would it all go? The day's balance sheet was already respectable: the landlady's anger, the private view already more than half missed, Pierre's uneasy irritability, the quarrel with Gerbert. In Françoise herself existed this uneasiness that had settled on her a week earlier; perhaps it was that which frightened her most of all.

'Are you angry?' Xavière murmured. Her face of dismay did not soften Françoise.

'Why did you do it?'

'I don't know,' said Xavière softly; she looked down. 'It's just as well,' she said in an even lower voice, 'at least you'll know what I'm worth, you'll be disgusted with me. It's just as well.'

'That I should be disgusted with you?'

'Yes. I'm not worth having anyone take an interest in me,' said Xavière with desperate vehemence. 'Now you know me. I told you, I'm worthless. You ought to have left me in Rouen.'

All the reproaches Françoise had on the tip of her tongue were futile in comparison with these impassioned self-accusations. Françoise was silent. The café was now filled with people and smoke. At one table a group of German refugees were attentively watching a game of chess; at a neighbouring table, alone with a glass of coffee, an eccentric woman who imagined she was a whore was making up to an invisible companion.

'He wasn't there,' said Pierre.

'You were away a long time,' said Françoise.

'I took the opportunity of going for a little walk. I wanted to get some air.'

He sat down and lit his pipe; he seemed to have relaxed.

'I'm going to leave,' said Xavière.

'Yes, it's time to go,' said Françoise.

No one moved.

'What I would like to know,' said Pierre, 'is why you told him that?'

He stared at Xavière with so keen an interest that it seemed to have swept away his anger.

'I don't know,' said Xavière once again. But Pierre did not give up so quickly.

'Of course you know,' he said gently.

Xavière shrugged her shoulders despondently.

'I couldn't help myself.'

'You had something in mind,' said Pierre. 'What was it?' He smiled.

'Did you want to be unkind to us?'

'Oh, how could you think that?'

'You thought that this little mystery gave Gerbert a slight advantage over you, didn't you?'

Xavière's eyes flashed with resentment.

'I find it very irritating always to have to conceal my feelings,' she said.

'Is that the reason?' said Pierre.

'No, of course not. I told you it just happened, that's all,' she said with a tortured look.

'You said yourself that this secret irritated you.'

'But that's beside the point,' said Xavière.

Françoise looked at the clock impatiently; Xavière's reasons were of no consequence, her behaviour was inexcusable.

'The idea that we owed some consideration to someone else annoyed you. I understand. It's unpleasant to feel that you are facing up to people who aren't free,' said Pierre.

'Yes, in a way,' said Xavière. 'And besides . . .'

'And besides what?' asked Pierre in a friendly tone. He looked as if he were quite ready to approve of Xavière.

'No, it's contemptible,' said Xavière. She hid her face in her hands. 'I'm contemptible. Leave me alone.'

'But there's nothing contemptible about it,' said Pierre. 'I would like to understand you.' He hesitated. 'Was it a little revenge because Gerbert hadn't been nice the other evening?'

Xavière uncovered her face: she seemed completely astonished.

'But he was very nice, at least as nice as I was.'

'Then it wasn't in order to hurt him?'

'Of course not.' She hesitated and then taking the plunge,

she said: 'I wanted to see what would happen.'

Françoise looked at her with increasing uneasiness. Pierre's face reflected such an intense curiosity that it looked almost like affection. Did he excuse jealousy, perversity, selfishness to which Xavière had all but confessed? With what determination she would have fought such feelings had she felt them dawning in herself. And Pierre was smiling.

Suddenly Xavière blurted out: 'Why do you make me say all this? To despise me even more? But you can't despise me any more than I despise myself!'

'How can you think that I despise you?' said Pierre.

'Yes, you do despise me,' said Xavière, 'and you're right. I don't know how to behave! I make trouble everywhere. Oh! there's a curse on me,' she wailed passionately.

She leant her head against the back of the banquette and turned her face towards the ceiling to prevent her tears from flowing. Her throat swelled convulsively.

'I'm certain this whole incident will be straightened out,' said Pierre in an urgent tone. 'Don't get so upset.'

'It's not only that,' said Xavière. 'It's . . . everything.'

She looked fiercely into space and said quietly: 'I'm disgusted with myself. I loathe myself.'

Whether she wished to be or not, Françoise was touched by her tone. She could feel that these words had not just come to her lips; she had torn them from the very depths of herself. For hours and hours during long sleepless nights she must bitterly have turned them over and over.

'You shouldn't,' said Pierre. 'We think so highly of you . . .'

'Not now,' said Xavière weakly.

'Yes we do,' said Pierre, 'I can well understand that you should have had a brainstorm.'

Françoise suffered a spasm of revulsion: she did not think so highly of Xavière, she did not excuse this brainstorm; Pierre had no right to speak for her. He went his own way without even looking at her and then would insist that she had followed him; this was just too presumptuous. She felt herself turning into a lump of lead from head to foot. This separateness hurt her cruelly, but nothing would induce her to set foot on this slippery slope of the imagination at the bottom of which yawned she knew not what abyss.

'Moods and brainstorms,' said Xavière, 'that's all I'm capable of.'

Her face was blanched and purple rings were showing under her eyes. She was extraordinarily ugly with her red nose and her streaming hair that suddenly seemed tarnished. There could be no doubt that she was genuinely upset, but it would be too convenient if remorse were to obliterate everything, thought Françoise.

Xavière continued, her voice dismally plaintive. 'When I was in Rouen, people could still find excuses for me, but what have I done since I've been in Paris?' She began to cry again. 'I no longer feel anything, I no longer am anything.'

She looked as if she were contending against some physical malady of which she was the helpless victim.

'All that will change,' said Pierre. 'Trust us and we'll help you.'

'No one can help me,' said Xavière in a burst of childlike despair. 'I'm branded!' Sobs choked her; sitting bolt upright, her face distorted in agony, she allowed her tears to flow freely, and at the sight of their disarming ingenuousness Françoise felt her heart soften. She wished she could find a gesture, a word, but that was not easy, she was returning from too far away. There ensued a long, weighty silence. In the café, between the tarnished mirrors, a weary day still hesitated to die. The chess players had not changed position. A man had come to sit down beside the lunatic woman: she seemed much less crazy now that her companion had found a body.

'I'm such a coward,' said Xavière, 'I ought to kill myself, I ought to have done it a long time ago.' She screwed up her face. 'I will do it,' she said, suddenly defiant.

Pierre looked at her, perplexed and woebegone, and turned sharply to Françoise. 'Well, don't you see what a state she's in? Try to calm her down,' he said indignantly.

'What do you want me to do?' said Françoise, whose pity immediately froze.

'You ought to have put your arm round her a long time ago and said – said something to her,' he added lamely.

Mentally, Pierre enfolded Xavière in his arms and rocked her soothingly, but respect, decency, and strict convention paralysed them, his warm compassion could be embodied only in Françoise. Inert, frozen, Françoise gave not the faintest hint of a movement; Pierre's imperious voice had drained her of her own will, but with all the strength of her stiffened muscles she shut herself off from any outside intrusion. Pierre, too, remained motionless, cluttered up with useless affection. For a moment Xavière's agony continued through the silence.

'Calm yourself,' Pierre repeated gently. 'You must trust us. Up till now you've lived haphazardly, but life is a big undertaking. We'll talk it over together and make our plans.'

'There's no plan to make,' said Xavière gloomily. 'No, all I can do is go back to Rouen. That's the best thing.'

'Go back to Rouen! That really would be clever!' said Pierre. 'You can see that we aren't angry with you.' He cast an impatient look at Françoise. 'Tell her at least that you're not angry with her.'

'Of course I'm not angry with you,' said Françoise in a flat voice.

With whom was she angry? She had the painful impression of being divided against herself. It was already six o'clock, but there was no question of leaving.

'Stop being tragic,' said Pierre. 'Let's talk sensibly.'

There was something so reassuring, so steady about him, that Xavière calmed down a little: she looked at him with a sort of submissiveness.

'What you need more than anything else,' said Pierre, 'is something to do.' Xavière made a gesture of derision. 'Not a job just to fill in time. I appreciate the fact that you are too exacting to be satisfied with disguising a void, you can't merely accept something that's just an amusement. You want something that will give your days some real meaning.'

Françoise heard Pierre's analysis with annoyance; she had never suggested anything but amusement to Xavière. Once again she had not taken her seriously enough. And now Pierre was trying to reach an understanding with Xavière over her head.

'But I tell you I'm not good at anything,' said Xavière.

'But then you haven't tried your hand at very much,' said Pierre. He smiled. 'I've got a good idea.'

'What is it?' she enquired.

'Why don't you go on the stage?'

Xavière's eyes opened wide.

'On the stage?'

'Why not? You have a very good figure, a keen sense of the effects of your attitudes and of facial expressions. That doesn't necessarily mean that you have talent, but it's a good reason for hoping so.'

'I could never do it,' said Xavière.

'Wouldn't it tempt you?'

'Of course, but that doesn't get me anywhere.'

'You're sensitive and intelligent – gifts that are not every-one's,' said Pierre. 'They're trump cards.' He looked at her seriously. 'Dash it, you've got to work. You'll come to the School. I take two courses myself, and Bahin and Rambert are as nice as can be.'

A flash of hope flickered in Xavière's eyes.

'I'll never manage it,' she said.

'I'll give you lessons myself to help you out. I promise you, that if you have the faintest shadow of talent I'll bring it out.'

Xavière shook her head.

'It's a beautiful dream,' she said.

Françoise made an effort to be co-operative. It was possible that Xavière might be talented; in any case it would be all to the good if they could succeed in getting her interested in something.

'You said that about your coming to Paris,' she said. 'And yet, you are here all right.'

'That's true,' said Xavière.

Françoise smiled.

'You're so wrapped up in the present, that any future at all seems to you like a dream. It's time itself that you mistrust.'

Xavière smiled faintly.

'It's so uncertain,' she said.

'Are you in Paris or not?' asked Françoise.

'Yes, but that's not the same thing,' said Xavière.

'You only have to get to Paris once,' said Pierre cheerfully. 'But in the theatre, you'll have to begin all over again each time. But you can rely on us. We have enough will-power for three.'

'Alas!' said Xavière smiling. 'You're bursting with it.'

Pierre pressed home his advantage.

'From Monday onwards, you'll attend the miming classes. It's just like the games you used to play when you were a little girl. You'll be asked to imagine that you're lunching with a friend, that you're caught shop-lifting. You have to improvise the scene as well as act it.'

'That must be good fun,' said Xavière.

'And then you'll choose a part which you begin to work on immediately; that is, selections from it.'

Pierre looked at Françoise questioningly.

'What do you think we ought to suggest to her?'

Françoise thought it over.

'Something that doesn't call for too much experience, but that doesn't let her simply act with her natural charm. Mérimée's *l'Occasion*, for example.'

The notion amused her, perhaps Xavière would become an actress; at any rate it would certainly be interesting to try.

'That wouldn't be at all bad,' said Pierre.

Xavière looked happily from one to the other.

'I would so love to be an actress! Could I act on a real stage like you?'

'Of course,' said Pierre, 'and perhaps by next year you'll be ready for a small part.'

'Oh!' said Xavière, ecstatically. 'Oh! I shall work. You'll see.'

Everything about her was so unpredictable, perhaps she would work, after all; Françoise once more began to take pleasure in the future she planned for her.

'Tomorrow is Sunday, so that's no good,' said Pierre, 'but on Thursday I can give you your first elocution lesson. Would you like to meet me in my dressing-room on Mondays and Thursdays from three to four?'

'But that will put you out,' said Xavière.

'On the contrary, I shall find it most interesting,' said Pierre.

Xavière's calm was completely restored, and Pierre was beaming. It had to be admitted that he had accomplished an almost gymnastic feat in pulling Xavière from the depths of despair to a state of confidence and joy. He had completely forgotten about Gerbert and the private view as well.

'You ought to ring up Gerbert again,' said Françoise. 'It would be better if you saw him before the show.'

'Do you think so?' said Pierre.

'Don't you think so?' she said a little dryly.

'Yes,' said Pierre reluctantly. 'I'll go.'

Xavière looked at the clock.

'Oh! Now I've made you miss the private view,' she said penitently.

'That's nothing,' said Françoise.

On the contrary, it mattered a good deal. She would have to go the very next day to apologize to Aunt, and the apologies would not be accepted.

'I'm ashamed,' said Xavière softly.

'But you mustn't be,' said Françoise.

Xavière's remorse and her resolutions had really touched her; she could not be judged by any rule of thumb. She put her hand on Xavière's hand.

'You'll see, everything will be all right.'

For a moment Xavière looked at her with devotion.

'When I look at myself and when I look at you,' she said fervently, 'I'm ashamed!'

'That's absurd,' said Françoise.

'You're perfect,' said Xavière ardently.

'Oh, that's certainly not true,' said Françoise. Formerly, these words would only have made her smile, but today they made her feel awkward.

'Sometimes, at night, when I think about you,' said Xavière, 'it dazzles me so, I can't believe that you really exist.' She smiled. 'And you do exist,' she said with charming tenderness.

Françoise had always known it. The love that Xavière bore her, she yielded to it at night, in the secrecy of her room; then no one could contend with her for the image she carried in her heart, and sitting comfortably in her arm-chair, her eyes fixed on space, she studied it in ecstasy. The flesh-and-blood woman who belonged to Pierre, to everyone, and to herself, could only perceive at odd moments faint hints of this jealous worship.

'I don't deserve that you should think that of me,' said Françoise with a kind of remorse.

Pierre was approaching cheerfully.

'He was there. I asked him to be at the theatre at eight o'clock and told him I wanted to speak to him.'

'What did he answer?'

'He said "Good".'

'Don't beat about the bush with him,' said Françoise.

'Just leave it to me,' said Pierre. He smiled at Xavière: 'Let's go to the Pôle Nord for a drink before saying goodbye.'

'Oh, yes, do let's go to the Pôle Nord,' said Xavière sweetly.

That was where they had sealed their friendship and the place had already become legendary and symbolic. When they left the café, Xavière, of her own accord, took Pierre's and Françoise's arms and, all three walking in step, they set out on their pilgrimage to the Pôle Nord.

Because of some latent uneasiness and also because she

objected to having any strange hand, even that of a divinity, touch her bits and pieces, it was clear that Xavière did not want Françoise to help her tidy her room. Françoise went up to her own room, put on a dressing-gown, and spread out her papers on her table. It was most often at this time of day, while Pierre was acting, that she worked on her novel; she began to read over the pages she had written the night before, but she had difficulty in concentrating. In the next room the Negro was giving the blonde tart a lesson in tap-dancing; with them was a little Spanish girl, who was a barmaid at the Topsy; Françoise recognized their voices. She took a nail file out of her bag, and began to file her nails. Even if Pierre succeeded in convincing Gerbert, wouldn't there always be a shadow between them? How angry would Aunt Christine be tomorrow? She couldn't get these irritating thoughts out of her head. But above all, she couldn't dismiss the thought that she and Pierre had not been at one during the afternoon. No doubt, when she talked it over with him, this unpleasant impression would be dissipated; but, in the meantime, it weighed heavily on her heart. She looked at her nails. It was stupid. She ought not to attach so much importance to a slight disagreement. She ought not to have felt herself so lost the minute Pierre's support failed her.

Her nails were not nicely shaped, she couldn't get them to match. Françoise picked up her file again. She was wrong to depend so entirely on Pierre: that was a real mistake, she ought not to thrust responsibility for herself upon someone else. With impatience, she shook from her dressing-gown the white nail dust clinging to it. In order to become totally responsible for herself, she had only to will it; but she did not really want to do so. She would still ask Pierre to sanction the very censure she inflicted on herself; her every thought was with him and for him; an act, self-initiated and having no connexion with him, an act that bespoke genuine independence, was beyond her imagination. Yet this was not disturbing; she would never find it necessary to fall back on herself in opposition to Pierre.

Françoise threw down her nail file. It was absurd to waste three precious working hours. This was not the first time Pierre had shown considerable interest in other women. Why, then, did she feel injured? What was disturbing was this feeling of rigid hostility which she had discovered in herself, and which

108

had not been completely dissipated. She hesitated, and, for a moment, she was persuaded to try to clarify her uneasiness; but really it took too much effort. She bent over her papers.

It was barely midnight when Pierre returned from the theatre. His face was red with the cold.

'Did you see Gerbert?' said Françoise anxiously.

'Yes, everything's all right,' said Pierre cheerfully. He took off his muffler and overcoat.

'He began by telling me that it didn't matter and that he didn't want any explanation; but I insisted. I argued that we never stood on ceremony with him and that if we'd wanted to chuck him we'd have said so roundly. He was a little mistrustful, but that was just to keep up appearances.'

'You really are a little Chrysostom,' said Françoise. There was a tinge of bitterness blended with her relief. It annoyed her to feel that she was conspiring with Xavière against Gerbert, and she would have liked Pierre himself to have felt it as well, instead of happily rubbing his hands together. A slight tampering with truth was next to nothing, but to repeat lies, from soul to soul, did spoil something between people.

'Still, Xavière's little trick was pretty rotten,' she said.

'I thought you were extremely severe,' said Pierre. He smiled. 'You'll be terribly stern when you get old!'

'At the outset you were more strict than I,' said Françoise, 'in fact you were almost insufferable.'

With a feeling of distress she recognized that it would not be so easy to blot out the day's misunderstandings by a friendly conversation; a persistent bitterness overwhelmed her as soon as she brought them back to mind.

Pierre began to undo the tie he had put on in honour of the private view.

'I consider it's unspeakably feather-brained that she should have forgotten an appointment with us,' he said in an offended tone, but with a smile that, in retrospect, mocked its significance. 'And besides, when I went to take a little walk to calm me down, I saw things in another light.'

His careless good humour only served to increase Françoise's edginess.

'I saw that her behaviour with Gerbert suddenly made you indulgent; you almost congratulated her.'

'It was becoming too serious to be merely feather-brained,' said Pierre. 'I thought that all that – her nervousness, her need for entertainment, the forgotten appointment and yesterday's betrayal, was part of the same thing and that there must have been some reason for it.'

'She told you the reason,' said Françoise.

'You mustn't believe what she says, just because she makes up stories for the fun of it,' said Pierre.

'Well, it isn't really worth the effort of insisting on them so much,' said Françoise, who was bitterly turning over in her mind his endless cross-questionings.

'She isn't really lying either. You have to interpret her words,' said Pierre.

It seemed almost as if they were talking about a Pythian oracle.

'Just what is your point?' asked Françoise impatiently.

Pierre smiled on one side of his mouth.

'Didn't it strike you that, all in all, she was blaming me for not having seen her since Friday?'

'Yes,' said Françoise, 'that proves that she's beginning to grow very fond of you.'

'For that girl, beginning and going on to the end are one and the same thing,' said Pierre.

'How so?'

'I feel that she is very well disposed towards me,' said Pierre in a fatuous manner, partly assumed, but all the same betraying deep personal satisfaction. Françoise was shocked by this; usually, Pierre's discreet caddishness amused her, but Pierre respected Xavière, the affection that had shone in his every smile, at the Pôle Nord, had not been affected. This cynical tone became disquieting.

'I am wondering how far the fact that Xavière's well disposed towards you excuses her?' she said.

'You must put yourself in her place,' said Pierre. 'She's a proud, emotional creature. I solemnly offered her my friendship, and the very first time that there was a question of seeing her again, I gave her the impression of having to move mountains to devote a few hours to her. That hurt her.'

'Not at the time, at any rate,' said Françoise.

'I dare say. But she thought it over, and since she didn't see me when she wanted to during the following days it became a terrible grievance. Add to that the fact that on Friday it was you who raised the objections about Gerbert. However much she may be devoted to you, in her possessive little soul you are still the biggest obstacle between her and me. Behind that secret we insisted on her keeping, she suddenly perceived a whole fate. And she behaved like a child who mixes up all the cards when it sees that it's losing the game.'

'You give her credit for a lot,' said Françoise.

'You don't credit her with enough,' said Pierre impatiently, and it was not the first time that day that he had used this biting tone on the subject of Xavière.

'I don't say that she put it all into just such precise words, but that was the meaning of what she did.'

'Perhaps,' said Françoise.

So, according to Pierre, Xavière regarded her as an undesirable of whom she was jealous. Françoise remembered with displeasure how moved she had been by Xavière's worshipping face; it now appeared to her as an act.

'That's an ingenious explanation,' she said, 'but I don't think there can ever be any such thing as a clear-cut explanation of Xavière; she lives far too much according to her moods.'

'Well, that's just it, her moods have a twofold basis,' said Pierre. 'Do you think she would have flown into a rage over a wash-hand basin if she hadn't already lost control of herself? This idea of moving was a form of escape; and I'm certain that she was escaping from me, because she was angry with herself for being fond of me.'

'In short, you think there's a key to her strange conduct and that key is a sudden passion for you?'

Pierre's lip jutted out slightly.

'I didn't say that it was a passion.'

Françoise's phrase had irritated him. In fact, it was the kind of brutal statement for which they so often criticized Elisabeth.

'A truly deep love!' said Françoise. 'I don't think that Xavière is capable of such a thing.' She thought a moment. 'Ecstasy, desire, resentment, unreasonable demands, most certainly; but the sort of assent that's needed to make a real emotion of all these feelings, that she'll never possess, to my way of thinking.'

'That's what the future will show,' said Pierre, whose profile became still sharper.

He took off his jacket and disappeared behind the screen. Françoise began to undress. She had spoken openly; she never hedged with Pierre, there was no self-pity about him, nor did he have any secrets which had to be handled with excessive care; and she had been in the wrong. This evening she had to think things over twice before speaking.

'Surely, she's never looked at you in the way she did tonight at the Pôle Nord,' said Françoise.

'Did you notice that, too?' said Pierre.

Françoise felt a lump in her throat. That sentence had been well thought out, a sentence for a stranger, and it had struck its mark. The man brushing his teeth behind the screen was a stranger. An idea flashed into her mind. Hadn't Xavière refused her help chiefly because she would all the sooner be left alone with Pierre's image? It was possible that he had guessed the truth; it was indeed a dialogue that had gone on all day between them; it was to Pierre that Xavière showed her inner self most willingly and there was a kind of conspiracy between him and her. Well, that was perfectly satisfactory, for it relieved her of the whole business, which was beginning to weigh on her. Pierre had already adopted Xavière to a far greater extent than Françoise had ever agreed to do; she was handing her over to him. Henceforth, Xavière belonged to Pierre.

'You can't drink better coffee than this anywhere,' said Françoise as she put her cup down on the saucer.

Madame Miquel smiled.

'Well, of course, this isn't what they give you in your cheap restaurants.'

She was looking through a fashion magazine and Françoise came over and sat down on the arm of her chair. Monsieur Miquel was reading *Le Temps*, sitting beside the fireplace in which a wood fire was crackling. Things had barely changed during the past twenty years, the atmosphere was oppressive. Whenever Françoise came back to this flat, she felt that all those years had led absolutely nowhere: time was spread out all round her in a quiet, stagnant pool. To live was to grow old, nothing more.

'Daladier really spoke very well,' said Monsieur Miquel. 'With great firmness, with great dignity; he won't give way an inch.'

'It's rumoured that Bonnet, personally, would be willing to make concessions,' said Françoise. 'It's even said that he embarked on secret negotiations over Djibouti.'

'Mind you, as such, the Italian demands aren't so outrageous,' said Monsieur Miquel, 'but it's their tone that's insufferable. After being told off like that, we couldn't agree to a compromise at any price.'

'All the same, you wouldn't start a war over a question of prestige?' said Françoise.

'No more can we resign ourselves to becoming a second-rate nation, huddled behind our Maginot Line.'

'No,' said Françoise. 'It's very difficult.'

By always avoiding questions of principle, she could easily come to a kind of understanding with her parents.

'Do you think I'd look well in this sort of dress?' asked her mother.

'Of course you would, Mother, you're so slim.'

She looked at the clock; it was almost two; Pierre would already be sitting at a table with a cup of that cheap coffee in front of him. Xavière had arrived so late for her lesson on the first two occasions that they had decided to meet an hour earlier at the Dôme today, and they could then be sure of beginning their work at the proper time. Perhaps she was already there – she was unpredictable.

'I must have a new evening gown for the hundredth performance of *Julius Caesar*,' said Françoise. 'I don't really know what to choose.'

'We'll have to think about it,' said Madame Miquel.

Monsieur Miquel put down his newspaper.

'Are you really counting on a hundred performances?'

'At least that. The house is full every night.'

She roused herself and walked over to the looking-glass; this atmosphere sapped her spirits.

'I'll have to be going,' she said, 'I have an appointment.'

'I don't like this fashion of going without a hat,' said Madame Miquel, as she fingered Françoise's coat. 'Why didn't you buy a fur coat as I told you? You've nothing to keep you warm.'

'Don't you like this three-quarter style? I think it's charming,' said Françoise.

'It's a between-season coat,' said her mother. She shrugged her shoulders. 'I can't imagine what you do with your money.'

'When are you coming again?' said Monsieur Miquel. 'Wednesday evening Maurice and his wife will be here.'

'Then I'll come on Thursday evening,' said Françoise, 'I'd rather see you alone.'

She walked slowly downstairs and out into the rue de Médicis. The air was sticky and damp, but once outside she felt better than in the warm library. Slowly, time had begun to move again: she was going to meet Gerbert; that at least gave some small meaning to these moments.

'Xavière must have arrived by now,' thought Françoise with a slight tightening of her heart. She would be wearing either her blue dress or her beautiful red-and-white striped blouse, with the smooth folds of her hair framing her face, and she would be smiling. What was this unknown smile? How was Pierre looking at her? Françoise stopped short on the edge of the pavement: she had the painful impression of being in exile. In the ordinary way, the centre of Paris was wherever she happened to be. Today, everything had changed. The centre of Paris was the café where Pierre and Xavière were sitting, and Françoise was wandering about in some vague suburb.

Françoise sat down near a brazier on the terrace of the Deux Magots. Tonight, Pierre would tell her the whole story, but for some little time now she hadn't altogether trusted the spoken word.

'A black coffee,' she said to the waiter.

Anguish pierced her: it was not a definite pain, she would have to delve very deep into the past to unearth a similar uneasiness. Then she remembered. The house was empty, the blinds had been drawn to shut out the sun, and it was dark; on the first-floor landing, a little girl was standing close up against the wall, holding her breath. It was funny to be there all alone when everyone else was in the garden, it was funny and frightening; the furniture looked just as it always did, but at the same time it was completely changed: thick and heavy and secret; under the book-stand and under the marble console there lurked an ominous shadow. She did not want to run away but her heart turned over.

Her old jacket was hanging over the back of a chair. Anna had probably cleaned it with petrol, or else she had just taken it out of camphor-balls and put it there to air; it was very old and it looked very worn out. It was old and worn but it could not complain as Françoise complained when she had hurt herself; it could not say to itself: 'I'm an old worn jacket.' It was strange; Françoise tried to imagine what it would be like supposing she couldn't say: 'I'm Françoise, I'm six years old, and I'm in Grandma's house,' if she could say absolutely nothing: she closed her eyes. It was as if she did not exist at all; and yet other people would be coming here, and would see her, and would speak about her. She opened her eyes again; she could see the jacket, it existed, yet it was not aware of it. There was something a little disturbing, a little frightening, about it all. What was the use of existing, if it wasn't aware of his own existence? She thought it over; perhaps there was a way. Since I can say: 'I', what would happen if I said it for the jacket? It was very disappointing; it was useless to look at the jacket, to see absolutely nothing but it, and to say very quickly: 'I'm old, I'm worn'; nothing happened. The jacket stayed there, indifferent, a complete stranger, and she was still Françoise. Besides, if she were to become the jacket, then she, Françoise, wouldn't know anything. Everything began to spin round in her head and she raced down and out into the garden.

Françoise emptied her coffee-cup in one gulp, it was almost stone cold; the incident was irrelevant, why had she remembered it? She looked at the clouded sky. What had happened now was that the present world was out of reach; not only was she exiled from Paris, she was exiled from the whole world. The people who were sitting on the terrace, the people who were walking in the street, were insubstantial, were shadows; the houses were nothing but painted back-cloths with no depth. And Gerbert, who was coming towards her with a smile, he too was nothing but a light and charming shadow.

'Greetings,' he said.

He was wearing his big beige overcoat, a shirt with small brown-and-yellow checks, and a yellow tie that set off his mat complexion. He always dressed gracefully. Françoise was happy to see him, but she knew immediately that she would not be able to count on him to help her to recover her place in the world; he would be just a pleasant companion in exile.

'Shall we still go to the flea-market in spite of the horrible weather?' said Françoise.

'It's only a thin drizzle,' said Gerbert, 'it's not really raining.'

They crossed the square and went down the steps to the métro.

'What can I talk to him about all day?' thought Françoise.

This was the first occasion for some little while that she had gone out alone with him and she wanted to be as friendly as she could in order to wipe out the last traces that Pierre's explanation might have left in him. But how? She worked, Pierre worked as well. Civil servants' lives – as Xavière had put it.

'I thought I'd never be able to get away,' said Gerbert. 'There was a crowd at lunch: Michel, and Lermière and the Abelsons, all top-notch, as you can see. And what talk! Real fireworks – it was agonizing. Péclard has written a new anti-war song for Dominique Oryol. It wasn't a bad effort, I must admit. Only their songs don't get them very far.'

'Songs – speeches –' said Françoise, 'never has there been such a flood of words.'

'Oh! the newspapers nowadays are terrific,' said Gerbert, and his face lighted up with a broad smile; indignation was always expressed by him in the form of jocularity. 'What a song and dance they're making about how France is standing firm! And all because Italy doesn't scare them out of their wits as much as Germany.'

'Well, they certainly won't go to war for Djibouti,' said Françoise.

'Suits me,' said Gerbert, 'but whether it's in two years or six months, it's not much encouragement to know that we're certain to get it in the neck in the end.'

'That's putting it mildly,' said Françoise.

With Pierre she was far more casual – 'We'll see what we'll see.' But Gerbert made her ill at ease: it wasn't amusing to be young these days. She looked at him somewhat uncomfortably. What was he really thinking? About himself, about his life, about the world? He never revealed anything personal. She would try to talk seriously with him in a little while; for the time being the noise of the métro made conversation difficult. She looked at a shred of yellow poster on the black wall of the tunnel. Even her curiosity lacked conviction today. It was a blank day, a worthless day.

'Did you know that there's a slight chance of my acting in the film *Déluges*?' said Gerbert. 'Nothing but a stand-in, but it would be good pay.' He frowned. 'As soon as I've put by a little cash, I'll buy an old car; I'd be able to get one second-hand for next to nothing.'

'That's a great idea,' said Françoise. 'You're sure to kill me, but I'll be driven by you.'

They emerged from the métro.

'Or else,' said Gerbert, 'I might set up a marionette theatre with Mollier. Begramian is still supposed to come in with us on *Images*, but you can't count on him.'

'Marionettes are great fun,' said Françoise.

'Only you have to pay through the nose to get a hall and the doings to yourself,' said Gerbert.

'You'll get it one day, perhaps,' said Françoise.

Today, Gerbert's plans did not amuse her; she even wondered why she found a quiet charm in the fact of his existence. He was there, he had come from a boring meal at Péclard's, tonight he would play the part of young Cato for the twentieth time, there was nothing specially exciting in that. Françoise looked about her; she wished she could find something that would make some slight appeal to her, but this long straight avenue had nothing to say to her. Only boring things were being sold in the little carts lined up along the edge of the pavement: cotton frocks, socks, or soap.

'Let's go down one of these little streets,' she said.

Here were old shoes, gramophone records, silks that were falling to pieces, enamel bowls, chipped crockery, all on the bare muddy ground. Dark-skinned women clothed in brightly-coloured tatters were sitting on newspapers or old rugs, leaning up against the hoardings. All that meant nothing to her either.

'Look,' said Gerbert. 'We're sure to find some props among all that junk.'

Françoise looked unenthusiastically at the bric-à-brac displayed at her feet; without a doubt, all these filthy òld objects could tell a strange story, but to the casual onlooker they were only bracelets, broken dolls, faded materials, devoid of any personal history. Gerbert picked up and ran his hand over a glass ball with multicoloured confetti like snowflakes inside it.

'It looks like a fortune-teller's crystal,' he said.

'It's a paper-weight,' said Françoise.

The vendor was watching them out of the corner of her eye; she was a fat, heavily-painted woman, with wavy hair, her body enveloped in woollen shawls and her legs wrapped in old newspapers; she, too, had no history, no future, she was nothing but a mass of chilled flesh. And the hoardings, the corrugated-iron huts, the wretched gardens with their dumps of rusting old iron, did not, as was usual, create a sordid and fascinating world for Françoise; it was there all round her, huddled and heaped together, inert and shapeless.

'What's this story about our going on tour?' said Gerbert. 'Bernheim talks as if it were settled for next year.'

'Bernheim has a bee in his bonnet about it,' said Françoise, 'that's obvious! He's only interested in money; but Pierre won't hear of it. Next year there'll be other things to do.'

She stepped over a puddle. It was just like the day when, years ago, she closed the door of her grandmother's house on the softness of the evening and the scents of the wild garden: she would always feel she had been cheated out of one of the solemn moments of the world. Elsewhere something was in the process of existing without her being there, and it was that thing only which really mattered. This time, she couldn't say: 'It doesn't know it exists, it doesn't exist.' For it did know. Pierre did not miss one of Xavière's smiles and Xavière gathered up, with entranced attentiveness, every word that Pierre was saying to her. Together at this moment, their eyes

118

were reflecting Pierre's dressing-room with Shakespeare's portrait hanging on the wall. Were they working? Or were they resting and talking about Xavière's father, about the aviary full of birds, about the smell of the stables?

'Did Xavière do anything yesterday in the elocution lessons?' said Françoise.

Gerbert laughed.

'Rambert asked her to repeat: "Round the rugged rock the ragged rascal ran!" She blushed furiously and looked down at her feet without uttering a sound.'

'Do you think she's got anything in her?'

'She's got a good figure,' said Gerbert. He seized Françoise by the elbow. 'Come and look,' he said suddenly, and pushed through the crowd. People were gathering around a large opened umbrella lying on the muddy ground; a man was spreading out cards on the black surface.

'Two hundred francs,' said an old grey-haired woman, casting distracted looks on all sides, 'two hundred francs!' Her lips were trembling; someone pushed her back roughly.

'They're thieves,' said Françoise.

'Everyone knows that,' said Gerbert.

Françoise looked with curiosity at the card-sharper with the deceptive hands, who was nimbly sliding three bits of grimy cardboard on the black cover of the umbrella.

'Two hundred on this one,' said a man, putting two notes on one of the cards; he winked insinuatingly: one of the corners was slightly bent and the king of hearts could be seen.

'And he wins,' said the card-sharper turning up the king. The cards slipped through his fingers again.

'Here it is – watch the cards – keep your eyes skinned – here it is, here it is: two hundred francs on the king of hearts.'

'That's the one, who'll go a hundred with me?' said the man.

'A hundred francs! Here's a hundred francs,' someone shouted.

'And he wins,' said the sharper, throwing four crumpled notes down in front of him. He was, of course, purposely letting them win in order to lead the crowd on. This would have been the time to bet, it was easy. Françoise guessed the whereabouts of the king at each deal. It was dazzling to watch the quick shuffling of the cards; they slipped and flipped to right, to left, to centre, to left.

'It's foolish,' said Françoise. 'You can see it every time.'

'Here it is,' said a man.

'Four hundred francs,' said the sharper.

The man turned to Françoise.

'I've only two hundred francs, here it is – put down two hundred francs with me,' he said suddenly.

Left, centre, left, that was certainly the one. Françoise put down her two notes on the card.

'Seven of clubs,' said the sharper. He snatched up the notes.

'How idiotic!' said Françoise.

She stood there dumbfounded, like the old woman a few moments beforehand; a quick little gesture – it wasn't possible that the money was really lost – surely she could win it back. If she really paid attention to the next deal . . .

'Come on,' said Gerbert, 'they're all stooges. Come on, or you'll lose your last sou.'

Françoise followed him.

'And yet I knew all the time that you can never win,' she said angrily.

This was just the sort of day for doing such stupid things. Everything was absurd – places, people, the things people said. How cold it was! Madame Miquel had been right, this coat was much too light.

'Suppose we go and have a drink,' she suggested.

'I'd like to,' said Gerbert. 'Let's go to the big café where there's singing.'

Night was already falling . . . The lesson was over now, but no doubt they had not yet said goodbye to each other. Where were they? Perhaps they had gone back to the Pôle Nord; when Xavière liked a place she immediately made it a home from home. Françoise called to mind the leather-covered banquettes with their big copper nail-heads, and the windows, and the red-and-white check lamp-shades, but it was useless; the faces and the voices and the honey-flavoured cocktails – everything had acquired a mysterious meaning which would have disappeared had Françoise come in through the door. Both would have smiled affectionately, Pierre would have continued their conversation and she would have drunk from a glass through a straw; but the secret of their tête-à-tête could never be revealed, not even by themselves.

'This is the café,' said Gerbert.

It was a kind of shed heated by enormous braziers, and very crowded; an orchestra was blaringly accompanying a man dressed as a soldier.

'I'll have a marc,' said Françoise, 'that will warm me up.'

The sticky persistent drizzle had permeated her very being, she shivered; she did not know what to do with her body or her thoughts. She looked at the women wearing clogs and wrapped in big shawls who were drinking coffee and brandy at the bar. 'Why are the shawls always mauve?' she wondered. The soldier had his face daubed with rouge; he was clapping his hands with a knowing look, though he had not yet come to the smutty couplet.

'Would you mind paying now?' said the waiter. Françoise took a sip from her glass; a violent flavour of petrol and mildew filled her mouth. Suddenly, Gerbert burst out laughing.

'What is it?' said Françoise; at that moment he didn't look a day over twelve.

'Smut always makes me laugh,' he said, embarrassed.

'What was the word that made you laugh all of a sudden?' asked Françoise.

'Squirt,' said Gerbert.

'Squirt!'

'Oh, but I really have to see it written out!' said Gerbert.

The orchestra broke into a paso doble. On the dais, next to the accordion player, stood a big doll in a sombrero, and it looked almost alive.

Not a word passed between the pair of them. 'He still thinks that he bores us,' thought Françoise regretfully. Pierre had not exerted himself very much to regain Gerbert's confidence; even into the most sincere friendship he put so little of himself! Françoise tried to shake herself out of this torpor; she must explain a little to Gerbert why Xavière had taken on so much importance in their life.

'Pierre thinks that Xavière might become an actress,' said Françoise.

'Yes, I know, he seems to think a lot of her,' said Gerbert, a little stiffly.

'She's a funny person,' said Françoise, 'to be friends with her is not easy.'

'She's a bit of an iceberg,' said Gerbert. 'I never know what to say to her.'

'She will not descend to plain civilities,' said Françoise. 'It's high-minded, but somewhat inconvenient.'

'At the School she never says a word to anyone: she stays

121

in a corner with her hair half over her face.'

'What exasperates her more than anything else,' said Françoise, 'is that Pierre and I are always on such good terms.'

Gerbert looked astonished.

'Still, she knows how things are between you, doesn't she?'

'Yes, but she thinks people should be untrammelled where their affections are concerned. She seems to think constancy can be achieved only by continual compromise and lies.'

'What a scream! She ought to be able to see that you get along all right without that,' said Gerbert.

'Of course,' said Françoise.

She looked at Gerbert with some annoyance: love was surely less simple than he thought. It was stronger than time, nevertheless it existed in time, and, from instant to instant, it was the cause of misgivings, self-denial, and minor despondencies; naturally that counted for very little, but only because she refused to let it count: a little effort was called for occasionally.

'Give me a cigarette,' she said, 'that will give me the illusion of being warm.'

Gerbert held out his packet with a smile; this smile was charming and nothing more, yet it would have been possible to discover a devastating charm in it; Françoise could guess how gentle she might have found these green eyes had she loved them; she had renounced all these precious qualities without even having known them; she would never know them. She granted them no regrets, however much they might merit them.

'It's a scream to watch Labrousse with Pagès,' said Gerbert. 'He looks as if he's treading on eggs.'

'Yes, a change has certainly come over him – Pierre who is usually so interested in what he can find in the way of ambition, desire and pluck in people,' said Françoise. 'No one cares less about her life than she does.'

'Is he really so fond of her?' said Gerbert.

'It's not so easy to say just what being fond of someone means to Pierre,' said Françoise. She stared in uncertainty at the tip of her cigarette. In the past, when she had spoken about Pierre, she had looked into herself; now, when she tried to discern his features, she had to stand back from him. It was almost impossible to answer Gerbert. Pierre always refused to compound with himself. He demanded progress from every minute of the day and with the fury of a renegade he offered up his past in sacrifice to his present. She might feel that he was anchored with her to a lasting passion of affection, sincerity, and suffering, yet he was already floating away like a sprite to the confines of time. He left behind him a phantom which he condemned out of hand from the height of his new virtues. The worst was that he was angry with his dupes for being content with a shell, and with an out-of-date shell at that. She crushed out her cigarette in the ash-tray. In the past, she used to find it amusing that Pierre could never be bound to any moment. But to just what extent was she herself protected against these vanished renegades? Of course, Pierre would never conspire against her with anyone in the world, but what went on in his own mind? It was understood that he had no secret life; all the same, a certain amount of credulity was required to give this theory full credence. Françoise was aware that Gerbert was observing her furtively, and she pulled herself together.

'What really matters is that she likes him,' she said.

'How's that?' said Gerbert.

He was very surprised; to him, too, Pierre seemed so complete, so outwardly protected, so perfectly shut up in himself: it was impossible to imagine any fissure through which misgivings could infiltrate. And yet, Xavière had breached this serenity. Or had she only revealed an imperceptible crack?

'I've often told you, that if Pierre stakes so much on the theatre, on art in general, it's because of some sort of decision he's made,' said Françoise. 'And when you begin to question a decision, it's always disturbing.' She smiled. 'Xavière is a living question mark.'

'Still, he's strangely stubborn on the subject,' said Gerbert.

'All the more reason. It stimulates him when someone argues to his face that it's just as significant to drink a cup of coffee as to write *Julius Caesar*.'

Françoise's heart contracted. Could she really assert that during all these years Pierre had never had any doubt? Or was it simply that she had not wanted to worry about it?

'What do you think?' said Gerbert.

'About what?'

'About the significance of a cup of coffee?'

'Oh, I!' said Françoise. She recalled a certain smile of Xavière's. 'I so want to be happy,' she said disdainfully.

'I don't see the connexion,' said Gerbert.

'Introspection is tiring,' she said. 'It's dangerous.'

Fundamentally she resembled Elisabeth. Once and for all time she had performed an act of faith, and she was now resting calmly on out-dated proof. She would have had to re-examine everything from the beginning; but that required a superhuman strength.

'And you? What do you think about it?'

'Oh, it's up to you,' said Gerbert with a smile. 'It depends on whether you feel like drinking or writing.'

Françoise looked at him.

'I've often wondered just what you expect to get out of your life,' she said.

'First of all, I would like to be sure that I'll still be allowed to live it for a little while,' he said.

Françoise smiled.

'That's fair enough. But supposing you have that amount of luck.'

'Then I don't know,' said Gerbert. He thought for a moment. 'Perhaps, in other times, I might have known better.'

Françoise assumed an air of detachment. Perhaps if Gerbert did not see the importance of the question he might answer.

'But are you satisfied with your life or not?'

'There are some good spells and others not so good,' he said.

'Yes,' said Françoise, a little disappointed. She hesitated a moment. 'If you limit yourself to that, it's a little depressing.'

'It depends on the day,' said Gerbert. Then he made an effort. 'Whatever you may say about life, it always seems to me to be just so many words.'

'To be happy or unhappy – are they simply words to you?'

'Yes, I don't really understand what it means.'

'But you're rather gay by nature,' said Françoise.

'I'm frequently bored,' said Gerbert.

He said it calmly. Long periods of boredom punctuated by short bursts of pleasure seemed completely natural to him. 'Good spells and others not so good.' Wasn't he right, after all? Wasn't the remainder of time just illusion and fiction? They were sitting on a hard wooden bench; it was cold, and there were soldiers and family parties all round them. Pierre was sitting at a different table with Xavière; they had smoked cigarettes and drunk a few glasses and spoken some words, and those sounds and that smoke had not been condensed into mysterious hours whose forbidden intimacy Françoise must envy; they would part, and nowhere would a bond remain that bound them one to the other. There was nothing anywhere to envy, or to regret, or to fear. The past, the future, love, unhappiness, were no more than a sound made with the mouth. Nothing existed except the musicians in their crimson blouses and the black-robed doll with a red scarf around its neck; its skirts, raised above a wide embroidered petticoat, revealed a pair of thin legs. It was there, it was enough to fill the eyes that could rest on it for an eternal present.

'Give me your hand, my beauty, and I'll tell your fortune.' Françoise shuddered and automatically held out her hand to a handsome gypsy dressed in yellow and purple.

'Things aren't going as well for you as you'd really like but have patience, you'll soon receive some news that will bring you happiness,' said the woman in one breath. 'You have money, my beauty, but not as much as people think. You're proud and that's why you have enemies, but you'll triumph over all your enemies. If you come with me, my beauty, I'll tell you a little secret.'

'Do go,' Gerbert urged her.

Françoise followed the gypsy, who produced a little piece of light-coloured wood from her pocket.

'I'll tell you a secret. There's a dark young man in your life, you're very much in love with him, but you're not happy with him because of a blonde girl. This is a charm. You must put it into a small handkerchief and keep it on you for three days and then you'll be happy with the young man. I wouldn't give it to anyone, for this is a very precious charm; but I'll give it to you for a hundred francs.'

'No, thank you,' said Françoise. 'I don't want the charm. Here's something for the fortune.'

The woman seized the coin.

'A hundred francs for your happiness is nothing. How much do you want to pay for your happiness, twenty francs?'

'Nothing at all,' said Françoise.

She came back and sat down beside Gerbert.

'What did she tell you?' said Gerbert.

'Just a lot of twaddle,' said Françoise. She smiled. 'She offered me my happiness for twenty francs, but I found that too dear, if, as you say, it's nothing but a word.'

'I didn't say that!' said Gerbert, startled to have been

involved to such an extent.

'Perhaps it's true,' said Françoise. 'With Pierre one uses so many words, and what exactly lies behind them?'

The anguish that suddenly overcame her was so violent that she wanted to scream. It was as if the world had suddenly become a void; there was nothing more to fear, nor was there anything to love. There was absolutely nothing. She was going to meet Pierre, they would exchange meaningless phrases and then they would part. If Pierre's and Xavière's friendship was no more than an unsubstantial mirage, then equally Françoise's and Pierre's love did not exist. There was nothing but an infinite accumulation of meaningless moments, nothing but a chaotic seething of flesh and of thought whose termination was death.

'Let's go,' she said abruptly.

Pierre was never late for an appointment. When Françoise walked into the restaurant, he was already sitting at their usual table. A wave of joy swept over her when she caught sight of him, but immediately she thought: 'We have only two hours ahead of us,' and her pleasure vanished.

'Have you had a pleasant afternoon?' said Pierre affectionately. A broad smile expanded his face and imparted a kind of innocence to his features.

'We went to the flea-market,' said Françoise. 'Gerbert was very nice, but the weather was so wretched. I lost two hundred francs by betting on the three-card trick.'

'What on earth made you do that? You are an idiot!' said Pierre. He handed her the menu. 'What will you have?'

'A Welsh rarebit,' said Françoise.

With a worried look, Pierre studied the menu.

'There's no egg mayonnaise,' he said. His puzzled and disappointed face did not soften Françoise; she noted coldly that it was a touching face.

'Well, two Welsh rarebits,' said Pierre.

'Would you like to know what we talked about?' said Françoise.

'Of course I would,' said Pierre warmly.

She looked at him warily. In the past, she would simply have thought: 'He wants to hear about it,' and she would have told him at once; when Pierre's words and smiles were directed to her, that was Pierre himself. Suddenly, she felt as if they were ambiguous symbols: Pierre had deliberately created them, he himself was behind them. All that was certain was that he had said that he would like to hear about it, and nothing more.

She put her hand on Pierre's arm.

'You tell me first,' she said. 'What did you do with Xavière? Did you manage to get some work done?'

Pierre looked at her a little sheepishly.

'Not much,' he said.

'Well, really!' said Françoise, making no secret of her annoyance. Xavière had to work for her own sake and for theirs; she could not go on living for years as a parasite.

'We spent three-quarters of the afternoon squabbling,' said Pierre.

Françoise felt she was controlling her expression, but was not too certain what it was that she feared might be revealed.

'About what?' she said.

'About her work,' said Pierre smiling into space. 'This morning in the miming class, Bahin asked her to walk in the woods and gather flowers; she told him with horror that she loathed flowers and she never budged an inch. She told me about it with great pride and it made me furious.'

Quite quietly Pierre was drowning his steaming Welsh rarebit with Worcester sauce.

'And then?' said Françoise with impatience. Pierre certainly was taking his time; he could have no suspicion of how important it was for her to know.

'Oh! Then the band played,' said Pierre, 'she became embittered. She arrived, all sweetness and smiles, certain that I was going to pat her on the hand, but I – well, I dragged her through the mud! Clenching her fists, she began to explain – but with that silky politeness that you know so well – that we were worse than bourgeois because we crave for moral comfort. She wasn't far out, but I got into a hell of a temper with her. We sat face to face at the Dôme for over an hour, without so much as uttering a word.'

All these theories about life without hope, about the futility of making an effort, became very irritating in the long run. Françoise held her peace; she did not want to spend her time criticizing Xavière.

'That must have been a pretty sight!' she said. This constraint, which made a lump rise in her throat, was so stupid. Surely she had not reached the stage where she had to keep up appearances in front of Pierre!

'It isn't so disagreeable to sit simmering with rage,' said Pierre, 'I don't think she dislikes it either; but she has less resistance than I, and in the end she broke down. Then I made an attempt at reconciliation. That was difficult because she had immured herself in her hatred, but I won in the end.' He added with a self-satisfaction: 'We signed a solemn peace and to seal the reconciliation she invited me to her room for tea.'

'To her room?' said Françoise. It was a long time since Xavière had invited her inside her room, she felt a little stab of resentment.

'Did you finally manage to drag some good resolutions out of her?'

'We talked about other things,' said Pierre. 'I told her stories about our travels and we pretended that we were on a trip together.' He smiled. 'We made up a number of little scenes. An encounter, in the heart of a desert, between an English woman on her travels and a famous adventurer – you know the sort of thing. She has imagination, if only she could make use of it.'

'She has to be handled firmly,' said Françoise a little reproachfully.

'I'll manage that,' said Pierre. 'Don't scold me.' He had a queer smile, humble and saint-like. 'All of a sudden she said to me: "I'm having a wonderful time with you!"'

'Well, that's a triumph,' said Françoise. 'I'm having a wonderful time with you . . .' Had she been standing with a vague look in her eyes, or had she been sitting on the edge of the sofa, looking straight at Pierre? There was no use in asking him. How could her exact tone of voice, the scent of her room at that moment, be described? Words could bring you nearer the mystery, but without making it any less impenetrable; it only masked the heart in a more chilling shadow.

'I can't quite make out her feelings towards me,' said Pierre, as if preoccupied, 'I think I'm gaining some ground, but the ground is constantly shifting.'

'You're progressing every day,' said Françoise.

'When I left her, the signs were ominous again,' he said. 'She was angry with herself for not having had her lesson, and she had a fit of self-disgust.' He looked gravely at Françoise. 'Be very nice to her when you see her later.'

'I'm always nice to her,' said Françoise a little stiffly. Whenever Pierre tried to tell her how she should behave to Xavière, she shrank into herself; she had no desire whatsoever to go and see Xavière and be nice, now that it was expected of her.

'That vanity of hers is terrible,' said Françoise. 'She has to be certain of an immediate and striking success before committing herself.'

'It's not only vanity,' said Pierre.

'Then what is it?'

'She's told me a hundred times that she loathes having to stoop to scheming and waiting for opportunities.'

'And do you consider that "stooping"?'

'I haven't any morals,' said Pierre.

'Do you honestly think that her behaviour is due to her moral sense?'

'In a way it is,' said Pierre with some annoyance. 'She has a very definite outlook on life, and she doesn't choose to compromise. That's what I call morals. She's looking for completeness; and that's the kind of exactingness we've always admired.'

'There's a lot of listlessness in her case,' said Françoise.

'Listlessness, what is listnessness?' said Pierre, 'a way of shutting yourself up in the present; it's the only way in which she can find completeness. If the present has nothing to offer, she buries herself in her lair like a sick animal. But you know, when you carry inertia to the point to which she carries it, the word listlessness is no longer valid; it assumes a kind of power. Neither you nor I would have the strength of mind to stay in a room for forty-eight hours without seeing a soul or doing a thing.'

'I don't deny it,' said Françoise. She felt a sudden, painful need to see Xavière; there was unusual warmth in Pierre's voice. Yet, admiration was a feeling which he maintained that he never experienced.

'On the other hand,' said Pierre, 'when something does appeal to her, it's quite amazing how she enjoys it; I feel very thin-blooded beside her; I almost feel humiliated.'

'That must surely be the first time in you life that you've experienced the feeling of humility,' said Françoise, with an attempt at a laugh.

'When I left her, I told her she was a little black pearl,' said Pierre gravely. 'She shrugged her shoulders, but I really meant what I said. Everything about her is so pure – and so violent.'

'Why black?' said Françoise.

'Because of that kind of perversity of hers. It almost seems as if she has moments when she must harm others and herself, when she must make herself hated.' He let his thoughts wander for a moment. 'You know, it's curious. Often, if you tell her that you think highly of her, she jibs as if she were afraid; she feels herself fettered by our esteem.'

'She was very quick about shaking off the fetters,' said Françoise.

She was beginning to be uncertain; she almost had a desire to believe in that seductive face. If she now so often felt estranged from Pierre, it was because she had allowed him to progress alone down these paths of admiration and affection. They no longer saw things eye to eye. Where she beheld no more than a capricious child, Pierre saw a wild and exacting soul. If she were willing to stand by his side once more, if she were to give up this obstinate resistance . . .

'There's some truth in all that,' she said. 'I very often feel something pathetic about her.'

Again, she felt herself stiffen from head to foot; that alluring mask was a trap, she would not yield to such witchcraft. Of what might happen to her if she were to yield, she had not the faintest idea: all she knew was that some danger was threatening her . . .

'But it's impossible to be true friends with her,' she said bitterly. 'Her selfishness is something monstrous. It isn't only that she considers herself superior to other people, she is utterly unaware of their existence.'

'Still, she's extremely fond of you,' said Pierre a little reproachfully. 'And you're quite hard enough with her, you know.'

'Hers isn't a very pleasant affection,' said Françoise, 'she treats me at one and the same time as an idol and as a doormat. Perhaps deep in her heart she worships me in the abstract, but she treats the poor flesh-and-blood creature that I am with an off-handedness that's rather embarrassing. It's quite understandable: an idol doesn't get hungry, or sleepy, or suffer from headaches, it is adored without being asked its opinion on the form of adoration it receives.'

Pierre began to laugh. 'There's some truth in that; but you'll soon think me biased. Her inability to have human relations with people makes me feel sorry for her.'

Françoise, too, smiled.

'I think you are slightly biased,' she said.

They left the restaurant. Once again they had talked about nothing but Xavière. When she was not with them, they spent the entire time talking about her; this was becoming an obsession. Françoise glanced sadly at Pierre; he had not asked her a single question, he was completely uninterested in the thoughts that had passed through her mind during the day; and when he did listen to her with interest, was that only out of politeness? She pressed her arm against him, so that she might at least feel some contact with him. Pierre gently squeezed her hand.

'You know, I'm a little sorry I'm not sleeping at your hotel any more,' he said.

'Still,' said Françoise, 'your dressing-room does look very handsome now that it has been repainted.'

It was a little frightening. In his tender phrases, his affectionate gestures, she saw only an intention of kindness: they were not wholly convincing, they did not register properly. She shivered: it was as if a stop-watch had been set going to check her feelings; and now that it had been started, could her doubting ever again be stopped?

'Have a pleasant evening,' said Pierre tenderly.

'Thank you. I'll see you tomorrow morning,' said Françoise.

She watched him disappear through the small side door of the theatre and an agony of doubt assailed her. What was there beneath the phrases and gestures? 'We are but one.' With the help of this convenient confusion she had always been relieved from worrying about Pierre – but these were only words: they were two separate persons. She had felt that one evening at the Pôle Nord. That was what she had held as a grievance against him several days later. She had not wanted to increase her qualms, she had taken refuge in anger, that she might not see the truth; yet Pierre was not at fault, he had not changed. It was she who had made the mistake of looking upon him only as a justification of herself. Now, she was aware that he lived his own life, and the result of her blind trust was that she suddenly found herself facing a stranger. She quickened her pace. The only way she could bring herself nearer to Pierre was by joining Xavière and trying to see her through his eyes. How far away was the time when Françoise only thought of Xavière as a part of her own life! Now it was

131

towards a strange world that would barely be opened to her that she was hurrying with an avid yet hopeless anxiety.

For a moment, Françoise stood motionless before the door. This room made her feel shy: it really was a holy place. Here more than one worship was held, but the supreme deity towards whom there rose the smoke of Virginian cigarettes, the scent of tea and of lavender, was Xavière herself, as she imagined herself to be.

Françoise knocked softly.

'Come in,' said a cheerful voice.

A little surprised, Françoise opened the door. Standing in her long green-and-white house-coat, Xavière was smiling, enjoying to the full the astonishment she had clearly intended to arouse. A lamp, shaded in red, threw a blood-coloured hue over the room.

'Would you like to spend the evening here?' said Xavière. 'I've made a little supper.'

Beside the wash-hand stand, the kettle was purring on a spirit stove and in the half-light Françoise was able to make out two plates of multicoloured sandwiches; refusal was out of the question: beneath their apparent timidity, Xavière's invitations were always imperious orders.

'How sweet of you,' she said. 'Had I known this was going to be a gala evening, I would have dressed for it.'

'You look very beautiful as you are,' said Xavière affectionately. 'Make yourself comfortable. Look, I've bought some green tea. The tiny leaves look as if they're still alive, and you'll see in a moment how strongly scented it is.'

She puffed out her cheeks and blew hard at the flame of the stove. Françoise was ashamed of her ill will. 'It's true that I'm hard,' she thought, 'I'm growing sour.' How bitter her voice had been just now, when she was talking to Pierre!

The rapt attention with which Xavière was bending towards the tea-pot was certainly very disarming.

'Do you like red caviare?' asked Xavière.

'Oh, very much,' said Françoise.

'Oh, that's good. I was afraid you might not like it.'

Françoise looked at the sandwiches a little apprehensively. Pieces of rye bread cut in rounds, squares and diamonds and spread with many coloured jams, and here and there between them peeped an anchovy, an olive, or a slice of beetroot.

'No two are alike,' said Xavière proudly. She poured the

steaming tea into a cup. 'I had to put a drop of tomato sauce on a few of them,' she added quickly, 'that made them so much prettier, but you won't even taste it.'

'They look delicious,' said Françoise with resignation; she loathed tomatoes. She chose the sandwich that looked the least red; it had a queer taste, but was not too bad.

'Did you notice that I have some new photographs?' said Xavière.

On the green-and-red flowered wallpaper she had pinned a set of artistic nudes. Françoise carefully studied the long curved backs, the proffered breasts.

'I don't think Monsieur Labrousse thought them very pretty,' said Xavière with a tight little pout.

'The blonde might perhaps be said to be a little too fat,' said Françoise, 'but that small brunette is charming.'

'She has a beautiful long neck like yours,' said Xavière in a caressing tone.

Françoise smiled at her. She suddenly felt relieved; all the evil poetry of the day had vanished. She looked at the couch, at the arm-chairs covered in a material patterned with yellow, green and red lozenges like a harlequin costume. She liked the varying values of strong and light colours, and this sombre light, and the scent of dead flowers and living flesh that always emanated from Xavière. Pierre had known no more than this, and Xavière had turned to him a face no more moving than the one she now raised to Françoise; these charming features went to make up the honest face of a child, and not the disquieting mask of a witch.

'Do eat some sandwiches,' said Xavière.

'I've really eaten enough,' said Françoise.

'Oh!' said Xavière, looking downcast, 'you don't like them!'

'Of course I like them,' said Françoise reaching towards the plate. Only too well did she know this gentle tyranny. Xavière did not try to make others happy; she selfishly delighted in the pleasure of giving pleasure. But was she to blame for that? Wasn't she lovable like this? Her eyes shining with satisfaction, she watched Françoise get down a thick tomato purée sandwich: one would have to be a stone not to be moved by her joy.

'I had a real thrill a little while ago,' said Xavière, in a confidential tone.

'What was that?' said Françoise.

133

'That handsome Negro dancer!' said Xavière. 'He spoke to me.'

'Take care that the blonde doesn't scratch your eyes out!' said Françoise.

'I met him on the stairs as I was coming back with my tea and all my little parcels.' Xavière's eyes sparkled. 'He was so nice! He had on a light-coloured overcoat and a pale grey hat – it went so well with his dark skin. My parcels fell out of my hands. He picked them up for me and with a big smile said: "Good evening, Mademoiselle, enjoy your dinner." '

'And what did you answer?' said Françoise.

'Nothing!' said Xavière in a shocked tone. 'I ran.' She smiled. 'He's as graceful as a cat, and he looks just as ruthless and treacherous.'

Françoise had never really taken a good look at this Negro; beside Xavière, she felt very barren: what reminiscences Xavière would have brought back with her from the flea-market! And all she had been able to see were filthy rags and tumble-down hovels.

Xavière refilled Françoise's cup.

'Did you work much this morning?' she asked with a fond look.

Françoise smiled. This was a deliberate advance that Xavière was making to her; usually, she loathed the work to which Françoise devoted most of her time.

'Quite a lot,' she said. 'But I had to leave at noon to go and lunch with my mother.'

'May I read your book some day?' Xavière asked with a coquettish pout.

'Of course,' said Françoise. 'I'll show you the first chapters whenever you like.'

'What's it about?'

She sat down on a cushion, tucked her legs up under her, and blew lightly on her scalding tea. Françoise looked at her with slight remorse, she was touched by the interest which Xavière was exhibiting in her; she should have tried more often to have a real talk with her.

'It's about my youth,' said Françoise. 'I want to explain in my story why people are so often misfits when they're young.'

'Do you think young people are misfits?'

'Not you,' said Françoise. 'You're a superior soul.' She thought a moment. 'You see, when you're a child, you very easily resign yourself to being regarded as of little account, but at seventeen things change. You begin to want to have a definite existence, and since you still feel the same inside yourself, you foolishly have recourse to external guarantees.'

'How do you do that?' asked Xavière.

'You seek the approbation of others, you write down your thoughts, you compare yourself with accepted models. Now, take Elisabeth,' said Françoise, 'in a sense, she has never passed that stage. She's a perennial adolescent.'

Xavière laughed. 'You are certainly not like Elisabeth,' she said.

'I am, in a way,' said Françoise. 'Elisabeth annoys us because she listens slavishly to Pierre and me, because she's constantly remodelling herself. But if you study her with a little sympathy you'll perceive in all that a clumsy attempt to give a definite value to her life and to herself as a person. Even her respect for the social formulas – marriage, fame – is still a form of this anxiety.'

Xavière's face clouded slightly.

'Elisabeth is a vain, pathetic jellyfish,' she said. 'That's all.'

'No, that isn't precisely all,' said Françoise. 'You still have to understand the cause of it.'

Xavière shrugged her shoulders.

'What's the good of trying to understand people who aren't worth it?'

Françoise repressed a movement of impatience. Xavière was affronted as soon as anyone but herself was spoken of indulgently or even fairly.

'In a way, no one is worth it,' she said to Xavière, who was listening with sulky attention. 'Elisabeth is completely bewildered when she looks into herself, because all she finds is an empty shell. She has no idea that it's the common fate. On the other hand, she sees other people from without, through the shape of words, gestures and faces. It produces a kind of mirage.'

'It's funny,' said Xavière. 'Usually, you don't make so many excuses for her.'

'But it's not a question of excusing or condemning,' said Françoise.

'I've already noticed that,' said Xavière. 'You and Monsieur Labrousse always make people out to be far too mysterious. But they're a lot simpler than that.'

135

Françoise smiled. That was the reproach she had once made to Pierre – of taking pleasure in complicating Xavière.

'They're simple if you look only at the surface!' she said.

'Perhaps,' said Xavière in a polite and careless tone that definitely closed the discussion. She pushed away her cup and gave Françoise a winning smile.

'Do you know what the chamber-maid told me?' she said. 'There's someone in Room 9 who's both a man and a woman.'

'Room 9. So that's why she has that craggy head and husky voice!' said Françoise. 'That strange creature does dress like a woman. Is that the one?'

'Yes, but he has a man's name. He's an Austrian. It seems that when he was born they couldn't make up their minds. Finally, they decided that he was a boy and when he was fifteen something happened to him that was decidedly feminine, but his parents didn't change his birth certificate.' Xavière lowered her voice and added: 'Besides, he has hair on his chest and other characteristics. He was famous in his own country. They made a film of him and he made a lot of money.'

'I should imagine that in the heyday of psycho-analysis and sexology, it must have been a godsend to be a hermaphrodite in Vienna,' said Françoise.

'Yes, but when there were all those political goings-on, you know,' said Xavière vaguely, 'he was driven out. Then she took refuge here. She's penniless and it seems that she's very unhappy because she's drawn to men, but men won't have anything to do with her.'

'Oh, the poor thing! That's true; she wouldn't even find favour with the homosexuals,' said Françoise.

'She weeps all the time,' said Xavière, seemingly heart-broken. She looked at Françoise. 'Still, it isn't her fault. How can you be driven out of a country because you're made one way or another? People have no right to do that.'

'Governments have the rights they take,' said Françoise.

'I don't understand that,' said Xavière accusingly. 'Isn't there any country where people can do as they like?'

'No.'

'Then I'll have to go to a desert island,' said Xavière.

'Even desert islands belong to people now,' said Françoise. 'You're cornered.'

Xavière shook her head.

136

'Oh, I'll find a way,' she said.

'I don't think so,' said Françoise. 'You'll have to accept a number of things you don't like, just like everyone else.' She smiled. 'Does that idea disgust you?'

'Yes,' said Xavière. She looked sideways at Françoise. 'Did Monsieur Labrousse tell you that he was not pleased with my work?'

'He told me that you had a long talk about it.' Françoise added cheerfully: 'He was extremely flattered at having been invited to your room.'

'Oh, it just happened,' said Xavière laconically.

She turned away to fill the kettle with water and there was a brief silence. Pierre was wrong if he thought she had forgiven him; with Xavière, the last impression was no true indication of her feelings. She must have thought over the events of the afternoon in anger and become enraged above all by the final reconciliation.

Françoise looked at her carefully. Wasn't this charming welcome just a form of exorcism? Hadn't she been taken in once again? Surely the tea, the sandwiches, the beautiful green gown were not intended to honour her, but rather to deprive Pierre of a privilege foolishly granted. Françoise felt a lump in her throat. No, it was impossible to proceed with this friendship unreservedly. Try as she would, it left an unwholesome taste in her mouth, a taste of metal shavings.

Chapter Seven

'Won't you have some fruit salad?' said Françoise. She elbowed a path to the buffet for Jeanne Harbley. Aunt Christine had never left the table for an instant; she was now smiling adoringly at Guimiot, who was eating a coffee ice with an air of condescension. Françoise ran her eyes over the plates of sandwiches and petits fours to make quite certain that they still looked presentable. There were twice as many people as at the previous Christmas-Eve party.

'The decorations are charming,' said Jeanne Harbley.

For the tenth time Françoise answered: 'Begramian is responsible for them: he's got excellent taste.'

He deserved no little credit for his rapid transformation of a Roman battlefield into a ballroom, but Françoise had no great liking for the profusion of holly, mistletoe and pine branches. She looked round the room, seeking new faces.

'It was so nice of you to have come! Labrousse will be so happy to see you!'

'Where is the dear master?'

'Over there, with Berger, you really had better go and rescue him.'

Blanche Bouguet could hardly be said to be any more amusing than Berger, but she would at least be a change. Pierre looked very far from being infected by any party spirit; from time to time his eyes roved apprehensively; he must be worried about Xavière, afraid that she would get drunk or disappear suddenly. At the present moment she was sitting beside Gerbert on the proscenium, their legs were dangling over the edge and they seemed horribly bored with each other. The gramophone was playing a rumba, but the stage was too crowded for anyone to dance.

'Well, it's just too bad about Xavière!' thought Françoise. The evening was trying enough as it was; it would become intolerable if her opinions and moods had to be taken into account. 'Just too bad!' repeated Françoise to herself, a little uncertainly.

'Are you leaving so soon? Oh, what a pity!'

She followed Abelson's retreating figure with some satisfaction; when all the important guests were gone, she could afford to relax a little. Françoise made her way towards Elisabeth; for the past half-hour, she had been leaning against an upright, smoking and staring abstractedly, without speaking to a soul. But to cross the stage was like going on a perilous voyage.

'It was so nice of you to have come! Labrousse will be so happy! He's in Blanche Bouguet's clutches, do try to rescue him.' Françoise gained a few inches. 'You look magnificent, Marie-Ange. That blue with the purple is really lovely. '

'It's a little ensemble I picked up at Lanvin's; it is pretty, isn't it?'

A few more handshakes, a few more smiles, and Françoise found herself at Elisabeth's side.

'That was tough going,' she said brightly. She suddenly felt very tired; she had been feeling tired very often lately.

'It's a real fashion parade tonight!' said Elisabeth. 'Do you notice what ugly complexions all these actresses have?'

Elisabeth's own skin, puffy and rather yellowish, was not particularly pretty, for that matter. 'She's letting herself go,' thought Françoise. It was hard to believe that six weeks earlier, at the dress rehearsal, she had been almost dazzling.

'It's the grease-paint,' said Françoise.

'Their figures are marvellous,' said Elisabeth impartially. 'When you think that Blanche Bouguet is over forty!'

The bodies were young and so was the too exact colouring of the hair, and even the firm outline of the faces, but this youth had none of the freshness of living things, it was an embalmed youth; not a wrinkle, not a crow's-foot marred this carefully massaged flesh; that stretched look round the eyes was only the more disturbing. They were ageing underneath, they could go on ageing for a long time before the glaze cracked; and then one day, suddenly, this flawless shell, grown thin as tissue paper, would crumble into dust. Then the effigy of an old woman would emerge, complete in every detail, with wrinkles, large brown moles, swollen veins, and knotted fingers.

'Well-preserved women,' said Françoise. 'That's a dreadful expression. It always makes me think of tinned lobster and of the waiter saying: "It's every bit as good as the fresh."'

'I don't think so very much of the young, either,' said Elisabeth. 'Those young people are so badly turned out that they look like nothing on earth.'

'Don't you think Canzetti looks charming in her wide gypsy skirt?' said Françoise. 'And look at the Eloy girl, and Chanaud! Obviously, the cut isn't perfection . . .'

These slightly clumsy dresses had all the charm of the tentative lives of those whose ambitions, dreams, hardships and resources they were the reflection: Canzetti's wide yellow belt, the embroidery Eloy had plastered over the bodice of her dress, were as intimate a part of them as their smiles. That was just the way Elisabeth used to dress.

'Believe me, these little ladies would give anything to look like Harbley or Bouguet,' said Elisabeth bitterly.

'They certainly would, and if they make good, they'll be exactly like the others,' said Françoise.

Françoise took in the scene at a glance; beautiful successful actresses, beginners, respectable failures, a whole host of separate fates went to make up this mixed congeries; it was almost enough to make her head spin. At certain moments, it seemed to Françoise that the orbits of these lives had intersected expressly for her at the particular point in time and space where she happened to be: at others, the very reverse; people seemed to be dotted about, each a separate entity.

'In any case, Xavière looks positively dowdy tonight,' said Elisabeth. 'Those flowers she's stuck in her hair are in the worst possible taste!'

Françoise had spent some little time with Xavière arranging that shy spray, but she did not want to contradict Elisabeth; there was hostility enough already in her expression even when she agreed with her.

'They're a riot, the two of them,' said Françoise.

Gerbert was about to light a cigarette for Xavière, but he carefully avoided catching her eye in the process; he looked very prim and proper in an expensive dark suit that he must have borrowed from Péclard. Xavière was obstinately staring at the tips of her small shoes.

'The whole time I've been watching them, they haven't exchanged a word,' said Elisabeth. 'They're as shy as two lovers.'

'They're frightened to death of each other,' said Françoise. 'It's a pity. They might have been good friends.'

Elisabeth's malice had no effect on her; her affection for Gerbert was completely devoid of jealousy, but it was not pleasant to feel herself so violently hated. It was almost an avowed hostility: Elisabeth had ceased to confide in her; her every word, her every silence was a living reproach.

'Bernheim told me that you were definitely going on tour next year,' said Elisabeth. 'Is it true?'

'Of course it isn't true,' said Françoise. 'He's got it into his head that Pierre would end up by giving in, but he's wrong. Next winter Pierre will put on his own play.'

'Are you going to open the season with that?' said Elisabeth.

'I don't know yet,' said Françoise.

'It would be a pity to go on the road,' said Elisabeth, looking preoccupied.

'That's just what I think,' said Françoise.

She wondered with some surprise whether Elisabeth still hoped to get something out of Pierre; perhaps she was making up her mind to approach him again on the question of opening with Battier's play in October.

'The place is beginning to empty a little,' she said.

'I must see Lise Malan,' said Elisabeth. 'I hear that she has something important to tell me.'

'I'm going to rescue Pierre,' said Françoise.

Pierre was shaking hands effusively, but try as he might, he could not put any warmth into his smiles: this was an art Madame Miquel had taken great pains to inculcate in her daughter.

'I wonder where she stands with Battier,' thought Françoise while showering goodbyes and regrets. Elisabeth had rid herself of Guimiot on the pretext that he had stolen some cigarettes from her, and she had taken up with Claude again, but that could not be going too well: she had never been more gloomy.

'Well, where's Gerbert gone to?' said Pierre.

Xavière, with her arms hanging loosely by her sides, was standing alone in the middle of the stage floor.

'Why doesn't anyone dance?' he added. 'There's plenty of room.'

There was a certain irritation in his voice. Her heart a little heavy, Françoise looked at this face that she had loved for so long in blind serenity; she had learned to read it; it was not reassuring tonight, for, tense and set, it had the appearance of being all the more brittle.

'Ten past two,' she said. 'Nobody else will come now.'

Pierre was so constituted that he did not take much pleasure in the moments when Xavière was pleasant to him; on the other hand, her slightest frown convulsed him with rage or remorse. To be at peace with himself, he had to feel that she was in his power. When people came between them, he was always disturbed and irritable.

'You're not too bored?' said Françoise.

'No,' said Xavière. 'Only it's wretched to listen to good jazz and not be able to dance.'

'But you can surely dance now,' said Pierre.

There was a moment's silence, during which all three smiled, but words failed them.

'Later, I'll teach you how to rumba,' Xavière said to Françoise with a shade too much animation.

'I'd rather stick to the slow steps,' said Françoise. 'I'm too old to rumba.'

'How can you say that?' said Xavière. She threw a slightly plaintive look at Pierre. 'She could dance so well if she wanted to.'

'It's fiddlesticks to say you're old!' said Pierre.

All at once, as he approached Xavière, he deliberately allowed his face and voice to brighten. He was regulating his slightest expression with disturbing precision; he must be on the alert, for he felt none of the light and tender gaiety that was sparkling in his eyes.

'Exactly the same age as Elisabeth,' said Françoise. 'I've just seen her. It's not very comforting.'

'Why are you talking to us about Elisabeth?' asked Pierre. 'You haven't looked at yourself.'

'She never looks at herself,' said Xavière, with a note of regret. 'Someone ought to take a cine-film of her one day without her knowing it, and then show it her as a surprise. Then she'd have to look at herself, and she'd be astounded!'

'She likes to think she's a big, middle-aged woman,' said Pierre. 'If you only knew how young you look!'

'But I have no wish to dance,' she said; this chorus of affection was making her feel ill at ease.

'Well, do you mind if we two dance?' said Pierre.

Françoise watched them; they were a pleasure to look at. Xavière danced, as light as a puff of smoke, seeming to skim over the floor; Pierre's body, though heavy, gave the impression of being released from the laws of gravity and

142

controlled by invisible threads; he had the miraculous ease of a marionette.

'I should like to know how to dance,' thought Françoise.

She had given it up ten years ago: now, it was too late to start over again. She lifted up a curtain and in the darkness of the wings she took out a cigarette; here, at least, she would have some slight respite.

Too late. She would never be the type of woman who had absolute mastery over her body. Whatever she might acquire today was not important; embellishments and adornments would remain external to her. That was what to be thirty years of age really meant: a mature woman! She was for ever a woman who did not know how to dance, a woman who had had only one love in her life, a woman who had not shot the Colorado Canyon by canoe, who had never crossed the Tibetan plateau. These thirty years were not only a past that she dragged along behind her; they had settled all about her, within her. That was her present, her future, that was the substance of which she was made. No heroism, no absurdity could change anything. Certainly, she had enough time before her death to learn Russian, read Dante, see Bruges and Constantinople; she could still dot her life now and then with unexpected incidents and new talents, but none the less it would still remain to the end this particular life, and none other; and her life could not be distinguished from herself. With a painful dizziness Françoise felt herself pierced by a barren, white light that left within her no recess of hope. She stood motionless for a moment watching the red tip of her cigarette glowing in the darkness. A light laugh, hushed whisperings, roused her from her torpor: these dark corridors were always very popular. Silently, she moved away and went back to the stage. Now people appeared to be enjoying themselves immensely.

'Where have you been?' asked Pierre. 'We've just been talking to Paule Berger. Xavière thinks she's very beautiful.'

'I saw her,' said Françoise. 'I even invited her to stay on until morning.'

She was fond of Paule, but it was difficult to see her without her husband and without the remainder of their group.

'She's amazingly beautiful,' said Xavière. 'She doesn't look like all these mannequins.'

'She looks a little too much like a nun or a missionary,' said Pierre.

Paule was talking to Inès; she was wearing a long, high-necked, black velvet dress. Red-gold hair, parted in the middle, framed her face with its wide, smooth forehead and deep-set eyes.

'The cheeks are a little ascetic,' said Xavière, 'but she has such a large generous mouth and such expressive eyes.'

'Transparent eyes,' said Pierre. He looked at Xavière and smiled. 'I like sultry eyes.'

It was rather dishonest of Pierre to speak of Paule in such a manner, for usually he praised her; he was taking a perverse pleasure in gratuitously sacrificing her to Xavière.

'She's marvellous when she dances,' said Françoise, 'but it is miming rather than dancing. Her technique isn't very elaborate, but she can express almost anything.'

'I'd love to see her dance!' said Xavière.

Pierre looked at Françoise. 'You ought to go and ask her,' he said.

'I'm afraid that might be tactless.'

'She doesn't usually need much persuasion.'

'She makes me feel shy.'

Paule Berger was delightfully affable with everyone, but one never knew what she was thinking.

'Did you ever hear of Françoise feeling shy?' said Pierre, laughing. 'It's the first time I have!'

'It would be so lovely!' said Xavière.

'All right, I'll do it,' said Françoise.

Smiling, she walked towards Paule Berger. Inès looked depressed. She was wearing a striking red moiré dress and a golden net over her fair hair. Paule was looking straight at her, talking in an encouraging and slightly motherly tone. She turned to Françoise vivaciously.

'Isn't it true that on the stage all the talent in the world amounts to nothing if you don't possess courage and faith?'

'Of course,' said Françoise.

That was not the question and Inès knew it only too well, but still she looked rather pleased.

'I've come to make a request,' said Françoise. She felt herself blushing, and was aware of a sudden fury against Pierre and Xavière. 'If it bores you in the least, please say so, but we would be so happy if you would dance for us.'

'I'd like to,' said Paule, 'but I have neither my music nor my props.' She smiled her apologies. 'I dance with a mask now, and a long dress.'

'That must be beautiful,' said Françoise.

Paule looked at Inès hesitantly.

'You could play the accompaniment for the dance of the machines,' she said, 'and then I'll do the charlady without music. But you already know that one.'

'That doesn't matter. I'd love to see it again,' said Françoise. 'It's so good of you. I'll go and turn off the gramophone.'

Xavière and Pierre were watching her with an air of conspiracy and amusement.

'She is going to,' said Françoise.

'You are a good ambassadress,' said Pierre.

He looked so childishly happy that Françoise was astonished. Her eyes fixed on Paule Berger, Xavière was waiting, entranced. This was the childlike joy reflected in Pierre's face.

Paule moved to the middle of the stage. She was not yet very well known to the general public, but everyone present admired her art. Canzetti was sitting on her heels, her wide mauve skirt spread out all round her. Eloy was lying catlike on the floor a few feet from Tedesco. Aunt Christine had disappeared, and Guimiot, standing beside Mark Antony, smiled at her mischievously. All seemed interested. Inès struck the first chords on the piano. Slowly, Paule's arm came to life, the slumbering machine was beginning to operate. Little by little the rhythm accelerated, but Françoise saw neither the driving rod, nor the rotating wheels, nor any motion of steel: it was Paule that she saw. A woman of her own age, a woman who also had her history, her work, and a life of her own, a woman who was dancing without giving Françoise a thought; and when, a little later, she would smile at her, it would only be to one among other spectators. To her, Françoise was no more than a piece of scenery.

'If only it were possible calmly to put oneself first,' thought Françoise with anguish.

At this moment, there were thousands of women scattered over the earth who were listening intently to the beating of their hearts; each her own, each for herself. How could she believe that she was standing at a vantage point of the world? There were Paule, and Xavière, and so many others. She could not even compare herself with them.

Françoise's hand slowly relaxed down the length of her skirt. 'Just what am I?' she wondered. She looked at Paule. She looked at Xavière whose face radiated unrestrained admiration. She knew what these women were: they had their own special memories, tastes and ideas which identified them, definitely formed characters that were expressed in their features. But in herself Françoise did not see any clear-cut shape. The light that had flashed through her a short while before had revealed nothing but a void. 'She never looks at herself,' Xavière had said. It was true. Françoise was heedful of her face only in so far as she took care of it as something impersonal. She searched her past for landscapes and people, but not for herself; and even her ideas and her tastes did not make her face what it was. It reflected the truths that had revealed themselves to her, and no more belonged to her than the bunches of mistletoe and holly that hung from the flies.

'I am no one,' thought Françoise. Often she had taken pride in not being circumscribed like other people in narrow little individual confines: – one night, not so very long ago, at the Prairie, with Elisabeth and Xavière – a naked conscience in front of the world, it was thus she thought of herself. She touched her face: to her it was no more than a white mask. And yet all these people saw it; and, whether she liked it or not, she too was in the world, a part of this world. She was a woman among other women and she had permitted this woman to grow at random without shaping her. She was utterly incapable of passing any judgement on this unknown. And yet Xavière had judged her, had compared her with Paule. Which of them did she prefer? And Pierre? When he looked at her what did he see? She turned her eyes towards Pierre, but Pierre was not looking at her.

He was looking at Xavière. With lips parted, and lack-lustre eyes, Xavière scarcely breathed; she no longer knew where she was; she seemed out of her body. Françoise looked away, embarrassed: Pierre's insistence was indiscreet and almost obscene, this rapt face was not for public view. Françoise could at least be certain of one thing – she would be incapable of going into such passionate trances. She did know with reasonable certainty what she was not: it was agonizing to know herself only as a series of negations.

'Did you see Xavière's face?' said Pierre.

'Yes,' said Françoise.

He had spoken without taking his eyes off Xavière.

'That's what it is,' thought Françoise; her features were no more distinct to him than they were to herself; amorphous, invisible; she was vaguely a part of him; he spoke to her as to himself, but his eyes remained fixed on Xavière. At this moment, with distended lips, and two tears trickling down her pale cheeks, Xavière was beautiful.

Applause broke out.

'I must thank Paule,' said Françoise. She thought: 'And as for me, I don't feel a thing.' She had hardly watched the dance; she had been gloating over her wild thoughts like an aged maniac.

Paule accepted her congratulations gracefully; Françoise admired her for knowing so perfectly how to behave.

'I'd like to send home for my dress, my records and masks,' she said. She turned her large candid eyes to Pierre. 'I'd very much like to know what you think of it.'

'I am very curious to know in what direction you are working at present,' said Pierre. 'There are so many and varied possibilities in what you've just shown us.'

The gramophone was playing a paso doble; couples were again taking the floor.

'Dance this one with me,' Paule said authoritatively to Françoise.

Françoise followed her docilely. She heard Xavière say sulkily to Pierre: 'No, I don't want to dance.'

A spasm of ill will shook her. Once again she was in the wrong. Xavière was fuming and Pierre was going to be angry with her because of Xavière's rage. Paule led so well that it was a pleasure to be guided by her; Xavière had no conception of how to lead.

There were some fifteen couples on the stage; others were scattered in the wings and in the boxes; one group was sitting in the balcony. Suddenly, Gerbert leapt up from the proscenium like a bounding elf; Mark Antony was in pursuit of him, miming a dance of seduction, and, considering his somewhat stocky build, with great vivacity and grace. Gerbert seemed a little drunk and his long black lock of hair kept falling over his eyes. He would stop with hesitant mock modesty, then dash away again, bashfully snuggling his head against his shoulder; he would flee and return again, faunlike and provoking.

'They're charming,' said Paule.

'The joke is,' said Françoise, 'that Ramblin really is that sort of fellow. What's more, he makes no bones about it.'

'I wondered whether that feminine quality he gave Mark Antony was due to art or nature,' said Paule.

Françoise glanced at Pierre. He was talking animatedly to Xavière who seemed hardly to be listening to him; she was watching Gerbert with a strangely avid, fascinated look. Françoise was hurt by this look, it seemed to derive from a secret and imperious possessiveness.

The music stopped and Françoise left Paule.

'I could make you dance, too,' said Xavière grasping hold of Françoise. She clasped her in her arms, her muscles taut, and Françoise wanted to smile as she felt the small hand tighten against her waist; with a certain tenderness, she inhaled the odour of tea, honey and flesh – Xavière's odour.

'If I could have her to myself, I would love her,' she thought. This domineering little girl, too, was nothing more than a tiny fragment of the warm, defenceless world.

But Xavière did not persevere in her efforts: she began, as usual, to dance for herself alone, without a thought for Françoise. Françoise could not attempt to follow her.

'It's not going so well,' said Xavière with a discouraged look. 'I'm dying of thirst,' she added. 'Aren't you?'

'Elisabeth is at the buffet,' said Françoise.

'What does that matter?' said Xavière. 'I want something to drink.'

Elisabeth was talking to Pierre. She had danced fairly often and seemed a little less gloomy; she giggled like a village gossip.

'I was telling Pierre that Eloy has spent the entire evening hanging round Tedesco,' she said. 'Canzetti is simply furious.'

'Eloy looks very well tonight,' said Pierre. 'That coiffure changes her. She has more physical attractions than I thought.'

'Guimiot told me that she throws herself at the head of every man,' said Elisabeth.

'At the head, that's one way of putting it,' said Françoise.

The words had slipped out: Xavière did not bat an eyelash, perhaps she had not understood. When conversation with Elisabeth was not formal, it easily became vulgar. It was annoying to feel this virtuous little madam at her side.

'They all treat her like the lowest of door-mats,' said Françoise. 'And what's so funny is that she's a virgin, and is determined to remain one.'

'Is it a complex?' said Elisabeth.

'It's for the sake of her complexion,' said Françoise with a laugh.

She stopped, for Pierre seemed to be in agony.

'Aren't you dancing any more?' he hurriedly asked Xavière.

'I'm tired,' said Xavière.

'Are you interested in the stage?' said Elisabeth in her most engaging manner. 'Do you really feel it to be your vocation?'

'You know, when you first start, it's rather thankless,' said Françoise.

There was a silence: Xavière was a mass of living resentment from head to foot. In her presence, everything assumed such tremendous importance that it became oppressive.

'What about you, are you working now?' said Pierre.

'Oh, yes, all's going well,' said Elisabeth; and she added casually: 'Lise Malan has just put out some feelers on behalf of Dominique, about decorating her night-club. I might accept.'

Françoise felt that she would have liked to keep the secret, but that she could not resist the longing to dazzle them.

'Accept it!' said Pierre. 'That's a job with a future. Dominique will make a fortune with that joint.'

'Little Dominique,' said Elisabeth laughing: 'That's funny!' For her, people were classified once and for all. All possibility of change was excluded from this rigid universe where she sought so stubbornly to find landmarks.

'She has a lot of talent,' said Pierre.

'She was charming to me. She's always had a tremendous admiration for me,' said Elisabeth in a matter-of-fact tone.

Françoise felt Pierre's foot kicking her under the table.

'You simply must keep your promise,' he said. 'You're far too lazy. Xavière is going to make you dance this rumba.'

'All right!' said Françoise in a tone of resignation. She rose and dragged Xavière off with her.

'It's just so that we can get away from Elisabeth,' she said. 'Let's dance for three minutes.'

With a business-like step Pierre crossed the stage.

'I'll wait for both of you in your office,' he said. 'We'll have a quiet drink up there.'

'Are we inviting Paule and Gerbert?' said Françoise.

'No, why? Let's just the three of us go,' said Pierre a little curtly.

He disappeared. Françoise and Xavière followed shortly afterwards. On the staircase, they passed Begramian who was feverishly kissing the Chanaud girl. There was a running farandole across the first-floor landing.

'At last we'll have a little peace,' said Pierre.

Françoise took a bottle of champagne from his cupboard; it was good champagne, kept for special guests. There were also some sandwiches and petit fours which would be served at dawn before the party finally broke up.

'Here, uncork this for us,' she said to Pierre. 'The amount of dust one swallows on that stage is amazing, it makes one's throat so dry.'

Pierre skilfully popped the cork and filled the glasses.

'Are you having a good evening?' he said to Xavière.

'A heavenly evening!' said Xavière. She drained her glass and began to laugh.

'Goodness, you looked so important when you were talking to that stout fellow. I thought I was looking at my uncle!'

'And now?' asked Pierre.

The tenderness that flitted across his face was still restrained and almost veiled; a slight change of expression would be enough to restore imperceptibly the mask of smooth indifference.

'Now, it's you again,' said Xavière, pouting.

The restraint vanished from Pierre's face, and Françoise eyed him with uneasy concern. In the past, whenever she had looked at Pierre, she had seen the whole world through him, but now she saw only him alone. Pierre was precisely where his body was, his body that could be focused in a single glance.

'That stout fellow?' said Pierre. 'Do you know who that was? Berger – Paule's husband.'

'Her husband?' For a second, Xavière looked disconcerted; then she said sharply: 'She does not love him.'

'She's strangely fond of him,' said Pierre. 'She was married, with a child, and she got a divorce so that she could marry him; all of which caused a great to-do because she comes from a very devout Catholic family. Did you ever read any of Masson's novels? He's her father. She's very much the great man's daughter.'

'She's not really in love with him,' said Xavière. Her pout was almost cynical. 'People get into such muddles!'

'I love your gems of worldly wisdom,' said Pierre, gaily. He smiled at Françoise. 'If you only heard her a little while ago. Young Gerbert is one of those fellows who are so deeply in love with themselves that they don't even take the trouble to make themselves pleasant . . . !'

He had imitated Xavière's voice to perfection and she looked at him half in amusement and half in anger.

'The worst of it is that she's often right,' said Françoise.

'She's a witch,' said Pierre tenderly.

Xavière laughed foolishly, as she did when she was very happy.

'What I think can be said about Paule Berger, is that she's a frigid enthusiast,' said Françoise.

'She can't possibly be frigid,' said Xavière. 'I liked her second dance so much. At the end, when she falters with fatigue, she gives the impression of such utter exhaustion that it becomes voluptuous.'

Her fresh lips slowly plucked off each syllable of the word: vol . . up . . tu . . ous.

'She knows how to evoke sensuality,' said Pierre, 'but I don't think she is sensual herself.'

'She's a woman who is aware of her body,' said Xavière with a smile of hidden connivance.

'I am not aware of my body,' thought Françoise. That was another lesson learnt, but it was no help in the long run to add to the sum total of negatives.

'In that long black dress,' said Xavière, 'when she stands motionless, she makes me think of those stiff, medieval virgins; but when she moves, she's like a bamboo in the wind.'

Françoise refilled her glass; she was not in the conversation; she, too, might have commented on Paule's hair, her lithe figure, the curve of her arms, but she still remained apart because Pierre and Xavière were so deeply engrossed in what they were saying. There was a long empty silence. Françoise had ceased to follow the ingenious arabesques which the voices were weaving in the air. Then, once more, she heard Pierre speaking.

'Paule Berger is pathos, and she expresses pathos entirely in yielding movements. To me, pure tragedy was in your face while you were watching her.'

Xavière blushed.

'I made a spectacle of myself,' she said.

'No one noticed it,' said Pierre. 'I envy you for feeling things so intensely.'

Xavière stared at the bottom of her glass.

'People are so funny,' she said, ingenuously. 'They clapped, but no one seemed really moved. Perhaps it's because you know so many things, but even you, too, do not seem to differentiate.' She shook her head and added sternly: 'It's very strange. You spoke to me about Paule Berger in an off-hand way, much as you speak about someone like Harbley, and you dragged yourself to this party tonight as if you were on your way to work. I have never had such a good time.'

'That's true,' said Pierre. 'I don't differentiate enough.'

He stopped. There was a knock at the door.

'Excuse me,' said Inès. 'I came up to tell you that Lise Malan is going to sing her latest numbers, and then Paule will dance. I went to fetch her music and her masks.'

'We'll come down in a moment,' said Françoise.

Inès closed the door.

'We were so comfortable here,' said Xavière grumpily.

'I don't give a damn for Lise's songs,' said Pierre. 'We'll go down in a quarter of an hour.'

As a rule, he never made a final decision without consulting Françoise; she felt the blood mounting to her cheeks.

'That's not very kind,' she said.

Her voice sounded more abrupt than she would have wished, but she had drunk too much to have perfect control. It was gross discourtesy not to go down; surely they were not going to start following Xavière along her wayward path.

'They won't even notice our absence,' said Pierre with finality.

Xavière smiled at him. Each time something, more especially someone, was sacrificed for her, a look of angelic sweetness spread over her face.

'We ought never, never to leave this room,' she said and she laughed. 'We'll lock the door, and we can have our meals sent up from outside on a rope.'

'And you'll teach me to differentiate,' said Pierre.

He smiled affectionately at Françoise.

'She's a little witch,' he said. 'She looks at things with virgin eyes, and lo and behold, the things come into existence for us exactly as she sees them. In the old days we would have clenched our fists; there used to be nothing but an endless series of little worries. Thanks to her, this is a real Christmas Eve that we're enjoying tonight!'

'Yes,' said Françoise.

Pierre's words were not intended for her, nor for Xavière either; Pierre had spoken for himself. There lay the greatest change: formerly, he had lived for the stage, for Françoise, for ideas; one could always collaborate with him; but there was absolutely no way of participating in his relations with himself. Françoise drained her glass. She would have to make up her mind once and for all to face up to all the changes that had taken place; for days and days now her thoughts had had a tinge of bitterness, Elisabeth must feel like that in her heart of hearts. She must not be like Elisabeth.

'I want to see clearly,' Françoise said to herself. But her head was filled with a flame-like, searing giddiness. 'We must go down,' she said brusquely.

'Yes, now we really must,' said Pierre.

Xavière's face tightened. 'But I want to finish my champagne,' she said.

'Drink it down,' said Françoise.

'But I don't want to pour it down. I want to drink it while I finish my cigarette.' She threw herself back in her chair. 'I don't want to go down.'

'You were so anxious to see Paule dance,' said Pierre. 'Come along, we simply must go down.'

'Go without me,' said Xavière. She wedged herself into her arm-chair and repeated stubbornly: 'I want to finish my champagne.'

'All right, we'll see you presently,' said Françoise, opening the door.

'She'll finish all the bottles,' said Pierre uneasily.

'She's intolerable with her fads and fancies,' said Françoise.

'Those weren't fads and fancies,' said Pierre acidly. 'She was happy to have us to herself for a while.'

The moment Xavière seemed fond of him, he found everything perfect, of course; Françoise almost told him so, but she held her tongue; there were so many thoughts that she now kept to herself.

153

'Am I the one who has changed?' she thought. She was suddenly appalled to feel how much hostility she had put into her thought.

Paule was wearing a kind of gandoura of white wool; she was holding in her hand a mask of closely woven mesh. 'I'm nervous, you know,' she said, smiling.

Very few people were left. Paule hid her face behind the mask. Wild music burst from the wings and she leapt on to the stage. She was miming a storm: she was a hurricane personified; sharp, pulsating rhythms, inspired by Hindu music, controlled her movements. Suddenly the fog in Françoise's head lifted; she saw clearly what lay between herself and Pierre; they had built beautiful, faultless structures in whose shadow they were sheltering, without giving any further thought to what lay behind them. Pierre still repeated: 'We are but one,' but now she had discovered that he lived only for himself. Without losing its perfect form, their love, their life, was slowly losing its substance, like those huge, apparently invulnerable cocoons, whose soft integument yet conceals microscopic worms that painstakingly consume them.

'I'll speak to him,' thought Françoise, and she felt relieved; there was a danger ahead, but together they would ward it off; they must above all pay more attention to each other at every moment. She turned towards Paule and concentrated on watching her beautiful gestures without allowing her mind to wander.

'You ought to give a recital as soon as possible,' said Pierre, warmly.

'Ah, I wonder,' said Paule with a note of uncertainty in her voice. 'Berger says that it is not an art which can stand by itself.'

'You must be tired,' said Françoise. 'I have some fairly good champagne upstairs, we'll drink it in the foyer; we'll be much more comfortable than here.'

The stage floor was far too vast for the few remaining people, and it was strewn with cigarette ends, fruit pips, and scraps of paper.

'You're going to carry the records and glasses,' said Françoise to Canzetti and Inès.

She drew Pierre towards the switch box and pulled down the levers.

'I want to break it up quickly, and then I'd like the two of

154

us to go for a walk together,' she said.

'Gladly,' said Pierre. He looked at her with a certain curiosity. 'Don't you feel well?'

'Of course I feel well,' said Françoise, with a shade of annoyance in her voice. Pierre did not seem to think that she could be hurt in any way but physically. 'But I would like to see you. This sort of party takes it out of you.'

They began to climb the stairs and Pierre took her by the arm.

'I thought you looked a little low,' he said.

She shrugged her shoulders; her voice trembled slightly.

'When you look at people's lives – at Paule, Elisabeth, Inès – they make a strange impression. You begin to wonder how you'd look at your own from without.'

'You're not satisfied with your life?' said Pierre anxiously.

Françoise smiled. It was not very serious; after all, as soon as she had explained things to Pierre, it would all be forgotten.

'The trouble is that you can't have proofs,' she began. 'You require an act of faith.'

She stopped. With a tense and almost agonized expression, Pierre was staring at the door at the head of the stairs behind which they had left Xavière.

'She must be dead drunk,' he said.

He dropped Françoise's arm and rushed up the last steps. 'There's not a sound.'

For a moment he stood motionless. The anxiety which now strained his face was not the same kind of anxiety Françoise had stirred in him, and to which he had calmly responded; this time he was shaken despite himself.

Françoise felt the blood ebbing from her cheeks; had he suddenly struck her, the shock could not have been more violent; she would never forget how his friendly arm had unhesitatingly withdrawn from her own.

Pierre pushed open the door. On the floor, in front of the window, Xavière lay sound asleep, curled up into a ball. Pierre bent over her. Françoise took a carton of food and a butler's basket filled with bottles from the cupboard and left without a word. She wanted to get away, anywhere, to try to think, and to be able to cry. So it had come to this: a pout from Xavière was more important than all her own distress; and yet Pierre kept on telling her that he loved her.

The gramophone was grinding out some old melancholy

refrain. Canzetti took the basket from Françoise's hands and sat down behind the bar. She passed the bottles to Ramblin and Gerbert who, along with Tedesco, were perched on stools. Paule, Berger, Inès, Eloy and Chanaud were seated near the big bay windows.

'I'd like a little champagne,' said Françoise.

Her head was throbbing. She felt as if something inside her – an artery, or her ribs, or her heart – were going to burst; she was not accustomed to suffering: it was, indeed, unbearable. Canzetti was stepping carefully towards her, carrying a brimming goblet; her long skirt gave her the dignity of a young priestess. Eloy, holding a glass in her hand, suddenly came in between her and Françoise. For a second, Françoise hesitated and then she took the glass.

'Thank you,' she said, and she smiled at Canzetti with a look of apology. Canzetti threw a mocking glance at Eloy.

'One gets one's own back where one can,' she muttered between her teeth; and also between her teeth, Eloy answered something that Françoise did not catch.

'How dare you! And in front of Mademoiselle Miquel!' cried Canzetti.

Her hand struck Eloy's pink cheek. Eloy looked at her for a moment, nonplussed, then she threw herself upon her; they grabbed each other by the hair and, then and there, began to struggle where they stood, their jaws set. Paule Berger jumped up.

'What's come over you?' she said, laying her beautiful hands on Eloy's shoulders.

A shrill laugh rang out. Xavière was coming towards them, staring with glazed eyes, and looking as white as chalk. Pierre was walking behind her. Every face turned towards them. Xavière's laugh stopped short.

'That music is horrible,' she said. With a sullen look of determination, she walked towards the gramophone.

'Wait, I'll put on a different record,' said Pierre.

Françoise looked at him in bewildered pain. Up to now, when she thought: 'We are separate,' that separation was still a mutual misfortune that struck both of them, and that together they would remedy. Now she understood: to be separate was to live out the separation alone.

Her forehead pressed against a window-pane, Eloy was quietly weeping. Françoise put her arm round her shoulder.

She felt some slight revulsion for this plump little body, so often pawed yet ever immaculate, but it was a convenient excuse.

'You mustn't cry,' said Françoise, her mind a blank; these tears and this warm flesh had something soothing about them. Xavière was dancing with Paule, Gerbert with Canzetti. Their faces were expressionless, their movements feverish. For every one of them, this night was already starting a legend which was turning into weariness, deception, regret, and which was bringing disillusion to their hearts. She felt that they dreaded the moment of departure, but that they found no pleasure in staying on there. All of them would have liked to have curled up on the floor and slept, as Xavière had slept. Françoise herself had no other desire. Outside, under a dawning sky, could be seen the black outlines of the trees.

Françoise shivered. Pierre was at her side.

'We ought to take a stroll before leaving,' he said. 'Will you come with me?'

'I'll come,' said Françoise.

'We'll see Xavière home and then we'll go to the Dôme, just the two of us,' said Pierre. 'It's so pleasant in the early morning.'

'Yes,' said Françoise.

There was no need for him to be so kind to her; what she would have liked him to do was to turn to her that open face that he had bent over the sleeping Xavière.

'What's the matter?' said Pierre.

The room was plunged in darkness and he could not see that Françoise's lips were trembling. She pulled herself together.

'Nothing, what should be the matter? I'm not ill, the evening went off well. Everything's all right.'

Pierre seized her wrist. Abruptly she freed herself.

'Perhaps I've drunk a little too much,' she said with an attempt at a laugh.

'Sit down here,' said Pierre; and he sat beside her in the first row of the stalls. 'And tell me what's come over you. It seems as if you're angry with me. What have I done?'

'You have done nothing,' she said softly. She took Pierre's hand. It was unfair to be angry with him, he behaved so perfectly with her. 'Of course you've done nothing,' she repeated in a choked voice. She dropped his hand.

'It isn't because of Xavière? She can't change anything

between us, you know that. But you also know that if this affair is in the very least distasteful to you, you need only say the word.'

'That's not the question,' she said quickly.

It was not by sacrifices that he could bring joy back to her; certainly, when they were acting jointly, he always put Françoise above everything; but today she was not looking to this man cloaked in scrupulous moral conduct and considerate tenderness; she would have liked to reach him, in his nakedness, over and beyond esteem and hierarchies and self-approbation. She forced back her tears.

'The trouble is that I feel that our love is growing old,' she said. As soon as she had uttered these words, her tears began to flow.

'Old?' said Pierre, shocked. 'But my love for you has never been stronger. What makes you think that?'

It was only natural for him to try at once to reassure her – and to reassure himself.

'You don't even begin to know what's happening,' she said, 'there's nothing surprising in that. You build so firmly on this love, that you've put it in safe keeping, beyond time, beyond life, beyond reach. From time to time, you think about it with satisfaction, but what has really and truly become of it, you never look to see.' She burst into sobs. 'But I – I want to look,' she said, swallowing her tears.

'Calm yourself,' said Pierre pressing her close against him. 'I think you're talking nonsense.'

She pushed him away; he was wrong, she was not talking to be calmed, it would be too simple if he could dismiss her thoughts in this way.

'I'm not talking nonsense. Perhaps it's because I'm drunk that I'm talking tonight, but I've thought it all over for days.'

'You might have said so sooner,' said Pierre, in an irritated tone. 'I don't understand: what are you reproaching me with?'

He was on the defensive; he had a horror of being in the wrong.

'I'm not reproaching you with anything,' said Françoise. 'You can have a perfectly clear conscience. But is that the ¹ˡ thing that counts?' she cried fiercely.

'ᵐⁿᵃake head or tail of this scene,' said Pierre. 'I love ⁿᵘght to know that, but if it pleases you not to I have no way to prove it to you.'

'Faith, always faith,' said Françoise. 'That's how Elisabeth succeeds in believing that Battier loves her and perhaps in believing that she still loves him. It's clear, that gives you a sense of security. Your feelings always have to keep the same outer significance, you have to have them ready for use, neatly lined up, immutable, and even if they're hollow inside it's all the same to you. They're like the whited sepulchres of the Bible: they dazzle outwardly. They're firm, they're faithful, they can even be whitewashed periodically with beautiful words.' She was again overcome by a flood of tears. 'Only, they must never be opened. You'll find only dust and ashes inside.' She repeated: 'Dust and ashes.' It was blinding evidence. 'Oh,' she said, hiding her face in the crook of her arm.

Pierre lowered his arm. 'Stop crying,' he said. 'I'd like to talk reasonably.'

Presently he would find lovely arguments and it would be so easy to give in to them. Françoise did not want to lie to herself, like Elisabeth; she saw that clearly. She kept on sobbing.

'But it's not so serious,' said Pierre gently. He brushed a light caress over her hair. She gave a start.

'It is serious. I'm sure of what I'm saying. Your feelings are unchangeable. They can endure for centuries because they are mummified. It's like this crowd of women,' she said suddenly, thinking with horror of Blanche Bouguet's face, 'it doesn't move; it's completely embalmed.'

'You are extremely unpleasant,' said Pierre. 'Either cry or talk, but not both at once.' He pulled himself together. 'Let's take it for granted that I don't swoon, or suffer from palpitations. I don't. But does true love consist of that? Why does that suddenly shock you today? You've always known that I was like that.'

'Look,' said Françoise, 'your friendship for Gerbert is the same. You never see much of him nowadays, but you shout to high heaven if I say that you've grown less fond of him.'

'I've no ardent desire to see much of people, that's quite true,' said Pierre.

'You have no desires at all,' said Françoise, 'it's all the same to you.'

She was crying desperately. She loathed the thought of that moment when she would cease crying and return to the world of merciful deception. She would have to find a spell that would fix the present minute for ever.

'Are you there?' said a voice.

Françoise sat up; it was astonishing how quickly those relentless sobs could stop. Ramblin's outline emerged from the shadow of the doorway and he came forward laughing.

'I'm being trailed. That Eloy girl dragged me into a dark corner, telling me how wicked the world was, and there she attempted to deliver a frontal attack upon my person.' He assumed the modest attitude of the Venus de Medicis. 'I had the greatest difficulty in defending my virtue.'

'She's out of luck tonight,' said Pierre. 'She tried in vain to seduce Tedesco.'

'If Canzetti hadn't been there, I don't know what would have happened,' said Françoise.

'Please note that I have no prejudices,' said Ramblin, 'but I find such behaviour unhealthy.'

He listened attentively.

'Do you hear?'

'No,' said Françoise. 'What is it?'

'I can hear someone breathing.'

A faint noise was coming from the stage. It did, indeed, sound like breathing.

'I wonder who it is?' said Ramblin.

They climbed on to the stage floor. It was pitch black.

'To the right,' said Pierre.

A body was lying behind the velvet curtain; they bent over it.

'Guimiot! It would have surprised me if he'd gone home before the last bottle had been emptied.'

Guimiot had a beatific smile, with his head resting on his crooked arm. He was really very pretty.

'I'll shake him,' said Ramblin, 'and I'll bring him upstairs for you.'

'We'll finish our stroll,' said Pierre.

The green-room was empty. Pierre shut the door.

'I'd like to talk things over,' he said. 'I find it very distressing that you should doubt our love.'

His face showed an honest concern, and Françoise, tempted, gazed at him.

'I don't think you've stopped loving me,' she murmured.

'But you said that we're dragging an old corpse at our heels. That's so unfair! First of all, it's not true that I don't need to see you. The minute you're not with me I'm bored, and when you're there I'm never bored; whenever anything happens to me, I at once think of telling you, for it happens to you as well as to me. You're my life, you know that. I don't often get upset about you, it's true; buf that's because we're happy. If you were ill, or if you were to double-cross me, I'd be at my wit's end.'

He spoke these words in a calm, earnest manner that forced a tender smile from Françoise. She took his arm and together they went up towards the dressing-rooms.

'I'm your life,' said Françoise, 'but you don't see what I feel so strongly tonight – that our lives are lying all about us, almost in spite of us, without our being able to choose them. And you don't choose me, you no longer choose me, either. You're no longer free not to love me.'

'The fact remains that I love you,' said Pierre. 'Do you really think that freedom consists in questioning things at every turn? We've often said, apropos of Xavière, that this was the way to become the slaves of our slightest moods.'

'Yes,' said Françoise.

She was too tired to find her way in her own thoughts, but she once again saw Pierre's face when he had dropped her arm: the evidence of that was irrefutable.

'And yet life *is* made up of moments,' she said vehemently. 'If every one of them were empty, you'd never convince me that it would make a full whole.'

'But I have hundreds of full moments with you,' said Pierre. 'Isn't that obvious? You speak as if I were a great callous brute.'

Françoise touched his arm.

'You are so sweet,' she said. 'Only, you see, full moments cannot be distinguished from empty ones, because you're always equally perfect.'

'From which you conclude that they're all empty!' said Pierre. 'How perfectly logical! Right! I presume that from now on, I'm allowed to be as temperamental as I like?' He looked reproachfully at Françoise. 'Why are you so morose when I'm so much in love with you?'

Françoise looked away.

'I don't know; I feel slightly bewildered.' She hesitated. 'For instance, you always listen to me very politely when I talk to you about myself, whether it interests you or not. Then, I ask myself, if you weren't being quite so polite would you listen to me?'

'It always interests me,' said Pierre with astonishment.

'But you never ask me questions spontaneously.'

'I feel that as soon as you have something to say, you say it to me,' said Pierre.

He stared at her a little uneasily.

'When did it happen?'

'What?' said Françoise.

'That I didn't ask questions?'

'Several times recently,' said Françoise with a little laugh. 'You looked as if you were thinking of something else.'

She hesitated, doubtful. Confronted with Pierre's trust, she was ashamed. Every time she had kept silence with regard to him she had prepared an ambush into which he had quietly fallen. He did not suspect that she had been laying traps for him. Wasn't she the one who had changed? Wasn't it she who was lying when she spoke of blissful love, of happiness, of jealousy overcome? Her words, her behaviour no longer corresponded fully to her deeper feelings. And he continued to believe her. Was that faith or indifference?

The dressing-rooms and corridors were empty and everything seemed in order. In silence, they went back to the green-room and on to the stage. Pierre sat down on the edge of the proscenium.

'I think I've neglected you lately,' he said. 'I think that had I really been perfect with you, you wouldn't have been worried about this perfection.'

'Perhaps,' said Françoise. 'It's not easy just to talk about that subject.' She took a little time to steady her voice. 'It seemed to me that during those moments when you let yourself go unrestrainedly, I didn't mean so very much to you.'

'In other words, I'm sincere only when I'm in the wrong?' said Pierre, 'and if I behave properly to you it's only through conscious effort? Does that make sense to you?'

'It's valid,' said Françoise.

'Certainly, because my attentions to you condemn me as much as my blunders. If you start from that basis you will always be right, whatever I do.'

Pierre seized Françoise by the shoulder.

'It's wrong, ridiculously wrong. I've no hidden spring of

162

indifference to you that intermittently wells to the surface. You mean everything to me, and when by chance, because of some worry or other, I am less aware of it for five minutes or so, you yourself say that anyone can notice it.' He looked at her. 'You don't believe me?'

'I believe you,' said Françoise.

She believed him; but that was not precisely the point. She did not really know any longer just what was the point at issue.

'That's sensible,' said Pierre, 'but don't start all over again.' He squeezed her hand. 'I think I understand all right the effect it has on you. We've tried to build our love beyond each individual moment, yet we can only be certain of the moments. For the rest, you do require faith. And is faith courage or laziness?'

'That's what I was wondering a little while ago,' said Françoise.

'Sometimes I wonder about that with regard to my work,' said Pierre. 'I get annoyed when Xavière tells me that I cling to it out of a desire for moral security – and yet?'

Françoise felt her heart contract. The one thing she could least bear was for Pierre to question the value of his work.

'In my case there's a certain blind obstinacy,' said Pierre. He smiled. 'You know, when you make a big hole in the back of a honeycomb, the bees continue spitting honey into it with the same cheerfulness. That's somewhat the impression I have of myself.'

'You don't really think that?' said Françoise.

'At other times I see myself as a little hero who keeps resolutely on his way through the oncoming night,' said Pierre, frowning and looking resolute yet stupid.

'Yes, you're a little hero,' said Françoise, laughing.

'I'd like to believe it,' said Pierre.

He had risen but he remained motionless, with his back against a piece of scenery. Above them the gramophone was playing a tango and people were still dancing; they would have to go up and join them.

'It's too awful,' said Pierre, 'she really makes me uncomfortable, that creature, with her philosophy which makes us less than the dust. It seems to me that if she loved me I'd be as sure of myself as I was before. I would feel that I'd compelled her approval.'

'You are odd,' said Françoise. 'She is allowed to love you and censure you at the same time.'

'Then it would be only an abstract censure,' said Pierre. 'To make her love me is to dominate her, to enter into her world and there conquer in accordance with her own values.' He smiled. 'You know this is the kind of victory for which I have an insane need.'

'I know,' said Françoise.

Pierre looked gravely at her.

'Only, I don't want this sinful mania to drag me into spoiling anything between us.'

'It can't spoil anything, you said so yourself,' said Françoise.

'It can't spoil anything vital,' said Pierre, 'but the fact is that when I'm worried because of her, I neglect you. When I look at her I don't look at you.' His voice grew urgent. 'I wonder if it wouldn't be better to call a halt to this affair. It's not love that I feel for her: it savours more of superstition. If she resists, I become obstinate, but as soon as I think I'm sure of her, I become indifferent about her. And if I decide not to see her any more, I know very well that from one minute to the next I'll stop thinking about her.'

'But there's no reason for that,' said Françoise quickly.

Surely, if Pierre took the initiative and broke with her, he would not regret it; life would go on again where it had left off before the advent of Xavière. With some astonishment, Françoise felt that this assurance awakened in her only some kind of disappointment.

'You know,' said Pierre smiling, 'I can't accept anything from anyone. Xavière offers me absolutely nothing. You need have no qualms.' He again became solemn. 'Think it over well; it's serious. If you think it holds any threat whatsoever to our love, you must say so. I don't want to run that risk at any price.'

There was a silence. Françoise's head felt heavy; she was conscious only of her head, she no longer felt a body. And her heart too was quiet: it was as if layers of fatigue and indifference had separated her from herself. Without jealousy, without love, ageless, nameless, confronted with her own life, she was no longer anything but a calm and detached spectator.

'I've thought it all over,' she said. 'There's no doubt about it.'

Pierre tenderly put his arm round Françoise's shoulders and they went up to the first floor. It was now daylight. Everyone's face was haggard. Françoise opened the bay window and stepped out on to the flat roof. The cold gripped her. A new day was beginning.

'And now what is going to happen?' she thought.

But whatever happened, she could not have decided in any other way than she had. She had always refused to live among dreams, nor would she agree now not to imprison herself in an incomplete world. Xavière existed and was not to be refuted, all the risks involved in her existence had to be accepted.

'Come inside,' said Pierre. 'It's too cold.'

She shut the window again. Tomorrow perhaps might bring suffering and tears, but she felt no compassion for that tormented woman whom she was to become again so soon.

She looked at Paule, Gerbert, Pierre, Xavière. She felt nothing but an impersonal curiosity, and a curiosity so violent that it had the warmth of joy.

Chapter Eight

'Naturally,' said Françoise, 'the character is not brought out quite clearly enough, you're giving much too much of your own self; but you do feel the character; all the finer shades are correct.' She sat down on the edge of the couch beside Xavière and seized her by the shoulders. 'I solemnly swear to you that you can do that scene for Labrousse. You're good, you know; you're really good.'

It was a triumph even to have persuaded Xavière to recite her monologue; she had had to be coaxed for an hour and Françoise felt completely exhausted; but it was useless if she could not now persuade her to work with Pierre.

'I don't dare,' said Xavière in despair.

'Labrousse is not so frightening,' said Françoise with a smile.

'But he is!' said Xavière. 'As a teacher, he frightens me.'

'Never mind,' said Françoise. 'You've been working on this scene for over a month now. You're turning into a neurasthenic, and you've got to get out of it.'

'There's nothing I'd like better,' said Xavière.

'Listen, you can trust me,' said Françoise, with great warmth. 'I wouldn't tell you to chance Labrousse's opinion if I didn't think you were ready. I'll take the responsibility.' She looked Xavière in the eyes. 'Don't you believe me?'

'I believe you,' said Xavière, 'but it is perfectly horrible to feel that you are being judged.'

'If you want to work, you must get rid of all false pride,' said Françoise. 'Be brave: do it before you even start on your first lesson.'

Xavière thought it over.

'I'll do it,' she said with a look of conviction. Her eyelids fluttered. 'I do so want you to be a little satisfied with me.'

'I'm sure you will become a real actress,' said Françoise tenderly.

'That was a good idea of yours,' said Xavière, her face brightening. 'The end is much more effective if I'm standing up.'

She rose and recited with vivacity: *'If this twig has an even number of leaves, I shall give him the letter ... Eleven, twelve, thirteen, fourteen ... even.'*

'You've got it perfectly,' said Françoise gaily.

The inflection in Xavière's voice and her facial expressions were still only hints, though natural and charming. 'If only it were possible to instil a little determination into her,' thought Françoise: it would be so wearing if she had to be spoon-fed to success.

'There's Labrousse,' said Françoise, 'he's scrupulously punctual as usual.'

She opened the door, she had recognized his step. Pierre smiled cheerfully.

'Greetings!' he said.

He was weighed down by a heavy camel-hair overcoat that made him look like a teddy-bear.

'Oh, what a boring time I've had! All day long I've been going through accounts with Bernheim.'

'Well, we certainly haven't wasted our time,' said Françoise. 'Xavière rehearsed her scene from *l'Occasion* for me. You'll see how well she's worked.'

Pierre looked encouragingly at Xavière.

'I'm at your disposal,' he said.

Xavière was so afraid of venturing out of doors that she had finally consented to take her lessons in her room; but she did not budge.

'Not now,' she implored. 'Can't we wait for a while?'

Pierre looked questioningly at Françoise.

'Would you mind if we stayed here for a little?'

'Stay until six-thirty,' said Françoise.

'Yes, no more than a half-hour,' said Xavière, looking at Françoise and Pierre in turn.

'You look a little tired,' said Pierre.

'I think I've caught a chill,' said Françoise. 'It's the weather.'

It was the weather, but it was also due to lack of sleep; Pierre was blessed with an iron constitution and Xavière was able to catch up on her sleep during the day; both of them gently teased Françoise if she wanted to go to bed before six o'clock.

'What did Bernheim have to say?' she asked.

'He spoke to me again about that plan for a tour,' said Pierre; he hesitated a moment. 'Of course the figures are very tempting.'

167

'But we aren't in such need of money,' said Françoise quickly.

'A tour? Where?' said Xavière.

'Greece, Egypt, Morocco,' said Pierre. He smiled. 'The day we do that, we'll take you with us.'

Françoise shivered; they were only building castles in Spain, but it was annoying that it should have occurred to Pierre to put them into words: his was a ready generosity. If ever this tour were to take place she was fiercely determined to go alone with him; the company had to be dragged about with them, but that did not count.

'That won't be for a long time,' she said.

'Do you think it would be so terrible if we allowed ourselves a short holiday?' said Pierre coaxingly.

This time a violent storm shook Françoise from head to foot; Pierre had never even envisaged this idea; now he was well away. Next winter his plays would be produced, his book would be published, and he had a whole heap of plans for the development of the Dramatic School. Françoise was so desperately anxious for him to reach the peak of his career, and at last give his work its definitive form, that she had difficulty in mastering the tremor in her voice.

'This is not the moment,' she said. 'You know perfectly well that in the theatre it is so much a question of seizing the opportunity. After *Julius Caesar*, your next season will be impatiently awaited. If you let a year go by, people will be thinking about something else.'

'Your words are golden, as always,' said Pierre with a shade of disappointment.

'How sensible you are!' said Xavière; her face expressed genuine but shocked admiration.

'Oh, but we'll surely do it some day,' said Pierre cheerfully. 'It will be so nice when we land at Athens, or Algiers, to play in their moth-eaten little theatres. At the end of the show, instead of going to the Dôme, we'll go and lie on the mats inside a Moorish café and smoke kief.'

'Kief?' said Xavière, fascinated.

'It's an opiate plant that they grow over there; it seems that it induces enchanting visions'; and he added with a disappointed air, 'but then – I've never tried it.'

'That doesn't surprise me about you,' said Xavière with affectionate indulgence.

'It's smoked in nice little pipes that the shopkeepers make to order for you,' said Pierre. 'You'd be proud to have a little pipe of your own.'

'I would certainly have visions,' said Xavière.

'Do you remember Moulay Idriss?' said Pierre smiling at Françoise. 'When we smoked that pipe which those Arabs – who were most certainly riddled with syphilis – passed around from mouth to mouth?'

'I remember very well,' said Françoise.

'You were scared,' said Pierre.

'You weren't too happy about it yourself,' said Françoise. She had difficulty in getting the words out, she was so tense with emotion. Still, these were far-off plans and she knew that Pierre would decide nothing without her consent. She would say no : that was simple, there was nothing to worry about. No. No, they would not leave next winter; no, they would not take Xavière with them. No. She shivered; she must be feverish, her hands were moist and her whole body was on fire.

'We'll go and work,' said Pierre.

'I'll do some work, too,' said Françoise.

She forced herself to smile. They must have been aware of the fact that something unusual was going on inside her; there had been a hint of embarrassment. Usually, she had better control over herself.

'We still have five minutes,' said Xavière with a sullen smile, and she sighed : 'Only five minutes.'

Her eyes turned again to Françoise's face, then rested on her hands with their tapering fingernails. In the past, Françoise would have been moved by that fervent if furtive look, but Pierre had pointed out to her how Xavière often made use of this excuse when she felt overwhelmed with affection for him.

'Three minutes,' said Xavière; she was now staring at the alarm clock, and reproach was barely disguised beneath regret.

'I don't think I grudge my time,' thought Françoise; evidently by comparison with Pierre, she seemed rapacious; of late, he hadn't been writing at all, he was wasting himself unconcernedly. She could not compete with him; she did not wish to. Once again, a burning shiver ran through her.

Pierre stood up. 'Shall I come back at midnight and pick you up?'

'Yes, I shan't move,' said Françoise, 'I'll expect you for

supper.' She smiled at Xavière. 'Be brave. It will soon be over.'

Xavière sighed. 'I'll see you tomorrow,' she said.

'Till tomorrow, then,' said Françoise.

She sat down at her table and joylessly looked at the blank sheets. Her head was heavy, and she ached all down her neck and back. She knew that she would work badly. Xavière had again nibbled off a half-hour: it was terrible, the amount of time she devoured. There was no longer any leisure or solitude, or even simple rest; one reached a state of inhuman tension. No, she would say no; with all the strength at her command she would say no; and Pierre would listen to her.

Françoise felt herself growing weak, something snapped inside her. Pierre would easily give up this trip, he wasn't so terribly keen on it; and then what? What good would it do? What was agonizing was that he had not, of his own accord, faced up to this proposal. Did he value his work so little? Had his dilemma given way to complete indifference? It was senseless to foist on him from without the semblance of a faith he no longer possessed. What use was it to try to achieve something for him, if it did not carry him along with it and was achieved in spite of him. The decisions Françoise expected of him must come from his own will; all her happiness rested on Pierre's free will, and over that she had no hold.

She shuddered. Someone was running up stairs and the next moment knocks shook the door.

'Come in!' she called.

Their two faces appeared together in the doorway, both smiling. Xavière had tucked her hair under a big plaid cowl: Pierre was holding his pipe in his hand.

'Would you really be cross with us if we went for a walk in the snow instead of doing the lesson?' he said.

Françoise's heart was in her mouth. She had taken such pleasure in imagining Pierre's surprise and Xavière's satisfaction at the praise he would bestow on her. She had tried with all her heart to make her work; she really was a fool, they never took the lessons seriously, and they still expected her to take the responsibility for their laziness.

'That's your concern,' she said. 'I have nothing to do with it.'

Their smiles vanished; this serious voice had been unexpected.

'Are you really cross with us?' said Pierre unabashed.

He looked at Xavière, who returned the look uncertainly; they had the appearance of two guilty people. For the first time, because of the complicity wherein Françoise was confining them, they were standing up to her like a pair of lovers. They felt it themselves, and they were ill at ease.

'No, no,' said Françoise, 'have a nice walk.'

She shut the door a little too quickly, and stood leaning against the wall while they went downstairs without speaking. She could see their guilty faces; they were certainly not likely to work, she had only ruined their walk; a kind of sob shook her. What good was it? She had only succeeded in poisoning their pleasures and making herself hateful in her own eyes; she could not will their actions – that was a dead certainty. Suddenly she threw herself face down on the bed and her tears flowed: it was too painful, this rigid will she persisted in preserving in herself. She had only to let things take their own course, and she would see what would happen.

'We'll see what will happen,' Françoise said aloud; she felt utterly at the end of her strength, all she longed for was that blissful peace that falls in white flakes on the weary traveller. She had only to give up everything – Xavière's future, Pierre's work, her own happiness – and she would know what true peace was; she would be protected from the palpitations of her heart, the spasmodic contraction of her throat, and the terrible dry burning at the back of her eyeballs.

All she had to do was to make the simplest of gestures – open her hands and let go her hold. She lifted one hand and moved the fingers of it; they responded, in surprise and obedience, and this obedience of a thousand little unsuspected muscles was in itself a miracle. Why ask for more? She couldn't make up her mind to let go her hold. She had no fears for tomorrow, there was no tomorrow; but she saw herself surrounded by a present so naked, so glacial, that her heart failed her. It was like the time in the big café with Gerbert: a scattering of individual instants, a worm-like wriggling of continual gestures and incoherent images. Françoise jumped up, it was unbearable; any suffering, no matter what, was better than this hopeless abandonment in the very centre of void and chaos.

She put on her coat and fitted her fur toque close down

over her ears; she must pull herself together: she needed to commune with herself, she ought to have done so long ago instead of throwing herself into her work whenever she had a spare moment. Tears had burnished her eyelashes and darkened the rings under her eyes. It would be easy to repair the damage, but it was not even worth the effort; between now and midnight she would not see a soul, she wanted to satiate herself with solitude during all these hours. For a moment she stood before the looking-glass, staring at her face, it was a face which conveyed no meaning; it was stuck on her head like a label: Françoise Miquel. Xavière's face, on the contrary, was the source of inexhaustible conjecture: that was unquestionably why she smiled to herself so mysteriously in mirrors. Françoise left her room and went downstairs. The pavements were covered with snow; the cold was biting. She boarded a bus. To recapture her solitude, her freedom, she must escape from this neighbourhood.

With the palm of her hand, Françoise wiped off the film that obscured the window. Brightly lit shop windows, streetlamps, passers-by, sprang out from the night; but she had no sensation of motion, these apparitions followed one another without her altering her own position; it was a voyage in time, outside space; she closed her eyes. She must somehow pull herself together. Pierre and Xavière had stood up to her; she in turn wanted to stand up to them. Pull herself together! But pull on what? Her ideas melted away. She found absolutely nothing to think about.

The bus stopped at the corner of the rue Damrémont and Françoise got off; the Montmartre streets were stark in whiteness and silence; Françoise hesitated, completely encumbered by her freedom. She could go anywhere she liked, but she had no desire to go anywhere. Mechanically, she began to climb up towards the Butte. At first the snow was slightly resilient to her tread and then subsided with an unctuous crunch: it was disappointing and tiresome to feel its resistance melt away before bearing the full pressure of her step. 'Snow – cafés – steps – houses . . . how do they concern me?' thought Françoise in a kind of daze; she felt seeping into her a despair so deadly that her legs seemed on the point of giving way. What could all these unfamiliar things mean to her? They were set at a distance; they had no contact with the whirling emptiness, the maelstrom which was sucking her under; she was being sucked down spirally, deeper and deeper. It seemed that in the end she must touch something: peace of mind or despair, something definite; but always she remained at the same level, on the brink of emptiness. Françoise looked round her in distress. No, nothing could help her; she would have to eradicate from within herself pride, self-pity, and tenderness. Her back and her temples ached, and even this pain was impersonal. Someone should have been there to say: 'I'm tired. I'm unhappy.' Then this vague and aching moment would worthily have taken its place in her life. But there was no one.

'It's my fault,' thought Françoise, as she slowly climbed the steps. It was her fault, Elisabeth was right, for many years now she had ceased to be an individual; she no longer even possessed a face. The most destitute of women could at least lovingly touch her own hand, and she looked at both her own with surprise. Our past, our future, our ideas, our love . . . never did she say: 'I.' And yet, Pierre determined his own future and his own heart: he disengaged himself, he retreated to the boundaries of his own life. She remained behind, separated from him, separated from everyone and without a link with herself; neglected, and finding in this abandonment no true aloneness.

She leaned against the balustrade and looked down at the big, cold, blue puff of smoke that was Paris; it lay sprawled out with insulting unconcern. Françoise sprang back. What was she doing here, in the cold, with these white domes above her head, and at her feet this pit that lay gaping to the stars? She ran down the steps. She must go to a cinema or telephone to somebody.

'It's pitiful,' she murmured to herself.

Aloneness was not something you could dissect into small portions, to be used up piecemeal. It had been childish of her to think that she could take refuge in aloneness for an evening. She must reject it totally until she could totally regain it.

A shooting pain cut short her breath; she stopped and put her hands to her sides. 'What's the matter with me?' A violent shiver shook her from head to foot. She was perspiring and her head was throbbing.

'I'm ill,' she thought with a kind of relief. She beckoned to

173

a taxi. All she could do was to return home, go to bed and try to sleep.

A door slammed on the landing and someone shuffled across the passage; it must be the blonde tart getting up. In the room above, the Negro's gramophone was softly playing 'Solitude'. Françoise opened her eyes, night had almost fallen; she must have been nearly forty-eight hours lying in the warmth of the sheets. That light breathing at her side came from Xavière, who had not moved from the big arm-chair since Pierre had left. Françoise took a deep breath: the stabbing pain had not left her lungs, she was rather thankful for it, as if it made her quite certain of being ill, it was so restful. There was nothing in the world to worry about, she was not even expected to talk. If only her pyjamas had not been drenched with sweat, Françoise would have felt completely well: as it was, they were glued to her body. On her right side, too, she felt a large smarting patch. The doctor had been indignant that the poultices had been so inefficiently applied; but that was his fault; he should have explained things better.

Someone was lightly tapping at the door.

'Come in,' said Xavière.

The hall-porter appeared in the doorway.

'Does Mademoiselle need anything?'

He timidly approached the bed. With a look of dolorous solicitude, he came every hour to offer his services.

'No, thank you very much,' said Françoise.

Her breath was so short, she could no longer speak.

'The doctor says that tomorrow, without fail, Mademoiselle must go to the nursing-home. Doesn't Mademoiselle wish me to make any telephone calls?'

Françoise shook her head.

'I don't intend to go,' she said.

A burning wave of blood rushed to her face and her heart began to pound violently. Why had this doctor stirred up the hotel staff? They would be bound to tell Pierre, and Xavière, too, would tell him: she herself knew that she could not lie to him. Pierre would force her to go. She did not want to, they would not, after all, take her away against her will. She watched the door close behind the hall-porter, and her eyes wandered over the room. It smelt like a sick-room. For two days, the housework had not been done, nor had the bed

174

been made; the window had not even been opened. On the mantelpiece, Pierre, Xavière, Elisabeth, had stacked appetizing foods in vain. The ham had begun to shrivel, the apricots had candied in their own juice, the custard had slumped into a morass of caramel. The room was beginning to look like a leper's lodging; but it was her room and Françoise did not want to leave it. She loved the squamous chrysanthemums on the wallpaper, and the threadbare carpet, and all the confused sounds of hotel life. Her room, her life. She was quite willing to stay there, prone and passive, but not to go into exile between white, anonymous walls.

'I don't want to be taken away from here,' she said in a choking voice; once again, scorching waves broke upon her and nervous tears started to her eyes.

'Don't lose heart,' said Xavière with an unhappy and earnest look. 'You're going to get well quickly.' She suddenly threw herself on the bed and, pressing her own cool cheek against the feverish cheek, she clung to Françoise.

'My darling Xavière,' whispered Françoise with emotion. She put her arms round the supple, warm body. Xavière pressed against her with all her weight, she could not draw a breath, but she did not want to let her go; one morning she had pressed her to her heart like this: why had she been unable to keep her? She was so fond of this worried face, now radiant with affection.

'My darling Xavière,' she repeated.

A sob rose in her throat. No, she would not go. There must have been some mistake, she wanted to begin everything afresh. Her morbid state had made her believe that Xavière had broken away from her, but this impulse that had thrown Xavière into her arms could not be deceptive. Françoise would never forget her eyes with their dark rings of anxiety, and this attentive, feverish love that Xavière had lavished on her without reserve during these last two days.

Xavière drew gently away from Françoise and left the bed.

'I'll go now,' she said. 'I hear Labrousse's step on the staircase.'

'I'm certain he'll want to send me to a nursing-home,' said Françoise nervously.

Pierre knocked and came into the room: he looked worried.

'How do you feel?' he said, pressing Françoise's hand in his. He smiled at Xavière. 'Has she been good?'

'I'm all right,' whispered Françoise. 'It's a little difficult to breathe.' She wanted to sit up, but a sharp pain stabbed her chest.

'Please, would you knock on my door when you leave,' said Xavière, giving Pierre a friendly look. 'I'll come back.'

'It's not necessary,' said Françoise. 'You ought to go out for a while.'

'Am I not a good nurse?' said Xavière reproachfully.

'The best possible nurse,' said Françoise affectionately.

Xavière noiselessly closed the door behind her and Pierre sat down at the side of the bed.

'Now then, have you seen the doctor?'

'Yes,' said Françoise suspiciously, and she grimaced; she did not want to start to cry but she felt herself completely lacking control.

'Send for a nurse, but let me stay here,' she said.

'Listen,' said Pierre putting his hand on her forehead. 'They told me downstairs that you have to be watched very closely. It's not critical, but as soon as the lungs are affected, it is serious all the same. You need injections, a lot of care, and a doctor within reach. A good doctor. That old man is an ass.'

'Find another doctor and a nurse,' she said.

The tears welled up; she continued to resist with what little strength remained to her; she did not give in. She would not let herself be torn from her room, from her past, from her life; but she had no longer any way in which to protect herself, even her voice was no more than a whisper.

'I want to stay with you,' she said. She began to cry in real earnest. Here she was at the mercy of others, just a body shivering with fever, without strength, without speech, even without thought.

'I'll be there all day long,' said Pierre. 'It will be exactly the same.'

He looked at her pleadingly and in great distress.

'No, it will not be the same thing,' said Françoise. She was choking with sobs. 'That's all.'

She was too weak to determine what exactly it was that was dying in the yellow light of the room, but she never wished to derive comfort from its loss. She had struggled so hard; she had felt menaced for so long a time; she had confused visions of a jumble of tables at the Pôle Nord, banquettes at the Dôme, Xavière's room, her own room, and she saw herself strained and intent – to what purpose, she hardly knew. Now the moment had come; it was useless to keep her hands clenched, and crouch for a last leap. She would be taken away despite herself. Nothing depended on her will now, and her only means of defence was tears.

Françoise was very feverish all through the following night. She fell asleep only at dawn. When she again opened her eyes a pale winter sun shone in the room, and Pierre was leaning over the bed.

'The ambulance is here,' he said.

'Ah!' said Françoise.

She recalled that she had cried the previous evening, but she did not really remember why: her mind was empty, she was completely calm.

'I'll have to take some things with me,' she said.

Xavière smiled.

'We packed your bag while you were asleep. Pyjamas, handkerchiefs, eau-de-Cologne – I don't think we've forgotten anything.'

'You needn't fuss,' said Pierre cheerfully. 'She managed to fill the big suitcase.'

'You would have let her go away like an orphan, with nothing but a toothbrush in a handkerchief,' said Xavière.

She came up to Françoise and looked at her anxiously.

'How do you feel? It won't tire you too much?'

'I feel all right,' said Françoise.

Something had happened while she was asleep; not for weeks and weeks had she known such peace. Xavière's features looked tortured. She took Françoise's hand and squeezed it.

'I hear them coming up,' she said.

'Will you come and see me every day?' said Françoise.

'Oh yes, every day,' said Xavière. She bent over Françoise and kissed her: her eyes were filled with tears. Françoise smiled at her. She still knew how to smile, but not how to be moved by tears, nor how to be moved by anything. She watched dispassionately as they entered, the two ambulance men who would raise her up and lay her on a stretcher. One last time she smiled at Xavière, who stood paralysed beside the empty bed. And then the door closed on Xavière, on her room, on the past. Françoise was hardly more than an inert mass, she was not even an organic body. She was carried down the stairs, head first, her feet in the air, nothing more than a heavy piece of luggage that the stretcher-bearers handled in accordance with the laws of gravity and their personal convenience.

'We'll see you back soon, Mademoiselle Miquel. Get well quickly.'

The proprietress, the hall-porter and his wife were lined up in the hall.

'I'll soon be back,' said Françoise.

A cold gust, striking her face, woke her to full consciousness. A number of people were assembled in front of the door. An invalid being carried away in an ambulance: Françoise had frequently seen this in the streets of Paris.

'But this time the invalid is *me*,' she thought, with astonishment; she did not quite believe it. Sickness, accidents, all those stories printed in thousands of copies, she had always thought it impossible for that to become her story; she had told herself that about war; these impersonal, anonymous misfortunes could not happen to her. How can I be just anybody? And yet there she was stretched out in an ambulance which was gliding smoothly away; Pierre was seated beside her. She was the invalid. It had happened after all. Had she become just anybody? Was that why she felt so light, released from herself, from her whole choking escort of joys and cares? She closed her eyes. Smoothly, the car drove on and time slipped by.

The ambulance drew up in front of a big garden. Pierre wrapped the blanket tightly round Françoise and she was carried along icy paths, along linoleum-covered corridors. She was laid on a big bed and she felt with delight under her cheek, against her body, the freshness of clean linen. Everything here was so clean, so restful. A small olive-complexioned nurse came to shake up the pillows and talk quietly to Pierre.

'I'll leave you,' said Pierre. 'The doctor will come in to see you. I'll be back presently.'

'I'll see you presently, then,' said Françoise.

She let him go without regret; she no longer needed him — she needed only the doctor and the nurse. She was just a patient, No. 31, just an ordinary case of congestion of the lungs. The sheets were fresh, the walls white, and she felt within her a tremendous sense of well-being. That was that! All she had to do was to let herself go, to give in — it was so simple, why had she hesitated so? Now, instead of the endless babbling of the streets, of faces, of her own head, she was surrounded by silence and she wanted nothing more. Outside, a branch snapped in the wind. In this perfect void, the slightest sound radiated in broad waves which could almost be seen and touched: it reverberated to the ends of eternity in thousands of vibrations which remained suspended in the ether, beyond time, and which entranced the heart more magically than music. On the night-table, the nurse had set a carafe of pink, transparent orangeade; it seemed to Françoise that she would never tire of looking at it; there it was; the miracle lay in the fact that something should be there, without any effort being made, this mild refreshment or anything else at all. It had come there without any fuss or bother, and there it was going to remain. Why then should her eyes cease to be enchanted by it? Yes, this was precisely what Françoise had not dared to hope for three days earlier: released, satisfied, she was lying in the lap of peaceful moments turned in upon themselves, smooth and round as shingle.

'Can you raise yourself a little?' said the doctor. He helped her sit up. 'That's all right like that. It won't take long.'

He had a friendly, efficient look: he took an instrument from his case and put it against Françoise's chest.

'Take a deep breath,' he said.

Françoise inhaled. Her breathing was so laboured that the effort exhausted her. When she tried to breathe deeply, a stab of pain pierced her.

'Count, one, two, three,' said the doctor.

He was now listening to her back. With a series of short taps he sounded the thoracic cavity, like a detective on the films tapping a suspicious wall. Obediently, Françoise counted, coughed, inhaled.

'There, that's all over,' said the doctor. He arranged the pillow under Françoise's head and surveyed her with a kindly look.

'It's a slight inflammation of the lungs. We'll start injections immediately to stimulate the heart.'

'Will it last a long time?' said Françoise.

'Normally, it takes about nine days, but you'll need a long convalescence. Have you ever had trouble with your lungs in the past?'

'No,' said Françoise. 'Why? Do you think I may have a patch on one of them?'

'One can never be sure,' said the doctor vaguely. He patted Françoise's hand. 'As soon as you feel better we'll X-ray you, and we'll see what has to be done for you.'

'Are you going to send me to a sanatorium?'

'I didn't say so,' said the doctor, smiling. 'In any case, a few months' rest won't hurt you. But above all, don't worry.'

'I'm not worrying,' said Françoise.

A patch on her lung! Months in a sanatorium! Years, perhaps. How strange it was. All these things could really happen. How far away was that Christmas Eve festivity when she believed herself to be safely settled in stability; there was as yet no indication of coming events. The future spread out in the distance, smooth and white like the sheets; the walls were a long soft expanse of peaceful snow. Françoise was just anyone, and just anything had suddenly become possible.

Françoise opened her eyes. She loved these awakenings that did not drag her from her repose but allowed her to become enchantedly aware of it; she did not even have to change her position, she was already sitting up. She had grown quite accustomed to sleeping in this way; for her sleep was no longer a fierce voluptuous retreat, it was one of many activities, carried out in the same posture as the others. Her eyes slowly took in the oranges and the books that Pierre had piled on the night-table; a peaceful day lay lazily ahead of her.

'Presently they'll X-ray me,' she thought.

That was the principal event round which all other events revolved. She felt indifferent about the results of the examination. What did interest her was to cross the threshold of this room in which she had been immured for three weeks. Today, she felt that she was completely recovered; surely she would have no difficulty in standing up or even walking.

The morning went by very quickly. While helping with her ablutions, the thin dark nurse who looked after Françoise delivered a long lecture on the fate of modern woman and the beauty of learning. Then the doctor called. Madame Miquel came at about ten o'clock: she brought with her two pairs of freshly ironed pyjamas, a pink angora bed-jacket, some tangerines and a bottle of eau-de-Cologne; she stayed on for lunch and lavished thanks on the nurse. When she left, Françoise stretched out her legs and, lying on her back with the upper part of her body almost straight, she let the world slip into darkness. It began to slip, then returned to the light; it slipped again; it was a very gentle swaying. Suddenly, the swaying ceased. Xavière was leaning over the bed.

'Did you have a good night?'

'I always sleep well when I have those drops,' said Françoise.

With her head thrown back and a faint smile on her lips, Xavière was undoing the scarf tied over her hair; when she was thinking about herself, there was always something mysterious and ritualistic in her gestures. The scarf slipped off, and she came back to earth. Cautiously, she picked up the bottle.

'You mustn't get into the habit,' she said, 'for then you won't be able to do without it. Your eyes will become glassy and your nostrils pinched. You'll frighten people.'

'And you'll conspire with Labrousse to hide all my little bottles,' said Françoise, 'but I'll outwit you.'

She began to cough, it tired her to talk.

'I didn't go to bed at all last night,' said Xavière proudly.

'You'll have to tell me all about it,' said Françoise.

Xavière's statement had affected her like a dentist's drill in a dead tooth; she felt nothing but the empty cavity of a pang that existed no more. Pierre tires himself out too much, Xavière will never accomplish a thing: these thoughts were still there, but ineffective and insensitive.

'I have something for you,' said Xavière.

She took off her raincoat and drew from the pocket a small cardboard box tied with a green ribbon. Françoise untied the knot and lifted the lid; it was stuffed with cotton wool and tissue paper. Under the light paper lay a bunch of snowdrops.

'How pretty they are!' said Françoise. 'They look both real and artificial at the same time.'

Xavière blew gently on the white corollas.

'They were up all night too, but this morning I put them on a special diet. They're in good health.'

She got up and filled a glass with water and arranged the flowers in it. Her black velvet suit made her lithe body look even more slender: no longer had she anything of the little peasant-girl about her. She was a perfect young lady and certain of her charm. She drew an arm-chair up to the bed.

'We really spent an amazing night,' she said.

Almost every evening she met Pierre at the close of the performance and there was now not a shadow between them; but never before had Françoise seen this rapt, excited expression on her face; her lips were parted slightly as if they were shaping an offering and her eyes were smiling. Under the tissue paper, under the cotton wool, carefully enclosed in a well-sealed box, lay the memory of Pierre and it was that which Xavière was caressing with her lips and her eyes.

'You know, I've wanted for a long time to see all the sights of Montmartre,' said Xavière, 'but somehow it could never be arranged.'

Françoise smiled; there was a magic circle round Montparnasse that Xavière could never bring herself to cross; almost at once cold and fatigue deterred her, and she timorously took refuge at the Dôme or the Pôle Nord.

'Labrousse really took things in hand yesterday evening,' said Xavière, 'he carried me off in a taxi and landed me at the Place Pigalle. We didn't really know where we wanted to go, we were on a voyage of exploration.' She smiled. 'There must have been tongues of flame over our heads, because in five minutes we were in front of a little red house with clusters of tiny panes and red curtains in the windows; it looked very intimate but a little dubious. I didn't dare to go in, but Labrousse blithely opened the door. It was as warm as toast and full of people, but we even managed to find a table in a corner. On it was a pink tablecloth and charming little pink napkins that looked like the small, folded silk handkerchiefs which young dandies arrange so carefully in their breast-pockets. So we sat down.' Xavière paused to gain her final effect. 'And we ate sauerkraut.'

'You ate sauerkraut?' said Françoise.

'Yes, we did,' said Xavière, in the seventh heaven at having created her effect. 'And I thought it was delicious.'

Françoise could see Xavière's bold, sparkling look. 'Sauerkraut for me too.' It was a mystical communion that she had offered to Pierre. They were seated side by side, a little apart; they looked at the people and then they looked at one another with mutual and happy affection. There was nothing disquieting in these thoughts: Françoise called them to mind with perfect calm. All this happened outside these bare walls, outside the garden of this nursing-home, in a world as chimerical as the black-and-white world of the films.

'There was such a funny crowd there,' said Xavière, puckering her lips in false prudishness. 'Dope-pedlars, I should say, and habitual criminals. The proprietor is a tall, very pale, dark-haired man with thick pink lips; he looks like a gangster. Not a brute, but a gangster refined enough to be cruel.' She added as if to herself, 'I would like to seduce a man like that.'

'What would you do with him?' said Françoise.

Xavière's lip curled back over her white teeth.

'I'd make him suffer,' she said voluptuously.

Françoise looked at her a little uneasily; it seemed sacrilegious to think of this virtuous little madam as a woman, with the desires of a woman. But how did she think of herself? What dreams of sensuality and amorous passion made her nose and mouth quiver? What picture of herself, concealed from the eyes of the world, was she smiling at with mysterious connivance? Xavière, at this moment, was aware of her body, she knew herself to be a woman, and Françoise felt that she was being duped by an ironical stranger hiding behind familiar features.

The strange smile left her face, and Xavière added in a childish tone: 'And then he'd take me to opium-dens and he'd introduce me to criminals.' She went into a brown study for a moment. 'Perhaps if one were to go back there every evening, one would end up by being accepted. We began to get to know some of the people: two women who were at the bar, completely drunk.' She added confidentially: 'Pansies.'

'You mean Lesbians?' said Françoise.

'Isn't it the same thing?' said Xavière raising her eyebrows.

'Pansy is the word used only about men,' said Françoise.

'In any case, they live together,' said Xavière with a shade of impatience. Her face brightened. 'One had her hair cut very short and looked just like a young man, a charming young man taking infinite pains to debauch himself. The other was the wife. She was a little older and rather pretty with a black silk dress and a red rose at her breast. The young chap entranced me. Labrousse told me that I ought to try to seduce him. I ogled him provocatively, and she came over to our table graciously enough, offering me a drink from her glass.'

'How do you ogle someone?' said Françoise.

'Like this,' said Xavière. She rolled her eyes in a provokingly immodest way in the direction of the carafe of orangeade. Again Françoise was embarrassed. It was not because Xavière proved so adept that she was disturbed: it was because she seemed to take delight in doing so and did it with such complete self-satisfaction.

'And then?' said Françoise.

'And then we asked her to sit down,' said Xavière.

The door opened noiselessly, and the young olive-complexioned nurse came up to the bed.

'It's time for the injection,' she said in a bright voice.

Xavière stood up.

'You needn't go,' said the nurse, as she filled the syringe with a green liquid. 'It will only take me a minute.'

Xavière gave Françoise an unhappy but faintly reproachful look.

'I don't scream, you know,' said Françoise with a smile.

Xavière walked to the window and pressed her forehead against the pane. The nurse turned back the blankets and uncovered Françoise's thigh. The skin was mottled with bruises, and underneath it were a number of tiny hard lumps. With a quick stroke she inserted the needle. She was dexterous and caused no pain.

'There, that's all,' she said. She looked at Françoise a little crossly. 'You mustn't talk too much. You'll tire yourself out.'

'I'm not doing the talking,' said Françoise.

The nurse gave her a smile and left the room.

'What a horrible creature!' said Xavière.

'She's nice,' said Françoise. She felt full of unreflecting indulgence towards this thoughtful, skilful young woman who took such good care of her.

'How can anyone be a nurse?' said Xavière. She threw a timorous but disgusted glance at Françoise.

'Did she hurt you?'

'Of course not. It doesn't hurt at all.'

Xavière shivered; she was capable of really shivering at a thought.

'A needle pricking its way into my flesh is something I couldn't bear.'

'If you were to take drugs . . .' said Françoise.

Xavière threw back her head and laughed a short scornful laugh.

'Ah, then I'd be doing it to myself. I can do anything in the world to myself.'

Françoise recognized that tone of superiority and rancour. Xavière judged people far less by their acts than by the situations in which they found themselves, even in spite of themselves. She would have liked to close her eyes to this particular

184

instance because Françoise was involved, but it was a serious fault to be ill; she suddenly remembered that.

'You'd have to bear it none the less,' said Françoise. She added a little mischievously: 'It may perhaps happen even to you one of these days.'

'Never,' said Xavière. 'I'd die rather than see a doctor.'

Her moral principles forbade the use of medicines, for it was contemptible to continue the struggle for life if life were failing. She loathed any kind of struggle on principle, regarding it as a lack of freedom and of pride.

'She'd allow herself to be cared for just like anyone else,' thought Françoise, with annoyance; but that was small consolation. For the moment, Xavière was there, fresh and free in her black suit; a high-necked plaid blouse set off the radiance of her face and her hair glistened. Françoise lay bound down, at the mercy of nurses and doctors. She was thin and ugly, an invalid; she could barely speak. Suddenly, she felt the illness in her as a humiliating blemish.

'Perhaps you'd like to tell me the rest of your story,' she said.

'Won't she come in again and interrupt us?' said Xavière irritably. 'She doesn't even knock.'

'I don't think she'll come back,' said Françoise.

'Well! She waved to her friend,' said Xavière with some effort, 'and they sat down beside us. The younger one finished her whisky and then suddenly collapsed on to the table, with her arms spread out and her cheek resting on her arm like a small child. She was laughing and crying at the same time. Her hair was all tousled, she had drops of perspiration on her forehead, but all the same she was absolutely clean and pure.'

Xavière stopped speaking, she was once again watching the scene in her mind's eye.

'It's magnificent – when someone goes to the limit in something, really to the limit,' she said. For a moment, she looked off into space, then she began again excitedly. 'The other girl shook her. She was determined to get her home. She looked like a maternal whore, you know, those whores who don't want to let any harm come to their boy-friend, both in their own interest and from possessive instinct, as well as from some disgusting sort of pity.'

'I see,' said Françoise. One might have thought that Xavière had spent years of her life among prostitutes. 'Didn't someone knock?' she added, listening. 'Would you mind telling them to come in?'

'Come in,' said Xavière in a clear voice: a shadow of displeasure came into her eyes.

The door opened.

'Greetings,' said Gerbert. With some slight confusion he shook hands with Xavière. 'Greetings,' he repeated. He walked up to the bed.

'How nice of you to have come,' said Françoise.

She had not dared to hope he would visit her, but she was surprised and delighted to see him. It seemed as if a fresh breeze had come into the room, sweeping away the odour of illness and the heavy warmth of the air.

'You do look funny,' said Gerbert, laughing sympathetically. 'You look like a Red Indian chief. Are you feeling better?'

'I'm well again,' said Françoise. 'These things reach their turning point in nine days; either you croak or the fever subsides. Do sit down.'

Gerbert took off his muffler, a woollen muffler with wide brilliant white ribbing. He sat down on a hassock in the middle of the room and turned from Françoise to Xavière with a slightly hunted look.

'The fever has subsided, but I'm still wobbly,' said Françoise. 'In a little while, I'm to be X-rayed, and I think it will give me a funny feeling to put my feet out of bed. They're going to examine my lungs to find out precisely what condition they're in. The doctor told me when I came here that my right lung was like a piece of liver and the other one, too, was slowly beginning to turn into liver.' She had a brief bout of coughing. 'I hope they've gone back to a decent condition. Can you imagine me having to spend years in a sanatorium?'

'That wouldn't be too dreadful,' said Gerbert. His eyes wandered over the room in search of an inspiration. 'Just look at all your flowers! It looks like a bridal chamber!'

'The basket is from the students at the School,' said Françoise. 'The pot of azaleas is from Tedesco and Ramblin. Paule Berger sent the anemones.'

Another coughing fit shook her.

'You see, you're coughing,' said Xavière with a slightly too intense compassion. 'The nurse forbade you to talk.'

'You are a wise nurse,' said Françoise. 'I'll shut up.'

There was a short silence.

'And then what happened to these women?' she asked.

'They left. That's all,' said Xavière affectedly.

With a look of heroic resolve, Gerbert tossed back the lock of hair that was falling over his face.

'I hope you'll be well in time to come and see my marionettes,' he said. 'It's going well, you know, the show will be ready in a fortnight.'

'But you'll put on others during the year, won't you?' said Françoise.

'Yes, now that we have a place. They're decent fellows, the *Images* chaps. I don't much care for what they're doing, but they're obliging all the same.'

'Are you satisfied?'

'Oh, I'm as pleased as Punch,' said Gerbert.

'Xavière told me that your marionettes are so pretty,' said Françoise.

'Oh hell, I should have brought you one,' said Gerbert. 'There they have marionettes on strings, but we use dolls like a Punch and Judy show – the ones you work on your hand. That's much harder. They're made of oilcloth with big flared skirts that hide your whole arm. You can slip them on like gloves.'

'Did you make them?' said Françoise.

'Mollier and I . . . But all the ideas were mine,' said Gerbert, importantly.

He was so wrapped up in his subject that he forgot his shyness.

'It's not so easy to manage, you know, because the movements have to have rhythm and expression; but I'm beginning to learn how to do it. You can't possibly imagine all the small problems of production involved. Just think,' he raised his hands, 'you have a doll on each hand. If you want to send one to the edge of the stage, you have to find an excuse for moving the other at the same time. That requires some ingenuity.'

'I'd love to see a rehearsal,' said Françoise.

'We've been working every day, from five to eight,' said Gerbert. 'We're doing a play with five characters, and three sketches, I've had them in my head for a long time now!' He turned to Xavière. 'We were more or less counting on you last night. Doesn't the part interest you?'

'What? I think it's great fun,' said Xavière in an offended tone.

'Well, then, come along with me later,' said Gerbert. 'Yesterday, Chanaud read the part, but she was terrible: she enunciates as if she were on a stage. It's very hard to find the proper pitch,' he said to Françoise. 'The voice has to sound as if it were coming from the dolls.'

'But I'm afraid I won't know how to do it,' said Xavière.

'Of course you will. The four cues you gave the other day were just right.' Gerbert smiled coaxingly. 'And you know we're dividing the proceeds among the actors. With a little luck, we'll certainly get something like five or six francs.'

Françoise dropped back against the pillows; she was happy that they had begun to talk to one another, she had begun to feel tired. She wanted to stretch out her legs, but the slightest movement required elaborate strategy; she was sitting on a rubber ring sprinkled with talcum powder and there was rubber under her heels, while a kind of wicker hoop held the sheets away from her knees, otherwise the friction would have irritated her skin. She managed to extend her feet. When they were gone, if Pierre did not come in immediately, she would sleep a little. Her mind was blank. She heard Xavière saying: 'The fat woman suddenly changed into a female Montgolfier, her skirts were pulled up to form the basket of the balloon and away she floated into the air.' She was talking about the marionettes she had seen at a fair in Rouen.

'When I was in Palermo, I saw *Orlando Furioso*,' said Françoise.

She did not go on with her story, she had no desire to recount anything. It was in a tiny little street near a grape-vendor's; Pierre had bought her a huge bunch of sticky muscat grapes. Seats were five sous and the audience was made up only of children – the width of the benches was just right for their small behinds. Between the acts, a fellow went round with a tray filled with glasses of cold water that he sold for one sou each, and then he sat down on a bench near the stage. He held a long pole in his hand with which he poked children who made a noise during the performance. On the walls, there were Epinal-type broad-sheets portraying the story of Roland. The dolls were superb and very stiff in their knights' armour. Françoise closed her eyes. It had been only two years ago, but it already seemed to belong to a prehistoric age. Everything had now become so complicated – feelings, life, Europe. To her it made no difference, because she was drifting passively like flotsam; but there were dark reefs everywhere on the horizon: she was drifting on a grey ocean, all round her stretched tarry, sulphurous waters, and she was floating, thinking of nothing, fearing nothing, desiring nothing. She opened her eyes again.

The conversation had stopped. Xavière was looking at the tips of her shoes and Gerbert was intently staring at the pot of azaleas.

'What are you working on at the moment?' he said at last.

'Mérimée's *l'Occasion*,' said Xavière.

She still had not been able to make up her mind to rehearse the scene with Pierre.

'And you?' she asked.

'Octave in *Les Caprices de Marianne*, but only so that I can give Canzetti her cue.'

Again there was a silence; Xavière pouted almost jealously.

'Is Canzetti any good as Marianne?'

'I don't think it's her kind of part,' said Gerbert.

'She's common,' said Xavière.

There was an embarrassed silence.

With a shake of his head, Gerbert tossed back his hair.

'You know, I might do a marionette number at Dominique Oryol's? That would be marvellous, because the place seems to have got off to a good start.'

'Elisabeth mentioned it to me,' said Françoise.

'It was she who introduced me. She's got terrific pull there.' He put his hand up to his mouth, looking half delighted, half shocked. 'No, really, the way she's carrying on these days, it's really unbelievable!'

'She's in the money. People are talking about her. It's changing her life,' said Françoise. 'She's become devastatingly smart.'

'I don't like the way she dresses,' said Gerbert, with determined prejudice.

It was strange to think that out there, in Paris, the days were not all alike; all sorts of things were happening, they moved, they changed. But all these far-off eddies, these jumbled flickerings, awakened no desire in Françoise.

'I have to be at the Impasse Jules-Chaplain at five o'clock,' said Gerbert. 'I must beat it.'

He looked at Xavière.

'Well, are you coming with me? Otherwise Chanaud won't

ever give up the part.'

'I'm coming,' said Xavière. She put on her raincoat and carefully tied her scarf under her chin.

'Will you be staying here much longer?' said Gerbert.

'One week, I hope,' said Françoise, 'and then I'll go home.'

'Goodbye, until tomorrow,' said Xavière a little coldly.

'Until tomorrow,' said Françoise.

She smiled at Gerbert, who waved to her. He opened the door and uneasily stepped back for Xavière; he must have been wondering what he could possibly talk about. Françoise dropped back against the pillows. It delighted her to think that Gerbert was fond of her. Naturally, he was far less fond of her than of Labrousse, but it was a personal affection that was really meant for her. She, too, was very fond of him. She could think of no more delightful relationship than this friendship, devoid of any demands and always so full. She closed her eyes; she was at ease; years in a sanatorium . . . even this thought inspired no rebellion in her. In a few moments, she would know; she felt prepared to accept any verdict whatsoever.

The door opened softly.

'How do you feel?' said Pierre.

The blood rushed to Françoise's cheeks; it was something more than pleasure that Pierre's presence brought her. In front of him alone her calm indifference disappeared.

'I'm getting better and better,' she said, holding Pierre's hand in hers.

'They're going to X-ray you in a little while, aren't they?'

'Yes. But you know, the doctor thinks that my lungs are completely healed.'

'I only hope they don't wear you out,' said Pierre.

'I'm full of beans today,' she said.

Her heart was filled with tenderness. How unfair she had been in comparing Pierre's love to an old whited sepulchre! Thanks to this illness, she had attained its living abundance. It was not only his constant presence, his telephone calls, his attentions, for which she was grateful to him. What had been unforgettably sweet to her was that, over and above his avowed tenderness, she had seen in him a passionate anxiety that was not volitional, but which overwhelmed him. At this moment, the face turned towards her was utterly without reserve; it was useless to tell him over and over that the X-ray was hardly more than a formality: worry had affected him deeply. He put a bundle of books on the bed.

'Look what I've chosen for you! Are they all right?'

Françoise looked at the titles: two detective stories, an American novel, a few magazines.

'They'll do splendidly, I'm sure,' she said. 'You're so kind.'

Pierre took off his overcoat.

'I passed Gerbert and Xavière in the garden.'

'He was taking her to rehearse a marionette show,' said Françoise. 'It's dreadfully funny to see them together. They pass from the wildest volubility to the bleakest silence.'

'Yes,' said Pierre, 'they are amusing.' He took a step towards the door. 'I think someone's coming.'

'Four o'clock. That was the time,' said Françoise.

The nurse entered, walking importantly ahead of two stretcher-bearers who were carrying a huge arm-chair.

'How's our patient doing?' she said. 'I hope she is going to stand her little expedition nicely.'

'She looks well,' said Pierre.

'I feel very well,' said Françoise.

To cross the threshold of this room, after these long days of incarceration, was a real adventure. She was lifted up, wrapped in blankets, and settled in the arm-chair. It was strange to find herself sitting: it was not the same thing as sitting up in bed; it made her somewhat dizzy.

'All right?' asked the nurse, turning the door handle.

'Fine,' said Françoise.

She looked with slightly shocked surprise at this door that was opening to the outside world; normally, it opened to let people in; now it had suddenly changed direction and was transformed into an exit. And the room too was shocking, with its empty bed. It was no longer the heart of the nursing-home, to which all corridors and stairs led: it was the corridor laid with sound-deadening linoleum that became the vital artery on to which a vague series of small cubicles opened. Françoise had the feeling of having come from the other side of the world. It was almost as strange as stepping through a looking-glass.

The arm-chair was set down in a tiled room filled with complicated apparatus. It was terribly hot. Françoise half-closed her eyes. This voyage into the beyond had tired her.

'Can you stand up for two minutes?' said the doctor, who

had just come in.

'I'll try,' said Françoise: she was no longer so sure of her strength.

Strong arms placed her in a standing position and guided her among the apparatus; the ground swirled out from under her feet, it made her feel sick. She could never have imagined that it was such an effort to walk, big beads of perspiration stood out on her forehead.

'Remain absolutely still,' said a voice. She was placed against a piece of the apparatus and a wooden screen was pressed against her chest. She was choking; she would never be able to hold out for two minutes without suffocating. Night fell suddenly and silently; she heard nothing more than the short, quick wheeze of her breathing. Then, there was a click, a sharp noise, and everything was blotted out. When she regained consciousness, she was again reclining in the arm-chair; the doctor was bending gently over her, and the nurse was sponging her dripping forehead.

'It's all over,' he said. 'Your lungs are in excellent condition. You can sleep in peace.'

'Are you feeling better?' asked the nurse.

Françoise nodded ever so slightly; she was exhausted, she felt as if she would never regain her strength, she would have to remain in bed all her life. She flopped against the back of the arm-chair and was carried off down the corridors; her head was empty and heavy. She saw Pierre marching up and down in front of the door of her room. He gave her an anxious smile.

'It's all right,' she murmured.

He started to move towards her.

'Just a second, please,' said the nurse.

Françoise turned to him, and seeing him so firmly on his own legs, she was overcome with distress. How weak and crippled she was! Nothing more than an inert bundle which was being carried by the strength of men's arms.

'Now you're going to have a good rest,' said the nurse. She settled the pillows and pulled up the sheets.

'Thank you very much,' said Françoise, stretching herself out with delight. 'Would you mind saying it's all right for him to come in?'

The nurse left the room. A short conference took place behind the door and Pierre entered. Françoise watched him enviously; it seemed so natural for him to move across the room.

'I'm so happy,' he said. 'It seems that you're as sound as a bell.'

He leaned over her and kissed her; the joy reflected in his smile warmed Françoise's heart; he had not invented it intentionally to bestow on her, he lived this joy for itself with complete freedom. His love had again become dazzlingly apparent.

'What a wild look you had when you were in that sedan-chair,' he said tenderly.

'I was almost sick,' said Françoise.

Pierre took a cigarette from his pocket.

'You may smoke your pipe, you know,' she said.

'Certainly not,' said Pierre. He looked longingly at the cigarette. 'I shouldn't even smoke this.'

'No, no, my lungs are completely cured,' said Françoise cheerfully.

Pierre lit his cigarette.

'And now we'll soon be taking you home; you'll see what a pleasant convalescence you'll have. I'll get you a gramophone and records, you'll have visitors, you'll be in clover.'

'Tomorrow, I'll ask the doctor when he'll let me leave,' said Françoise. She sighed. 'But I feel as if I shall never be able to walk again.'

'Oh! That will soon come back,' said Pierre. 'We'll put you in your arm-chair for a little while every day, and then we'll get you to stand up for a few minutes, and you'll end up by taking real walks.'

Françoise smiled at him trustingly.

'It seems you had a wonderful time last night, you and Xavière,' she said.

'We found a rather amusing place,' said Pierre.

He suddenly became glum. Françoise felt that she had all at once thrust him back into a world of unpleasant thoughts.

'She told me about it with her eyes popping out of her head,' she said, with disappointment in her voice.

Pierre shrugged his shoulders.

'What is it?' she said. 'What are you thinking?'

'Oh! It's of no interest,' said Pierre with a reticent smile.

'How strange you are! Everything interests me,' said Françoise, a little anxiously.

Pierre hesitated.

'Well?' said Françoise. She looked at Pierre. 'Please tell me what's in your mind.'

Pierre still hesitated, then he seemed to take the plunge.

'I wonder if she isn't in love with Gerbert.'

Françoise stared at him dumbfounded.

'What do you mean?'

'Just what I said,' said Pierre. 'That would be only natural. Gerbert is young and charming. He has the sort of charm that appeals to Xavière.' He looked vacantly at the window. 'It's even more than likely,' he said.

'But Xavière is much too absorbed in you,' said Françoise. 'She seemed bowled over by the evening she'd just had.'

Pierre thrust his lip forward and Françoise, with discomfort, again saw that sharp and slightly caddish profile which she had not noticed for a long time.

'Naturally,' he said arrogantly. 'I can always give someone a wonderful time if I want to take the trouble. What does that prove?'

'I don't understand why you think that,' said Françoise.

Pierre seemed hardly to hear her.

'We are dealing with Xavière and not Elisabeth,' he said. 'It's quite clear that I have a certain intellectual attraction for her, but surely she doesn't make the mistake of confusing the issue.'

Françoise felt a slight jolt of dismay. It was Pierre's intellectual charm that formerly had made her fall in love with him.

'She's sensual,' he continued, 'and her sensuality is unadulterated. She quite likes my conversation, but her desires are for a handsome young man's kisses.'

Françoise's dismay was deepened; she liked Pierre's kisses, did he despise her for that? But she was not the person under discussion.

'I'm sure Gerbert isn't making up to her,' she said. 'First of all, he knows that you're interested in her.'

'He doesn't know anything,' said Pierre. 'He only knows what he is told. Anyway, that's beside the point.'

'All the same, did you notice anything between them?' said Françoise.

'When I caught a glimpse of them in the garden just now, it struck me as obvious,' said Pierre, who had begun to gnaw one of his nails. 'You've never seen the way she looks at him when she thinks she's not being watched. She looks as if she'd like to eat him.'

Françoise recalled a particularly avid look which she had caught sight of on the night of the Christmas Eve party.

'Yes,' she said, 'but she was also in a trance over Paule Berger. Those are snapshots of passion, they don't really amount to feeling.'

'And you don't remember how furious she was when we joked once about Aunt Christine and Gerbert?' said Pierre; at the rate he was going, he would gnaw his finger down to the bone.

'That was the day she first met him,' said Françoise. 'You aren't going to suggest that she was already in love with him?'

'Why not?' said Pierre. 'He appealed to her at first sight.'

Françoise thought for a moment: she had left Xavière alone with Gerbert that evening, then, when she had rejoined her, Xavière had been in a strange mood. Françoise had asked if he had been rude to her, but perhaps, quite the contrary, she was angry with him because she was too attracted by him. Several days later, there had occurred that strange indiscretion . . .

'What are you thinking?' said Pierre nervously.

'I'm trying to remember,' she said.

'You see, you're hesitating,' said Pierre in an urgent tone. 'Oh! There are any number of indications. What did she have in mind when she deliberately went and told him that we had gone off without him?'

'You thought that that was the first time she felt drawn to you?'

'There was something of that in it – it was then that she began to take an interest in me; but it must have been more complicated than that. Perhaps she really was sorry not to have spent the evening with him: perhaps she was looking for a momentary complicity with him against us. Or further, she wanted then to take revenge on him for the desire he aroused in her.'

'In any case, that gives no indication one way or the other,' said Françoise. 'It's all too ambiguous.'

She raised herself a little on the pillows: this discussion was tiring her, the perspiration was beginning to ooze in the small of her back and the palms of her hands. She, who had thought that all these interpretations, these analyses, in which Pierre could circle round and round for hours on end, were over and done with . . . She would have liked to remain peaceful and detached, but Pierre's feverish agitation was infecting her.

'She didn't give me that impression a little while ago,' she said.

Pierre's lip was again thrust forward. He had a strange expression, as if he were congratulating himself on keeping back the very spiteful words he was, in fact, uttering.

'You see only what you want to see,' he said.

Françoise flushed.

'I've been away from the world for three weeks now.'

'But there had been many signs already.'

'Which ones do you mean?'

'All those we've talked about,' said Pierre vaguely.

'That's not much,' said Françoise.

Pierre looked annoyed.

'I tell you I know what's up,' he said.

'Then don't ask me,' said Françoise; her voice quavered a little. Faced with an unexpected harshness in Pierre, she felt weak and utterly miserable.

Pierre looked at her with self-reproach.

'I'm tiring you with my talk,' he said, in a burst of tenderness.

'How can you think that?' said Françoise. He seemed so tormented, she would very much have liked to help him. 'Frankly, your evidence seems to me to be a little weak.'

'At Dominique's, on the opening night, she danced once with him. When Gerbert put his arm round her, she shivered from head to foot, and she had a voluptuous smile that could not be misinterpreted.'

'Why didn't you say so?' said Françoise.

'I don't know.' He thought for a moment. 'Yes, I know. It's the most unpleasant memory I have, the one that carries the most weight with me. In a way, I was afraid that if I told you, I would be sharing my proof with you and thus be making it final.' He smiled. 'I didn't think I'd come to that.'

Françoise recalled Xavière's face when she was talking about Pierre, her caressing lips, her tender look.

'It doesn't seem to me to be so conclusive,' she said.

'I'll speak to her tonight,' said Pierre.

'She'll fly into a rage.'

Pierre smiled, with a somewhat irritating air,

196

'Of course not, she loves me to talk to her about herself. She thinks I can appreciate all her subtleties. In fact, that's my greatest attraction in her eyes.'

'She very fond of you,' said Françoise. 'I think Gerbert appeals to her for the moment, but it doesn't go any further than that.'

Pierre's face brightened a little, but he remained tense.

'Are you sure of what you're saying?'

'Sure? No, one can never be sure,' said Françoise.

'You see, you're not sure,' said Pierre. He looked at her almost threateningly. He had to hear her say the calming words, that he might as if by magic feel reassured. Françoise set her teeth. She did not want to treat Pierre like a child.

'I'm not an oracle,' she said.

'What are the odds, in your opinion, that she's in love with Gerbert?'

'They can't be calculated,' said Françoise, rather impatiently. It was painful to her that Pierre should be so puerile, she refused to be his accomplice.

'Still, you can make a shot at them,' said Pierre.

Her temperature must have risen considerably during the course of the afternoon: Françoise felt that her whole body was going to dissolve into sweat.

'I don't know. Ten to one,' she said in an off-hand way.

'No more than ten to one?'

'How on earth should I know?'

'You're not even making an effort,' said Pierre tartly.

Françoise felt a lump rise in her throat. She felt like crying; it would be easy to say what he wanted to hear, to give in. But an obstinate resistance once more came to life within her, again things had meaning and value and were worth fighting for. Only, she was not equal to the fight.

'It's stupid,' said Pierre. 'You're right. Why should I come and pester you with all this?' His face cleared. 'Please note that I want nothing more from Xavière than what I have, but I could not bear that anyone else should have more.'

'I fully understand,' said Françoise.

She smiled, but peace did not return to her; Pierre had broken into her isolation and her repose. She was beginning to catch sight of a world filled with riches and obstacles, a world in which she wanted to join him, that she might desire and fear at his side.

'I'll speak to her this evening,' he repeated. 'Tomorrow, I'll tell you everything that happens, but I won't torment you any more, I promise.'

'You haven't been tormenting me,' said Françoise. 'It was I who made you talk. You didn't want to.'

'It was a sore point,' said Pierre with a smile. 'I was certain that I'd be incapable of discussing it cold-bloodedly. It wasn't that I didn't want to talk to you about it, but when I came in and saw you with your pathetic thin face, everything else seemed ridiculous to me.'

'I'm no longer ill,' said Françoise. 'There's no need for you to handle me carefully any longer.'

'You see very clearly that I'm not particularly careful how I handle you,' said Pierre. He smiled. 'I'm really ashamed. All we do is to talk about me.'

'Well, one can't say that you never mention your own affairs,' said Françoise. 'In fact, you're amazingly honest. You, who can be such a complete sophist in discussions, you never cheat about yourself.'

'I don't deserve any credit for that,' said Pierre. 'You know that I never feel compromised by what goes on within me.' He looked up at Françoise. 'The other day, you told me something that struck me – that I put my feelings beyond time, beyond space, and that in order to keep them intact, I did not live them. That was a little unfair. But where I myself am concerned, it seems to me that I do behave rather in that way: I always think that I'm elsewhere, and that each particular moment is of no importance.'

'That's true,' said Françoise. 'You always think that you're above anything that happens to you.'

'And therefore, I can do anything I want,' said Pierre. 'I take refuge in this notion that I am the man who is accomplishing a certain amount of work, the man who, with you, has achieved so perfect a love. But that's too convenient. Everything else exists too.'

'Yes, the rest does exist,' said Françoise.

'You see, my honesty is still a means of cheating with myself. It's amazing how cunning one can be,' Pierre added with an earnest expression.

'Oh! We'll foil your tricks,' said Françoise.

She smiled at him. What was she uneasy about? He could easily cross-examine himself, he could question the world. She knew she had nothing to fear from this freedom that separated him from her. Nothing would ever change their love.

Françoise rested her head against the pillow. Noon. She still had a long period of solitude before her, but it was no longer the steady white loneliness of the morning. A warm anxiety had crept into the room; the flowers had lost their brilliance, the orangeade its freshness; the walls and the polished furniture seemed naked. Xavière . . . Pierre . . . Wherever her eyes fell, they caught only absences. Françoise closed her eyes. For the first time for weeks anxiety came to life in her. How had the night gone? Pierre's indiscreet questions must have hurt Xavière. Perhaps, in a little while, they would be reconciled at Françoise's bedside. And then what? She became aware of that burning in her throat, that feverish beating of her heart. Pierre had brought her back from the depths of limbo, and she did not want to plunge back there again. She did not want to remain here: this nursing-home was now nothing but an exile. Even illness was not enough to enable her to stand alone. The future that was taking shape on the horizon was her future beside Pierre – our future. She listened. During the past days, quietly settled at the core of her invalid's life, she welcomed visits as a simple distraction. Today, it was different. Pierre and Xavière were approaching, step by step, along the corridor. They had climbed the stairs. They were coming from the station, from Paris, from the centre of their life; it was a portion of this life that they would spend here. The steps halted outside the door.

'May we come in?' said Pierre, as he opened the door. There he was, and Xavière was with him. The transition from their absence to their presence had, as always, been imperceptible.

'The nurse told us that you had slept very well.'

'Yes, as soon as the injections are stopped, I'll be able to leave,' said Françoise.

'Provided you behave and don't get too excited,' said Pierre. 'Relax and don't talk. We'll do the talking.' He smiled at Xavière. 'We have lots of things to tell you.'

He sat down on a chair beside the bed, and Xavière sat on the big square hassock; she must have washed her hair that morning, a thick golden fuzz framed her face: her eyes and her pale mouth had a caressing and secretive expression.

'Everything went very well at the theatre last night,' said

Pierre. 'The house was responsive, and we had a great many curtain calls. But for some unknown reason I was in a filthy mood after the performance.'

'You were nervy during the afternoon,' said Françoise with a half-smile.

'Yes, and then I no doubt felt the lack of sleep – I don't know. Whatever it was, when I was walking down the rue de la Gaieté, I suddenly became intolerable.'

Xavière gave a queer little triangular pout.

'He was a real little asp, hissing and poisonous,' she said. 'I was very cheerful when I arrived. I had rehearsed the Chinese princess very nicely for two hours. I had purposely slept for a little while, so that I'd really be fresh,' she added reproachfully.

'And in my filthy mood, I did nothing but look for excuses to lose my temper with her!' said Pierre. 'Crossing the boulevard Montparnasse, she had the bad luck to let go of my arm . . .'

'Because of the traffic,' said Xavière quickly, 'it was impossible to walk in step. It wasn't at all convenient.'

'I took that as a deliberate insult,' said Pierre, 'and I was shaken by a fit of temper that made my bones rattle.'

Xavière looked with consternation at Françoise.

'It was terrible. He wouldn't talk to me, except that now and then out came an acidly polite remark. I didn't know what to do with myself. I felt so unjustly attacked.'

'I can well imagine it,' said Françoise, smiling.

'We had decided to go to the Dôme, because we had not been there for so long,' said Pierre. 'Xavière seemed happy to be back there and I thought that it was her way of running down the recent evenings we had spent together looking for adventure. That added to my fury, and for nearly an hour I sat, tied up in knots with anger, over my glass of beer.'

'I tried various topics of conversation,' said Xavière.

'Her patience was really angelic,' said Pierre, embarrassed, 'but all her efforts at goodwill only made me the more furious. I know, when I'm in such a state, that I can get out of it if I want to, but on the other hand I never see any reason to want to. I ended up by bursting into accusations. I told her that she was as inconsistent as the wind; that it was certain that if anyone spent one pleasant evening with her, the next was sure to be execrable.'

Françoise burst out laughing.

'But what comes over you to make you so mistrustful?'

'I actually believed sincerely that she had greeted me in a standoffish and reticent way. I believed it because, out of surliness, I had made up my mind in advance that she would be on the defensive.'

'Yes,' said Xavière querulously. 'He explained that he was in that charming temper because he was afraid that he might not spend as perfect an evening with me as the night before.'

They smiled at one another with affectionate understanding. It seemed that Gerbert had not entered into it; in the end, of course, Pierre had not dared to talk about him, and he had got out of it with half-truths.

'She looked so pathetically shocked,' said Pierre, 'that I was promptly disarmed. I felt completely ashamed. I told her everything that had gone through my mind from the time we left the theatre,' then smiling at Xavière, 'and she was magnanimous enough to forgive me.'

Xavière returned his smile. There was a brief silence.

'And then we agreed the fact that for a long time now our evenings had been perfect,' said Pierre. 'Xavière was kind enough to tell me that never once had she been bored with me, and I told her that the moments I spent with her counted among the most precious of my life.' He added quickly, in a playful tone that did not ring quite true, 'and we agreed that this was not so surprising since we were in love.'

Despite the gaiety in his voice, the last word fell heavily on the room and silence closed over it. Xavière wore a forced smile: Françoise composed her features with difficulty; it was only a matter of a single word, it was a long time since things had reached this stage, but it was a decisive word and before saying it, Pierre really might have talked it over with her. She was not jealous of him, but not without a fight would she lose this little sleek, golden girl whom she had adopted early one chilly morning.

Pierre continued easily and calmly, 'Xavière told me that until that moment she had never been conscious that it was love.' He smiled. 'She knew well enough that the moments we spent together were happy and important ones, but she had not understood that it was owing to my presence.'

Françoise glanced at Xavière, who was gazing non-committally at the floor. She was unfair, Pierre had talked it over with her; she had been the first to tell him a long time ago:

201

'You may fall in love with her.' The night of the New Year's Eve party he had offered to give up Xavière. He had every right to feel his conscience clear.

'Did you think it was an extraordinary coincidence?' said Françoise clumsily.

Xavière quickly looked up.

'Of course not,' she said. She looked at Pierre. 'I knew quite well that it was thanks to you, but I thought that it was simply because you were so interesting and so pleasant. Not because – not because of anything else.'

'But what do you think now? You haven't changed your mind since yesterday?' said Pierre with a winning air which did reveal a slight uneasiness.

'Certainly not, I'm not a weather-vane,' said Xavière stiffly.

'You might have made a mistake,' said Pierre, whose voice wavered between curtness and gentleness. 'Perhaps in a moment of exaltation, you mistook friendship for love.'

'Did I look exalted last night?' said Xavière with a twisted smile.

'You seemed caught up by the moment,' said Pierre.

'No more than usual,' said Xavière. She clutched a strand of her hair and began to squint at it with a stupid, vicious look. 'The trouble is,' she drawled, 'that big words immediately make everything so oppressive.'

Pierre's face froze.

'If the words are apt, why be afraid of them?'

'Quite so,' said Xavière continuing to squint atrociously.

'Love is not a disgraceful secret,' said Pierre. 'To me, it's a weakness to refuse to look squarely at what goes on inside you.'

Xavière shrugged her shoulders.

'You can't change human nature,' she said. 'I haven't got a public soul.'

Pierre had a disconcerted and helpless look that pained Françoise; he could be so fragile, if he chose to cast away all his defences and all his weapons.

'Do you find it disagreeable that all three of us should discuss the matter?' he said. 'Still, that's what we decided yesterday evening. Perhaps it might have been better had we each talked alone with Françoise.' He look hesitatingly at Xavière. She threw him a vexed glance.

'It's all the same to me whether we're two or three or a

202

whole crowd,' she said. 'What seems strange to me is to hear you talk to me about my own feelings.' She began to laugh nervously. 'It's so strange, I can hardly believe it. Am I actually the person you're talking about? Is it me you've been dissecting? And do you expect me to put up with it?'

'Why not? It's you and I who are involved,' said Pierre. He smiled timidly. 'It seemed quite natural to you last night.'

'Last night . . .' said Xavière, and she had an almost painful sneer, 'you seemed to live things, for once, and not just to talk about them.'

'You're being extremely unpleasant,' said Pierre.

Xavière ran her hands through her hair and pressed them against her temples.

'It's crazy to be able to talk about oneself as if one were a piece of wood,' she said fiercely.

'You can only experience things in the dark, secretly,' said Pierre in a rasping voice. 'You're incapable of thinking them and wanting them in broad daylight. It's not the words that upset you. What does irritate you is that, today, I'm asking you to agree, of your own free will, to what you accepted last evening when it was sprung upon you.'

Xavière's face fell, and she glanced at Pierre with a hunted look. Françoise would have liked to stop Pierre. She could easily understand that people were afraid of, and wanted to escape from, this domineering tenseness which hardened his features. He himself was not happy at this moment either, but despite his fragility, Françoise could not help seeing him as a man fighting desperately for his masculine triumph.

'You've just let me say that you loved me,' said Pierre. 'It's not too late for you to correct yourself. It would not surprise me in the least to discover that you experience nothing deeper than passing emotions.' He gave Xavière a nasty look. 'Go ahead, tell me frankly that you don't love me.'

Xavière threw a desperate glance at Françoise.

'Oh! I wish none of this had ever happened,' she said, in obvious distress. 'Everything was going so well before! Why must you spoil it all?'

Pierre seemed moved by this outburst. He looked first at Xavière, then at Françoise, unable to make up his mind.

'Give her time to breathe,' said Françoise, 'you're badgering her.'

To love, not to love – how laconic and rational Pierre was

becoming in his thirst for certainty! In a sisterly way, Françoise understood Xavière's bewilderment. In what words could she herself have described her feelings? Everything was in such confusion within her.

'Forgive me,' said Pierre. 'I was wrong to lose my temper. It's all over. I don't want to think that anything is spoilt between us.'

'But it is spoilt, you can see that!' said Xavière. Her lips were trembling, her nerves were on edge. Suddenly, she buried her face in her hands.

'Oh! What can we do now? What can we do?' she said in a whisper.

Pierre bent towards her.

'No, no, nothing has happened. Nothing has changed,' he said insistently.

Xavière let her hands fall to her knees.

'Everything's so heavy now. It's like a strait-jacket round me.' She was trembling from head to foot. 'It's so heavy.'

'Don't think that I expect anything further. I ask nothing more of you. It's just as it was before,' said Pierre.

'Look what's happened already,' said Xavière. She sat bolt upright and threw her head back to check her tears. Her throat swelled convulsively. 'It's a disaster, I'm sure of it. I'm not up to it,' she said in a broken voice.

Françoise looked at her, helpless and heartbroken: this reminded her of one such occasion at the Dôme; now, however, it was even more dangerous than then for Pierre to make any gesture, for it would have been not only an effrontery but an outrage. Françoise wished she might put her arms round the trembling shoulders and find something to say, but she lay paralysed between the sheets. No contact was possible; she could only utter brittle words which were doomed not to ring true. Xavière, with no help available, was standing face to face with a menacing avalanche, alone, like one hallucinated.

'There's no disaster to fear between the three of us,' said Françoise. 'You must have confidence. What are you afraid of?'

'I'm afraid,' said Xavière.

'Pierre is a little snake, but his hiss is worse than his bite, and besides we'll tame him. You'll let yourself be tamed, won't you?'

'I won't even hiss any more,' said Pierre. 'I swear to that.'

'Well?' said Françoise.

Xavière took a deep breath.

'I'm afraid,' she repeated in a weary tone.

Just as on the evening before, at the same time, the door opened softly and the nurse entered, a syringe in her hand. Xavière jumped up and walked to the window.

'It won't take long,' said the nurse.

Pierre got up and took a step forward as if he wanted to join Xavière, but he stopped in front of the fireplace.

'Is this the last injection?' said Françoise.

'We'll give you one more tomorrow,' said the nurse.

'And after that, I can just as easily convalesce at home?'

'Are you in such a hurry to leave us? You'll have to wait until you're a little stronger, before you can be moved.'

'How long? Another week?'

'A week or ten days.'

The nurse inserted the needle.

'There, that's all,' she said. She pulled up the sheets and left the room with an expansive smile. Xavière whirled round on her heel.

'I loathe her, with her honeyed voice,' she said with bitter hatred. For a moment she stood motionless at the far end of the room; then she walked to the arm-chair on which she had thrown her raincoat.

'What are you doing?' said Françoise.

'I'm going out to get a little air. I'm suffocating in here.' Pierre made a gesture. 'I must be alone,' she said fiercely.

'Xavière! Don't be obstinate!' said Pierre. 'Come back and sit down and let's talk sensibly.'

'Talk! We've already talked too much!' said Xavière. She quickly put on her coat and walked towards the door.

'Don't go like this,' said Pierre gently. He put out his hand and lightly touched her arm. Xavière started back.

'You're not going to issue orders to me now,' she said tonelessly.

'Go and get some air,' said Françoise, 'but come back and see me at the end of the day. Will you do that?'

Xavière looked at her.

'I'd like to,' she said with a kind of docility.

'Shall I be seeing you at midnight?' said Pierre in a curt tone.

'I don't know,' said Xavière, almost in a whisper. She

suddenly opened the door and closed it behind her.

Pierre walked to the window and for a moment remained motionless, pressing his forehead against a pane. He was watching her leave the building.

'Now we're in a fine mess,' he said, walking back to the bed.

'And how clumsy you were!' said Françoise nervously, 'what ever came over you? The last thing in the world you should have done was to come back like that with Xavière to tell me at once all about your conversation. The situation was embarrassing for everyone. Even a less sensitive girl would not have stood it.'

'Eh! What else could I have done?' said Pierre. 'I made the suggestion that she should come and see you alone, but of course she felt that that was more than she could cope with. She said that it would be far better for us to come together. And as for me, there was never any question of my speaking to you without her. We would have looked like a couple of grown-ups making our own arrangements for her over her head.'

'I don't deny it,' said Françoise. 'It was a very delicate matter.' She added with a strange stubborn pleasure: 'In any case, your solution was not a happy one.'

'Last night it seemed so simple,' said Pierre. He assumed a far-away look. 'We discovered our love. We came to tell it to you as a beautiful story that had happened to us.'

The blood rushed to Françoise's cheeks and her heart was filled with resentment. She hated this role of a dispassionate benevolent divinity which they obliged her to play to suit their own convenience, on the pretext of revering her.

'Yes, and the story was thereby hallowed in advance,' said Françoise. 'I quite understand; it was even more important for Xavière than for you to think that I would be told about last night.' She recalled their delighted look of mutual understanding when they came into her room; they were bringing her their love, like a beautiful gift, that she might return it to them transformed into a virtue. 'Only, Xavière can never picture things in detail. She did not understand that words had to be used. She was horrified as soon as you opened your mouth. I am not surprised that she was, but you ought to have foreseen the result.'

Pierre shrugged his shoulders.

'I didn't think of taking it into account,' he said. 'I had no suspicions. That little fiend! If you could have seen how submissive and yielding she was last night. When I said the word "love", she trembled a little, but her face gave immediate consent. I took her home.'

He smiled, but he looked as if he did not feel that he was smiling. His gaze remained vague.

'When I was about to leave her, I took her in my arms and she held her lips up to me. It was a completely chaste kiss, but there was so much tenderness in her gesture.'

The picture seared Françoise like a burn. Xavière – her black suit, her plaid blouse and her white neck; Xavière – supple and warm in Pierre's arms, her eyes half closed, her mouth proffered. Never would she see that face. She made a determined effort; she was going to be unfair, she did not want to allow herself to be submerged by this increasing resentment.

'You're not offering her an easy love,' she said. 'It was only natural for her to be frightened for a moment. We don't usually look at her from that point of view; but after all, she's a young girl and she has never loved. That does count, in spite of everything.'

'I only hope she doesn't do anything foolish,' said Pierre.

'What do you think she might do?'

'With her, you never know. She was in such a state.'

He looked anxiously at Françoise.

'Will you try to reassure her? Explain everything to her. You're the only one who can put matters right.'

'I'll try,' said Françoise.

She looked at him, and their conversation of the previous evening flooded back into her mind. She had loved him too blindly, and for too long, for what she received from him; but she had promised herself to love him for himself, and even in that condition of freedom of which he was now availing himself to escape from her; she would not stumble over the first obstacle. She smiled at him.

'What I shall really try to get into her head,' she said, 'is that you are not one man between two women, but that all three of us form something very special, something difficult, perhaps, but something which could be beautiful and happy.'

'I wonder if she'll come at midnight,' said Pierre. 'She was so unlike herself.'

'I'll do my best to persuade her,' said Françoise. 'It isn't really so serious.'

'And Gerbert?' said Françoise, after a short silence. 'Is he right out of it now?'

'We hardly mentioned him,' said Pierre, 'but I think you were right. He attracts her for the moment, and a minute later she no longer gives him a thought.' He rolled a cigarette between his fingers. 'Still, it was that which brought the whole thing to a head. I found our relationship delightful, such as it was. I wouldn't have tried to change a thing if jealousy hadn't aroused my domineering instinct. It's chronic, as soon as I feel I'm being met with resistance, I lose my head.'

It was true that he had within him a dangerous mechanism of which he was not master. Françoise felt a tightening in her throat.

'You'll end up by sleeping with her,' she said.

No sooner were the words out of her mouth than she was overwhelmed by an unbearable certainty – Pierre, with his caressing masculine hands, would turn this black pearl, this austere angel, into a rapturous woman. He had already crushed his lips to her soft lips. She looked at him with a kind of horror.

'You know that I'm no sensualist,' said Pierre. 'All I ask is to be able at any time to see an expression like the one I saw last night, and moments when I alone in this world exist for her.'

'But it's more or less inevitable,' said Françoise. 'Your domineering isn't going to be content with half-measures. To make sure that she always loves you as much, you'll ask a little more of her each time.'

In her voice there was a harsh hostility that wounded Pierre. He made a slight grimace.

'You're going to make me disgusted with myself,' he said.

'It always seems a sacrilege to me,' said Françoise more gently, 'to think of Xavière as a sexual woman.'

'But it does me, too,' said Pierre. Resolutely, he lit his cigarette. 'The point is, that I won't tolerate her sleeping with another man.'

Again Françoise felt that unbearable searing in her heart.

'That's just why you'll be brought to sleeping with her,' she said. 'I don't say at once, but in six months, in a year.'

She envisaged each step along the fatal path that led from kisses to caresses, from caresses to complete surrender. Through Pierre's failing, Xavière would end up there like anyone else. For a moment she frankly hated him.

'Do you know what you are going to do now?' she said, taking care to control her voice. 'You're going to sit down in your corner, as you did the other day, and do some work. I'll rest for a while.'

'I tire you out, I know,' said Pierre. 'I forget far too often that you're ill.'

'It's not you,' said Françoise.

She closed her eyes. She was suffering from unpleasant suspicions. Exactly what did she want? What could she want? She did not know; but it was absurd to have imagined that she could escape by renunciation; she was too fond of Pierre and Xavière; she was too involved. A thousand painful recollections swirled through her head and battered at her heart; she felt that the blood coursing through her veins was poisoned. She turned to the wall and began to cry silently.

Pierre left Françoise at seven o'clock. She had finished her supper and she was too tired to read; she could do nothing else but wait for Xavière. But would she come? It was terrible to be dependent on that capricious will, without having the means to influence it. A prisoner. Françoise looked at the bare walls; the room smelt of fever and night, the nurse had taken away the flowers and turned off the ceiling light. There remained nothing but a shell of pale light round her bed.

'What do I want?' Françoise asked herself again in anguish. She had only been able to cling obstinately to the past; she had let Pierre proceed alone. And now that she had let go, he had gone too far for her to reach him. It was too late. 'And if it weren't too late?' she thought. If in the end she were to decide to throw all her reserves into action instead of standing stock-still, with limp and empty arms? She pulled herself up a little on the pillows. She, too, must give herself without reservation, that was her only chance: perhaps then she, in her turn, would be caught up by this new future into which Pierre and Xavière had preceded her. She looked excitedly at the door. She would do that; she made up her mind to do that: there was absolutely nothing else to do. If only Xavière would come! Half-past seven. It was no longer Xavière she was awaiting, her hands moist and her throat dry; it was her life, her future, and the resurrection of her happiness.

There was a soft knock.

'Come in,' said Françoise.

Nothing happened. Xavière must have been afraid that Pierre was still there.

'Come in,' cried Françoise as loudly as she could; but her voice was strangled. Xavière would go away without hearing her and she had no way of recalling her.

Xavière came in.

'I'm not disturbing you?' she said.

'Certainly not, I was looking forward to seeing you,' said Françoise.

Xavière sat down beside the bed.

'Where have you been all this time?' said Françoise gently.

'I've been for a walk,' said Xavière.

'How upset you were,' said Françoise. 'Why do you torment yourself like that? What are you afraid of? There's no reason for it.'

Xavière lowered her head; she seemed to be completely worn out.

'I was perfectly foul just now,' she said. She added timidly: 'Was Labrousse very angry?'

'Of course not,' said Françoise. 'He was just worried.' She smiled. 'But you'll reassure him.'

Xavière stared at Françoise with a look of terror.

'I don't dare go and see him,' she said.

'But that's absurd,' said Françoise. 'Because of that scene just now?'

'Because of everything.'

'You've worked yourself up over a word,' said Françoise, 'but a word doesn't change anything. You don't think he'll feel he has any rights over you?'

'You saw just now,' said Xavière. 'It's already caused a row.'

'It was you who made the row, because you became panic-stricken,' said Françoise. She smiled. 'Anything new always upsets you. You were afraid to come to Paris, afraid of the theatre. And after all, so far, you've met with no great trouble.'

'No,' said Xavière with a shadow of a smile.

Her face, drawn with fatigue and anguish, seemed even more impalpable than usual; still, it was made of soft flesh against which Pierre had pressed his lips. For a while Françoise gazed with loving eyes at this woman whom Pierre loved.

'On the contrary, everything could be so easy,' she said. 'A couple who are closely united is something beautiful enough, but how much more wonderful would be a trio who loved each other with all their being.' She waited a while. Now the moment had come for her, too, to commit herself and to take her risks. 'Because, after all, it is certainly a kind of love that exists between you and me.'

Xavière threw her a quick glance.

'Yes,' she said in a low voice. Suddenly, an expression of childlike tenderness softened her face and impulsively she leaned towards Françoise and kissed her.

'How warm you are,' she said. 'You are feverish.'

'I'm always a little feverish at night,' said Françoise. She smiled. 'But I'm so happy you're here.'

It was so simple; this love, which of a sudden swelled her heart with sweetness, had always been within her reach; she had only to stretch out her hand, her timid and avaricious hand.

'You see, if there is also love between you and Labrousse, what a beautiful well-balanced trio that makes,' she said. 'It's not a recognized way of living, but I don't think it will be too difficult for us. Do you share my view?'

'Oh yes,' said Xavière, who seized Françoise's hand and squeezed it.

'Just let me get well, and you'll see what a beautiful life we'll have, the three of us,' said Françoise.

'You'll be back at the end of a week?' said Xavière.

'If all goes well,' said Françoise.

She suddenly became aware of the painful stiffening of her whole body. No, she would not stay in this nursing-home any longer, this was the end of any peaceful detachment; she had regained her keen zest for happiness.

'That hotel is so dismal without you,' said Xavière. 'In the old days, even when I didn't see you for a whole day, I felt you were up there above me and I heard your step on the staircase. It's so empty now.'

'But I'll be coming back,' said Françoise, with emotion.

She had never suspected that Xavière paid such particular attention to her presence. How she had misjudged her! How she would love her, to make up for time lost! She pressed her hand and looked at her in silence. Now when her temples were throbbing with fever and her throat was dry, she understood at last what miracle had entered her life. She had been slowly withering away under the protection of painstakingly

211

built patterns and leaden-heavy thoughts, when suddenly, in a burst of purification and freedom, all this too-human world had collapsed into dust. One open childlike look from Xavière had sufficed to destroy that prison, and now, on this liberated earth a thousand marvels would come to life, thanks to this exacting young angel. A sad angel with gentle feminine hands, as red as those of a peasant woman, with lips perfumed with honey, Virginian tobacco and green tea.

'My precious Xavière,' said Françoise.

PART TWO

Chapter One

Elisabeth's eyes ran over the upholstered walls, and came to rest on the miniature theatre painted in red at the far end of the room. For a time she had thought with pride: 'This is my work.' But it was not so very much to be proud of; it had, after all, to be the work of somebody's hands.

'I must go home,' she said. 'Pierre is coming to supper with Françoise and the Pagès girl.'

'Ah! Pagès is walking out on me,' said Gerbert with a slightly mortified expression.

He had not taken the trouble to remove his make-up; with his green eyelids and the thick layer of ochre covering his cheeks, he looked much more handsome than he actually was. Elisabeth had brought him and Dominique together, and made her accept his marionette number. She had played an important part in the organization of the night-club. She smiled bitterly. With the aid of drinking and smoking she had had, during the discussions, the intoxicating feeling of playing an active part, but it was like the rest of her life – her actions had no real value. This she had understood, during these three gloomy days; nothing that happened to her was ever real. Sometimes, far into the fog, it was possible to catch a glimpse of something which faintly resembled an event or an act; some people could let themselves be taken in by it, yet it was nothing but blatant deception.

'She'll walk out on you more often than you think,' said Elisabeth.

In Xavière's absence, Lise had resumed her part and, in Elisabeth's opinion, played it at least as well. Still, Gerbert appeared put out. Elisabeth studied him closely.

'That child has some talent,' she continued, 'but she seems to lack conviction in whatever she does, and that's a pity.'

'I can understand that it isn't much fun for her having to come here every night,' said Gerbert, slightly on the defensive, a fact not lost on Elisabeth. She had for a long time suspected that Gerbert had a soft corner for Xavière. It was amusing.

Did Françoise suspect this?

'Which day shall we meet to make a start on your portrait?' she said. 'Tuesday evening? I only want to make a few sketches.'

What she would very much like to know was what Xavière thought of Gerbert. She could not be very interested in him, they kept her too close in hand; still, her eyes had had a strange sparkle that opening night while she danced with him. If he were to make advances to her, how would she react?

'Tuesday, if you like,' said Gerbert.

He was so shy. He would never dare to take the initiative: he did not even suspect that he stood a chance.

Elisabeth lightly pecked at Dominique's forehead.

'Goodbye, darling.'

She went out into the street. It was late; she would have to walk quickly if she wanted to get there before them: she had delayed sinking back into herself until the very last minute. She would manage to speak to Pierre somehow; the game was lost in advance, yet she wanted to take this one last chance. She pursed her lips. Suzanne was triumphant; Nanteuil had just accepted *Partage* for next winter, and Claude was oozing fatuous satisfaction from every pore. Never had he been so tender as during the past three days, and never had she hated him more. He was a careerist – vain and weak; he was eternally bound to Suzanne and eternally Elisabeth would remain the licensed and clandestine mistress. During these past few days, the truth, in all its unbearable crudity, had become obvious to her: she had nursed her vain hopes out of cowardice, she could expect nothing of Claude; and yet she would bear anything to keep him, for she could not live without him. She had not even the excuse of a generous love, her suffering and bitterness had killed all love. Had she really ever loved him? Was she capable of loving? She quickened her pace. There had been Pierre. If he had devoted his life to her, perhaps she would never have grown up with these discords or these lies within her. Perhaps for her, too, the world would have been complete and she would have known peace in her heart. But that was all in the past. She was hurrying to him without finding within herself anything but a desperate desire to do him harm.

She climbed the stairs and turned on the light. Before going out she had laid the table, and the supper really did present a handsome spread. She, too, looked handsome in her pleated skirt, plaid jacket, and careful make-up. Anyone looking at this whole scene in a mirror might well have felt confronted with an old dream come true. When she was twenty, in her dreary little bedroom, she used to set out pork-sausage canapés and carafes of rough red wine for Pierre: then she used to take pleasure in imagining that she was giving him a delicious repast of pâté de foie gras and old Burgundy. Now the foie gras was on the table, together with caviare canapés, and there was sherry and vodka in the bottles; and now she had money, any number of connexions, and a dawning reputation. And yet, she continued to feel herself on the outskirts of life: this supper was only a Barmecide feast in a counterfeit smart studio, and she was only a living caricature of the woman she pretended to be. She crumbled a petit four between her fingers. The pretence used to be fun in the old days: it was the anticipation of a brilliant future. Now she no longer had a future. She knew that in no way would she ever reach the authentic ideal of which her present self was only a copy. Never would she know anything other than these shams. It was the curse which had been cast upon her: everything she touched turned into papier-mâché.

The doorbell shattered the silence. Did they know that everything was spurious? Surely they knew. She gave a final glance at the table and at her face. She opened the door. Françoise was framed in the doorway, a bunch of anemones in her hand. It was Elisabeth's favourite flower – at least that was what Elisabeth had decided ten years previously.

'These are for you, I found them at Banneau's just now,' said Françoise.

'You are sweet,' said Elisabeth, 'they're so pretty.' Something softened inside her. Besides, it wasn't Françoise she hated.

'Come in quickly,' she said, as she led them into the studio.

Hidden behind Pierre was Xavière, with that timid, foolish expression on her face. Elisabeth was prepared for it, but it irritated her none the less. They were making fools of themselves, dragging this child with them wherever they went.

'Oh, how pretty!' said Xavière.

She looked at the room and then at Elisabeth with undisguised astonishment. She had a look which said: 'I would never have expected this of her.'

'This studio is a dream, isn't it?' said Françoise. She took off

215

her coat and sat down.

'Take off your coat, you'll be cold when you leave,' said Pierre to Xavière.

'I'd rather wear it,' said Xavière.

'It's very warm in here,' said Françoise.

'I assure you I'm not too warm,' said Xavière with gentle persistence. They both stared at her unhappily and then looked questioningly at each other. Elisabeth repressed a shrug. Xavière would never know how to dress; she was wearing an old lady's coat, much too big and drab for her.

'I hope you're hungry and thirsty,' said Elisabeth invitingly. 'Help yourselves. You've got to do justice to my supper.'

'I'm dying of hunger and thirst,' said Pierre. 'Besides, I make no bones about my atrocious appetite.' He smiled, and the others smiled too. All three of them looked hilarious and conspiratorial, almost to the point of seeming drunk.

'Sherry or vodka?'

'Vodka,' they said in chorus.

Pierre and Françoise preferred sherry, she was well aware; had Xavière gone so far as to impose her tastes on them? She filled the glasses. Pierre was sleeping with Xavière, there was not the slightest doubt; and the two women? That was quite possible – it made such a perfectly symmetrical trio. Sometimes they were to be seen in pairs – they must have arranged a rotation – but most often the complete outfit was to be seen arm in arm, walking in step.

'I saw you yesterday crossing the street at Montparnasse,' she said. She smiled slightly. 'You looked so funny.'

'Why funny?' said Pierre.

'You were holding each other by the arm, and you were hopping about from one foot to the other, the three of you together.'

When he became infatuated with someone or something, Pierre lost all sense of proportion; he had always been like that. What could he see in Xavière? – with her yellow hair, her expressionless face, her red hands – there was nothing attractive about her.

She turned to Xavière.

'Don't you want to eat anything?'

Xavière suspiciously examined the plates.

'Have one of these caviare canapés,' said Pierre. 'It's all delicious. Elisabeth, you're entertaining us royally.'

'And she's dressed like a princess,' said Françoise. 'It is certainly becoming to you to be smart.'

'It's becoming to everyone,' said Elisabeth. Françoise surely had more than adequate means to be just as chic, had she bothered.

'I think I'll try the caviare,' said Xavière after due consideration, and she took a sandwich and bit into it. Pierre and Françoise were watching her with passionate interest.

'How do you like it?' said Françoise.

Xavière took her time. 'It's good,' she said decisively.

The two faces relaxed. In view of their behaviour, it was obviously not this child's fault if she considered herself a goddess.

'Are you really recovered now?' Elisabeth asked Françoise.

'I've never felt so full of beans,' said Françoise. 'My illness obliged me to take a good long rest, and that has done me the world of good.'

She had even put on a little weight. She looked flourishing. With a suspicious glance, Elisabeth watched her swallow a foie gras canapé. Was there really no flaw in this happiness which they were so ostentatiously parading?

'Could I see your latest canvases? I'd like to very much,' said Pierre. 'It's such a long time since I've seen anything of yours. Françoise told me that you'd changed your style.'

'I'm in the very middle of a transition,' said Elisabeth, with ironic emphasis. Her pictures! Pigment spread on canvas so as to give the appearance of pictures; she spent her days painting in order to convince herself that she was a painter, but it was still nothing but a lugubrious game.

She took out one of her canvases, put it on an easel, and turned on a blue light. There, that was all part of the ritual! She would show them her fraudulent paintings and they would bestow fraudulent praise on her. They would not know that she knew: this time they were the dupes.

'Well yes, that's a radical change!' said Pierre.

He studied the picture with a look of genuine interest. It was a section of a Spanish arena with a bull's head in one corner, and rifles and corpses in the middle.

'That's not in the least like your first sketch,' said Françoise. 'You ought to show that to Pierre too, so that he can see the development.'

Elisabeth took out her 'Firing Party'.

'That's interesting,' said Pierre, 'but it's not as good as the other. I think you're quite right to avoid any kind of realism in the treatment of such subjects.'

Elisabeth turned searching eyes on him, but he seemed genuinely sincere.

'As you have seen, this is the line along which I'm now working,' she said. 'I'm trying to use the incoherence and freedom of the surrealists, but by giving them direction.'

She took out 'Concentration Camp', 'Fascist Landscape', and 'The Night of the Pogrom', which Pierre studied approvingly. Elisabeth threw a puzzled look at her pictures. After all, taking all things into consideration, wasn't it only a public that she lacked to become a real artist? Didn't every exacting artist regard himself in private as a dauber? The real artist is one whose work is real. In a sense, Claude was not completely wrong when he panted to have his play put on. A work of art only becomes real by becoming known. She chose one of her most recent canvases, 'The Game of Massacre'. As she was putting it on the easel, she caught a look of dismay which Xavière had directed at Françoise.

'Don't you care for pictures?' she said with a surface smile.

'I don't understand anything about it,' said Xavière apologetically.

Pierre turned to her quickly with an uneasy look, and Elisabeth felt a sudden wave of anger. They must have warned Xavière that this was part of the evening's entertainment, but she was beginning to grow impatient, for her slightest whim was accounted more important than Elisabeth's entire fate.

'What do you say to this?' she said.

It was a daring and complex painting which called for considerable comment. Pierre glanced at it hastily.

'I like it very much, too,' he said.

It was obvious that he only wanted to get it over and done with. Elisabeth took away the canvas.

'That's enough for today,' she said. 'We mustn't make a martyr of this child.'

Xavière cast a saturnine glance at her; she understood perfectly well that Elisabeth was not blind where she was concerned.

'You know, if you want to put on a record,' said Elisabeth to Françoise, 'you can easily do so. Only take a fine needle, because of the tenant below.'

'Oh, yes!' said Xavière eagerly.

'Why don't you try exhibiting this year?' said Pierre, lighting his pipe. 'I'm sure you'd interest a large public.'

'It's not the right moment,' said Elisabeth. 'In these uncertain times it would be madness to launch a new name.'

'Still, theatres are doing very well,' said Pierre.

Elisabeth looked at him, hesitated, then said point-blank: 'Did you know that Nanteuil has taken Claude's play?'

'Oh, yes,' said Pierre with a vague look. 'Is Claude pleased?'

'Not terribly,' said Elisabeth. Slowly, she inhaled the smoke of her cigarette. 'I'm absolutely heart-broken. It's one of those snap decisions that can ruin a man permanently.' She took her courage in both hands. 'Oh, if only you had taken *Partage*, Claude would have been made.'

Pierre looked embarrassed; he hated to refuse anyone anything. Only as a rule he managed to wriggle out of it when someone wanted to ask him for a favour.

'Listen,' he said. 'Would you like me to try to talk to Berger about it once more? It so happens that we're lunching with them.'

Xavière had put her arm round Françoise and was making her dance a rumba. Françoise's face was knit with concentration, as if her soul's salvation depended on her prowess.

'Berger won't go back on his rejection,' said Elisabeth. A flash of absurd hope struck her. 'He needn't come into it at all. You're the only one. Listen, you're putting on your play next winter; but not until October? If only you would put on *Partage* for a few weeks!'

She waited, her heart pounding. Pierre puffed at his pipe. He seemed uncomfortable.

'You know what's most likely to happen,' he said at last, 'is that next year we'll go on an extended tour.'

'Bernheim's famous plan?' said Elisabeth suspiciously. 'But I thought that you didn't want to have anything to do with it.'

She was defeated, but she would not let Pierre get out of it so easily.

'It's quite tempting,' said Pierre. 'We'll make money. We'll see the world.' He glanced at Françoise. 'Of course, it's not finally settled.'

Elisabeth thought a moment. Obviously, they would take Xavière with them. Pierre seemed capable of doing anything for a smile from her: perhaps he was ready to give up his work to treat himself to a triangular idyll travelling round the Mediterranean for a year.

'But if you didn't go?' she continued.

'If we didn't go . . .' Pierre repeated lackadaisically.

'Yes, would you put on *Partage* in October?'

She wanted to force a definite reply from him. He did not like to go back on his word.

Pierre drew at his pipe a few times.

'After all, why not?' he said without conviction.

'Do you mean that seriously?'

'Of course,' said Pierre in a more decided tone. 'If we stay, we can very easily open the season with *Partage*.'

He had agreed very quickly; he must be absolutely certain of going on that tour. In spite of everything, it was rash. If he did not carry out this plan, he would be committed.

'That would be absolutely marvellous for Claude!' she said. 'When will you be quite certain?'

'In another month or two,' said Pierre.

Silence fell.

'If there were some way of preventing this departure,' thought Elisabeth excitedly.

Françoise, who had been watching them out of the corner of her eye for some time, quickly joined them.

'It's your turn to dance,' she said to Pierre. 'Xavière never tires, but, as for me, I'm worn out.'

'You danced very well,' said Xavière. She smiled good-naturedly. 'You see, all that was needed was a little effort.'

'You have enough for two,' said Françoise gaily.

'We'll try again,' said Xavière in a gently threatening tone.

This highly affected badinage which they had begun to use among themselves had become irritating in the extreme.

'Excuse me,' said Pierre.

He went with Xavière to choose a record. She had finally decided to take off her coat. She had a slender body, but one in which the experienced eye of the painter could detect a tendency to stoutness: she would put on weight very quickly if she did not keep herself to a strict diet.

'She's quite right to watch herself,' said Elisabeth. 'She could easily fill out.'

'Xavière?' Françoise laughed. 'She's a reed.'

'Do you think it's quite fortuitous that she eats nothing?' said Elisabeth.

'It's certainly not because of her figure,' said Françoise; she seemed to find the idea completely ridiculous. She had been lucid about her for a while, but now she had become as complacently foolish as Pierre. As if Xavière were not a woman like any other! Elisabeth had seen through her. She saw that beneath the mask of a golden-haired virgin, she was susceptible to every human weakness.

'Pierre told me that you may go on a tour next winter,' she said. 'Is that serious?'

'There's some talk of it,' said Françoise; she seemed embarrassed. She did not know what Pierre had said and must be on her guard against blundering.

Elisabeth filled two glasses with vodka.

'What are you going to do with that child?' she said, shaking her head. 'I very much wonder!'

'Do with her?' said Françoise; she seemed dumbfounded. 'She's on the stage, you know.'

'First of all, she isn't,' said Elisabeth, 'and besides, that isn't what I mean.' She half-emptied her glass. 'She isn't going to spend her life hanging on to your coat-tails?'

'No, probably not,' said Françoise.

'Hasn't she any desire for a life of her own – love, adventure?'

Françoise gave her a one-sided smile.

'I don't think she's giving it much thought just now.'

'Not just now, naturally,' said Elisabeth.

Xavière was dancing with Pierre. She danced very well. She had on her face a smile so flirtatious that it was actually indecent. How could Françoise tolerate all that? A coquette, a sensualist, Elisabeth had seen it clearly. Certainly she was in love with Pierre, but she was a sly, fickle girl; she was capable of sacrificing everything to the pleasure of the moment. It was in her that the flaw could be found.

'What's become of your lover?' said Françoise.

'Moreau? We had a terrible row,' said Elisabeth. 'About pacifism. I teased him and then he got angry. He ended up by almost strangling me.' She rummaged in her bag. 'Here, look at his last letter.'

'I don't think he's so very stupid,' said Françoise. 'You've said so much to me against him.'

'Everyone thinks a lot of him,' said Elisabeth.

She had found him interesting in the beginning, and she

had enjoyed encouraging his love. Why was she so completely disgusted with him? She emptied out the contents of her bag. It was because he was in love with her. That was the best way to lose value in her eyes: she had at least kept the pride of being able to scorn any ridiculous feelings that she might inspire.

'His letter is most correct,' said Françoise. 'What did you answer?'

'I was really embarrassed,' said Elisabeth. 'It was very difficult to explain to him that I hadn't taken this affair seriously for one single minute. Besides . . .'

She shrugged her shoulders. How could she know what to think? She herself was bewildered. This sham friendship, which she had created for lack of anything better to do, might well have as much reality as painting, politics, or rows with Claude. It was all just like everything else – pointless play-acting.

She continued: 'He followed me as far as Dominique's, pale as a ghost, his eyes popping out of his head. He was furious. There was no one in the street. I was terrified.'

She gave a short laugh. She could not help speaking about him; however, she had not been afraid, there had been no scene. Just a poor fellow at his wits' end, attempting to express himself in words and awkward gestures.

'Just imagine, he pinned me against a lamp-post, grabbed me by the throat, while he shouted dramatically: "I'll have you, Elisabeth, or I'll kill you."'

'He really almost strangled you?' said Françoise. 'I thought that was only figurative.'

'Oh no,' said Elisabeth. 'He really seemed on the point of murder.'

It was irritating; if things were related just as they happened, people did not believe that they had ever happened at all; and then, as soon as they began to pay attention, they believed something other than what had actually taken place. She remembered his glassy eyes quite close to her face and his pale lips coming nearer and nearer to her mouth.

'I said to him: "Strangle me, but don't kiss me," and his hands tightened around my neck.'

'Well,' said Françoise, 'that would have been a fine *crime passionel*.'

'Oh, he let go at once,' said Elisabeth. 'I said: "This is

ridiculous," and he let go.'

She had almost felt disappointed, but even had he tightened his grip, held on until she collapsed, it would not really have been a crime. Just a clumsy accident. Never, never did anything decisive happen to her.

'Was it because of his passion for pacifism that he wanted to murder you?' said Françoise.

'He was incensed when I said that war was the only way of getting out of the mess in which we're living,' said Elisabeth.

'I feel for him in that,' said Françoise. 'I'd be afraid that the cure might be worse than the disease.'

'Why?' said Elisabeth.

She shrugged her shoulders. War. Why were they all so afraid of it? War at least was something solid; it did not turn into papier-mâché in your hand. Something real, at last: real deeds would be possible. Make ready the revolution: against that day she had begun to learn Russian. Perhaps at last she would be able to show what she had in her; perhaps it really was that circumstances were too insignificant for her.

Pierre had come over to them.

'Are you quite sure that war will lead to revolution?' he said. 'And even then, don't you think that that would be a very high price to pay?'

'It's because she's a fanatic,' said Françoise, with an affectionate smile. 'She would plunge Europe into a blood-bath to serve the cause.'

Elisabeth smiled.

'A fanatic . . .' she said quietly, and her smile fell abruptly. Surely they weren't letting themselves be fooled. They knew: she was quite hollow; there was no conviction except in words, and they, too, were artificial and theatrical.

'A fanatic!' she repeated, bursting into a strident laugh: that was a new one!

'What's up?' said Pierre with a look of annoyance.

'Nothing,' said Elisabeth. She said no more. She had gone too far. 'I've gone too far,' she thought. Too far – but then that, too, had been done deliberately, hadn't it? – that cynical disgust with herself – and this contempt for that disgust that she was in the process of working up, wasn't that also theatrical? And this doubt about the contempt . . . It was becoming maddening, if one set about being sincere, was there

223

really no end to it?

'We're going to say goodbye,' said Françoise. 'We must run along.'

Elisabeth started. They were all three standing before her, and they seemed very ill at ease: she must have had a strange look on her face during that silence.

'Goodbye. I'll drop in to the theatre one of these evenings,' she said as she accompanied them to the door. She went back to her studio. She walked to the table and poured out a large glass of vodka, and drank it in one go. And if she had gone on laughing? If she had shouted at them: 'I know, I know that you know!' They would have been astonished. But of what use was it? Tears and revulsions: they would have been theatrical, too, but more tiring and just as futile. There was no way out. In no place in the world, or within herself, had a vestige of truth been allotted to her.

She looked at the dirty plates, at the empty glasses, at the ash-tray filled with cigarette ends. They would not always triumph: there was something that could be done, something in which Gerbert was mixed up. She sat down on the edge of the couch. She remembered Xavière's pearly cheeks and fair hair, and Pierre's blissful smile while he was dancing with her. It was all whirling in her head like a saraband, but tomorrow she would be able to sort out her thoughts. Something that could be done; an authentic act that would make genuine tears flow. At that moment, perhaps, she would feel that she, too, was living in real earnest. Then, they would not go on tour: they would put on Claude's play. Then . . .

'I'm drunk,' she murmured.

There was nothing to do but sleep and wait for the morning.

Chapter Two

'Two black coffees, and one white, with croissants, please,'
Pierre said to the waiter. He smiled at Xavière. 'You're not
too tired?'

'I'm never tired when I'm enjoying myself,' said Xavière.
She had put down in front of her a bag of pink shrimps, two
huge bananas and three raw artichokes. None of them had
wanted to go home to bed after leaving Elisabeth's. They had
gone to the rue Montorgueil to have some onion soup and
then, to Xavière's delight, they had walked all round les Halles.

'How pleasant the Dôme is at this hour,' said Françoise.
The café was almost empty. A man in blue overalls was kneel-
ing on the floor wiping the soapy tiles, and this made the
place smell like a laundry. As the waiter was putting their
order on the table, a tall American woman in evening dress
threw a paper pellet at his head.

'She's had a bit too much,' he said with a smile.

'It's wonderful to see a drunk American woman,' said
Xavière in a serious tone. 'They're the only people who can
get dead drunk without at once going to pieces.'

She took two lumps of sugar, held them uncertainly for a
moment above her glass, and then dropped them into her
coffee.

'What are you doing, you little wretch?' said Pierre. 'Now
you won't be able to drink it.'

'But I did it deliberately, to neutralize it,' said Xavière. She
looked at Françoise and Pierre as if they were at fault. 'You
don't seem to know that you're poisoning yourselves with all
the coffee you drink.'

'You're a nice one to talk,' said Françoise. 'You guzzle tea;
that's still worse!'

'Ah, but I'm systematic,' said Xavière. She shook her head.
'But you, you drink that stuff without even thinking about it,
as if it were only skimmed milk.'

She really looked refreshed. Her hair was lustrous, her eyes
sparkled like enamels: Françoise noticed that the clear iris
was surrounded by a dark blue ring; there were always new

225

discoveries to be made in her face. Xavière had something fresh every time she looked at her.

'Just listen to them!' said Pierre.

A couple near the window were carrying on in whispers. The young woman was coquettishly fingering her black hair, held in place by a hair-net.

'That's how it is,' she was saying, 'nobody has ever really seen my hair. It belongs only to me.'

'But why?' said the young man in a passionate voice.

'Those women!' said Xavière with a scornful pout. 'They have to invent something unusual about themselves, otherwise they would feel so very ordinary.'

'That's true,' said Françoise. 'This girl is withholding her hair. With Eloy it's her virginity, and with Canzetti her art. It enables them to throw the rest to the wind.'

Xavière smiled faintly and Françoise noticed the smile with a little envy; it must give one a sense of power to feel of such high value to oneself.

Pierre had been staring at the bottom of his glass for some little while. His muscles had relaxed, his eyes were clouded and a look of childish suffering had spread over his features.

'Don't you feel a little better than you did earlier on?' asked Xavière.

'No,' said Pierre. 'No, poor Pierre doesn't feel any better.'

They had started this game in the taxi. Françoise was always amused when he improvised an act, but she took only the minor parts for herself.

'Pierre isn't poor. Pierre feels very well,' said Xavière with gentle authority. She thrust a threatening face very close to Pierre's.

'You do feel well, don't you?'

'Yes, I feel well,' said Pierre quickly.

'Then smile,' said Xavière.

Pierre's lips flattened out till they were stretched almost from ear to ear; at the same time his eyes became wild, and his contorted face tightened round his smile: it was amazing what he could do with his face. Suddenly, as if a spring had broken, his smile collapsed into a tearful pout. Xavière almost choked with laughter, and then, with all the pomposity of a hypnotist, she passed her hand over Pierre's face from forehead to chin. The smile came back. With a sly look, Pierre moved his finger downward across his mouth and the smile vanished. Xavière shook with laughter almost to the point of tears.

'Exactly what method do you use, Mademoiselle?' Françoise asked.

'A method all my own,' said Xavière modestly. 'A mixture of suggestion, intimidation and reasoning.'

'And you obtain good results?'

'Amazing!' said Xavière. 'If only you knew what a state he was in when I first took him in hand!'

'Yes, yes, of course,' said Françoise, 'it's most important to pay the strictest attention to the initial symptoms.' At this moment, the patient appeared to be very far gone. He was greedily munching tobacco straight from his pipe, like a donkey from its manger; his eyes were popping out of their sockets and he was really chewing the tobacco.

'Good God!' said Xavière in horror. Then she adopted a level tone of voice. 'Listen carefully,' she said, 'you ought to eat only what is edible. Pipe tobacco is not edible, therefore you are making a big mistake by eating tobacco.'

Pierre listened obediently, then he began eating from his pipe again.

'It's good,' he said earnestly.

'You'll have to try psycho-analysis,' said Françoise. 'Perhaps his father whipped him with an elder branch when he was a child?'

'What has that to do with it?' asked Xavière.

'Took a hiding, took to a smoke screen,' said Françoise. 'He eats tobacco to sublimate the hiding. The tobacco is also the pith of the elder which he is destroying through symbolic assimilation.'

Pierre's face was changing dangerously: it had become puce. His cheeks were swelling visibly and a pinkish blur was beginning to spread over his eyes.

'It's no longer good,' he said angrily.

'Stop that,' said Xavière. She took the pipe out of his hands.

'Oh!' said Pierre. He looked at his empty hands. 'Oh! oh, oh,' he wailed. He snivelled and quite suddenly tears rolled down his cheeks. 'Oh! I'm so unhappy!'

'You frighten me,' said Xavière, 'Stop it.'

'Oh! I'm so unhappy,' said Pierre. He was bawling, and had the terrifying face of a child undergoing a paroxysm.

'Stop,' said Xavière whose features were tense with fright.

Pierre began to laugh and wiped his eyes.

'What a poetic idiot you'd make,' said Françoise. 'It would be perfectly possible to fall in love with an idiot with a face like that.'

'You still have a chance,' said Pierre.

'Aren't there ever any idiot's parts on the stage?' said Xavière.

'I know of one superb one, in a play by Valle Inclam, but it's a silent part,' said Pierre.

'What a pity,' said Xavière with tender irony.

'Did Elisabeth pester you again about Claude's play?' Françoise asked. 'I thought I understood that you'd dodged it by saying that we were going on tour next winter.'

'Yes,' said Pierre absent-mindedly, as he stirred the remains of his coffee. 'In point of fact, why are you so set against this plan?' he said. 'If we don't go on tour next year, I'm very much afraid that we never shall.'

Françoise had a feeling of displeasure, but so slight that it almost surprised her. Everything was blurry and muted within her, as if an injection of cocaine had desensitized her soul.

'But there's also the risk that the play itself will never be produced,' she said.

'No doubt we'll still be able to work, even if we can no longer leave France,' said Pierre insincerely. He shrugged his shoulders. 'And besides, my play is not an end in itself. We've spent our lives working so hard, wouldn't you like a little change?'

Just at the very moment that they were nearing their goal! In the course of next year she would finish her novel, and Pierre would at last reap the fruits of ten years' work. She was acutely aware of the fact that a year's absence would entail some kind of disaster, but she remembered this with a listless indifference.

'Oh! as far as I'm concerned, you know how much I like travelling,' she said.

It wasn't even worth the effort to fight, she knew she was defeated; not by Pierre, however, but by herself. This shadow of resistance which still survived in her was not strong enough to give her any hope for carrying the fight through to a finish.

'Doesn't it thrill you to think of the three of us watching the coast of Greece draw nearer and nearer as we stand on the deck of the *Cairo-City*!' said Pierre. He smiled at Xavière.

'In the distance, we can see the Acropolis looking like any silly little monument. We'll jump into a taxi and go jolting into Athens: the road is very bumpy.'

'Then we'll dine and go afterwards to the Zapeion Gardens,' said Françoise. She looked happily at Xavière. 'It's quite likely that she'll love the grilled shrimps and lamb tripe, and even the resinous wine.'

'Of course I'll love it,' said Xavière. 'What disgusts me is the sensible cooking in France. Once there, I'll eat like an ogress, you'll see.'

'As far as that goes, it's nearly as disgusting as the food at that Chinese restaurant where you stuffed yourself full,' said Françoise.

'Shall we stay in one of those districts built over with little wood and corrugated-iron huts?' said Xavière.

'We can't. There's no hotel there,' said Pierre. 'They're just emigrant quarters. But we'll spend a lot of time there.'

It would be fun to see all that with Xavière; she would transfigure the most insignificant objects when she looked at them. Just now, while showing her the bistros round les Halles, with their piles of carrots and their beggars, Françoise felt she was discovering their full flavour for the first time. She took a handful of shrimps and began to shell them. Through Xavière's eyes, the swarming quays of the Piraeus, the blue boats, the dirty children, the taverns smelling of olive oil and grilled meat, would reveal a wealth of riches yet unknown. She looked at Xavière, then at Pierre. She loved them; they loved each other; they loved her. For weeks all three of them had been living in happy enchantment. And how precious was this moment, with the light of dawn on the empty banquettes of the Dôme, the smell of the soapy tiles, and this faint scent of fresh fish!

'Berger has some superb photographs of Greece,' said Pierre. 'I must ask him for them later.'

'Of course, I forgot that you're going to lunch with those people,' said Xavière, with a tender sulkiness.

'If it were only Paule, we would take you with us,' said Françoise. 'But with Berger there, it becomes formal.'

'We'll leave the whole company in Athens,' said Pierre, 'and we'll make a grand tour across the Peloponnese.'

'On mules?' asked Xavière.

'Partly on mules.'

'And we'll have lots of adventures,' said Françoise.

'We'll kidnap a beautiful little Greek girl,' said Pierre. 'Do you remember that little girl at Tripolis whom we felt so sorry for?'

'I remember her very clearly,' said Françoise. 'It's terrible to think that she'll probably spend the whole of her natural life stagnating in that kind of desert cross-roads.'

Xavière was beginning to look sullen. 'And after that, we'll have to drag her about with us. That'll be an awful nuisance,' she said.

'We'll send her off to Paris,' said Françoise.

'But she would be there when we got back,' said Xavière.

'Do you mean to say,' said Françoise, 'that if you were told that in some corner of the world someone very nice indeed was imprisoned and in utter misery, you wouldn't lift a finger to go and rescue him?'

'No,' said Xavière with a stubborn look, 'it wouldn't matter to me.' She looked at Pierre and Françoise, and suddenly added with bitterness: 'I don't want anyone else with us.'

It was childish, but Françoise felt as if a heavy cape had fallen on her shoulders. She ought to have felt free after all these renunciations, and yet she had never experienced the taste of freedom less than during these last few weeks. For the moment she felt as if she were bound hand and foot.

'You're right,' said Pierre. 'We three have enough to do as things are. Now that we've achieved a very harmonious trio, we've got to take advantage of it without bothering about anything else.'

'Still, supposing one of us met someone exciting?' said Françoise. 'It might well be to the common benefit; it's always a pity to limit oneself.'

'But what we've just built up is still so new,' said Pierre. 'We must first put a good long period behind us: after that any of us will be able to have adventures, leave for America, or adopt a Chinese child. But not before . . . let's say five years.'

'Yes,' said Xavière excitedly.

'Shake hands on that,' said Pierre, 'it's a pact. For five years each of us will devote himself exclusively to the trio.' He put his hand palm up on the table. 'I forgot that you don't like that gesture,' he said smiling.

'But I do,' said Xavière solemnly, 'it's a pact.' She put her hand on Pierre's,

'Agreed,' said Françoise, putting her hand out too.

Five years! How heavy those words sounded! She had never been afraid to commit herself to the future; but because the future had changed in character, it was not a free impulse of her whole being. What was it? She could not think, 'my future,' because she could not separate herself from Pierre and Xavière. But now she found it impossible to say, 'our future,' for that implied a future with Pierre alone. Together they had planned the same future for both: planned one life, one work, one love. But with Xavière there all that became meaningless. It was not possible to live with her, but only beside her. Despite the sweetness of the past few weeks Françoise was gripped with fear at the thought of long unchanging years ahead of them both: strange and fateful, they stretched into infinity like a black tunnel in which the twists and bends would have to be endured blindfold. This was not a proper future: it was a shapeless and unpeopled extension of time.

'It seems odd to be making plans at this time of day,' said Françoise. 'We've grown so used to living from day to day.'

'Then you've never really believed there'd be a war,' said Pierre. He smiled. 'Don't start now that things seem just about settled.'

'I don't think about it positively,' said Françoise, 'but the future is utterly obstructed.'

It was not so much because of the war; but it did not matter. She was happy enough, thanks to this ambiguity, to have had a chance to express her thoughts; she had long since ceased to be so scrupulously honest.

'It's true that we've imperceptibly begun to live without thinking of a tomorrow,' said Pierre. 'Almost everyone has reached that stage, even the most extreme optimists, I think.'

'That takes the meaning out of everything,' said Françoise. 'Nothing can be said to have any future now.'

'Wait! I don't think so,' said Pierre with an air of interest. 'On the contrary, it makes everything more precious, to my mind, to be menaced on all sides.'

'Everything seems pointless to me,' said Françoise. 'How can I explain it to you? In the old days, whatever I did, I had the impression of being thoroughly involved in things: for instance, in my novel. It existed. It demanded to be written. Nowadays, writing is simply heaping up pages.'

She pushed away the mound of tiny pink shells she had

emptied of their flesh. The young woman with her precious hair was now alone with two empty glasses; she had lost her animated look and was thoughtfully applying lipstick to her mouth.

'The point is that we've been torn from our own personal history,' said Pierre, 'but that seems to me to be all to the good.'

'Of course,' said Françoise with a smile. 'Even if there's war, you'll still find a way of getting something out of it.'

'But how can you expect a thing like that to happen?' said Xavière suddenly. She had an air of superiority. 'Surely people aren't stupid enough to wish to get themselves killed.'

'They aren't asked for their opinion,' said Françoise.

'All the same, it's the public who decide, and they're not all fools,' said Xavière with angry contempt.

Conversations about war or politics always irritated her, because of their empty frivolity. Nevertheless, Françoise was surprised by her aggressive tone.

'They're not all fools,' said Pierre, 'but they're abused. Society is a strange piece of mechanism; nobody can control it.'

'Well! I don't understand why people let themselves be crushed by that machine,' said Xavière.

'What do you want them to do?' said Françoise.

'Not to bow down their heads like sheep,' said Xavière.

'Then you must join a political party,' said Françoise.

Xavière interrupted her.

'Good God! I wouldn't want to dirty my hands by doing that.'

'In that case, you'll be one of the sheep,' said Pierre. 'It's always the same. You can't fight society except by social means.'

'In that case,' said Xavière, whose face had grown florid with rage, 'if I were a man, I wouldn't go when they came to get me.'

'That would be a great help,' said Françoise. 'They'd march you off between two policemen, and, if you were stubborn about it, they'd shove you up against a wall and shoot you.'

Xavière made a faint pout.

'Does it really seem to you so terrible to die?' she asked.

Xavière must be in a blind rage to argue with such deep dishonesty. Françoise felt that this outburst had been directed particularly at her, but she had no notion as to what fault

232

she had committed. She looked at Xavière in horror. What venomous thoughts had suddenly transformed this fragrant face which was lately redolent with tenderness? Malignantly they blossomed beneath her stubborn little forehead, under the shelter of her silky locks, and Françoise was defenceless against them. She loved Xavière. She could no longer stand her hatred.

'You said a little while ago that it was disgusting to let yourself be killed,' she said.

'But it's not the same if you die intentionally,' said Xavière.

'Killing yourself in order not to be killed is not dying intentionally!' said Françoise.

'In any case, I would prefer it,' said Xavière. She added with a faraway, weary air: 'And besides, there are other ways. It's always possible to desert.'

'That's not so easy, you know,' said Pierre.

Xavière's eyes softened, and she gave Pierre an ingratiating smile.

'Would you do it, if it were possible?' she said.

'No,' said Pierre, 'for a thousand reasons. First of all, I'd have to give up the idea of ever returning to France, and that's where I have my theatre, my public, that's where my work has a meaning and a chance of leaving some trace.'

Xavière sighed.

'That's true,' she said with a sad and disappointed expression. 'You drag so much dead weight about with you.'

Françoise shuddered. Xavière's words always held a double meaning. Did she also include Françoise in that dead weight? Did she resent Pierre's still loving her? Françoise had at times noticed sudden silences were she to break into a tête-à-tête, short spells of surliness were Pierre to speak to her for a little too long. These she had disregarded; but today, they seemed obvious. Xavière would have liked to feel that Pierre was free and alone in front of her.

'The dead weight,' said Pierre, 'why, it's myself! You can't differentiate between what a man feels and loves, and the life he's built for himself.'

Xavière's eyes were glistening.

'Well, as far as I'm concerned,' she said with a slightly theatrical shiver, 'I'd go anywhere, at any time. One should never be bound to a country or a profession: or to anybody or anything,' she concluded impetuously.

'But that's because you don't understand what a person does and what a person is. It's one and the same thing,' said Pierre.

'That depends on who the person is,' said Xavière. She was smiling to herself and bristling with defiance; she did nothing and she was Xavière; she was irrevocably Xavière.

After a short silence she said with vindictive modesty: 'Of course you know more about these things than I.'

'But you think that a little common sense is worth more than all this knowledge?' said Pierre cheerfully. 'Why did you suddenly decide to hate us?'

'I, hate you?' said Xavière. She stared with wide-eyed innocence, but her mouth remained tight. 'I'd have to be insane.'

'Did it irritate you to hear us drivelling on again about the war, when we were busy making such pleasant plans?'

'You surely have the right to talk about whatever you choose,' said Xavière.

'You think we enjoy creating a tragedy out of nothing,' said Pierre, 'but I assure you that it's not so. The situation demands careful consideration; the course of events is equally important to us and to you.'

'I know,' said Xavière with some embarrassment. 'But what good does it do to talk about it?'

'That we may be ready for anything,' said Pierre. He smiled. 'It's not bourgeois prudence. But if you really have a horror of being crushed in this world, if you don't want to be a sheep, there's nothing to do but to begin by weighing up your position very carefully.'

'But I don't understand anything about it,' said Xavière in a plaintive voice.

'No one can begin to understand in one day. First of all, you'll have to start reading the newspapers.'

Xavière pressed her hands against her temples.

'Oh! That's so boring,' she said. 'I don't know what to make of them.'

'That's quite true,' said Françoise. 'If you're not already well informed, the news slips between your fingers.'

Her heart was constricted by suffering and anger; it was through jealousy that Xavière hated these adult conversations in which she was unable to participate. The origin of all this fuss was that she could not bear Pierre's attention not to be directed to her every moment.

'Well, I know what I'll do,' said Pierre. 'One of these days, I'll give you a long lecture on politics, and after that I'll keep you regularly informed. It's really not so complicated, you know.'

'I'd like you to do that,' said Xavière happily. She leaned over towards Françoise and Pierre. 'Have you noticed Eloy? She's sat herself down at a table near the door, so that she can wheedle a few words out of you when you pass her.'

Eloy was dipping a croissant into her cup of coffee, and she was not made up. She looked shy and lonely and the effect was not unpleasing.

'Anyone seeing her like that and not knowing her would think her attractive,' said Françoise.

'I feel sure that she comes here for breakfast with the express purpose of meeting you,' said Xavière.

'She's quite capable of that,' said Pierre.

The café had been filling up. At a near-by table, a woman was writing letters with one eye on the cashier's desk, obviously haunted by the fear that a waiter would discover her and insist on her ordering something. But no waiter put in an appearance, even though a man near the window was rapping on his table with increasing vigour.

Pierre looked at the clock.

'We'll have to go home,' he said. 'I still have a hundred and one things to do before going to lunch with Berger.'

'Yes, now you've got to go just when everything's coming right again,' said Xavière resentfully.

'But everything was all right,' said Pierre. 'What's a little five-minute disagreement compared with the full enjoyment of this night?'

Xavière smiled shyly and they left the Dôme, waving a faint greeting to Eloy from a distance. Françoise found little pleasure in the thought of going to Berger's for lunch, but she was happy to have the opportunity of seeing Pierre by himself for a while, or at least of seeing him without Xavière. It was a brief glimpse of the outside world: she was beginning to feel stifled in this trio, which was in danger of becoming hermetically sealed.

Xavière amiably linked her arms with Françoise and Pierre, but her face was still downcast. They crossed over the road and reached the hotel without a word being spoken. There was an express letter in Françoise's pigeon-hole.

'It looks like Paule's handwriting,' said Françoise, as she opened the envelope.

'She's put us off,' she said. 'She has invited us to supper on the sixteenth instead.'

'Oh! What a godsend!' said Xavière, her eyes sparkling.

'It's a real bit of luck,' said Pierre.

Françoise said nothing. She kept turning the paper over in her hand. If only she had not opened it in front of Xavière, she might have withheld its message and spent the day alone with Pierre. Now it was too late.

'We'll go upstairs and freshen ourselves up a bit, and meet at the Dôme later,' she said.

'It's Saturday,' said Pierre. 'We can go to the flea-market, and we'll have lunch in the big blue shed.'

'Oh yes! That will be wonderful! What a godsend!' Xavière repeated with delight.

There was an almost tactless insistence in her joy.

They went upstairs. Xavière went into her room, and Pierre followed Françoise into hers.

'Aren't you sleepy?' he said.

'No, when we walk like that, a sleepless night isn't too tiring,' she said.

She began to wipe off her make-up. A nice cold sponge would soon put her right again.

'The weather is wonderful, we'll have a delightful day,' said Pierre.

'If Xavière is pleasant,' said Françoise.

'She will be; she always gets sullen when she thinks we're going to leave her behind.'

'That wasn't the only reason.' She hesitated, she was afraid that Pierre might think her accusations outrageous. 'I think she was angry because we'd had five minutes' conversation together.' Again she hesitated. 'I think she's a little jealous.'

'She's terribly jealous,' said Pierre. 'Have you only just noticed it?'

'I was wondering if I mightn't be wrong,' said Françoise. It always shocked her to see Pierre welcome with approval feelings she had been determinedly fighting within herself. 'She's jealous of me,' she added.

'She's jealous of everything,' said Pierre. 'Of Eloy, of Berger, of the theatre, of politics, of the fact that we think about war. She feels that it's disloyal of us. We're not supposed to worry about anything but her.'

'She was angry with me today,' said Françoise.

'Yes, because you expressed reservations about our future plans. She's jealous of you, not only because of me, but of you yourself.'

'I know,' said Françoise.

If Pierre had the intention of making her feel better, he was going the wrong way about it. She felt more and more oppressed.

'I find it wretched,' she said, 'for it means a love without any friendship. It makes you feel that you are simply an object of love, and not being loved for yourself alone.'

'That is her way of loving,' said Pierre.

He adjusted himself very nicely to this love. He even felt he had gained a victory over Xavière, while Françoise felt painfully at the mercy of this passionate, touchy heart, and she now existed only through Xavière's capricious feelings for her. This sorceress had taken possession of her wax image and was sticking pins into it to her heart's content. At this moment, Françoise was an undesirable, wretched, withered creature. She must wait for a smile from Xavière before regaining some self-respect.

'Well, we'll see what sort of mood she's in,' she said.

But it was true anguish to be dependent to this extent on that strange and rebellious conscience for her happiness and for her very being itself.

Joylessly, Françoise bit into a thick slice of chocolate cake: every mouthful stuck in her throat; she was furious with Pierre. He knew that Xavière, weary after a night without sleep, would be sure to go to bed early; and he might have guessed that, after the morning's misunderstanding, Françoise was eager to spend some time with her alone. When Françoise had recovered from her illness, they had drawn up certain hard and fast rules. On alternate days, she was to go out with Xavière from seven in the evening till midnight; and every other day Pierre was to see Xavière from two till seven. Each was free to spend the rest of the time as desired, but any tête-à-tête with Xavière was taboo. Françoise, at least, kept scrupulously to this curriculum: Pierre was more apt to suit his convenience. This evening he had really gone too far, in asking in a plaintive if playful tone not to be sent away before he had to go back to the theatre; he seemed to have no feeling of guilt. Perched on a high stool next to Xavière, he was telling her the story of Rimbaud's life with great animation. This story had been in the telling ever since they had been to the flea-market, but it had been interspersed with so many digressions that Rimbaud had not yet met Verlaine. Pierre was speaking. His words were giving a description of Rimbaud, but his voice seemed enriched by countless intimate allusions and Xavière was watching him with a kind of voluptuous docility. Their relationship was virtually chaste, and yet, through a few kisses and light caresses, he had established between them a sensual understanding, which was clearly visible beneath their reserve. Françoise looked away; she, as a rule, loved Pierre's story-telling, but tonight neither the inflections of his voice, nor his enchanting figures of speech, nor his unexpected turns of phrase affected her: she felt too much bitterness towards him. He was careful to explain almost daily to Françoise that Xavière was as fond of her as she was of him, but he deliberately behaved as if this feminine friendship seemed unimportant to him. It was certain that he easily held the first place, but that was no justification of his indiscreetness. Of course, there was no question of refusing him what he asked: he would have flown into a rage, and perhaps so would Xavière also. Yet, by cheerfully accepting Pierre's presence, Françoise seemed to take little account of Xavière. Françoise glanced into the floor-to-ceiling looking-glass behind the bar; Xavière was smiling at Pierre; she was obviously pleased that he was trying to monopolize her, but that was no good reason for her not to be angry with Françoise for permitting him to do so.

'Ah! I can just imagine how furious Madame Verlaine was,' said Xavière with a burst of laughter.

Françoise felt as if her heart were drowning in misery. Did Xavière always hate her? She had been amiable throughout the afternoon, but in some superficial way, because the weather was heavenly and the flea-market had enchanted her. It was all meaningless. 'And what can I do if she does hate me?' thought Françoise. She lifted her glass to her lips and noticed that her hands were trembling; she had drunk too much coffee during the day, and impatience was making her jittery. She could do nothing, she had no real hold on this stubborn little soul, not even on the beautiful living body protecting it: a warm, lithe body, not aloof to a man's hands, but one which now confronted Françoise like a rigid suit of armour. She could only wait, without stirring, for the verdict that would acquit or condemn her; and she had now been waiting ten hours.

'It's squalid!' she thought suddenly.

She had spent the day watching Xavière's every frown, her every intonation; at this moment, she was still absorbed in this despicable anguish, separated from Pierre and the delightful surroundings reflected back to her by the looking-glass, and separated from herself.

'And if she hates me, what then?' she thought defiantly. Was it not possible to consider Xavière's hatred exactly as she did the cheese-cakes on a plate? They were a beautiful pale yellow, decorated with pink arabesques; she might also have been tempted to eat one, had she not known their taste too well, as sour as that of a new-born child. Xavière's small round head did not occupy much more space in the world, it could be enveloped in a single glance; and if this haze of hatred issuing from it in clouds could only be forced back into its container, then it, too, could be kept under control. She had only to say the word, and, with the sound of crumbling plaster, the hatred would dissolve into a cloud of dust, to be perfectly contained in Xavière's body, and become as harmless as the familiar taste hidden under the yellow cream of the cakes. She felt that she existed, but that made very little difference, for she was writhing hopelessly in whorls of rage: she could see passing over Xavière's defenceless face only a few faint eddies, as unexpected and steadily errant as clouds in the sky. 'They're simply thoughts passing through her head,' thought Françoise. For a moment she thought the words must have taken effect, for nothing but little trails were now flitting in disorder over her face beneath its fair tresses, and, if she took her eye off them, even for an instant, they were no longer to be seen.

'Unfortunately, I've got to go! Look here, I am late already,' said Pierre.

He jumped down from his stool and put on his trench-coat: he had given up wearing his old man's soft silk scarf, and he looked very young and gay. Françoise put her hand out to him with tenderness, but it was a tenderness as lonely as her rancour. He was smiling, and his smile hung poised before her eyes without becoming one with the beating of her heart.

'I'll see you tomorrow; ten o'clock at the Dôme,' said Pierre.

'Good, see you tomorrow,' said Françoise. Indifferently, she shook his hand, and then she watched it close round Xavière's hand. And she could see from Xavière's smile that the pressure of his fingers was a caress.

Pierre departed and Xavière turned to Françoise. 'Thoughts passing through her head . . .' That was easy to say, but Françoise did not believe in those thoughts, they were only a delusion; the magic word would have had to spring from the depths of her soul, but her soul was too numbed. The maleficent mist still remained suspended across the world, poisoning sounds and lights, and penetrating to the very marrow of her bones. She would have to wait until it dissipated of itself: wait, and watch, and suffer, squalidly.

'What shall we do?' she said.

'Whatever you like,' said Xavière with a charming smile.

'Would you prefer a walk or shall we go to some place?'

Xavière hesitated. She must have had a very definite idea in the back of her mind.

'What would you say to going to the Negro dance-hall?' she said.

'Why, that's a wonderful idea,' said Françoise. 'It's ages since we've been there.'

They left the restaurant and Françoise took Xavière's arm. This was a very solemn occasion that Xavière was suggesting: whenever she wanted particularly to show her affection for Françoise she made a point of inviting her to dance. It was also possible that she quite simply felt in the mood to go to the Negro dance-hall for her own amusement.

'Shall we walk a little?' she said.

'Yes, let's go up the boulevard Montparnasse,' said Xavière. She disengaged her arm. 'I'd rather I gave you my arm,' she explained.

Françoise complied submissively, and as Xavière's fingers touched her own, she gently squeezed them; the velvety suède-gloved hand surrendered to her hand with tender trust. Happiness began to dawn for Françoise, but she did not yet know if she ought really to believe in it.

'Look, there's the beautiful dark girl with her Hercules,' said Xavière.

They were holding hands; the wrestler's head looked minute

on the top of his tremendous shoulders; the girl was laughing resplendently.

'I'm beginning to feel at home,' said Xavière, as she glanced with pleasure over the terrace of the Dôme.

'You've taken your time over it,' said Françoise.

Xavière breathed a faint sigh.

'Ah! When I think of the old streets in Rouen – in the evening – all round the Cathedral, my heart breaks!'

'You weren't so fond of it when you were there,' said Françoise.

'It was so poetic,' said Xavière.

'Are you going back to see your family?'

'Of course. I'm definitely going there this summer.' Her aunt wrote to her every week. In the end, they had taken things far better than could have been expected. Suddenly, the corners of her mouth dropped, and she had the tired look of a much older woman. 'I knew how to live alone in those days. I'm amazed when I think how I used to feel things.'

Xavière's regrets always covered up some resentment. Françoise put herself on the defensive.

'And yet I can remember that even then you complained of being dried up,' said Françoise.

'Things weren't as they are now,' said Xavière in a hollow voice. She looked down and murmured: 'Now, I'm diluted.'

Before Françoise could reply she gaily squeezed her arm.

'Why don't you buy some of those lovely caramels?' she said, stopping in front of a shop as pink and shiny as a baptismal gift of sugared almonds.

In the window, a huge wooden tray was turning on its own axis, proffering to tempted eyes stuffed dates, glazed nuts and chocolate truffles.

'Do buy something,' said Xavière.

'If we are to make it a wonderful solemn occasion, we mustn't make ourselves sick, as we did the last time,' said Françoise.

'Oh! One or two tiny caramels,' said Xavière, 'would be quite safe.'

She smiled. 'This shop has such really beautiful colours, I feel as if I'm walking into a picture come to life.'

Françoise opened the door. 'Don't you want anything?' she said.

'I'd like some Turkish Delight,' said Xavière. She studied the sweets with a look of enchantment. 'Suppose we take some of that too,' she said, pointing to some thin sticks of barley sugar wrapped in transparent paper. 'It has such a pretty name.'

'Two of caramels, one of Turkish Delight, and half a pound of "fairy fingers",' said Françoise.

The shop assistant put the sweets into a little crinkly paper bag tied with a pink ribbon run through the top as a draw-string.

'I'd buy the sweets just for the bag,' said Xavière. 'It looks like an alms-purse. I've got half a dozen of them already,' she added proudly.

She offered Françoise a caramel, and then bit into one of the tiny gelatinous squares.

'We look like two little old women offering each other delicacies,' said Françoise. 'It's shameful.'

'When we're eighty, we'll slowly totter along to the sweet-shop, and we'll stand for two hours in front of the window arguing about the flavour of the Turkish Delight and slobber-ing a little,' said Xavière. 'The people of the neighbourhood will point their fingers at us.'

'And we'll shake our heads and say: "These aren't like the caramels we used to buy!"' said Françoise. 'We won't be going along much more slowly than we are now.'

They smiled at each other. Whenever they strolled along the boulevard, they were apt to slip into an octogenarian's pace.

'Would it bore you to look at those hats?' said Xavière stopping in front of a milliner's shop.

'Would you by any chance like to buy yourself one?'

Xavière laughed.

'It's not that I dislike them, it's my face that objects. No, I was looking for you.'

'Would you like me to wear a hat?' said Françoise.

'You'd look so lovely in one of those little sailor hats,' said Xavière in a pleading tone. 'Just think of your face under it. And when you go to a smart party you could put on a big veil and tie it in a huge bow at the back.' Her eyes were shining. 'Oh! Do promise that you'll do it.'

'A veil! I'm a little frightened of that,' said Françoise.

'But you can wear anything,' said Xavière, back to her pleading. 'Ah! If only you'd let me choose your clothes!'

'Well!' said Françoise gaily. 'You'll choose my spring wardrobe. I'll put myself in your hands.'

She squeezed Xavière's hand. How delightful she could be! One had to excuse her abrupt changes of mood; the situation was not an easy one, and she was so young. Françoise looked at her with tenderness: she did so want Xavière to have a beautiful, happy life.

'What exactly did you mean just now when you complained you were being diluted?' she asked softly.

'Oh! No more than that,' said Xavière.

'But what did you mean?'

'Just that.'

'I do so want you to be satisfied with your existence,' said Françoise.

Xavière did not reply. All her cheerfulness had suddenly faded.

'Do you find that by living so intimately with other people you lose something of yourself?' Françoise enquired.

'Yes,' said Xavière. 'You become a parasite.'

Her voice was deliberately cutting. Françoise thought that, in point of fact, it had not been so displeasing to her to live among people. She even grew quite angry when Pierre and Françoise went out without her.

'And yet you still have a great many moments alone,' she said.

'But that's no longer the same thing,' said Xavière. 'That's no longer truly being alone.'

'I understand,' said Françoise. 'Now, these are only blank intervals, while before they were filled.'

'That's quite right,' said Xavière sadly.

Françoise thought for a moment. 'But don't you think it would be different if you tried to make something of yourself? That's the best way of not becoming diluted.'

'And what am I to do?' said Xavière.

She looked quite crestfallen. Françoise wanted with all her heart to help her; but it was difficult to help Xavière. She smiled.

'Become an actress, for example,' she said.

'Ah! an actress,' said Xavière.

'I'm so sure that you could be one, if only you would work,' said Françoise warmly.

'Oh! no,' said Xavière wearily.

'You can't be certain of it.'

'That's just it. It's so pointless to work without knowing,' Xavière shrugged her shoulders. 'Even the most insignificant of those girls believes that she will be an actress.'

'It doesn't prove that you won't be one.'

'The chances are one in a hundred,' said Xavière.

Françoise squeezed her arm more tightly.

'What strange reasoning,' she said. 'Listen, I don't think it's possible to calculate your chances. On the one hand, there's everything to gain, and on the other, nothing to lose. You must bank on success.'

'Yes, you've already told me that,' said Xavière. She shook her head mistrustfully. 'I don't like acts of faith.'

'It's not an act of faith. It's a bet.'

'It's all the same thing.' Xavière made a little face. 'That's how Canzetti and Eloy console themselves.'

'Yes, those are the compensatory myths; it's nauseating,' said Françoise. 'But it's not a question of dreaming, it's a question of willing. That's different!'

'Elisabeth wants to be a great artist,' said Xavière. 'That's a pretty sight!'

'I wonder,' said Françoise. 'I have a feeling that she puts the myth into action the better to believe it, but that she's incapable of really willing anything.' She thought for a moment. 'You think that you're something ready-made once and for all, but I don't think so. I think you make yourself what you are of your own free will. It wasn't pure chance that Pierre was so ambitious in his youth. You know what was said about Victor Hugo? That he was a lunatic who thought he was Victor Hugo'

'I can't bear Victor Hugo,' said Xavière. She quickened her pace. 'Couldn't we walk a little faster? It's cold, don't you think?'

'Let's walk faster,' said Françoise. She continued: 'I do so want to convince you. Why have you so little confidence in yourself?'

'I don't want to lie to myself,' said Xavière. 'I think it's disgraceful to have blind faith; nothing is certain except what you can put your hand on.'

She looked at her closed fist with a queer bitter sneer. Françoise looked at her uneasily. What was going on in her mind? Surely during these weeks of peaceful happiness she had not been dormant. A thousand things had been going on inside her, behind her smiles. She had forgotten none of them; they were all there, tucked away, and after throwing off a few sparks, they would cause an explosion one fine day.

They turned the corner of the rue Blomet. The big red cigar of the café-tobacco-shop came into view.

'Have one of these sweets,' said Françoise, by way of a diversion.

'No, I don't like them,' said Xavière.

Françoise pressed one of the thin transparent sticks of barley sugar between her fingers.

'I think they have a pleasant taste,' she said. 'A dry, pure taste.'

'But I loathe purity,' said Xavière, screwing up her mouth.

Again Françoise was struck with anguish. What was too pure? The life in which they were imprisoning Xavière? Pierre's kisses? She herself? 'You have such a pure profile,' Xavière had said to her from time to time. They had reached a door on which was written in bold white letters: *Bal Colonial*. They went in. A crowd was surging round the pay desk: black, pale yellow, and café-au-lait faces: Françoise got in line to buy two tickets: seven francs for ladies, nine francs for men: the rumba going on behind the wooden partition was throwing all her thoughts into confusion. What precisely had happened? Naturally, it was always inadequate to explain Xavière's reactions on the basis of a momentary caprice: to find the key to it, she would have had to think back over the events of these past two months; all the same, the old, carefully buried grievances never came to life except through the perversity of the moment. Françoise tried to remember. Along the boulevard Montparnasse, the conversation had been light and easy: and then, instead of continuing, Françoise had suddenly jumped to serious subjects. It happened to be prompted by tenderness, but did she know how to be tender only with words at a time when she had Xavière's velvety hand in her own and her perfumed hair brushing against her cheek? Was that it? Was it that, was it really her ill-adjusted sense of purity?

'Look, there's the whole crowd from Dominique's,' said Xavière as she walked into the large hall.

There was the Chanaud girl, Lise Malan, Dourdin, Chaillet ... Françoise nodded to them and smiled, while Xavière cast a sleepy glance in their direction; she had not let go of

Françoise's arm, for she did not dislike having people take them for a couple when they entered a place: it was the kind of provocation which gave her amusement.

'That table over there will be fine,' she said.

'I'll have a Martinique punch,' said Françoise.

'I'll have one too,' said Xavière. She added contemptuously: 'I can't understand how people can stare at one with such bovine vulgarity. And I don't care a damn, anyway.'

Françoise experienced real pleasure at feeling herself included in the stupid spite of the whole of that bunch of gossips; she felt that they were being cut off together from the rest of the world and imprisoned in an impassioned tête-à-tête.

'You know, I'll dance as soon as you like,' said Françoise. 'I feel inspired this evening.' Excepting rumbas, she danced well enough not to look foolish. Xavière's face brightened.

'Really? It won't bore you?'

Xavière put her arm firmly around her. She danced with an absorbed look and without glancing about her, but she was not bovine: she knew how to see without appearing to look; it was even one of the talents in which she took such pride. She found it very gratifying to attract attention and she was not unintentionally holding Françoise tighter than usual, and smiling at her with decided assurance. Françoise returned her smile. Dancing made her head spin a little. She felt Xavière's beautiful warm breasts against her, she inhaled her sweet breath. Was this desire? But what did she desire? Her lips against hers? Her body surrendered in her arms? She could think of nothing. It was only a confused need to keep for ever this lover's face turned towards hers, and to be able to say with passion: 'She is mine.'

'You danced extremely well,' said Xavière as they reached their table.

She remained on her feet: the orchestra had struck up a rumba and a mulatto came over and bowed to her with a courteous smile. Françoise sat down at the table with the punch now on it and drank a mouthful of the syrupy liquid. In this huge room, decorated with pale frescoes and resembling in its banality a private banqueting room, most of the faces were coloured; from ebony to pinkish ochre, every shade of skin could be found here. These Negroes danced with untrammelled obscenity, but their movements had such pure rhythm that in its elemental simplicity the rumba kept the sacred character of a primitive rite. The whites who mingled with them were far less happy; the women, in particular, resembled either inflexible machines or hysterical creatures in a trance. Xavière was the only one whose perfect grace gave the lie to both the obscenity and the decorum.

Xavière refused a second invitation with a shake of her head and she returned to sit down beside Françoise.

'These Negresses have the very devil in them,' she said angrily. 'I'll never be able to dance like that.'

She touched her glass with her lips.

'Oh! how sweet that is! I can't drink it,' she said.

'You dance extremely well, you know,' said Françoise.

'Yes, for a civilized person,' said Xavière scornfully. She was staring at something in the middle of the dance floor. 'She's still dancing with that litle creole,' she said. Her eyes indicated Lise Malan. 'She hasn't let go of him since we arrived.' She added dolefully: 'He's disgracefully pretty.'

It was quite true. He was attractive, and looked very slender in his tight-fitting fawn-pink jacket. An even more doleful groan escaped from Xavière's lips.

'Ah!' she said, 'I'd give one year of my life to be that Negress for just one hour.'

'She's beautiful,' said Françoise. 'She hasn't got negroid features. Don't you think she must have Indian blood?'

'I don't know,' said Xavière with a downcast look. But her admiration had brought a gleam of hatred into her eyes.

'Or else, I'd have to be rich enough to buy her and keep her locked up in the house,' said Xavière. 'Baudelaire did that, didn't he? Just think, when you came back home, instead of finding a dog or a cat, this magnificent creature would be purring in front of the fireplace!'

A naked, black body stretched out in front of a fireplace . . . Was that what Xavière was dreaming of? How far did her dreams go?

'I loathe purity.' How could Françoise have overlooked the sensual line of her nose, of her mouth? Her avid eyes, her hands, her sharp teeth visible between her partly opened lips were in search of something to seize, something tangible. Xavière did not yet know what; sounds, colours, perfumes, bodies, everything was her prey. Or did she know?

'Come, let's dance,' she said suddenly.

Her hands grasped hold of Françoise, but it was not Fran-

247

çoise and her well-meaning tenderness which they coveted. The very first evening they had met, there had been a vacillating blaze in Xavière's eyes. It had died. It would never come to life again. 'How could she love me?' thought Françoise with pain. Delicate and dry, like the scorned taste of the barley sugar, with stern, too placid features, a transparently pure soul, Olympian – as Elisabeth used to say – Xavière would not have given one hour of her life to feel within herself this cold perfection she piously worshipped. 'And this is I,' thought Françoise with some disgust. In the past, when she had taken no notice of it, this blundering clumsiness barely existed: now it pervaded her whole person, and her gestures – her thoughts even – were angular and sharp, cutting; her perfectly adjusted equilibrium had turned into empty sterility. This mass of bare and translucent whiteness with its jagged edges was, for all she might think to the contrary, herself; irrevocably herself.

'You aren't tired?' she said to Xavière as they reached their table.

There were faint rings under Xavière's eyes.

'Yes, I am tired,' said Xavière. 'I'm getting old.' She pouted. 'And what about you?'

'A little,' said Françoise. Dancing, drowsiness and the sweet taste of light rum were turning her stomach.

'Of course we always see each other in the evening,' said Xavière. 'We can't be fresh.'

'That's true,' said Françoise. She added hesitantly: 'Labrousse is never free in the evening. We have to keep the afternoons for him.'

'Yes, naturally,' said Xavière, her face contracting.

Françoise looked at her with a sudden hope, more painful than her regrets. Did Xavière resent her discreet self-effacement? Had she hoped that Françoise would compel and force her love on her? Still, she should have understood that Françoise was not wantonly resigning herself to the fact that Pierre was preferred to her.

'We could perhaps make other arrangements,' said Françoise.

Xavière cut her short.

'No, everything's fine just as it is,' she said quickly.

She made a grimace. This idea of making arrangements was loathsome to her; she would have liked to see Pierre and Françoise completely at her beck and call, without any programme attached: that, after all, was asking too much.

Suddenly she smiled.

'Ah! He's fallen into the trap,' she said.

Lise Malan's creole was coming towards them with a shy and winning air.

'Did you make up to him?' she said.

'Oh! Not for his good looks,' said Xavière. 'I did it just to annoy Lise.'

She got up and followed the young man to the middle of the dance floor. It had been discreetly accomplished, for Françoise had not noticed either the slightest glance or the faintest smile. Xavière would never cease to astonish her.

She picked up the glass Xavière had barely touched and drank half of it: if only it could have revealed the thoughts in that mind! Was she angry with her for having accepted her love for Pierre? . . . 'Yet I did not ask her to love him,' she thought with anger. Xavière had made a free choice. What exactly had she chosen? What sincerity lay beneath her cajolery, her displays of tenderness, her jealousies? Was there indeed any sincerity? Françoise suddenly felt she was on the verge of hating her: there she was dancing, and dazzling in her white blouse with its wide sleeves, a tinge of pink glowing in her cheeks. She was looking at the creole, beaming with delight, and she was beautiful. Beautiful, alone, carefree, she was living her personal history, with the sweetness or cruelty dictated by each instant; her story, into which Françoise had put her whole being. And Françoise had to struggle unaided in front of her, while she smiled contemptuously or approvingly. What exactly did she want? Françoise had to guess; she had to guess everything: what Pierre felt, what was good, what was evil, and what she herself really and truly wanted. Françoise emptied her glass. She saw nothing clearly any more, nothing at all. Shapeless wreckage lay all about her; within her a great emptiness and darkness without.

The orchestra stopped playing for a minute and then the dancing was resumed. Xavière stood facing her creole, a few paces away from him. They were not touching one another, and yet a single shudder seemed to pass through both their bodies. At this moment, Xavière wanted to be nothing other than herself: her own charm filled her to the full. And suddenly, Françoise found that she, too, was overwhelmed. Now, she was nothing but a woman lost in a crowd, a minute particle of the world, wholly drawn towards that infinitesimal golden-haired flake, of which she was indeed incapable of catching hold; but here, in this abject state into which she had fallen, she was vouchsafed what she had vainly desired six months earlier, at the height of her happiness: this music, these faces, these lights changed into regret, into waiting, into love. They commingled with her, and gave an irreplaceable meaning to each beat of her heart. Her happiness was shattered, but it was falling all round her in a shower of impassioned moments.

Xavière came back to the table, staggering a little. 'He dances divinely,' she said. She leaned back in her chair and suddenly her face fell. 'Oh! I'm so tired,' she said.

'Do you want to go home?' said Françoise.

'Oh, yes! I do so want to go,' said Xavière pleadingly.

They left the dance-hall and got into a taxi. Xavière collapsed on to the seat and Françoise slipped her arm round her; as she closed her hand over the small, limp hand, she felt torn by a kind of joy. Whether she wanted to be or not, Xavière was bound to her by a bond stronger than hatred or love; to her, Françoise was not prey along with the rest, she was the very substance of her life, and moments of passion, of pleasure, of covetousness could not have existed without this firm web that supported them. Whatever happened to Xavière, happened through Françoise, and even if she wanted it or not, Xavière belonged to her.

The taxi stopped in front of the hotel, and they hurried upstairs. Despite her weariness, Xavière's walk had lost nothing of its majestic spring. She opened the door of her room.

'I'll come in for just a moment,' said Françoise.

'Just coming home makes me feel less tired,' said Xavière. She took off her jacket and sat down beside Françoise, and all Françoise's precarious calm was wrecked. Xavière was sitting there, bolt upright, in her dazzling blouse, close beside her and smiling, yet beyond reach: no bond fettered her except that which she decided to forge for herself: she could only be held by her own consent.

'It was a delightful evening,' said Françoise.

'Yes,' said Xavière. 'We'll have to do that again.'

Françoise looked around her anxiously; solitude would close in on Xavière, the solitude of her room, and of sleep, and of her dreams. There would be no way of breaking in.

'You'll end up by dancing as well as the Negress.'

'Oh no! That's impossible,' said Xavière.

Silence fell again, heavily, words were powerless; paralysed by the frightening grace of this beautiful body that she could not even desire, Françoise was at a loss for a gesture.

Xavière's eyes closed and she smothered a childlike yawn. 'I think I'm falling asleep where I am,' she said.

'I'll leave you now,' said Françoise. She stood up; she had a lump in her throat, but there was nothing else to do; there was nothing else she could do.

'Good night,' she said.

She was standing near the door. Impulsively, she took Xavière in her arms.

'Good night, dear Xavière,' she said brushing her lips over her cheek.

Xavière yielded, and for a moment she was light and taut against her shoulder. What was she waiting for? For Françoise to let her go, or for her to embrace her more tightly? She gently withdrew her arms.

'Good night,' she said in a completely natural voice.

There was nothing else to be done. Françoise climbed the stairs. She was ashamed of that futile gesture of tenderness. She dropped on to her bed with a heavy heart.

Chapter Three

'April, May, June, July, August, September, six months' training and I'll be ready for the slaughter,' thought Gerbert.

He stood planted in front of the bathroom mirror, adjusting the wings of the magnificent bow tie he had just borrowed from Péclard: he wanted very much to know whether or not he would be afraid, but in matters of that sort it was impossible to tell; the most dreadful thing imaginable was the cold . . . when you take off your shoes and see that your toes have remained inside.

'There's no further hope this time,' he thought with resignation. It seemed unbelievable that people could be warped enough to decide in cold blood to commit the world to fire and slaughter. But the fact remained that German troops had entered Czechoslovakia, and England was being rather obstinate on the subject.

With an expression of satisfaction, Gerbert studied the beautiful bow he had just tied: he disapproved of neckties, but he had no idea where Labrousse and Françoise would take him for dinner. They both had a vicious passion for cream sauces and, Françoise could say what she liked, one did attract attention when one wore a sweater in any of those restaurants with check tablecloths. He put on his jacket and went into the living-room. The room was empty; he carefully selected two cigars from Péclard's desk and then went into Jacqueline's bedroom. Gloves, handkerchiefs, rouge, Lanvin's *Arpeggio* – an entire family could have been fed on the money paid for these frivolities. Gerbert stuffed a packet of Greys and a bag of chocolates into his pocket; Françoise's only weakness was her passion for sweets; one could allow her that. Gerbert was grateful to her for so often unashamedly wearing down-at-heel shoes and caught stockings. In her room at the hotel, no impeccable elegance affronted the eye; she owned neither knick-knacks nor embroideries, nor even a tea service; and besides, one never had to play up to her. She was not given to coquetry, to headaches, to abrupt changes of mood; she demanded no special consideration: one could even remain silent and in peace by her side.

Gerbert slammed the door behind him and dashed down the three flights of stairs at top speed: forty seconds – Labrousse could never have precipitated himself down that dark, winding staircase so speedily; sometimes he did win the race unfairly by a stroke of luck. Forty seconds; Labrousse would surely accuse him of exaggerating. 'I'll say thirty seconds,' Gerbert decided. 'In that way, we can work back to the truth.' He crossed the place Saint-Germain-des-Prés; they had arranged to meet him at the Café de Flore; they liked the place because they did not go there very often, but as far as he was concerned, he was fed up to the teeth with all that intellectual elite. 'Next year I'll have a change of air,' he said fiercely. 'If Labrousse arranges that tour, it will be great.' He looked quite determined. Gerbert pushed open the door. Next year, he would be in the trenches, there could be no question about it. He walked through the café smiling vaguely all around him, then his smile broadened. Considered singly, each one of the three was slightly comic, but when they were all together, then it was a real scream.

'What are you splitting your face about?' said Labrousse.

Gerbert waved his hand helplessly.

'Why, because I caught sight of you,' he said.

They were sitting in a row on a banquette, with Françoise and Pierre on either side of Pagès. He sat down opposite them.

'Are we so comical?' said Françoise.

'You've no idea,' said Gerbert.

Labrousse looked at him out of the corner of his eye.

'Well, how does the idea of a lively little holiday along the Rhine strike you?'

'Lousy,' said Gerbert. 'And you it was who kept on saying that it looked as if everything were being settled.'

'This last blow has come as a complete surprise,' said Labrousse.

'We're in for it this time, that's certain,' said Gerbert.

'I think we have far less chance of escaping it than in September. England explicitly guaranteed Czechoslovakia. She can't back out.'

There was a short silence. Gerbert always felt embarrassed in Pagès's presence: even Labrousse and Françoise seemed ill at ease. Gerbert pulled the cigars out of his pocket and handed them to Labrousse.

'Take 'em,' he said. 'They're big 'uns.'

Labrousse breathed a low whistle of approval.

'Péclard does himself well! We'll smoke them after dinner.'

'Here's something for you,' said Gerbert, putting down the cigarettes and chocolate in front of Françoise.

'Oh! Thank you,' said Françoise.

The smile which lit her face was a little like those in which she so often tenderly included Labrousse: it made Gerbert feel good to see it; there were moments when he almost thought Françoise was fond of him; yet, she had not seen him for a very long time; she hardly gave him a thought: she was concerned only with Labrousse.

'Help yourself,' she said, offering the bag to the table at large.

Xavière shook her head with a guarded look.

'Not before dinner,' said Pierre. 'You'll spoil your appetite.'

Françoise bit into a chocolate; she would probably devour the full contents in a few munches: it was fantastic, the quantity of sweets she could get down without making herself sick.

'What will you have?' said Labrousse.

'A Pernod,' said Gerbert.

'Why do you drink Pernod when you don't like it?'

'I don't like Pernod, but I do like drinking Pernod,' said Gerbert.

'That's just like you,' said Françoise, laughing.

Again silence fell; Gerbert had started to smoke his pipe; he leant over his empty glass and slowly blew smoke into it.

'Do you know how to do that?' he said to Labrousse, as a challenge.

The glass filled with creamy, curling spirals.

'It looks like ectoplasm,' said Françoise.

'You've only to blow gently,' said Pierre. He took a pull at his pipe and then he too bent over with an air of concentration.

'Well done,' said Gerbert with condescension. 'Here's to you.'

He clinked his glass against Pierre's and in one gulp inhaled the smoke.

'You are proud of yourself,' said Françoise, smiling at Pierre whose face was beaming with satisfaction. She looked regretfully at the remains of the chocolates, then resolutely put them in her bag. 'You know, if we want to have enough time to eat, we ought to leave now,' she said.

Once again, Gerbert wondered why people usually thought she looked stern and intimidating; she did not try to act girlishly, but her face was full of gaiety, life and healthy zest; she seemed so completely at ease that it made you feel perfectly at ease when you were near her.

Labrousse turned to Pagès and looked at her anxiously.

'You did understand? You are to take a taxi and say to the driver: "To the Apollo, rue Blanche." He'll put you down right in front of the cinema and all you'll have to do is go inside.'

'Is it really a cowboy film?' Pagès asked suspiciously.

'It's super,' said Françoise. 'It's full of wonderful chases and round-ups.'

'And shootings, and terrific brawls,' said Labrousse.

They were leaning towards Pagès like two tempting devils, and their voices had a ring of supplication. Gerbert made a heroic effort to suppress a burst of laughter which he could barely restrain. He took a sip of Pernod: every time he hoped that by some miracle he would suddenly develop a taste for aniseed, but every time that same nauseating tremor ran through him.

'Is the hero handsome?' said Pagès.

'He's the most attractive,' said Françoise.

'But he's not handsome,' said Pagès obstinately.

'It's not the usual sort of good looks,' Labrousse admitted. Pagès pouted disappointedly.

'I'm suspicious. The one you took me to see the other day looked like a seal. That was unfair.'

'You mean William Powell,' said Françoise.

'Oh, but this one's quite different,' said Labrousse imploringly. 'He's young, and well built and utterly primitive.'

'Well, all right, I'll go to see it,' said Pagès with resignation.

'Will you be at Dominique's at midnight?' asked Gerbert.

'Of course,' said Pagès with an offended look.

Gerbert took her answer sceptically, for Pagès hardly ever turned up.

'I'll stay five minutes longer,' she said as Françoise rose.

'Do enjoy your evening,' said Françoise warmly.

'Enjoy yourself too,' said Xavière. Her face had a queer expression and she quickly looked down.

'I wonder if she'll go to the cinema,' said Françoise while

255

walking out of the café. 'It's too silly of her, I'm sure she'd love it.'

'Did you see?' said Labrousse. 'She did her best to remain pleasant, but she didn't hold out till the end. She's annoyed with us.'

'Why?' said Gerbert.

'For not spending the evening with her,' said Labrousse.

'Well, then, take her along,' said Gerbert. He found it very unpleasant that this dinner should seem a complicated affair to Labrousse and Françoise.

'Certainly not,' said Françoise. 'It wouldn't be at all the same thing.'

'That girl is a little tyrant, but we do manage to keep our ends up,' said Pierre cheerfully.

Gerbert's serenity returned, but he wanted very much to understand precisely what Pagès stood for in the eyes of Labrousse. Was it out of affection for Françoise that he was fond of her? Or what? He would never dare to ask him. He was very happy when Labrousse happened to give him a little bit of himself, but it was not his place to question him.

Labrousse stopped a taxi.

'What do you say to dinner at the Grille?' said Françoise.

'That's fine,' said Gerbert. 'Maybe there'll still be some *jambon aux haricots rouges*.' He suddenly noticed that he was hungry, and he tapped his forehead. 'Ah! I knew I'd forgotten something.'

'What?' said Labrousse.

'At lunch, I forgot to take a second helping of beef. That was a big mistake!'

The taxi pulled up in front of the little restaurant; a heavy grill covered the front windows; inside, to the right of the entrance, was a zinc-topped bar with a number of tempting bottles on it; the dining-room was empty. The proprietor and the cashier, with napkins tied around their necks, were eating their dinner together at one of the marble-topped tables.

'Ah!' said Gerbert, tapping his forehead.

'You frighten me,' said Françoise. 'What else have you forgotten?'

'I forgot to tell you before that I went down my stairs in thirty seconds.'

'You're a liar,' said Labrousse.

'I was sure you wouldn't want to believe it,' said Gerbert.

'Exactly thirty seconds.'

'You'll have to do it again, with me there as witness,' said Labrousse. 'Anyway, I did beat you down the Montmartre steps.'

'I slipped,' said Gerbert. He picked up the menu: *jambon aux haricots rouges* was on it.

'This place is quite deserted,' said Françoise.

'It's too early,' said Labrousse. 'And besides, you know people stay shut up at home whenever things take a bad turn. We'll play to an audience of ten tonight.' He had ordered egg mayonnaise, and, with a maniacal look, was squashing the yolks into the dressing: he called this making *œufs Mimosa*.

'I'd still prefer to see it settled once and for all,' said Gerbert. 'It's no life, to say to yourself every day that it's going to happen tomorrow.'

'But there's always that amount of time gained,' said Françoise.

'That's what everyone said at the time of Munich,' said Labrousse. 'But I'm convinced that it was rubbish. There's nothing to be gained by climbing down.' He picked up the bottle of Beaujolais already on the table and filled their glasses. 'No, these avoiding actions can't go on for ever.'

'After all, why not?' said Gerbert.

Françoise hesitated.

'Isn't anything better than war?' she said.

Labrousse shrugged his shoulders.

'I don't know.'

'If it gets too ghastly here, you could always slip off to America,' said Gerbert. 'You'd certainly get a welcome there. You've already made a name for yourself.'

'And what would I do?' said Labrousse.

'I think a lot of Americans speak French. And besides, you'd learn English. You'd produce your plays in English,' said Françoise.

'That wouldn't interest me in the least,' said Labrousse. 'What meaning would it have for me to work in exile? If I want to leave my mark on this world, I must accept my responsibility.'

'America is a world, too,' said Françoise.

'But it's not mine.'

'It will be, the day you adopt it.'

Labrousse shook his head.

257

'You're talking like Xavière. But I can't, I'm too involved in this one.'

'You're still young,' said Françoise.

'Yes, but don't you see, creating a new theatre for the Americans is a task that doesn't appeal to me. What does interest me is to carry out my own work, the work I began with my own sweat and labour in my hovel near the Gobelins on the money I wheedled out of Aunt Christine.' Labrousse looked at Françoise. 'Don't you understand that?'

'I do,' said Françoise.

She was listening to Labrousse with a passionate attention that filled Gerbert with a kind of regret. He had often seen women turn ardent faces toward him; he was only embarrassed by it: such fulsome tenderness seemed to him either indecent or tyrannical. But the love blazing in Françoise's eyes gave no consent and made no demand. It almost made him hope to be the inspiration of such a love.

'I've been moulded by my past life,' Labrousse continued. 'The Ballets Russes, the Vieux Colombier, Picasso, surrealism – I'd be nothing without all that. And certainly I hope that art will gain a fresh inspiration from me, but one that will be the continuation of that tradition. It's impossible to work in a vacuum, it leads nowhere.'

'Obviously, to move in bag and baggage, to work for a development that is not yours, would hardly be satisfying,' said Françoise.

'Personally, I prefer to go and put up barbed wire somewhere in Lorraine rather than to go and eat corn-on-the-cob in New York.'

'Well, I'd prefer the corn-on-the-cob, especially if it's grilled,' said Françoise.

'Well,' said Gerbert, 'I can assure you that if there were any way of getting the hell out of here to Venezuela, or to San Domingo . . .'

'If war breaks out, I wouldn't want to miss it for anything,' said Labrousse. 'I must even confess that I feel rather curious about it.'

'You're not half depraved!' said Gerbert.

He had been dreaming about the war all day long, but it chilled him to the marrow to hear Labrousse talk about it so calmly, as if it had already come. Indeed, it was already there, tucked away between the roaring stove and the zinc-topped bar with its yellow reflections, and this meal was a Reunion Dinner for the dead. Helmets, tanks, uniforms, grey-green trucks – a vast muddy tide was breaking over the world. The earth was being submerged in this blackish quagmire, that sucked down everyone, the leaden garments on their shoulders reeking like a wet dog, while fierce lights burst in the night sky.

'I wouldn't either,' said Françoise. 'I wouldn't like something important to happen without me.'

'At that rate, you should have joined up in Spain,' said Gerbert. 'Or even gone to China.'

'That's not the same thing,' said Labrousse.

'I don't see why not,' said Gerbert.

'It seems to me that it's a question of where you are,' said Françoise. 'I remember when I was at the Pointe du Raz, and Pierre tried to force me to leave before the storm, I was mad with despair; I would have felt in the wrong had I given in. Whereas, at the moment, all the storms in the world could rage there.'

'There you are, that's exactly it,' said Labrousse. 'This particular war is part of my own personal history, and that's why I couldn't bring myself to miss it.'

His face was burning with joy. Gerbert looked enviously at both of them; it must give them a sense of security to feel so important to each other. Perhaps he himself, if he were really of very great importance to someone, would have counted for a little more in his own eyes; he could set no proper value on either his life or his thoughts.

'Just imagine,' said Gerbert. 'Péclard knows a doctor who went completely potty from cutting men up; as he was operating on one, the next guy passed out. It seems that one of them – all the time they were hacking at him – never stopped yelling: "Oh! the pain in my knee! Oh! the pain in my knee!" That couldn't have been too funny.'

'When you've reached that point, there's nothing to do but yell,' said Labrousse. 'But, you know, I don't find even that too bad. It's just something you've got to put up with in life.'

'If you take that line, anything can be justified,' said Gerbert. 'All you have to do is just sit back.'

'Oh, no,' said Labrousse. 'To put up with something doesn't mean accepting life blindly. I'd be willing to live through almost anything, precisely because I'd always have it in me to live freely.'

'A strange kind of freedom,' said Gerbert. 'You wouldn't be able to do any of the things that interest you.'

Labrousse smiled.

'You know, I've changed. I'm no longer imbued with any mysticism about art. I can easily face up to other activities.'

Gerbert thoughtfully drained his glass. It was strange to think that Labrousse could change: Gerbert had always regarded him as being immutable. He had an answer to every question, it was hard to imagine what questions were left that he could still ask himself.

'Well, then, nothing stands in the way of your going to America,' he said.

'For the moment,' said Labrousse, 'it seems to me that the best use to which I can put my freedom is to defend a civilization that is bound up with all the values that mean a lot to me.'

'Still, Gerbert is right,' said Françoise. 'You'd regard any world in which there was a place for you as justified.' She smiled. 'I've always suspected that you think you're God the Father.'

They both looked happy. It always amazed Gerbert to see them becoming so excited over words. What difference did it make? What good were all these words in comparison with the glow of the Beaujolais he was drinking, in comparison with the gas that would stain his lungs green, and the fear that was clutching at his throat?

'Just what do you hold against us?' said Labrousse.

Gerbert shuddered. He had not expected to be caught out in the very process of thinking.

'Why, nothing at all,' he said.

'You had your magisterial look,' said Françoise. She handed him the menu. 'Don't you want any dessert?'

'I don't like dessert,' said Gerbert.

'There's tart. You like tart,' said Françoise.

'Yes, I do like it, but I don't feel up to it,' said Gerbert.

They burst out laughing.

'Are you too tired for a glass of old brandy?' said Labrousse.

'No, that's always easy to drink,' said Gerbert.

Labrousse ordered three brandies and the waitress brought a big, dust-coated demi-john. Gerbert took out his pipe. This was awful; even Labrousse had to invent something to which he could cling! Gerbert could not believe that his calmness was completely sincere; he valued his ideas rather as Péclard valued his furniture. And Françoise leaned on Labrousse. In that way, people managed to surround themselves with an impervious world in which their lives had meaning, but there was always a little cheating at the bottom of it all. If one looked carefully, without trying to deceive oneself, one would find beneath all these imposing appearances nothing but a sprinkling of small, futile impressions – the yellow light on the bar-top, the taste of rotten medlars at the bottom of the glass of marc. It could not be caught in words: it had to be borne in silence and then it disappeared without leaving any trace, and something else, equally elusive, arose in its place. Nothing but sand and water, and it was folly to try to build anything on it. Even death did not deserve all the fuss that was made over it. Of course it was terrifying, but only because one couldn't imagine how one would feel.

'Being killed, even that would be all right,' said Gerbert, 'but you might also have to go on living with a bashed-in face.'

'I'd sooner lose a leg,' said Labrousse.

'I'd rather an arm,' said Gerbert. 'I saw a young Englishman in Marseilles who had a hook instead of a hand: well, it made him look rather distinguished.'

'An artificial leg isn't so obvious,' said Labrousse. 'An arm would be impossible to disguise.'

'It's true that in our profession we can't afford to go too far,' said Gerbert. 'Having your ear torn off would ruin your whole career.'

'But that's not possible,' Françoise broke in. Her voice was choking, her face became transformed, and quite suddenly tears rose to her eyes. Gerbert thought she looked almost beautiful.

'It's also possible to come back without a scratch,' said Labrousse, in a soothing tone. 'And besides, we haven't gone yet.' He smiled at Françoise. 'You mustn't start having nightmares now.'

With effort, Françoise also smiled.

'The one thing quite certain is that you'll be playing before an empty house tonight,' she said.

'Yes,' said Labrousse. His eyes wandered over the deserted restaurant. 'I must go all the same. I ought to be there now.'

'I'm going home to do some work,' said Françoise. She

shrugged her shoulders. 'Though I don't how how much enthusiasm I'll have for it.'

They went out and Labrousse hailed a taxi.

'No, I'd rather walk home,' said Françoise. She shook hands with Labrousse and then with Gerbert.

He watched her walk away, her hands in her pockets, with long but rather unsteady strides. Now he probably would not see her again for the best part of a month.

'Get in,' said Labrousse, pushing him into the taxi.

When Gerbert reached his dressing-room he found Guimiot and Mercaton already at their dressing tables, their arms and necks daubed with ochre; he absent-mindedly shook hands with them, he did not really like them. The small, over-heated room reeked of the nauseating smell of cold cream and brilliantine. Guimiot stubbornly insisted on keeping the windows closed, he was afraid of catching cold. Gerbert walked to the window with marked determination.

'If he says anything, I'll smash that little pansy's face,' he thought.

He would have loved to have it out with somebody, it would have eased the strain, but Guimiot never turned a hair; he was dabbing his face with a huge mauve puff and the powder was flying all over the place: it made him sneeze twice most distressingly. Gerbert was so glum that this did not even make him laugh. He began to undress – coat, tie, shoes, socks; and in a little while they would all have to be put on again. He was fed up by the mere thought of it, and besides, he did not like to exhibit his naked body in front of other fellows.

'What the hell am I doing here!' he suddenly asked himself, looking round about him with an almost pained astonishment. He knew these states of mind all too well, they sometimes reached the height of unpleasantness, as if everything within him were transformed into stagnant water: he often used to have these attacks during his childhood, especially when he saw his mother bent over a tub of steaming washing. In a few days, he would be polishing a gun; he would be marching on the barrack square; and then he would be made to mount guard in some icy hole; it was absurd: but meanwhile, he was smearing his thighs with a coat of coppery pigment, which it would be no end of trouble to scrape off; and that was no less absurd.

'Oh! Hell!' he said aloud. He had suddenly remembered that Elisabeth was coming to sketch him that evening. She certainly had picked a good day!

The door opened and Ramblin's head appeared.

'Has anyone got some spirit-gum?'

'I've got some,' said Guimiot eagerly. He regarded Ramblin as a wealthy and influential person, and shamelessly licked his boots.

'Thanks,' said Ramblin coldly. He seized the jar containing a quivering pink jelly and turned to Gerbert. 'It's going to be dead tonight! There are three stray cats in the orchestra stalls, and no more in the dress circle.' He suddenly burst out laughing and Gerbert laughed with him. He liked these outbursts of lone gaiety that frequently shook Ramblin, and besides he was grateful to him, homosexual that he was, for never having made up to him.

'Tedesco's in a blue funk,' said Ramblin. 'He believes all foreigners are going to be clapped into concentration camps. Canzetti is holding his hand and sobbing. Chanaud has already called her a dirty wop and now she's ranting that French women will know how to do their duty. It's well worth seeing, I can assure you.'

He was carefully sticking on the curls round his face, smiling at himself in the glass with an approving and quizzical expression.

'Gerbert, darling, would you give me a little of your blue pencil?' said Eloy.

That Eloy girl always managed to think of some excuse to come into the men's dressing-room when they were naked. She was half undressed; a transparent shawl barely concealed her enormous breasts.

'Scram, we're not presentable,' said Gerbert.

'And cover those up,' said Ramblin, twitching her shawl; he watched her leave with disgust. 'She says she's going to volunteer as a nurse. Just think what a godsend she'll be to those poor defenceless devils who fall into her clutches.'

He disappeared. Gerbert put on his Roman costume and began to make up his face. This was much more fun, he loved detailed work; he had discovered a new way of making up his eyes by lengthening the line of the lids with a kind of star that had a most charming effect. He cast a satisfied last-minute glance at the glass and went downstairs. With her portfolio under her arm, he found Elisabeth sitting on a bench in the green-room.

'Have I come too early?' she said suavely. She was very smart tonight, there was no denying it: her jacket had certainly been cut by an expert tailor; Gerbert was a connoisseur.

'I'll be with you in ten minutes,' said Gerbert.

He glanced at the scenery. Everything was in place and the props were all arranged within reach. Through a slit in the curtain he studied the audience: there were no more than twenty people; that spelt disaster. With a whistle between his teeth he proceeded along the passages to summon the actors; then he went and sat down resignedly beside Elisabeth.

'Are you sure this isn't going to disturb you?' she said, starting to unwrap her sheets of paper.

'Oh no, I just have to be here to see that no one makes any noise,' said Gerbert.

The three strikes of the gong reverberated in the silence with ominous solemnity. The curtain rose. Caesar's procession was gathered near the door opening on to the stage. Labrousse entered, draped in his white toga.

'Fancy you being here!' he said to his sister.

'Well, I am,' said Elisabeth.

'But I thought you weren't doing any portraits these days,' he said, looking over her shoulder.

'This is a study,' said Elisabeth. 'If I did nothing but composition I'd spoil my touch.'

'Come and see me later,' said Labrousse.

He went on through the door and the procession fell in behind him.

'It's strange to watch a play from the wings,' said Elisabeth. 'You can see how it's put together.'

She shrugged her shoulders and Gerbert looked at her in embarrassment. He was always ill at ease with her, for he did not understand very clearly what she expected of him; every once in a while, he felt that she was slightly crazy.

'Stay just like that. Don't move,' said Elisabeth. She smiled, concerned. 'Is it a tiring pose?'

'No,' said Gerbert.

It was not tiring in the least, but it certainly made him feel a damned fool. As Ramblin walked through the green-room he gave him a quizzical look. Silence ensued. All the doors were closed and not a sound could be heard. Out there, the actors were moving about in front of an empty house. Elisabeth was obstinately sketching in order not to lose her touch, and Gerbert was there, looking like a fool. 'There's no rhyme or reason,' he thought in a rage. As in his dressing-room a short while before, he felt an emptiness in the pit of his stomach. One memory always came back to him when he was in this mood – that of a fat spider he had seen in Provence one evening when on a walking tour. Attached to its thread, it hung dangling from a tree; it would climb, then let itself drop back in sharp jerks; it would climb up again with such harrowing patience that it was impossible to understand whence it derived this continuing courage: it seemed so terribly alone in the world.

'Is your marionette show going to last a little while longer?' asked Elisabeth.

'Dominique said until the end of the week,' said Gerbert.

'Did Pagès finally turn down the part?' said Elisabeth.

'She promised me she'd come tonight,' said Gerbert.

Pencil in air, Elisabeth stared Gerbert in the eye.

'What do you think of Pagès?'

'She's all right,' said Gerbert.

'Anything else?' said Elisabeth. She had a curious, insistent smile; she looked as if she were putting him through an examination.

'I don't know her very well,' said Gerbert.

Elisabeth laughed candidly.

'Well, of course, if you're as shy as she is . . .'

She bent over her sketch and began to work with an air of concentration.

'I'm not shy,' said Gerbert. He felt, with rage, that he was blushing; it was ridiculous, but he hated that anyone should talk to him about himself, and he could not even move to hide his face.

'I can't help thinking you are,' said Elisabeth with evident amusement.

'Why?' said Gerbert.

'Because otherwise it wouldn't have been very hard for you to become better acquainted with her.' Elisabeth looked up and stared at Gerbert with apparently genuine curiosity. 'You really haven't noticed anything? Or are you pretending?'

'I don't know what you mean,' said Gerbert, put out of countenance.

'You're really delightful,' said Elisabeth. 'This shrinking violet modesty is so rare.' She was talking into space, self-confidently. Perhaps she really was on the verge of insanity.

'But Pagès doesn't give me a thought,' said Gerbert.

'Do you think so?' said Elisabeth with a touch of irony.

Gerbert did not answer. It was true that Pagès had acted strangely in his company at times, but that did not prove much; she took no interest in anyone, except in Françoise and Labrousse. Elisabeth was trying to make fun of him,' sucking the point of her pencil with an impatient look.

'She doesn't appeal to you?' she said.

Gerbert shrugged his shoulders.

'You've got things wrong,' he said.

He looked round in embarrassment. Elisabeth had always been tactless. She talked irresponsibly, just for the pleasure of talking. But this time, really, she was going too far.

'Five minutes,' he said, getting up. 'It's time for the acclamations.'

The members of the crowd had come in and sat down at the other end of the green-room. He motioned to them and slowly opened the door on to the stage. The actors' voices could not be heard, but Gerbert took his cue from the muted music which accompanied the dialogue between Cassius and Casca. Every evening he felt the same excitement while he waited for the theme indicating that the people were offering the crown to Caesar: he almost believed in the deceptive and dubious solemnity of this moment. He raised his hand and a great outcry drowned the last chords of the piano. Once more he watched in the silence emphasized by a far-away murmur of voices, then the short melody was heard again and a shout rose from every throat; the third time, a few words barely outlined the theme and the voices rose with redoubled volume.

'Now, we'll be undisturbed for a while,' said Gerbert, resuming his pose. He was intrigued, no matter what he might say; he was likeable, that he knew; he was even too likeable, but Pagès! – that would be flattering!

'I saw Pagès this evening,' he said after a pause. 'I can assure you she didn't seem to feel too kindly towards me.'

'How was that?' said Elisabeth.

'She was fuming because I was to dine with Françoise and Labrousse.'

'Ah! I see,' said Elisabeth. 'She's as jealous as a cat, that young woman. She must really have hated you, but that doesn't prove anything.' Elisabeth made a few pencil strokes in silence. Gerbert wanted to question her more closely, but he was unable to put into words any question that he did not consider indiscreet.

'It's a nuisance to have a child like that in one's life,' said Elisabeth. 'Devoted as Françoise and Labrousse may be, she's still a burden to them.'

Gerbert remembered the incident that had occurred that evening, and Labrousse's good-natured tone. 'That girl is a little tyrant, but we do manage to keep our ends up.'

He remembered people's faces and intonations very clearly, only he was unable to go further and grasp what they were thinking; the incident stood out before him, distinct and precise, without his being able to arrive at any clear idea. He hesitated. This was a heaven-sent opportunity to gather a little information.

'I don't understand very clearly just how they feel about her,' he said.

'You know what they're like,' said Elisabeth. 'They're so taken up with one another that their relationships with other people are always superficial or else a game.' She bent over her sketch with a look of complete absorption. 'They like having an adopted daughter, but I think that it's also beginning to act as a poison.'

Gerbert hesitated a moment.

'Labrousse stares at Pagès with such solicitude at times.'

Elisabeth laughed.

'Surely you don't think Pierre is in love with Pagès?' she said.

'Of course not,' said Gerbert. He was choking with rage. This woman was a perfect trollop with her elder sister act.

'Just you watch her,' said Elisabeth, becoming serious again. 'I'm certain of what I'm saying. You only have to lift a finger.' She added with heavy irony: 'It's quite true that you do have to lift your finger.'

Dominique's cabaret was as deserted as *Les Tréteaux*; the show had been performed in front of six gloomy-faced habitués. Gerbert felt a lump rise in his throat as he laid the little oil-cloth princess in a suitcase; this was perhaps the last evening. Tomorrow, a rain of grey dust would descend on Europe, drowning the fragile dolls, the settings, bistro bars, and all those rainbows of light glowing in the streets of Montparnasse. His hand rested for a moment on the cool, smooth face: a funeral in all conscience.

'She looks almost like a corpse,' said Pagès.

Gerbert shuddered. Pagès was tying a silk neckerchief under her chin as her eyes rested on the tiny cold bodies laid out on the bottom of their box.

'It was nice of you to come tonight,' he said. 'It goes so much better when you're here.'

'But I said that I would come,' she said with offended dignity.

She had arrived just as the show was about to begin, and they had not had time even to exchange a few words. Gerbert glanced at her: if only he could find something to say to her, he was very anxious to keep her with him for a while. After all, she was not as intimidating as all that. With the neckerchief over her head, she even looked good-natured.

'Did you go to the movie?' he asked.

'No,' said Xavière. She was twisting the fringe of her scarf. 'It was too far.'

Gerbert laughed.

'By taxi it's a lot nearer.'

'Oh!' said Xavière with a knowing look. 'I wouldn't be too sure.' She smiled amiably. 'Did you have a good dinner?'

'I had *jambon aux haricots rouges* which was really a miracle,' said Gerbert with enthusiasm. He stopped, embarrassed. 'But, talk about grub sickens you.'

Pagès raised her eyebrows, and they looked as if they might have been put on with a paint brush, as on a Japanese mask.

'Who told you that? That's a silly story.'

Gerbert thought with satisfaction that he was becoming a psychologist, for it seemed clear to him that Xavière was still furious with Françoise and Labrousse.

'You aren't going to pretend that you like feeding your face?' he said, laughing.

'It's because I'm a blonde,' said Xavière with a hurt look. 'It makes everyone think I'm ethereal.'

'Bet you won't come and eat a Hamburg steak with me?' said Gerbert. He said it without thinking and was immediately aghast at his boldness.

Xavière's eyes sparkled gaily.

'Bet you I will,' she said.

'Well, let's go,' said Gerbert. He stepped back to let her pass. 'What in the world can I say to her?' he thought uneasily. Still, he was quite proud of himself, no one could say he had not lifted a finger. This was really the first time he had taken so much initiative. Usually, he always found he had been left behind.

'Oh! How cold it is!' said Pagès.

'Let's go to the Coupole. It's only a five-minute walk,' said Gerbert.

Pagès looked around with a pained expression.

'Isn't there any place nearer?'

'Hamburg steak is eaten at the Coupole,' said Gerbert firmly.

These women were all the same, they were too hot or too cold, they required too much attention to be good companions. Gerbert had been fond of some of them because he liked to be liked, but it was hopeless, he felt bored in their company: if he had had the good fortune to be a homosexual, he would have associated only with men. On top of that, there was the hell of a to-do if you wanted to be rid of them, especially as he did not like to hurt anyone's feelings. They understood in the long run, but they took their time about it. Annie was beginning to understand: this was now the third time he had failed to keep an appointment without letting her know. Gerbert looked fondly at the façade of the Coupole: the play of the lights gave him even as great a thrill of melancholy as did a jazz melody.

'You see, it wasn't far,' he said.

'That's because you have long legs,' said Xavière glancing at him approvingly. 'I like people who walk fast.'

Before pushing the revolving door, Gerbert turned to her.

'Do you still feel like a Hamburger?' he asked.

Xavière hesitated.

'To tell the truth, I don't really and truly want one. But I am thirsty.'

She looked at him apologetically. She was really attractive with her glowing cheeks and her childish fringe showing under her neckerchief. A daring notion struck Gerbert,

269

'In that case, shall we go downstairs where there's dancing?'
he said. He ventured a timid smile which often carried the
day. 'I'll give you a lesson in tap-dancing.'

'Oh! That would be wonderful!' said Pagès, with such
enthusiasm that he was a little taken aback. She tore the
neckerchief off her head and dashed down the red stairs two
at a time. Gerbert wondered in amazement whether there was
not some truth in Elisabeth's insinuations. Pagès was always
so reserved with people! But tonight she welcomed the slightest
advance with such alacrity.

'We can sit here,' he said, pointing to a table.

'Yes, that will be just perfect,' said Pagès. She looked round
her with delight: it seemed that, faced with the threat of
possible disaster, a dance-hall was considered a better refuge
than the theatre, for there were several couples on the floor.

'Oh! I adore this kind of decoration,' said Pagès. She
wrinkled her nose. When he saw her tricks of facial expression
he frequently found it difficult to keep a straight face.

'At Dominique's everything is so select, what they call good
taste.' She pouted a little and gave him a conspiratorial look.
'Don't you think it has a niggardly look? Their humour too,
their jokes, the whole thing seems so rigidly controlled.'

'Oh, yes,' said Gerbert. 'There's precious little they can
afford to laugh at. They remind me of that philosopher
Labrousse told me about, who laughed when he saw a line
drawn at a tangent to a circle; because it looks like an angle
and it isn't one.'

'You're making fun of me,' said Pagès.

'I promise you,' said Gerbert, 'it seemed to him to be the
height of comedy, but nothing could have fallen flatter.'

'Yet you'd say he didn't want to miss a single chance of
enjoying himself,' said Pagès.

Gerbert began to laugh.

'Did you ever hear Charpini? Now there's a fellow whom
I call funny, especially when he sings *Carmen.* "My mother,
I perceive her," while Brancanto looks all over the place.
"Where? Here? Where is she, poor woman?" I laugh till I
cry at every line.'

'No,' said Pagès, looking downcast. 'I've never heard anything really funny. I'd so love to.'

'Well, we'll have to go some time,' said Gerbert. 'And
Georgius? Don't you know Georgius?'

'No,' said Pagès, looking at him wretchedly.

'Perhaps you'd find him a bore,' said Gerbert hesitantly. 'His songs and even his wisecracks are very near the knuckle, he's up to all the tricks of his trade.' He could hardly imagine Pagès listening to Georgius with pleasure.

'I'm sure I'd enjoy it,' she said eagerly.

'What would you like to drink?' said Gerbert.

'A whisky,' said Pagès.

'Two whiskies, then,' Gerbert said to the waiter. 'Do you like it?'

'No, said Pagès with a grimace. 'It smells like tincture of iodine.'

'But you like drinking it, it's just like me with Pernod,' said Gerbert. 'But I like whisky,' he added with misgivings. He smiled boldly. 'Shall we dance this tango?'

'Surely,' said Pagès. She got up and smoothed her skirt with the palm of her hand. Gerbert put his arm around her: he remembered that she danced well, better than Annie, better than Canzetti, but tonight, the perfection of her movements seemed miraculous to him; a light and delicate perfume rose from her fair hair, and for a moment Gerbert stopped thinking and yielded to the rhythm of the dance, to the singing of the guitars, to the orange haze of the lights, to the pleasurable satisfaction of holding a lithe body in his arms.

'I've been a fool,' he thought suddenly. He should have asked her to go out with him weeks ago, and now the barracks were waiting for him. It was too late, this evening would have no tomorrow. He was filled with regret. In his life, nothing had ever had a tomorrow. He had admired from afar all beautiful and passionate love-affairs; but a great love was like ambition, it would have been possible only in a world in which things were important, in which the words one spoke, and the things one did, left their mark; and Gerbert felt as if he were being cooped up in a waiting-room whose exit no future would ever open for him. Suddenly, as the orchestra paused, the anguish which had hung over him all evening changed to panic. All these years that had slipped between his fingers had never seemed to be anything but a wasted period of marking time, but they made up his sole existence, and he would never know any other. When he was stretched out in a field, stiff and muddy, with his identification disc on his wrist, then indeed there would be absolutely nothing more.

'Come, let's go and drink another whisky,' he said.

Xavière smiled at him submissively. As they reached their table, they caught sight of a flower-girl who was offering them a basket filled with flowers. Gerbert stopped and picked out a red rose. He laid it down in front of Xavière, who pinned it to her bodice.

Chapter Four

Françoise gave one last fleeting glance at the looking-glass and, for once, no single detail displeased her. She had carefully plucked her eyebrows and brushed her hair straight up from the nape, thus accentuating the clear line of her neck, her white nails shone like rubies. She was looking forward to this evening: she was very fond of Paule Berger and she always enjoyed herself when she went out with her. Paule had agreed to take them to a Spanish night-club, an exact replica of a dance-restaurant in Seville, and Françoise was elated at the thought of a few hours' escape from the strained, passionate, cloying atmosphere in which Pierre and Xavière had imprisoned her. She felt fresh and full of life and ready to enjoy at their proper value Paule's beauty, the attractions of the performance, and the poetry of Seville which the music of the guitars and the taste of the Manzanilla would so soon bring to life.

Five minutes to midnight: she could hesitate no longer; if the evening was not to be spoiled, she must go down and knock at Xavière's door. Pierre was expecting them at the theatre at midnight, and he would panic if they did not arrive at the appointed time. Once again, she re-read the pink sheet of paper on which, in green ink, Xavière had scribbled in her sprawling hand:

'Please let me off this afternoon, but I would like to rest so that I can be fresh this evening. I shall be in your room at eleven-thirty. Much love, Xavière.'

Françoise had found this note under her door in the morning and she, together with Pierre, had anxiously speculated on what Xavière could possibly have been up to the night before to want to sleep all day. 'Much love' did not mean anything, it was an empty formula. When they had left her at the Flore, the previous evening, before going to dinner with Gerbert, Xavière had been very much on edge and it was impossible to foresee her present mood. Françoise threw a new, light-weight wool cape over her shoulders. She gathered up her bag and the beautiful pair of gloves her mother had given her, and went downstairs. Even if Xavière turned out to be in a bad mood, and if Pierre seemed offended as a result of it, she was determined not to take their quarrelling seriously. She knocked. From the other side of the door there came a faint rustling sound; it seemed almost as if she were listening to the vibrations of the secret thoughts in which Xavière indulged when alone.

'What is it?' said a sleepy voice.

'It's Françoise.' This time there was not the slightest sound. In spite of her joyous resolutions, Françoise, with a sinking heart, was aware of the anguish that she always felt when waiting expectantly for the expression on Xavière's face. Would she be smiling or scowling? Whichever it might be, the course of this evening, the course of the entire world tonight, would depend on the light in her eyes. A minute passed before the door opened.

'I'm not nearly ready,' said Xavière, in a dismal voice.

It was the same story every time, and every time it was just as disconcerting. Xavière was in her dressing-gown; her tousled hair fell over a puffy, yellowish face Behind her the un-made bed looked as if it were still warm, and it was obvious that the shutters had not been opened all day. The room was filled with smoke and the acrid smell of methylated spirits. But what made this air unbreathable, to an even greater extent than the methylated spirits and tobacco, were all the unsatisfied desires, the boredom and bitterness accumulated in the course of hours, in the course of days, of weeks, between these walls as speckled as a feverish fantasy.

'I'll wait for you,' said Françoise irresolutely.

'But I'm not dressed,' said Xavière. She shrugged her shoulders with an air of hopeless resignation. 'No,' she said, 'you had better go without me.'

Françoise remained on the threshold of the room, inert and appalled. Since she had watched the growth of jealousy and hatred in Xavière's heart, this place of refuge frightened her. It was not only a sanctuary where Xavière celebrated her own worship; it was a hothouse in which flourished a luxuriant and poisonous vegetation; it was the cell of a bedlamite, in which the dank atmosphere adhered to the body.

'Look,' she said, 'I'll go and fetch Labrousse and in twenty minutes we'll come and pick you up. You can be ready in twenty minutes, can't you?'

274

Xavière's face suddenly showed signs of animation.

'Of course I can. You'll see, I can hurry when I want to.'

Françoise went down the last two flights. This was annoying: the evening was starting badly. For several days there had been a storm brewing and now it must come to a head; it was between Xavière and Françoise in particular that things were not going well. That clumsy burst of affection on Saturday, after they had returned from the Negro dance-hall, had in no way cleared the air. Françoise walked faster. Things happened almost imperceptibly: a misplaced smile, an equivocal phrase, were sufficient to ruin any happy outing. This evening she would again pretend not to notice anything, but she knew that Xavière let nothing slip unintentionally.

It was barely ten past twelve when Françoise walked into Pierre's dressing-room. He had already put on his overcoat and was sitting on the edge of the couch, smoking his pipe. He looked up and stared at Françoise with angry suspicion.

'Are you alone?' he said.

'Xavière is waiting for us. She wasn't quite ready,' said Françoise. Although she had steeled herself, a lump rose in her throat. Pierre had not even given her a smile: never before had he welcomed her in this way.

'Have you seen her? How was she?'

She stared at him in astonishment. Why did he seem distraught? As far as he was concerned, things were progressing favourably. Whatever the quarrels Xavière might pick with him, they were never more than lovers' tiffs.

'She looked depressed and tired. She's spent the day in her room, sleeping, smoking and drinking tea.'

Pierre got up.

'Do you know what she was doing last night?' he said.

'What?' said Françoise, stiffening. Something unpleasant was coming.

'She was out dancing with Gerbert until five o'clock in the morning,' said Pierre, almost in triumph.

'Oh! And what else?' said Françoise.

She was disconcerted. This was the first time that Gerbert and Xavière had gone out together, and in the feverish and complex life whose proper adjustment was her continuing concern, the slightest novelty was pregnant with threats.

'Gerbert looked delighted, even slightly smug,' Pierre continued.

'What did he say?' said Françoise. She could not define this equivocal feeling that had just come upon her, but its gloomy quality did not surprise her. In all her pleasures these days there was a musty flavour, and her worst difficulties gave her a kind of pleasure that set her teeth on edge.

'He thinks she dances magnificently and that she's quite likeable,' said Pierre dryly. He looked deeply chagrined, and Françoise was relieved to think that his uncivil greeting was not without excuse.

'She went into retirement all day,' continued Pierre. 'That's what she always does when she's been stirred up by something. She shuts herself up in order to have plenty of time to ruminate at leisure.'

He closed the door to his dressing-room behind him and they left the theatre.

'Why don't you tell Gerbert that you're fond of her?' said Françoise, after a silence. 'All you'd have to do is say the word.'

Pierre's profile sharpened.

'I really think he tried to sound me out,' he said, with an unpleasant laugh. 'He looked embarrassed, as if feeling his way, which I found slightly amusing.' Pierre added on an even more rasping note, 'I showered encouragement upon him.'

'Well, what do you expect? How can you expect him to guess?' said Françoise. 'You've always put on such an air of unconcern when he's about.'

'You surely can't expect me to hang a sign on Xavière's back saying, "Trespassers forbidden",' said Pierre in a scathing tone. He started to bite one of his fingernails. 'He can certainly guess.'

The blood rushed to Françoise's face. Pierre took pride in being a good sport, but he was not accepting the prospect of a failure like a true sportsman. At this moment he was stubborn and unjust, and she respected him too much not to hate him for this weakness.

'You know very well that he's no psychologist,' she said. 'And besides,' she added bitterly, 'you yourself told me, in connexion with our own relationship, that when you respect someone deeply, you refuse to pry into their soul without their permission.'

'But I'm not blaming anyone for anything,' said Pierre icily. 'Everything's all right as it is.'

She looked at him with bitterness. He was deeply troubled, but this suffering was too manifestly aggressive to inspire pity. Nevertheless, she tried to be understanding.

'I wonder whether Xavière was nice to him largely because she was angry with us,' she said.

'Perhaps,' said Pierre, 'but the fact remains that she had no desire to return home before dawn and that she put herself out for him.' He angrily shrugged his shoulders. 'And now we'll have Paule on our hands and we won't even be able to have it out with Xavière.'

Françoise felt her heart sink. Whenever Pierre was forced to run through his misgivings and his grievances in silent thought, he had the power of transforming the passage of time into a slow and refined torture: nothing was more dreadful than these inward explanations. This evening to which she had so greatly been looking forward was no longer a pleasure. With a few words, Pierre had already changed it into heavy drudgery.

'Stay here, I'll go up and get Xavière,' she said, as they arrived at the hotel.

She hurried up the two flights. Was no escape to liberty ever to be possible again? Would she once more be allowed only furtive glances at faces and their background? She wanted to smash this magic circle in which she found herself confined with Pierre and Xavière and which cut her off from the rest of the world.

Françoise knocked. The door opened immediately.

'You see. I did hurry,' said Xavière.

It was difficult to believe that this was the yellow-faced and feverish recluse of a short while ago. Her face was smooth and clear; her hair fell in even waves on her shoulders. She had put on her blue dress and pinned a slightly faded rose to her bodice.

'I think it's such fun to go to a Spanish night-club,' she said brightly. 'We'll see real Spaniards, won't we?'

'Of course,' said Françoise. 'There'll be beautiful creatures, and guitarists, and castanets.'

'Let's hurry,' said Xavière. She lightly touched Françoise's wrap. 'I do love this cape,' she said. 'It makes me think of a domino at a masked ball. You look beautiful,' she added with admiration.

Françoise couldn't help giving her an embarrassed smile;

Xavière was completely out of tune, she was going to be painfully surprised when she caught sight of Pierre's stony face. She was now bounding joyously down the stairs.

'And now I've kept you waiting,' she said gaily, as she shook hands with Pierre.

'It doesn't matter in the least,' said Pierre, so curtly that Xavière looked at him in astonishment. He turned away and signalled to a taxi.

'First we'll pick up Paule so that she can take us there,' said Françoise. 'Apparently it's very hard to find the place if you don't know it.'

Xavière sat down beside her on the back seat.

'You can sit between us, there's lots of room,' said Françoise to Pierre, with a smile.

Pierre pulled down the folding seat.

'Thanks,' he said. 'I'm all right here.'

Françoise's smile fell. If he were going to be stubborn and sulk, there was nothing to do but leave him alone; he would not succeed in ruining this evening for her. She turned to Xavière.

'Well, I hear you were out dancing last night. Did you have a good time?'

'Oh, yes! Gerbert dances magnificently,' said Xavière, in a completely natural tone. 'We went to the Coupole, downstairs. Did he tell you? There was a wonderful orchestra.' She flickered her eyelids a little, and moved her lips as if to offer her smile to Pierre. 'Your cinema frightened me,' she said. 'I stayed at the Flore until midnight.'

Pierre eyed her malevolently. 'But you were quite free to do so.'

Xavière was bewildered for a moment. Then a haughty tremor ran over her face and once more she turned her eyes towards Françoise.

'We must go there together,' she said. 'After all, it's quite all right for women to dance together. At the Negro dance-hall on Saturday, it was great fun.'

'I'd very much like to,' said Françoise. She looked gaily at Xavière. 'You're getting quite debauched! This will make two nights running without sleep.'

'That's just why I rested all day,' said Xavière. 'I wanted to be fresh to go out with you.'

Françoise met Pierre's sarcastic look without turning a hair.

Really he was overdoing it. There was no reason for him to look like that because Xavière had enjoyed dancing with Gerbert. Besides, he knew he was in the wrong; but he was taking refuge in a peevish superiority, from which eminence he assumed the right to trample on good faith, good manners and every moral value.

Françoise had made up her mind to love him even in his freedom, but there was still too easy an optimism in such a resolve. If Pierre was free, it no longer depended on her alone to love him, for he was also free to make himself detestable. At this moment that was just what he was doing.

The taxi stopped.

'Do you want to come up to Paule's with us?' Françoise asked Xavière.

'Oh yes! You told me her flat was so lovely.'

Françoise opened the taxi door.

'You two go up. I'll wait for you,' said Pierre.

'As you like,' said Françoise.

Xavière took her arm and they stepped through the main doorway.

'I'm so excited to see her beautiful flat,' said Xavière.

She looked like a happy little girl, and Françoise pressed her arm. Even if this tenderness arose from spite against Pierre, it was pleasant to receive it. Moreover, during this long day of seclusion, Xavière had perhaps purified her heart. From the joy this hope had instilled in her, Françoise gauged to what extent Xavière's hostility had wounded her.

Françoise rang the bell. A maid opened the door and conducted them into a huge high-ceilinged room.

'I will tell Madame that you are here,' she said.

Xavière slowly turned round and said ecstatically, 'How beautiful it is!'

Her eyes rested in turn on the multicoloured chandeliers, on the pirate's chest studded with tarnished copper, on the state-bed covered with old red silk embroidered with blue caravels, on the Venetian mirror hanging at the back of the alcove. All round the polished surface of this mirror curled glass arabesques, brilliant and capricious as the blossoming of hoar-frost. A vague sense of envy seized Françoise. It was a wonderful gift to be able to write one's personality in silk, spun glass, and precious wood; for permeating these judiciously disparate objects which her unerring taste had brought together, was the personality of Paule Berger. It was she whom Xavière was rapturously studying when she looked at the Japanese masks, the small glaucous decanters, the shell dolls rigid under a glass dome. As she had on the last occasion at the Negro dance-hall, as at the New Year's Eve party, Françoise, by contrast, felt as smooth and naked as the faceless heads in a picture by Chirico.

'Good evening. I'm so glad to see you,' said Paule.

With both hands held out in front of her, she walked in with a brisk step that contrasted with the majesty of her long black dress. A swathe of dark velvet tinged with yellow accentuated her waist. With arms outstretched, she seized Xavière's hands and held them for a moment in her own.

'She looks more and more like a Fra Angelico,' she said.

Xavière looked down in embarrassment. Paule dropped her hands.

'I'm quite ready,' she said, throwing a short silver fox coat over her shoulders.

They went downstairs. As Paule approached, Pierre managed to force a smile.

'Did you have a crowd at the theatre tonight?' asked Paule, as the taxi was driving off.

'Twenty-five people,' said Pierre. 'We're going to close. In any case, they're going to start rehearsals on *Monsieur le Vent*, and we're supposed to end the run a week from today.'

'We're less fortunate,' said Paule. 'The play was about to open. Don't you think it's a little strange, the way people have of retiring into their shells when times are troublous? Even the woman who sells violets near my house told me that she hadn't sold three bunches in the last two days.'

The taxi stopped in a steep, narrow street. Paule and Xavière walked ahead a few paces while Pierre paid the driver. Xavière was studying Paule with a look of fascination.

'I'm not going to look too good walking into this joint flanked by three women,' muttered Pierre between his teeth.

He looked resentfully at the ill-lit blind-alley into which Paule was turning. All the houses seemed asleep. At the far end, on a small wooden door, was painted the word *Sevillana* in weather-worn lettering.

'I telephoned to ask them to keep a good table for us,' said Paule.

She went in first, and walked swiftly up to a dark-skinned

man who must be the proprietor, and they smilingly exchanged a few words. The main room was small. In the middle of the ceiling was a spotlight that cast a rosy glow on the crowded dance floor. The rest of the room was plunged in shadow. Paule walked towards one of the tables against the wall, separated from one another by wooden partitions.

'How nice it is here,' said Françoise. 'It's arranged just as it is in Seville.'

She was on the point of turning to Pierre. She remembered the wonderful evenings they had spent, two years earlier, in a cabaret near Alameda, but Pierre was in no mood to conjure up memories. He cheerlessly ordered a bottle of Manzanilla. Françoise looked round her. She loved these first moments, when surroundings and people had not yet formed anything more than a vague congeries, half-hidden in tobacco smoke. It was a pleasure to think that this confused scene would little by little become clarified and resolve into a number of separate details and enthralling episodes.

'What I love about this place,' said Paule, 'is that there's no artificial quaintness.'

'Yes, it couldn't be more authentic,' said Françoise.

The tables were of rough wood, as were the stools, used in place of chairs, and the bar with kegs of Spanish wine stacked behind it. Nothing held the eye, except the balcony with the piano and the beautiful shining guitars which the musicians, dressed in light colours, were holding across their knees.

'You ought to take off your coat,' said Paule, touching Xavière's shoulder.

Xavière smiled. Ever since they had stepped into the taxi, she had not taken her eyes from Paule. She took off her coat with the docility of a somnambulist.

'What a lovely dress!' said Paule.

Pierre turned his piercing gaze on Xavière.

'Why do you keep that rose? It's wilted,' he said tersely.

Xavière stared at him. Slowly she unpinned the rose from her bodice and put it in the glass of Manzanilla the waiter had just brought.

'Do you think that will revive it?' said Françoise.

'Why not?' said Xavière, gazing out of the corner of her eye at the drooping flower.

'The guitarists are good, aren't they?' said Paule. 'They have the real flamenco style. They create the whole atmosphere.'

She looked at the bar. 'I was afraid it might be empty, but the Spaniards aren't so affected by events.'

'These women are amazing,' said Françoise. 'They are covered with layers of make-up and yet it doesn't make them look artificial; their faces are still completely alive and sensual.'

One by one she was studying the short, fat, Spanish women, their heavily painted faces crowned with thick black hair. They were all like the women of Seville who, on summer evenings, wore clusters of richly scented spikenard flowers behind their ears.

'And how they dance!' said Paule. 'I often come here to admire them. When they're standing still, they look rather dumpy and short-legged. They appear clumsy, but as soon as they begin to move, their bodies become so light and so full of grace.'

Françoise took a sip from her glass. The flavour of dried nuts brought back at once the merciful shade of the Seville bars where she and Pierre had stuffed themselves with olives and anchovies, while the sun beat down pitilessly on the streets. She turned to look at him, she wanted him to join her in recalling that wonderful holiday. But Pierre kept a malevolent eye fixed on Xavière.

'Well, it didn't take long,' he said.

The rose was drooping sadly on its stem, as if it had been poisoned; it had turned yellow and its petals were tinged with brown. Xavière picked it up gently.

'Yes, I think it's quite dead,' she said.

She threw it on the table and then looked at Pierre defiantly. She seized her glass and drained it at one draught. Paule gaped in astonishment.

'Does the soul of a rose have a pleasant taste?' said Pierre.

Xavière leaned back and lighted a cigarette without answering. There was an awkward silence. Paule smiled at Françoise.

'Would you like to try this paso doble?' she said, obviously trying to change the subject.

'When I dance with you, I almost have the illusion of knowing how,' said Françoise, rising.

Pierre and Xavière sat side by side without exchanging a word. Xavière was gazing at the smoke of her cigarette with an entranced look.

'How far advanced are the plans for your recital?' asked Françoise, after a short space of time.

'If the situation clears up I'll try something in May,' said Paule.

'It will certainly be a success,' said Françoise.

'Perhaps.' A shadow passed over Paule's face. 'But that does not particularly interest me. I would so like to find a way of introducing my dance technique to the stage.'

'But you're doing that to a certain extent,' said Françoise. 'Your plasticity is so perfect.'

'That's not enough,' said Paule. 'I'm sure there must be something else to discover, something really new.' Again her face clouded over. 'Only I would have to feel my way, take risks . . .'

Françoise looked at her with warm appreciation. When Paule had renounced her past to throw herself into Berger's arms, she thought she was starting upon an adventurous, heroic life at his side; and now Berger, like a good man of business, was doing nothing more than exploit an established reputation. Paule had sacrificed too much for him to admit her disappointment to herself. But Françoise could guess the painful flaws in this love, in this happiness which she continued to assert. Something bitter rose in her throat. In the recess where she had left them Pierre and Xavière were still not speaking. Pierre was smoking, his head slightly bowed. Xavière was staring at him with a furtive and woebegone expression. How free she was! Free in heart, free in thought, free to suffer, to doubt, to hate. No past, no pledge, no loyalty to herself to shackle her.

The music of the guitars died away. Paule and Françoise came back to their places. Françoise noticed a little anxiously that the bottle of Manzanilla was empty, and that Xavière's eyes had a too brilliant lustre beneath their blue-tinged lashes.

'You're going to see the dancer,' said Paule. 'I think she's first-rate.'

A plump, mature woman, in Spanish costume, was moving towards the middle of the dance floor. Her features were suddenly animated and assumed the fullness of youth beneath her black hair parted in the middle and crowned by a comb as red as her shawl. She smiled to everyone around her while the guitarist plucked out a few staccato notes on his instrument. He began to play. Slowly the woman straightened her torso. Slowly she raised her two beautiful arms; her fingers clicked the castanets, and her body began to spring with childlike lightness. The wide flowered skirt whirled about her muscular legs.

'How beautiful she became all of a sudden,' said Françoise turning to Xavière.

Xavière did not reply. Deep in her enraptured contemplation, she was oblivious to everyone near her. Her cheeks were flushed, her features were no longer under control and her eyes followed the movements of the dancer in dazed ecstasy. Françoise emptied her glass. Although she knew well that no one could ever be at one with Xavière in any single thought or action, it was hard, after the earlier joy she had felt at regaining her affection, not to exist for her any longer. She again turned her attention to the dancer. She was now smiling at an imaginary gallant. She enticed him; she spurned him; finally, she fell into his arms; then she became a sorceress, every movement suggesting dangerous mystery. Following that dance, she mimed a joyful peasant woman at some village festivity, whirling dizzily, her eyes starting out of her head. All the youth and reckless gaiety evoked by her dancing acquired a moving purity as they sprang, transmuted, from her no longer youthful body. Françoise could not help taking a surreptitious glance at Xavière: she gave a gasp of amazement. Xavière was no longer watching, her head was lowered. In her right hand she held a half-smoked cigarette which she was slowly moving towards her left hand. Françoise barely repressed a scream. Xavière was pressing the glowing brand against her skin with a bitter smile curling her lips. It was an intimate, solitary smile, like the smile of a half-wit; the voluptuous, tortured smile of a woman possessed by secret pleasure. The sight of it was almost unbearable, it concealed something horrible.

The dancer had finished her repertoire, and she was bowing amid applause. Paule had turned towards the table, and now gaped speechlessly with questioning eyes. Pierre had noticed Xavière's performance some time before. Since no one thought fit to speak, Françoise held her tongue, and yet what was going on was intolerable. With her lips rounded coquettishly and affectedly Xavière was gently blowing on the burnt skin which covered her burn. When she had blown away this little protective layer, she once more pressed the glowing end of her cigarette against the open wound. Françoise flinched. Not only did her flesh rise up in revolt, but the wound had injured her more deeply and irrevocably to the very depths of her being. Behind that maniacal grin, was the threat of a danger more positive than any she had ever imagined. Something was there that hungrily hugged itself, that unquestionably existed on its own account. Approach to it was impossible even in thought. Just as she seemed to be getting near it the thought dissolved. This was no tangible object, but an incessant flux, a never-ending escape, only comprehensible to itself, and for ever occult. Eternally shut out she could only continue to circle round it.

'That's idiotic,' she said. 'You will burn yourself to the bone.'

Xavière raised her head and gazed about her with a slightly wild look.

'It doesn't hurt,' she said.

Paule took her wrist.

'In a few moments it's going to hurt terribly,' she said to her. 'How childish!'

The burn was as large as a sixpenny-piece and seemed to be very deep.

'I assure you I don't feel it at all,' said Xavière, pulling her hand away and looking at Paule in a self-satisfied and mysterious way. 'A burn is voluptuous.'

The dancer came to the table. In one hand she was holding a plate, and in the other one of those double necked *porrons* from which the Spaniards drink on festive occasions.

'Who wants to drink my health?' she asked.

Pierre put a note on the plate and Paule took the *porron* between her hands. She said a few words to the woman in Spanish. She threw back her head and skilfully directed a jet of red wine into her mouth, and then cut off the flow with a quick jerk.

'Your turn,' she said to Pierre.

Pierre took the contraption and examined it warily. Then he tilted his head back, bringing the nozzle to the very edge of his lips.

'No, not like that,' said the woman.

With a steady hand, she drew the *porron* away. For a short moment Pierre let the wine run into his mouth, and then in an effort to catch his breath he moved and the liquid drenched his tie.

'Hell!' he said furiously.

The dancer laughed and began to rail at him in Spanish. He looked so upset that a great burst of laughter softened Paule's grave features.

Françoise barely achieved a feeble grin. Fear had penetrated into her, and nothing could take her mind off it. This time she felt imperilled above and beyond her own happiness.

'We're staying on for a while, aren't we?' said Pierre.

'If it doesn't bore you,' said Xavière timidly.

Paule had just left. It was to her calm gaiety that this evening had owed all its charm. She had initiated them, one by one, in the more unusual steps of the paso doble and the tango. She had invited the dancer to their table and had induced her to sing for them some beautiful folk songs, which the whole audience had taken up in chorus. They had drunk a considerable amount of Manzanilla. Pierre had finally brightened up and had fully regained his good humour. Xavière did not seem to be suffering from her burn; innumerable violent and contradictory feelings had been successively reflected in her face. Only for Françoise had the time passed slowly. Music, songs, dancing, nothing had succeeded in allaying the anguish that paralysed her. From the moment Xavière had burnt her hand she had been unable to detach her thoughts from that tortured, ecstatic face, the memory of which made her shudder. She turned to Pierre; she needed to regain a contact with him, but she had separated herself too decisively from him. She could not succeed in attuning herself to him. She was alone. Pierre and Xavière were talking and their voices seemed to be coming from a very great distance.

'Why did you do that?' Pierre was saying as he touched Xavière's hand.

Xavière looked at him in supplication; her whole expression was one of tender pleading. It was because of her that Françoise had stood up to Pierre to the extent of being unable now to smile at him; and yet Xavière had already silently made it up with him, and seemed prepared to fall into his arms.

'Why?' said Pierre. He stared for a moment at the injured hand. 'I'd swear that it's a holy burn.'

Xavière was smiling, as she turned a guileless face towards him.

'A penitential burn,' he continued.

'Yes,' said Xavière. 'I was so disgustingly sentimental about

286

that rose. I was ashamed of it.'

'You wanted to bury deep within you the memory of last night, didn't you?' Pierre's tone was friendly, but he was tense.

Xavière stared with admiring eyes.

'How do you know?' she said. She seemed spellbound by this sorcery.

'That wilted rose. It was easy to guess,' said Pierre.

'That was a ridiculous, a theatrical gesture,' said Xavière. 'But it was you who provoked me,' she added archly.

Her smile was as warm as a kiss, and Françoise wondered uncomfortably what she was doing there, witnessing this amorous tête-à-tête. She did not belong here; but where did she belong? Surely nowhere else. At this moment she felt expunged from the face of the world.

'I!' said Pierre.

'You were looking sarcastic, and you were staring at me threateningly,' said Xavière tenderly.

'Yes, I was unpleasant,' said Pierre. 'I apologize. But it was because I felt that you were interested in anything rather than in us.'

'You must have antennae,' said Xavière. 'You were bristling before I even opened my mouth,' she shook her head, 'only they're not very good ones.'

'I at once suspected that you'd become infatuated with Gerbert,' said Pierre bluntly.

'Infatuated?' said Xavière. She frowned. 'But what on earth did that young man tell you?'

Pierre had not done it intentionally. He was incapable of anything so contemptible, but his words contained an unpleasant insinuation against Gerbert.

'He didn't tell me anything,' said Pierre, 'but he enjoyed his evening, and it's unusual for you to make the effort to charm anyone.'

'I might have guessed as much,' said Xavière with rage. 'No sooner is one a little civil to a fellow than he gets ideas! God knows what he's gone and concocted in that empty little brain of his!'

'And besides, if you stayed shut up all day,' said Pierre, 'it was surely to ruminate over last evening's romance.'

Xavière shrugged her shoulders.

'It was inflated romance,' she said testily.

'That's how it seems to you now,' said Pierre.

'Not at all. I knew it all the time,' said Xavière impatiently. She looked straight at Pierre. 'I wanted yesterday evening to seem wonderful to me,' she said. 'Do you understand?'

There was a silence. One would never know precisely what Gerbert had been to her during those twenty-four hours, and she herself had already forgotten it. What was certain was that now she was openly denying him.

'It was to revenge yourself on us,' said Pierre.

'Yes,' said Xavière, in a low voice.

'But we hadn't had dinner with Gerbert for ages. We have to see him occasionally,' said Pierre, in an apologetic tone.

'I know,' said Xavière, 'but it always aggravates me when you allow yourselves to be preyed upon by all these people.'

'You're a possessive little person,' said Pierre.

'I can't help it,' said Xavière dejectedly.

'Don't try,' said Pierre tenderly. 'Your possessiveness is not petty jealousy. It goes with your inflexibility, with the violence of your feelings. You'd no longer be the same person if it were taken away from you.'

'Ah! It would be so nice if we three were alone in the world!' said Xavière. Her eyes had a passionate gleam. 'Only the three of us!'

Françoise's smile was forced. She had often been hurt by Pierre's and Xavière's collusion, but tonight she detected her own condemnation in it. Jealousy and resentment were feelings she had always spurned; yet this pair were now discussing them as if they were beautiful, cumbersome, precious objects to be handled with respectful care. She, too, might have enshrined these disturbing riches within herself. Why had she preferred to them the old, empty precepts which Xavière brazenly kicked aside? On many occasions she had been transfixed with jealousy. She had been tempted to hate Pierre, to wish Xavière ill; but, under the futile pretext of keeping herself pure, she had created a void within herself. With calm audacity Xavière chose to assert herself. Her reward was that she had a definite place in the world, and Pierre turned to her with passionate interest. Françoise had not dared to be herself, and she understood, in a passion of suffering, that this hypocritical cowardice had resulted in her being nothing at all.

She looked up. Xavière was speaking.

'I like you when you look tired,' she was saying; 'you become very ethereal.' She gave Pierre a quick smile. 'You look like your ghost. You were beautiful as a ghost.'

Françoise studied Pierre. It was true that he was pale. That nervous fragility, reflected at this moment in his drawn features, had often moved her to tears, but she was too detached from him to be touched by his appearance. It was only through Xavière's smile that she could sense its romantic charm.

'But you know I don't want to be a ghost any more,' said Pierre.

'Ah! But a ghost isn't a corpse,' said Xavière. 'It's a living thing, only it gets its body from its soul. It hasn't any unnecessary flesh; it doesn't get hungry, thirsty, or sleepy.' Her eyes rested on Pierre's forehead, then on his hands, long, firm, slender hands Françoise had often lovingly touched, but that she never thought to look at. 'And besides, what I find poetic is that it's not earthbound. Wherever it may be, it is also elsewhere at the same time.'

'I'm nowhere else but here,' said Pierre.

He smiled fondly at Xavière. Françoise called to mind with what joy she had so often been the recipient of such smiles, yet she was now incapable of coveting them.

'Yes,' said Xavière, 'but I don't know how to put it exactly; you are here because you want to be. You don't look confined.'

'Do I often look confined?'

Xavière hesitated.

'Sometimes,' she smiled conquettishly. 'When you talk with dull old fogies you almost seem to be one of them yourself.'

'I remember when you met me, you were inclined to take me for a tiresome pompous ass!'

'You've changed,' said Xavière.

She ran her eyes over him with a proud and happy possessive look. She thought she had changed him. Could it be true? It was no longer for Françoise to judge. Tonight her troubled heart allowed the greatest riches to sink into indifference: she felt obliged to trust this intense fervour that shone with new brilliance in Xavière's eyes.

'You look completely worn out,' said Pierre.

Françoise shuddered. It was to her that he was speaking, and he seemed worried. She tried to control her voice.

'I think I've drunk too much,' she said. The words stuck in her throat.

Pierre looked at her with distress. 'You've thought me

completely hateful this evening, haven't you?' he said remorsefully.

Spontaneously he laid his hand on hers. She managed to smile at him. She was touched by his solicitude, but even this tenderness that he was reawakening in her could not tear her out of her solitary anguish.

'You were a little hateful,' she said, taking his hand.

'I'm sorry,' said Pierre, 'for losing control.' He was so upset at having hurt her, that if their love alone had been at stake Françoise would have been at peace again. 'Now I've spoiled your evening for you,' he said, 'and you were so looking forward to it.'

'Nothing's been spoiled,' said Françoise, and with an effort she added more cheerfully, 'we still have some time ahead of us. It's delightful to be here.' She turned to Xavière. 'Isn't it? Paule was not fibbing. It is a nice place.'

Xavière wore a peculiar smile. 'Don't you think we look a little like American tourists seeing the night-life of Paris? We're sitting by ourselves so that we won't be contaminated, and we're sight-seeing without coming into contact with anything . . .'

Pierre's face clouded over. 'What! Do you expect us to snap our fingers and shout "Olle!" What do you expect?'

'I don't expect anything,' said Xavière coldly, 'I'm stating a fact.'

It was beginning all over again. Dense vapours of hatred, as corrosive as an acid, were once more emanating from Xavière, and there was no defence against its excruciating bite. There was nothing to do but to endure it and wait. But Françoise felt completely exhausted. Pierre was not so resigned: Xavière did not frighten him.

'Why do you suddenly hate us?' he said harshly.

Xavière burst into a strident laugh.

'No, no! You're not going to begin all over again,' she said. Her cheeks were aflame and her mouth was set. She seemed on the point of exasperation. 'I don't spend my time hating you. I'm listening to the music.'

'You do hate us,' Pierre insisted.

'Definitely not,' said Xavière. She caught her breath. 'It's not the first time that I've been astonished at the pleasure you take in looking at things from the outside as if they were stage sets.' She touched her breast. 'I,' she continued with an eloquent smile, 'I'm made of flesh and blood. Do you understand?'

Pierre threw a despairing glance at Françoice. He hesitated, then seemed to be trying to get control of himself.

'What happened?' he said, in a conciliatory tone.

'Nothing happened,' said Xavière.

'You thought we were behaving like lovers?'

Xavière looked him in the eye.

'Precisely,' she said arrogantly.

Françoise clenched her teeth. She was struck with a wild desire to thrash Xavière, to trample upon her. She spent hours listening patiently to her duets with Pierre, and Xavière was refusing her the right to exchange the slightest token of friendship with him! That was too much. It could not go on in this way. She would stand it no longer.

'You're utterly unfair,' said Pierre angrily. 'If Françoise was depressed it was because of my behaviour with you. I don't think that can be called behaving like lovers.'

Without answering Xavière leaned forward. At a neighbouring table, a young woman had just sprung to her feet and in a raucous voice was beginning to recite a Spanish poem. A great silence fell, and every eye was turned towards her. Even without full knowledge of the meaning of the words, her impassioned accent, and her face illuminated by emotional fervour were deeply moving. The poem was about hatred and death, about hope too perhaps, and by virtue of the rhythmic ebb and flow the fate of ravaged Spain was vividly evoked to every mind. Fire and sword had driven the guitars from the streets, gone were the songs, the dazzling shawls, and the spikenard blossoms. The cabarets were flat, and the bombs had ripped open the goatskin bottles swelled with wine; in the warm evening sweetness, fear and hunger stalked. The flamenco songs and the taste of intoxicating wines were now no more than funeral trappings veiling a dead past. For a little while, her eyes fixed on the red and tragic mouth, Françoise yielded to the power of the desolate pictures evoked by this rasping incantation: she longed to lose herself, body and soul, in these lamentations; in the nostalgia throbbing beneath these mysterious resonances. She turned her head. She was able to stop thinking about herself, but she could not forget that Xavière was beside her.

Xavière was no longer watching the woman: she was staring

into space. A cigarette was alight between her fingers and the glowing end was beginning to touch her flesh without her seeming to be aware of it, she seemed to be in the grip of hysterical ecstasy. Françoise passed her hand across her forehead, she was dripping with perspiration. The atmosphere was stifling, and deep down her thoughts were burning like a torch. This hostile presence, which earlier had betrayed itself in a lunatic's smile, was approaching closer and closer: there was now no way of avoiding its terrifying disclosure. Day after day, minute after minute, Françoise had fled the danger; but the worst had happened, and she had at last come face to face with this insurmountable obstacle which she had sensed, behind a shadowy outline, since her earliest childhood. At the back of Xavière's maniacal pleasure, at the back of her hatred and jealousy, the abomination loomed, as monstrous and definite as death. Before Françoise's very eyes, and yet apart from her, something existed like a sentence without an appeal: detached, absolute, unalterable, an alien conscience was taking up its position. It was like death, a total negation, an eternal absence, and yet, by a staggering contradiction, this abyss of nothingness could make itself present to itself and make itself fully exist for itself. The entire universe was engulfed in it, and Françoise, for ever excluded from the world, was herself dissolved in this void, of which the infinite contour no word, no image could encompass.

'Beautiful!' said Pierre.

He bent over Xavière and lifted the red-hot stub from her fingers. She stared at him as if waking from a nightmare, then looked at Françoise. Abruptly she took them each by the hand. The palms of her hands were burning. Françoise shuddered when she came in contact with these feverish fingers which tightened on hers; she wanted to withdraw her hand, but she was now unable to move. Riveted to Xavière she contemplated in amazement this body which allowed itself to be touched, and this beautiful face behind which the abomination was concealed. For a long time Xavière had been only a fragment of Françoise's life, and suddenly she had become the only sovereign reality, and Françoise now possessed no more than the colourless contours of a reflection.

'Why should it be she rather than I?' thought Françoise, with anger. She need only say one word, she need only say, 'It is I.' But she would have to believe in that word; she would have to know how to choose herself. For many weeks Françoise had no longer been able to dissolve Xavière's hatred, her affection, her thoughts, to harmless vapours. She had let them bite into her; she had turned herself into a prey. Freely, through her moments of resistance and revolt, she had made use of herself to destroy herself. She was witnessing the course of her own life like an indifferent spectator, without ever daring to assert herself, whereas Xavière, from head to foot, was nothing but a living assertion of herself. She made herself exist with so sure a power, that Françoise, spellbound, had allowed herself to be carried away so far as to prefer Xavière to herself, and thus to obliterate herself. She had gone so far as to be seeing places, people, and Pierre's smiles, through Xavière's eyes. She had reached the point of no longer knowing herself, except through Xavière's feelings for her, and now she was trying to merge into Xavière. But in this hopeless effort she was only succeeding in destroying herself.

The guitars kept up their monotonous thrumming and the air was throbbing like a sirocco. Xavière's hands had not let go their prey: her set face bore no expression. Pierre had not moved either. It was as if the same spell had transmogrified all three of them into marble. Visions were flitting through Françoise's mind: an old jacket, a deserted glade, a corner of the Pôle Nord where Pierre and Xavière were carrying on a mysterious tête-à-tête far apart from her. It had happened to her before, as now it was happening tonight, that she had felt her being dissolve to the advantage of inaccessible other beings; but never had she been aware of her own annihilation with such perfect lucidity. Had she perchance become a complete void! Yet there remained a faint phosphorescence hovering over the surface of things, attended by an infinity of deceptive will-o'-the-wisps. The tension which had been reducing her to rigidity snapped suddenly, and she burst into silent sobs.

The spell was broken. Xavière withdrew her hands. Pierre spoke.

'Suppose we leave,' he said.

Françoise rose. In a flash she was drained of all thought, and her body submissively set itself in motion. She put her cape over her arm and crossed the room. The cold outdoor air dried her tears, but her inner trembling never ceased. Pierre touched her shoulder,

'You aren't well,' he said anxiously.

Françoise gave a ghost of an apologetic smile.

'I've definitely drunk too much,' she said.

Xavière was walking a few paces ahead of them, as stiff as an automaton.

'She's also had all she can hold,' said Pierre. 'We'll take her home, and then we can talk undisturbed.'

'Yes,' said Françoise.

The cool of the night and Pierre's tenderness helped to restore her calm. They caught up with Xavière and each took her by an arm.

'I think it would do us good to walk a short way,' said Pierre.

Xavière said nothing. Against a livid face, her lips were set in a stony grin. They walked down the street in silence; day was dawning. Xavière stopped suddenly.

'Where are we?' she said.

'At la Trinité,' said Pierre.

'Ah!' said Xavière. 'I think I was a little tipsy.'

'I think so too,' said Pierre cheerfully. 'How do you feel?'

'I don't know.' said Xavière. 'I don't know what's happened.' She frowned as if in pain. 'I remember a very beautiful woman who was talking in Spanish; after that there's a blank.'

'You watched her for a while,' said Pierre. 'You were smoking cigarette after cigarette, and you had to have the stubs taken from between your fingers. You were letting them burn you without feeling anything. And then you seemed to wake up a little. You took our hands.'

'Ah! Yes,' said Xavière. She shuddered. 'We were in the depths of hell. I began to think we'd never get out again.'

'You sat there for some time, as if you'd been turned into a statue,' said Pierre. 'And then Françoise began to cry.'

'I remember,' said Xavière, with a vague smile. She lowered her eyelids and said, in a faraway voice, 'I was so glad when she cried, for that's just what I wanted to do.'

For a second Françoise looked with horror at this delicate but implacable face in which she had not once seen reflected any of her own joys and sorrows. Not for one minute during the whole evening had Xavière given a thought to her distress. She had seen her tears only to rejoice at them. Françoise snatched her arm from Xavière's and began to run on ahead as if carried away by a tornado. Sobs of revulsion shook her: her anguish, her tears, this night of torture, belonged to her and she would not allow Xavière to rob her of them. She would flee to the end of the world to escape the avid tentacles with which she wanted to drain her of her lifeblood. She heard hurrying steps behind her and a firm hand stopped her.

'What is it?' said Pierre. 'I beg of you, calm yourself.'

'I don't want to,' said Françoise. 'I don't want to.' Weeping, she fell against his shoulder. When she looked up she saw Xavière, who had caught up with them and was now looking at her with dismayed curiosity. But she had lost all sense of shame; nothing could affect her now. Pierre pushed them both into a taxi and she continued to weep without restraint.

'We're home,' said Pierre.

She rushed upstairs without looking back, and collapsed on to the couch. Her head was hurting her. There was a sound of voices on the floor below, and almost immediately the door opened.

'What's happening?' said Pierre. Quickly he came to her and took her in his arms. She pressed tightly to him, and for a long while there was nothing but emptiness and night, and a caress that lightly touched her hair.

'My dear love, what's happening to you? Speak to me,' said Pierre's voice.

She opened her eyes. In the light of dawn the room had an unusual freshness; she felt that it had not come under the influence of the night. With surprise Françoise found herself once again in the presence of familiar shapes which her eyes could take in with composure. This idea of rejected reality was no more indefinitely tenable than the idea of death. She must return to the full consciousness of material objects and of herself. But she remained as overwhelmed as if she had just come out of a death agony. Never more would she forget.

'I do not know,' she said. She smiled at him feebly. 'Everything was so unbearable.'

'Did I hurt you?'

She seized his hands. 'No,' she said.

'Is it because of Xavière?'

Françoise shrugged her shoulders helplessly. It was too difficult to explain, and her head was aching too much.

'It was hateful for you to witness her jealousy of you,' said

Pierre. There was a touch of remorse in his voice. 'I myself found her insufferable. This cannot go on; I shall speak to her tomorrow.'

Françoise started. 'You can't do that,' she said. 'She'll hate you.'

'I don't care.' He got up, took a few steps round the room, then came back to her.

'I feel guilty,' he said. 'I stupidly relied on the good feelings that girl has for me, but there was no question of a stupid little attempt at seduction. We wanted to build a real trio, a well-balanced life for three in which no one would be sacrificed. Perhaps it was taking a risk, but at least it was worth trying! But if Xavière behaves like a jealous little bitch, and you are an unfortunate victim while I play the gallant lover, it becomes a dirty business.' His face was stern and his voice harsh. 'I shall speak to her.'

Françoise looked at him tenderly. He judged any weakness he may have shown as severely as she had done. Once more he was himself again, in his strength, in his clarity of thought, and in his proud rejection of everything base. But even the return to this perfect agreement between them did not give her back happiness. She felt exhausted and cowardly at the thought of new complications.

'You don't expect to get her to admit that she's jealous of me out of love for you?' she said warily.

'I shall no doubt look like a conceited ass and she will be insanely angry,' said Pierre, 'but I'll take my chance.'

'No,' said Françoise. If Pierre were to lose Xavière, she in her turn would feel unbearably guilty. 'No, please. Besides, that wasn't why I cried.'

'Why did you, then?'

'You'll laugh at me,' she said, with a weak smile. There was a glimmer of hope: perhaps if she managed to encompass her anguish in words she might be rid of it. 'It's because I discovered that she has a conscience like mine. Have you ever felt, in your inmost being, the conscience of others?' Again she was trembling, the words were not releasing her. 'It's intolerable, you know.'

Pierre was looking at her a little incredulously.

'You think I'm drunk,' said Françoise. 'In one way, I am. It's true, but it makes no difference. Why are you so astounded?' She rose suddenly. 'If I were to tell you that I'm

296

afraid of death, you would understand. Well, this thing is just as real and just as terrifying. Of course, we all know that we're not alone in the world. We say these things, just as we say that we'll die some day. But when we begin to believe in it . . .'

She leaned against the wall, the room was swirling round her. Pierre took her by the arm.

'Listen, don't you think you ought to rest? I am not making light of what you're telling me, but it would be better to talk about it calmly after you've slept a little.'

'There's nothing to say about it,' said Françoise. Again the tears began to flow. She was dead tired.

He laid her on the bed, took off her shoes and threw a blanket over her.

'I'd rather like to get a breath of air,' he said, 'but I'll stay until you've fallen asleep.'

He sat down beside her, and she pressed his hand against her cheek. Tonight Pierre's love no longer sufficed to bring her peace, he could not defend her against this thing that had revealed itself during the day and evening. It was beyond reach. Françoise no longer even felt its mysterious emanation and yet it continued inexorably to exist. The weariness, the worries, even the disasters, brought by Xavière when she came to Paris, all these Françoise had accepted wholeheartedly because they were moments of her own life. But what had happened during the course of this night was something utterly different. She could not sublimate it. The world now stood before her like a gigantic interdict. The failure of her very existence was now brought to completion.

Chapter Five

Françoise smiled at the concierge and walked on across the courtyard where the old scenery had been left to rot, and ran up the little green wood steps. During the past few days the theatre had suspended performances and she was looking forward to having a long evening with Pierre; twenty-four hours had passed since she had last seen him, and a slight anxiety tempered her impatience. She never succeeded in waiting unmoved for the account of his excursions with Xavière, yet these were all alike: there were kisses, quarrels, tender reconciliations, passionate conversations, and lengthy silences. Françoise opened his door. Pierre was bending over a chest of drawers, rummaging about among bundles of papers.

He ran towards her. 'Ah! How slowly the time has passed without you!' he said. 'How I cursed Bernheim and his business luncheons! They didn't let me go until rehearsal time.' He took Françoise by the shoulders. 'What have you been doing with yourself?'

'I've a hundred and one things to tell you,' said Françoise. She touched his hair and the nape of his neck. Every time she saw him again, she liked to make certain that he was made of flesh and blood.

'What were you doing? Having a good tidy?'

'Oh! I give up. It's hopeless,' said Pierre, casting a vindictive glance at the chest of drawers. 'Anyhow, it's not so urgent now.'

'The atmosphere was certainly much less tense at that dress rehearsal,' said Françoise.

'Yes, I believe that we've escaped once again; for how long, is another matter.' Pierre rubbed his pipe against his nose to make it shine. 'Was it a success?'

'People laughed a lot. I'm not sure that that was the effect intended; but, in any case, I really enjoyed myself. Blanche Bouguet wanted me to stay for supper, but I escaped with Ramblin. He trotted me round to I don't know how many bars. I kept my end up, and it hasn't stopped me from working hard all day.'

'You must give me a detailed account of the play, and of Bouguet and Ramblin. Would you like something to drink?'

'Give me a little whisky,' said Françoise. 'And then you tell me first what you've been doing. Did you spend a pleasant evening with Xavière?'

'Whew!' said Pierre. He threw up his hands. 'You never saw such a bear-garden. Luckily, it's all over, but for two hours we sat side by side in a corner at the Pôle Nord, quivering with hatred. We've never before had such high tragedy.'

He took a bottle of Vat 69 from his cupboard, and half filled two glasses.

'What happened?' said Françoise.

'Well, I finally broached the question of her jealousy towards you,' said Pierre.

'You shouldn't have,' said Françoise.

'I told you that I had made up my mind to do so.'

'How did you lead up to it?'

'We talked about her exclusiveness, and I told her that, on the whole, it was something strong and estimable in her, but that there was one place where it did not fit, and that was within the trio. She willingly agreed with me, but when I added that she was, nevertheless, showing signs of being jealous of you, she turned scarlet with surprise and anger.'

'You were in a difficult position,' said Françoise.

'Yes,' said Pierre. 'I might easily have appeared ridiculous or obnoxious to her. But her mind's not petty – it was only the basis of the accusation that bowled her over. She fought like a tigress, but I didn't budge. I pointed out a number of instances to her. She wept with rage. She hated me so much that it frightened me. I thought she was going to die of suffocation.'

Françoise looked at him anxiously.

'Are you at least quite sure that she doesn't bear you any grudge?'

'Absolutely sure,' said Pierre. 'I lost my temper, too, at the beginning. But later, I made it abundantly clear to her that I was only trying to help her because she was beginning to become odious in your eyes. I gave her to understand that what we had set out minds on, all three of us, was something difficult to achieve, and that it required the complete good will of each one of us. When she was quite convinced that my words had carried no censure, that I'd only warned her against a danger, she stopped being angry with me. I believe that not only did she forgive me, but that she has decided to try her utmost to control herself.'

'If it's true, it does her great credit,' said Françoise. She felt a sudden surge of confidence.

'We talked far more sincerely than usual,' said Pierre. 'And I had the feeling that after this conversation something was released within her. You know that look she has, of always withholding the best of herself, had disappeared. She seemed to be completely at one with me, without any reserve, as if she saw no objections to loving me openly.'

'By honestly acknowledging her jealousy, she was perhaps delivered from it,' said Françoise. She took a cigarette and looked fondly at Pierre.

'Why are you smiling?' said Pierre.

'I'm always amused at the way you have of regarding the good feelings anyone may have for you as a sign of grace. It's one more way of taking yourself for God in person.'

'There's something in that,' said Pierre with embarrassment. He smiled abstractedly and his face was wreathed in the happy innocence that Françoise had seen on it only in sleep. 'She invited me to have tea with her, and for the first time, when I kissed her, she returned my kisses. In a state of complete submission, she stayed in my arms until three o'clock in the morning.'

Françoise felt a stab in her heart. She, too, would have to learn to become mistress of herself. It had always pained her that Pierre could embrace that body, whose bestowal she would not even have known how to accept.

'I told you you'd end up by sleeping with her.' She tried to mitigate the brutality of these words by smiling.

Pierre made an evasive gesture.

'It will depend on her,' he said. 'I, certainly . . . but I wouldn't want to lead her into anything that might be displeasing to her.'

'She's not got the temperament of a virgin,' said Françoise. From the moment she uttered them these words entered cruelly into her and she blushed. She hated to look upon Xavière as a woman with the desires of a woman, but the truth forced itself upon her. 'I loathe purity. I'm made of flesh and blood.' With all the strength at her command, Xavière was in revolt against this uneasy chastity to which she had been sentenced. In her bad moods, her bitter resentment was apparent.

'Certainly not,' said Pierre. 'And I even go so far as to think that she'll never be happy until she has achieved a sensual equilibrium. She's in a state of crisis at this present moment, don't you think?'

'Yes, I believe it implicitly,' said Françoise.

Perhaps Pierre's kisses, his caresses, were precisely what had awakened Xavière's senses: surely, matters could not rest at their present stage. Françoise was carefully examining her fingers: she would grow accustomed to this idea in the end, the unpleasantness of it already seemed a little less sharp. Since she was certain of Pierre's love and of Xavière's tenderness, no thought could now be obnoxious.

'What we're demanding of her is most unusual,' said Pierre. 'We were able to envisage such a way of living only by reason of the exceptional love between us two, and she can only conform to it because she herself is exceptional. It's quite understandable that she should have moments of uncertainty and even of revolt.'

'Yes, you must give us time,' said Françoise.

She got up, walked over to the drawer Pierre had left open and plunged her hands among the scattered papers. She herself had sinned through mistrust. She had not forgiven Pierre his shortcomings which were frequently very minor: she had kept to herself a mass of thoughts she should have shared with him, and often, she had sought less to understand him than to oppose him. She picked out an old photograph and smiled. Dressed in a Greek tunic and wearing a curled wig, Pierre was gazing at the heavens with a youthful and stern expression.

'That's how you looked when I first set eyes on you,' she said. 'You've hardly aged at all.'

'Neither have you,' said Pierre. He came to her side and bent over the drawer.

'I'd like to go through all that with you,' said Françoise.

'Yes,' said Pierre. 'It's full of amusing things.' He straightened himself up and ran his hand along Françoise's arm. 'Do you think we were wrong to embark on this affair?' he asked anxiously. 'Do you think we'll succeed in carrying it through?'

'I've sometimes had my doubts,' said Françoise. 'But this

evening hope is returning.'

She walked away from the chest of drawers and went back to sit down by her glass of whisky.

'And where have you got to?' said Pierre, sitting down beside her.

'I?' said Françoise. When she was in her ordinary state of mind, it always frightened her a little to talk about herself.

'Yes,' said Pierre. 'Do you still feel Xavière's existence to be an abomination of evil?'

'You know that idea never comes to me except in moments of inspiration,' said Françoise.

'But still it does recur from time to time?' Pierre insisted.

'It's bound to,' said Françoise.

'You amaze me,' said Pierre. 'You're the only living being I know who's capable of shedding tears on discovering in someone else a conscience similar to your own.'

'Do you consider that stupid?'

'Of course not,' said Pierre. 'It's quite true that everyone experiences his own conscience as an absolute. How can several absolutes be compatible? The problem is as great a mystery as birth or death, in fact, it's such a problem that all philosophers break their heads over it.'

'Well then, why are you amazed?' said Françoise.

'What surprises me is that you should be affected in such a concrete manner by a metaphysical problem.'

'But it is something concrete,' said Françoise. 'The whole meaning of my life is at stake.'

'I don't say it isn't,' said Pierre. He surveyed her with curiosity. 'Nevertheless, this power you have to live an idea, body and soul, is unusual.'

'But to me, an idea is not a question of theory,' said Françoise. 'It passes the test or, if it remains theoretical, it has no value.' She smiled. 'Otherwise, I wouldn't have waited for Xavière's arrival to be certain that my conscience is not unique in this world.'

Pierre ran his finger over his lower lip as he thought this over.

'I can readily understand you making this discovery apropos of Xavière,' he said.

'Yes,' said Françoise. 'I've never had any difficulty with you, because I barely distinguish you from myself.'

'And besides, there's give and take between us.'

'How do you mean?'

'The moment you acknowledge my conscience, you know that I acknowledge one in you, too. That makes all the difference.'

'Perhaps,' said Françoise. She stared in momentary perplexity at the bottom of her glass. 'In short, that is friendship. Each renounces individual self-importance. But what if either refuses to renounce it?'

'In that case, friendship is impossible,' said Pierre.

'Well then, what can be done about it?'

'I don't know,' said Pierre.

Xavière never renounced any part of herself. No matter how high she placed one, even if it amounted to worship, one remained an object to her.

'It can't be remedied,' said Françoise.

She smiled. One would have to kill Xavière . . . She rose and walked to the window. Tonight, Xavière did not weigh heavily on her mind. She drew back the curtain. She loved this small peaceful square where the people of the neighbourhood came to get a breath of fresh air. An old man seated on a bench was taking some food out of a paper bag; a child was running round a tree, of which the leaves were silhouetted, with metallic clarity, by a street lamp. Pierre was free. She was alone. But, within this separateness, they could re-establish a union as essential as the one she used to dream of too easily.

'What are you thinking about?' said Pierre.

She took his face between her hands and, without answering, kissed it again and again.

'What a wonderful evening we've had,' said Françoise.

She squeezed Pierre's arm happily. They had looked at old photographs together, re-read old letters, and then made a grand tour by the river, le Châtelet and les Halles, discussing Françoise's novel, and their youth, and the future of Europe. It was the first time for weeks that they had had such a long, unrestricted, and objective conversation. At last the circle of violent emotion and anxiety, in which Xavière's sorcery imprisoned them, had been broken, and they found themselves once more at one at the central point of the vast world. Behind them stretched the limitless past. Continents and oceans were spread like huge sheets over the surface of the globe, and the miraculous certainty of existing amid this incalculable wealth overran even the too narrow bounds of space and time.

'Look, there's a light in Xavière's room,' said Pierre.

Françoice shuddered. After that untrammelled flight, she was coming down to earth in this dark little street, in front of her hotel, and the shock was painful. It was two o'clock in the morning. Pierre, like a detective on the watch, was staring at a lighted window in the black façade.

'What's so surprising about that?' asked Françoise.

'Nothing,' said Pierre. He opened the door and hurried up the stairs. On the third-floor landing he stopped. A murmur of voices broke the silence.

'Someone's talking in her room,' said Pierre. He stood stock still, his ears cocked. A few paces behind him, her hand on the banister, Françoise stood motionless. 'Who on earth can it be?' he said.

'With whom was she to go out tonight?' said Françoise.

'She had no plans,' said Pierre. He took a step. 'I want to know who it is.'

He took another step and a floor-board creaked.

'They'll hear you,' said Françoise.

Pierre hesitated. Then he bent down and began to untie his shoe laces. Françoise was overwhelmed by despair more bitter than any she had ever known. Pierre had begun to tip-toe along between the yellow walls of the corridor. He was pressing his ear to the door. Everything had been obliterated at one stroke: the happy evening, Françoise herself, the whole world. There was nothing but the silent landing, the wooden door panels, and those whispering voices behind them. Françoise looked at him in distress. In his haunted, maniacal features, she could barely recognize the beloved face that had been smiling at her so tenderly only a short while ago. She mounted the last few steps. She felt that she had allowed herself to be deluded by the precarious lucidity of some lunatic, for whom a breath would suffice to topple him back into madness. Those rational hours of relaxation had been merely a temporary alleviation. There would never be a cure. Pierre tip-toed back to her.

'It's Gerbert,' he said in a low voice. 'I suspected as much.' Shoes in hand, he climbed up to the top floor.

'Well, there's nothing so mysterious about that,' said Françoise, walking into her room. 'They went out together, and he came home with her.'

'She didn't tell me she was going to see him,' said Pierre. 'Why did she hide it from me? Or else she decided on the spur of the moment.'

Françoise had taken off her coat. She slipped off her dress and put on her dressing-gown.

'They must have run into each other,' she said.

'They no longer go to Dominique's. No, she must have deliberately gone to look for him.'

'Unless it was he,' said Françoise.

'He would never have dared to ask her to go out with him at the last minute.'

Pierre was sitting on the edge of the divan, gazing at his stockinged feet in apparent perplexity.

'In all probability she suddenly felt like going out dancing,' said Françoise.

'Yes, so violent a feeling that she rang him up, she, who's frightened to death of a telephone! Or else she went all the way down to Saint-Germain-des-Près, she, who's incapable of walking three steps away from Montparnasse!' Pierre kept staring at his feet. The right sock had a hole in it, and the protruding tip of his little toe seemed to fascinate him. 'There's something behind all this,' he said.

'What should there be?' said Françoise. She was resignedly brushing her hair. How long was this indefinite and perpetually new discussion to last? What has Xavière done? What would she do? What was she thinking? Why? How? Evening after evening, the obsession was revived, always as harassing, always as futile, and with the same hasty feverish taste in her mouth, the same desolation in her heart, the same weariness in her sleepy body. When these questions had finally been answered, a new series of identical questions would take up their relentless round. What does Xavière want? What will she say? How? Why? There was no way of putting a stop to them.

'I don't understand,' said Pierre. 'She was so affectionate last night, so yielding, so trusting.'

'Well, who says that she's changed?' said Françoise. 'Whatever you may say, going out with Gerbert is no crime.'

'No one, except you or me, has ever entered her room,' said Pierre. 'If she did invite Gerbert, it's either in revenge against me, which means that she's begun to hate me; or else she had a sudden desire for him to come up to her room. And that means that he attracts her very strongly.' He was twitching his

305

feet in a puzzled and foolish manner. 'It could be both.'

'Probably it's a mere whim,' said Françoise without conviction. Last night's reconciliation with Pierre had certainly been sincere, that was one kind of pretence of which Xavière was incapable: but, with her, the latest smiles were not to be trusted, they were only the forerunners of lulls of uncertain duration. As soon as she had parted from anyone, Xavière immediately began to review the situation, and it very often happened that after leaving her, following a calm, reasonable, and affectionate talk, one returned to find her blazing with hatred.

Pierre shrugged his shoulders. 'You know very well that it isn't,' he said.

Françoise took a step towards him. 'Do you think she's angry with you because of that conversation? I really am sorry.'

'There's nothing for you to be sorry about,' said Pierre brusquely. 'She ought to be able to stand hearing someone tell her the truth.'

He got up and took a few steps across the room. Françoise had often seen him worried, but on this occasion he seemed to be fighting some intolerable suffering. She longed to release him from it: the bitter defiance, which she usually felt towards him when he inflicted anxiety and worry upon himself, had dissolved before the distress in his face. But nothing depended on her any more.

'Aren't you going to bed?' she asked.

'Yes,' said Pierre.

She stepped behind the screen and smeared some orange-scented cream on her face. Pierre's anxiety was infecting her. Directly below her, separated only by a few boards and a little plaster, was Xavière's unpredictable face, with Gerbert looking at it. She had switched on the bedside lamp, a faint glow beneath its blood-red shade, and muffled words were forcing their way through the smoke-laden darkness. What were they saying? Were they sitting side by side? Were they touching each other? She could imagine Gerbert's face, he always presented a true image of himself; but what became of him in Xavière's heart? Was he desirable, touching, cruel, indifferent? Was he good to look upon, was he an enemy or a prey? Their voices did not penetrate to the bedroom. Françoise was listening only to the rustle of clothes on the other side of the screen and the ticking of the alarm clock, amplified in the silence, as if heard through the uncertain haze of a high temperature.

'Are you ready?' said Françoise.

'Yes,' said Pierre. Barefoot and in pyjamas, he was beside the door. He opened it softly. 'You can't hear anything now,' he said. 'I wonder if Gerbert is still there.'

Françoise walked over to him.

'No, you can't hear a thing.'

'I'll go and see,' said Pierre.

Françoise laid her hand on his arm.

'Be careful. It would be so unpleasant if they were to find you there.'

'Don't worry,' said Pierre.

For a moment, Françoise watched him through the half-open door. Then she picked up a scrap of cotton-wool and a bottle of nail-polish remover, and began meticulously to rub her nails. First one finger, then another: all round each cuticle were little specks of pink. If it were possible to lose oneself in each minute, tragedy would never force its way through to one's heart: it must have assistance. Françoise gave a start. Two bare feet were brushing over the floor.

'Well?' she said.

'There was absolutely no sound,' said Pierre. He stood leaning against the door. 'They are certainly making love.'

'Or were; probably Gerbert has left,' said Françoise.

'No, if the door had opened or closed, I would have heard it.'

'In any case, they could be quiet without making love,' said Françoise.

'If she did bring him home with her, it's because she wanted to throw herself into his arms,' said Pierre.

'Not necessarily,' said Françoise.

'I'm sure of it,' said Pierre.

This peremptory tone was not usual with him. Françoise stiffened.

'I can't see Xavière bringing a man home with her to make love with him: or if she did, he'd have to be in a dead faint. Why, she'd go mad if she thought that Gerbert suspected that she'd fallen for him! You saw how she decided to hate him when she suspected him of being in the least bit pleased with himself.'

Pierre gave Françoise a queer look.

'Can't you trust my psychological sense? I tell you that they were making love.'

'You're not infallible,' said Françoise.

'That may be, but where Xavière is concerned, you are wrong every time,' said Pierre.

'That remains to be proved,' said Françoise.

Pierre gave her a sly, almost spiteful smile.

'What if I were to tell you that I saw them?' he said.

Françoise was taken aback. Why had he made such game of her?

'Did you see them?' she asked in an unsteady voice.

'Yes, I looked through the key-hole. They were on the divan and they were making love.'

Françoise felt more and more ill at ease. There was something shame-faced and shifty in Pierre's expression.

'Why didn't you tell me so at once?'

'I wanted to know if you'd take my word for it,' said Pierre with a short, unpleasant laugh.

Françoise could hardly keep back her tears. Pierre had deliberately tried to put her in the wrong. All this strange manoeuvring presupposed a hostility that she had never suspected. Was it possible that he was nursing secret resentments against her?

'You seem to think you're an oracle,' she said curtly.

She got into bed and Pierre disappeared behind the screen. Her throat was on fire. After such an unclouded and tender evening this sudden burst of hatred was inconceivable. But was he really the same man? Was he in fact the man who a short while ago was talking to her about herself with such solicitude, or was he this furtive Peeping Tom who bent over a key-hole with the smirk of a jealous lover? She could not restrain a feeling of real horror in the face of this stubborn, hot-headed indiscretion. Lying on her back, with her arms folded under her head, she held back her thoughts as one holds back one's breath in an attempt to postpone the moment of suffering, but this wincing was in itself far worse than a real and definite pain. She turned her eyes to Pierre who was now approaching her. Fatigue softened the flesh of his face without making his features any the more gentle; beneath his hard stubborn head, the whiteness of his neck appeared obscene.

She turned towards the wall. Pierre lay down beside her and put his hand on the switch. For the first time in their life together, they were about to go to sleep as enemies. Françoise kept her eyes open. She was afraid of what might happen when she gave way to sleep.

'Aren't you sleepy?' said Pierre.

She did not stir. 'No,' she said.

'What are you thinking?'

She did not answer. She could not utter a single other word without beginning to cry.

'You think I'm hateful,' said Pierre.

She controlled herself. 'I think that you are well on the way to hating me,' she said.

'I!' said Pierre. She felt his hand on her shoulder, and she saw that the face he was turning towards her was full of distress. 'I don't want you even to think such a thing; that would be the bitterest blow.'

'It began to look like it,' she said in a choking voice.

'How could you believe such a thing?' said Pierre. 'That I should hate you?'

His tone betrayed a poignant despair, and suddenly, with a spasm of joy and pain, Françoise saw that there were tears in his eyes. She threw herself towards him without restraining her sobs. Never had she seen Pierre cry.

'No, I don't believe it,' she said. 'It would be so horrible.'

Pierre hugged her to him. 'I love you,' he said in a low voice.

'And I love you, too,' said Françoise.

Lying against his shoulder she continued to weep, but now her tears were sweet. She would never forget how Pierre's eyes had become moist because of her.

'You know,' said Pierre, 'I lied to you just now.'

'How?' said Françoise.

'It wasn't true that I wanted to put you to the test. I was ashamed for having looked. That's why I didn't tell you at once.'

'Ah!' said Françoise, 'that's why you looked so shifty!'

'I wanted you to know that they were in each other's arms, but I thought you'd take my word for it. I was angry with you for forcing the truth out of me.'

'I thought you were acting out of pure spite,' said Françoise, 'and that seemed appalling to me.' Gently, she ran her hand over his forehead. 'It's funny, I never thought you could feel ashamed.'

'You can't imagine how sordid I felt, creeping along the corridor in my pyjamas and peeping through the key-hole.'

'I know; passion is sordid,' said Françoise.

Her calm was restored. Pierre no longer seemed a monster to her, since he was capable of lucidly passing judgement on himself.

'It is sordid,' repeated Pierre. He was staring at the ceiling. 'I can't bear the thought that she's making love with Gerbert.'

'I understand,' said Françoise. She pressed her cheek against his. Until tonight, she had always tried to keep outside Pierre's annoyances. Perhaps that had been an instinctive prudence, because now that she was trying to live his distress with him, the suffering which came upon her was unbearable.

'We ought to try to sleep,' said Pierre.

'Yes,' she said. She closed her eyes. She knew that Pierre had no desire to sleep, nor could she take her thoughts from the divan below her, where Gerbert and Xavière were locked in each other's arms, mouth to mouth. What was Xavière trying to find in his arms? Revenge against Pierre? Sensual satisfaction? Was it by chance that she had chosen this prey rather than another? Or was it him she coveted when she passionately demanded something to touch? Françoise's eyelids were growing heavy. In a sudden flash, she recalled Gerbert's face, his bronzed cheeks, his long feminine eyelashes. Was he in love with Xavière? Was he capable of being in love? Would he have loved her, Françoise, if she had wished it? Why had he been unable to will this? How hollow all those old reasons seemed! Or was it she who could no longer fathom their difficult meaning? In any case, it was Xavière he was embracing. Her eyes became as hard as stone. For a moment or two, she still heard the even breathing beside her; then she heard nothing more.

Suddenly, Françoise regained consciousness. There was a thick layer of fog behind her: she must have slept for a long time. She opened her eyes. In the room, night had given way to morning. Pierre was sitting up in bed; he looked wide awake.

'What time is it?' she asked.

'It's five o'clock,' said Pierre.

'Didn't you sleep?'

'Yes, a little.' He looked at the door. 'I'd like to know if Gerbert has gone.'

'He couldn't have stayed all night,' said Françoise.

'I'm going to have a look,' said Pierre.

He threw back the sheets and got out of bed. This time Françoise did not try to hold him back; she, too, wanted to know. She got out of bed and followed him on to the landing. A grey light had filtered into the stair-well; the whole house was asleep. She leaned over the banisters; her heart was thumping. What would happen now?

A moment later Pierre reappeared at the foot of the stairs and beckoned to her. She went down to him.

'The key is in the lock; you can't see anything now, but I think she's alone. She seems to be crying.'

Françoise went up to the door. She heard the faint clink of china, as if Xavière had put down a cup on a saucer. This was followed by a muffled sound and a sob; then another heavier sob, then a torrent of desperate, unrestrained sobbing. Xavière must have fallen on her knees in front of the divan or thrown herself full length on the floor. She was always so circumspect in her greatest sorrows that it was impossible to believe that this animal groan came from her body.

'You don't think she's drunk?' said Françoise.

Alcohol was the only thing that could have made Xavière lose control of herself so completely.

'I suppose she must be,' said Pierre.

They stood in front of the door, anguished and helpless. There was no pretext for knocking at this hour of the morning, and yet it was agonizing to think of Xavière prostrate and sobbing, a prey to all the nightmares of drunkenness and aloneness.

'Don't let's stay here,' said Françoise at last. The sobs had subsided; they had changed into short, painful gasps. 'We'll know everything in a few hours' time,' she added.

Slowly, they went upstairs to their room. Neither one nor the other had the strength to evolve fresh conjectures. Words would not serve to free them from this nebulous fear in which Xavière's wailing reverberated endlessly. What was the cause of her suffering? Could she be healed? Françoise threw herself on the bed, and unresistingly let herself drift into the depths

311

of weariness, fear and grief.

When Françoise awoke, daylight was filtering through the shutters. It was ten o'clock in the morning. Pierre was asleep, with his arms interlaced above his head, and he had an angelic and innocent look on his face. Françoise propped herself up on her elbow. From under the door there protruded part of a sheet of pink paper. Suddenly, the whole night came back to her mind, with its feverish comings and goings, and its throbbing uncertainties. She jumped out of bed. The sheet of paper had been torn in half, and on the jagged slip were scrawled words formed by large, untidy, overlapping strokes. Françoise deciphered the beginning of the note. 'I am so disgusted with myself – I ought to have jumped out of the window – but I shan't have the courage. Don't forgive me. Tomorrow morning you ought to kill me yourself if I've been too cowardly.' The last sentences were totally illegible. At the bottom of the sheet, in huge shaky letters, was written: 'No forgiveness.'

'What is it?' said Pierre.

He was sitting on the edge of the bed, with his hair tousled and his eyes still drugged with sleep; but behind his apparent miasma, his anxiety was distinct.

Françoise handed him the paper. 'She was well and truly sozzled,' she said. 'Look at the writing.'

' "No forgiveness," ' Pierre read aloud. He quickly glanced over the green ink scratches. 'Quick, go and see what's happening to her. Knock on her door.' There was panic in his eyes.

'I'm going,' said Françoise. She popped on her slippers and hurried downstairs. Her legs were shaking. What if Xavière had suddenly become insane? Would she be stretched out, lifeless, behind her door? Or huddled wild-eyed in a corner?

There was a pink patch on the door. Françoise hurried up to it. A piece of paper was fixed on the panel by a drawing-pin: it was the other half of the torn sheet.

Xavière had written in large letters: 'No forgiveness,' and beneath it was a jumbled mass of illegible scribbles. Françoise bent over the key-hole, but the key blocked the aperture: she knocked. There was a faint creaking, but no one answered. Xavière was probably asleep.

Françoise hesitated for a moment. Then she tore down the paper and went back to her room.

'I didn't dare knock,' she said. 'I think she's asleep. Look what she had pinned to her door.'

'It's illegible,' said Pierre, as he studied the mysterious marks for a moment. 'There's the word "unworthy". One thing is certain, she was completely beside herself.' He thought for a moment. 'Was she already drunk when she made love to Gerbert? Did she do it deliberately to give herself courage, because she thought she was playing a dirty trick on me? Or did they get drunk together without premeditation?'

'She must have cried, then written this note, and after that she must have fallen asleep,' said Françoise. She wished she could be sure that Xavière was lying peacefully in her bed.

She opened the shutters and daylight poured into the room. Almost with amazement, she gazed down for a moment on to the busy, sane street where everything had its normal appearance. And then she turned back into the anguish-ridden room in which the usual obsessive thoughts were ceaselessly pursuing their course.

'I'll go and knock all the same,' she said. 'It's impossible to stay like this without knowing for certain. Supposing she's swallowed some drug! God knows what state she's in.'

'Yes, knock until she answers,' said Pierre.

Françoise went downstairs. For hours past she had not stopped going down and coming up, either in reality or in her thoughts. Within her Xavière's sobbing still echoed. She must have lain prone for a long time, and then gone over to lean out of the window: the dizziness of disgust that had wrung her heart was frightful to imagine. Françoise knocked. Her heart was racing; but there was no answer. She knocked louder. A muffled voice murmured:.

'Who's there?'

'It's I, Françoise.'

'What is it?' said the voice.

'I wanted to know if you were ill,' said Françoise.

'No,' said Xavière. 'I was asleep.'

Françoise felt extremely awkward. It was broad daylight, Xavière was in bed in her room, and she was speaking in a voice which was very much alive. It was a normal morning in which the tragic memories of the night seemed entirely out of place.

'It's because of last night,' said Françoise. 'Do you really feel all right?'

'Of course I feel all right, I want to sleep,' said Xavière crossly.

Françoise hesitated a moment longer. She was still aware in her heart of the empty space created by disaster, which these sullen replies were far from filling and which left her with a misleading and insipid feeling of disappointment. She could carry her insistence no further, so she went back to her room. After the plaintive moans and the pathetic pleas, she found the utmost difficulty in resigning herself to embarking upon a dull and ordinary day.

'She was asleep,' she said to Pierre. 'She seemed to think it quite uncalled for that I should come and wake her up.'

'Didn't she open her door to you?' said Pierre.

'No,' said Françoise.

'I wonder if she'll keep her appointment at noon? I don't think so.'

'I don't think so, either.'

They dressed in silence. There was no point in putting into words thoughts that led nowhere. When they were ready, they left the room and, by mutual consent, started off for the Dôme.

'You know that what we ought to do,' said Pierre, 'is to ring up Gerbert and ask him to come and meet us. He'll be able to tell us what went on.'

'On what pretext?' said Françoise.

'Tell him exactly what's happened: that Xavière has written us a fantastic note, and is now barricading herself in her room; that we're worried and would like to be enlightened.'

'Good. I'll go,' said Françoise, walking into the café. 'Order me a black coffee.'

She went downstairs and gave the operator Gerbert's number: she felt as nervous as Pierre. What exactly had taken place last night? Only kisses? What did they want from each other? What was going to happen?

'Are you there?' said the operator. 'Hold on. Here's your number.'

Françoise stepped into the booth. 'Hullo. May I speak to Monsieur Gerbert, please.'

'Speaking,' said Gerbert. 'Who's that?'

'It's Françoise. Could you come and meet us at the Dôme? We'll explain why.'

'Right you are,' said Gerbert. 'I'll be there in ten minutes.'

'Good,' said Françoise. She dropped forty sous on the plate

and went up to the café. At one of the tables some way down the room sat Elisabeth, with the daily papers spread out in front of her and a cigarette between her lips. Pierre was sitting beside her, his face puckered with annoyance.

'Well! You here?' said Françoise. Elisabeth was not unaware of the fact that they came there almost every morning and she had certainly come there to spy on them. Did she know anything?

'I came to read the newspapers and write a few letters,' said Elisabeth. She added with a hint of satisfaction: 'Things aren't going so well.'

'No,' said Françoise. She noticed that Pierre had not ordered anything; obviously he wanted to get away as soon as possible.

Elisabeth gave an amused laugh. 'What's the matter with the two of you this morning? You look like a pair of mutes.'

Françoise hesitated.

'Xavière got drunk last night,' said Pierre. 'She wrote a demented note saying that she wanted to kill herself, and now she refuses to open her door to us.' He shrugged his shoulders. 'She's capable of any kind of idiocy.'

'In fact, we must get back to the hotel as quickly as possible,' said Françoise. 'I don't feel at all easy.'

'Go on! She won't kill herself' said Elisabeth. She stared at the tip of her cigarette. 'I met her last night in the boulevard Raspail; she was skipping along with Gerbert. I can assure you that she had no thoughts of suicide.'

'Did she seem to be drunk then?' said Françoise.

'She always looks more or less doped,' said Elisabeth. 'I can't tell you.' She shook her head. 'You take her far too seriously. I know what she really needs. You ought to make her join a sports club, where she'd be obliged to do eight hours' exercise a day and eat steaks. She'd feel a lot better for that, believe me.'

'We'll go back and see what's happening to her,' said Pierre, getting up.

They shook hands with Elisabeth and left the café.

'I told her at once that we'd only come to telephone,' said Pierre.

'Yes, but I told Gerbert to meet us here,' said Françoise.

'We'll wait for him outside,' said Pierre, 'and catch him as he arrives.'

They began to walk up and down the pavement in silence,

'If Elisabeth comes out and finds us here, what will we look like?' said Françoise.

'Oh! to hell with her!' said Pierre nervously.

'She ran into them last night, and she came along to find out what's going on,' said Françoise. 'How she hates us!'

Pierre did not answer. His eyes never left the métro exit. Françoise was apprehensively watching the café terrace. She had no wish to be caught by Elisabeth in this moment of agitation.

'There he is,' said Pierre.

Gerbert was coming towards them with a smile. Beneath his eyes, two huge blue circles discoloured half his cheeks. Pierre's face brightened.

'Greetings. We've got to make a quick getaway,' he said with a pleasant smile. 'Elisabeth's watching us from in there. We'll go and hide in the café opposite.'

'It wasn't inconvenient for you to come?' Françoise asked him.

She was embarrassed. Gerbert would think the step they had taken very odd. He already looked constrained.

'No, not at all,' he said.

They sat down at a table and Pierre ordered three coffees. He alone looked at his ease.

'Look at what we found under our door this morning,' he said, taking Xavière's message from his pocket. 'Françoise knocked at her door and she refused to open it. Perhaps you can enlighten us. We heard your voice last night. Was she drunk, or what? What condition was she in when you left her?'

'She wasn't drunk,' said Gerbert. 'But we brought back a bottle of whisky with us. Maybe she drank it afterwards.' He paused and tossed back his forelock with an embarrassed look. 'I'll have to tell you. I slept with her last night,' he said.

There was a brief silence.

'That's no reason for her wanting to jump out of the window,' said Pierre, with freedom and vigour.

Françoise looked at him almost with admiration. How well he could act! She might almost have been taken in herself.

'It's easy to understand that, from her point of view, it is world-shaking,' she said stiffly. Surely this news had not taken Pierre unawares: he must have sworn to himself that he would put a good face on it. But when Gerbert left them, what form of anger, what outburst of suffering might be expected?

316

'She came to look for me at the Deux Magots,' said Gerbert. 'There we talked for a while, until she asked me to come back to her room. After we got there, I don't know any more just how it happened, but she fell on my mouth, and finally – well, we slept together.'

He was staring fixedly at the bottom of his glass with a sheepish and somewhat annoyed expression.

'Has this been brewing for some time?' said Pierre.

'And you think that she attacked the whisky after you left?' said Françoise.

'Probably,' said Gerbert. He raised his head. 'She threw me out. But I swear to you that it wasn't I who wanted it,' he said defiantly. His face relaxed. 'How she cursed me! I was petrified! You'd have thought I'd raped her.'

'That's just what she would do,' said Françoise.

Gerbert looked at Pierre with sudden timidity. 'You don't blame me?'

'For what?' said Pierre.

'I don't know,' said Gerbert with embarrassment. 'She's young. I don't know,' he concluded with a faint blush.

'Don't make her pregnant, that's all I ask of you,' said Pierre.

Françoise crushed her cigarette in the saucer. She was ill at ease. Pierre's duplicity made her uncomfortable: it was more than play-acting. He was sneering at himself and at everything that meant most to him; but this fierce calm was achieved only at the cost of a strain which it was painful to imagine.

'Oh! You can rest assured of that,' said Gerbert. He added with a preoccupied look: 'I wonder if she'll come back.'

'If she'll come back – where to?' asked Françoise.

'I told her when I left that she would know where to find me, but that I wouldn't go looking for her,' said Gerbert with dignity.

'Oh! you'll go all the same,' said Françoise.

'Certainly not,' said Gerbert indignantly. 'She's not going to get the idea into her head that she can run me.'

'Don't get excited. She'll come back,' said Pierre. 'She's proud when it suits her, but she has no consistent principles. If she feels like seeing you, she'll rake up some good reason to do so.' He puffed at his pipe.

'Do you think she's in love with you, or what?'

'I can't quite make it out,' said Gerbert. 'I had kissed her now and then, but she didn't always seem to like it.'

'You ought to go and see what's happening to her,' said Pierre.

'But she's already sent me flying,' said Françoise.

'Well, never mind that. Go on insisting until she lets you in. She mustn't be left alone. God knows what ideas she's got into her head.' Pierre smiled. 'I'd gladly go myself, but I don't think it would be wise.'

'Don't tell her you have seen me,' said Gerbert anxiously.

'Don't worry,' said Françoise.

'And remind her that we're expecting her at noon,' said Pierre.

Françoise left the café and turned into the rue Delambre. She detested this role of go-between which Pierre and Xavière had all too often made her play and which made her hateful to each of them in turn. But today, she had made up her mind to throw herself into it wholeheartedly. She was really frightened on their account.

She went upstairs and knocked. Xavière opened the door. Her skin was yellow, her eyelids swollen, but she had dressed carefully. She had put lipstick on her mouth and mascara on her eyelashes.

'I've come to ask how you are,' said Françoise gaily.

Xavière cast a gloomy look in her direction. 'How I am? I'm not ill.'

'You wrote me a note that gave me a terrible fright,' said Françoise.

'Did I write a note?' said Xavière.

'Look,' said Françoise, handing her the pink slip.

'Ah! I do vaguely remember,' said Xavière. She sat down on the divan beside Françoise. 'I got disgracefully drunk,' she said.

'I thought that you really intended to commit suicide,' said Françoise. 'That's why I knocked this morning.'

Xavière stared at the paper in disgust.

'I must have been even more drunk than I thought,' she said. She passed her hand across her forehead. 'I met Gerbert at the Deux Magots, and I don't really remember why, but we came back to my room with a bottle of whisky. We had a few drinks together, and after he left, I finished the bottle.' She was staring into space, her mouth partly opened in a faint sneer. 'Yes, I remember now. I stayed at the window for a long time thinking I ought to jump out. And then I felt cold.'

'Well! It would have been cheerful if they'd brought your little corpse back to me,' said Françoise.

Xavière shivered. 'In any case, that's not the way I'd kill myself,' she said.

Her face fell. Françoise had never seen her look so miserable. She felt her heart go out to her. She so much wanted to help her! But Xavière would have to be willing to accept this help.

'Why did you think of committing suicide?' she said softly. 'Are you so unhappy?'

Xavière showed the whites of her eyes, and her features were transformed by a spasm of suffering. Françoise suddenly felt torn asunder, and overcome herself by this unbearable pain. She put her arms round Xavière and hugged her.

'My darling little Xavière, what's the matter? Tell me.'

Xavière fell limply against her shoulder and burst into sobs.

'What is it?' repeated Françoise.

'I'm ashamed,' said Xavière.

'Why ashamed? Because you got drunk?'

Xavière swallowed her tears and said in a lisping childish voice: 'Because of that, because of everything. I don't know how to behave. I quarrelled with Gerbert: I threw him out: I was loathsome. And then I wrote that stupid letter. And then . . .' She moaned and began to weep again.

'And then what?' said Françoise.

'And then nothing. Don't you think that's enough? I feel filthy,' said Xavière. She blew her nose pitifully.

'All that isn't so serious,' said Françoise. The beautiful, generous suffering which had, for a moment, filled her heart, had become cramped and bitter. In the depths of her despair, Xavière was keeping herself under such absolute control . . . How richly she was lying!

'You mustn't get so upset.'

'I'm sorry,' said Xavière. She dried her eyes, and said in rage: 'I'll never get drunk again.'

It had been folly to hope for a moment that Xavière would turn to Françoise as to a friend, in order to unburden her heart: she had too much pride and too little courage. Silence ensued. Françoise was filled with compassion at the thought of the inevitable future that was threatening Xavière. She would undoubtedly lose Pierre for ever and her relationship with Françoise would itself be affected by such a rupture. Françoise would not succeed in saving them if Xavière spurned all her advances.

'Labrousse is expecting us for lunch,' said Françoise.

Xavière drew back. 'Oh! I don't want to go.'

'Why?'

'I feel so clammy and tired,' said Xavière.

'That's no reason.'

'I don't want to,' said Xavière. She pushed Françoise away from her with a hunted look. 'I don't want to see Labrousse just now.'

Françoise put her arm round her. How she wished she might drag the truth from her! Xavière did not suspect to what extent she was in need of help.

'What are you afraid of?' she said.

'He'll think that I got drunk on purpose, because of the night before, because I was so intimate with him,' said Xavière. 'There'll be more explanations, and I've had enough, enough, enough.' She resolved into tears.

Françoise hugged her tighter, and said noncommittally: 'There's nothing to explain.'

'Yes, there's everything to explain,' said Xavière. The tears were pouring down her cheeks and her face became the essence of human misery.

'Whenever I see Gerbert, Labrousse thinks that I've turned against him, and he gets angry with me. I can't bear it any more. I never want to see him again,' she cried in a paroxysm of despair.

'On the contrary, if you were to see him,' said Françoise, 'if you were to speak to him yourself, I'm sure everything would be cleared up.'

'No, it's hopeless,' said Xavière. 'Everything's finished. He'll hate me.' She let her head sink on Françoise's knees. She was sobbing violently. How unhappy she would be! And how Pierre was suffering at this very moment . . .

Françoise felt utterly miserable and tears came to her eyes. Why was all their love put to no better use than to torture each of them? A black hell lay in wait for them now.

Xavière raised her head and looked at Françoise in amazement.

'You're crying because of me,' she said. 'You're crying! Oh! I don't want you to.'

320

Impulsively, she took Françoise's face between her hands and began to kiss her with fanatical devotion. These were sacred kisses, purifying Xavière of all her defilement and restoring her own self-respect. With these kisses, Françoise felt so noble, so ethereal, so sublime, that her heart swelled. She longed for a human friendship, and not this fanatical and imperious worship of which she was forced to be the docile idol.

'I don't deserve that you should cry over me,' said Xavière. 'When I see what you are and what I am! If you only knew what I am! And it's because of me that you're crying!'

Françoise returned her kisses. Despite everything, this violent tenderness and humility were intended for her. On Xavière's cheeks, mixed with a salty taste of tears, she found the memory of those hours in a sleepy little café, when she had vowed to make her happy. She had not made a success of it, but if only Xavière were to consent, she could, whatever the cost, protect her from the entire world.

'I don't want any harm to come to you,' she said passionately.

Xavière shook her head. 'You don't know me. You're wrong to love me.'

'I do love you. I can't help it,' said Françoise with a smile.

'You're wrong,' repeated Xavière sobbing.

'You do find life so difficult,' said Françoise. 'Let me help you.'

She wanted to say to Xavière: 'I know everything, and it doesn't make any difference,' but she could not speak without betraying Gerbert. She remained encumbered by her useless mercy, which sought in vain a precise wound to heal. If only Xavière would bring herself to confess, she could console her and reassure her. She would protect her even from Pierre himself.

'Tell me what is upsetting you so much,' she said in an urgent tone. 'Tell me.'

In Xavière's face something wavered. Françoise was waiting, hanging on her lips. In one sentence, Xavière was on the verge of bringing about what Françoise had so long desired: the complete union, which would encompass their joys, their worries, their torments.

'I can't tell you,' said Xavière in despair. She recovered her breath and said more calmly: 'There's nothing to say.'

Her frustration flared into anger and Françoise longed to crush that obstinate little head between her hands until it split open. Was there no way of breaking down Xavière's seclusion? For all the gentleness, for all the vehemence expended, she remained obstinately entrenched behind her aggressive reserve. An avalanche was about to crash down on her, and Françoise was condemned to remain in the background as a helpless witness.

'I could help you, I'm sure,' she said in a voice trembling with anger.

'No one can help me,' said Xavière. She threw back her head and tidied her hair with her finger-tips. 'I've already told you that I'm worthless. I warned you,' she added impatiently. Her wild, faraway look had returned.

Françoise could not insist any further without becoming indiscreet. She had felt ready to give herself to Xavière unreservedly, and had this gift been accepted, she would have been freed both from herself and from this woeful alien presence which constantly barred her path. But Xavière had repelled her. She was willing to weep in Françoise's presence, yet not to permit her to share her tears. Françoise was alone, faced by a solitary and stubborn conscience. Her finger brushed lightly over Xavière's hand disfigured by a large lump.

'Is the burn quite healed?' she said.

'It's gone,' said Xavière. She looked at her hand. 'I would never have thought that it could hurt so.'

'No wonder! You gave it a queer treatment,' said Françoise. In her dejection, she could find no more to say. Then she added: 'I'll have to go. Are you sure you don't want to come with me?'

'I don't,' said Xavière.

'What shall I tell Labrousse?'

Xavière shrugged her shoulders, as if the question were none of her concern. 'Whatever you like.'

Françoise got up.

'I'll try to manage something,' she said. 'Goodbye.'

'Goodbye,' said Xavière.

Françoise did not let go of her hand.

'It makes me very sad to leave you here so tired out and despondent.'

Xavière smiled feebly.

'Hangovers are always like that,' she said. She remained

seated on the edge of the divan as if petrified, and Françoise left the room.

Despite everything, she would try to protect Xavière. It would be a solitary and joyless struggle, since Xavière herself was refusing to stand by her, and she anticipated – not without some apprehension – the hostility she was about to arouse in Pierre by protecting Xavière from him. But she felt tied to Xavière by a bond she had not chosen. With slow steps, she went down the street. She wanted to press her forehead against a lamp-post and cry.

Pierre was sitting where she had left him. He was alone.

'Well, did you see her?' he said.

'I saw her. She sobbed without stopping. She was terribly upset.'

'Is she coming?'

'No, she's frightened to death of seeing you.' Françoise looked at Pierre and chose her words carefully. 'I think she's afraid that you might guess everything, and it's the thought of losing you that's making her so desperate.'

Pierre sneered. 'She's not going to lose me before we've had a nice little explanation. I've got a thing or two to say to that girl. She, of course, told you nothing?'

'No, nothing. She only said that Gerbert had come to her room, that she had thrown him out, and that she got drunk after he left.' Françoise shrugged her shoulders dejectedly. 'For a moment, I thought she was going to talk.'

'I'll make her come out with the truth, all right,' said Pierre.

'Be careful,' said Françoise. 'Thought-reader though she may believe you to be, she'll suspect that you really do know, if you insist too much.'

Pierre's face froze.

'I'll manage,' he said. 'If need be, I'll tell her that I looked through the key-hole.'

Françoise lit a cigarette to maintain her composure; her hand was unsteady. She pictured with horror Xavière's humiliation if she were to believe that Pierre had seen her. He would know only too well how to find ruthless words.

'Don't drive her too hard,' she said. 'She'll do something desperate.'

'Oh no, she's much too cowardly,' said Pierre.

'I don't say she'll commit suicide, but she'll go back to Rouen and her life will be ruined,' said Françoise.

'She can do what she pleases,' said Pierre angrily. 'But I swear to you that I'll pay her back in her own coin.'

Françoise looked down. Xavière was guilty towards Pierre, she had wounded him to the depths of his soul and Françoise keenly felt this wound. Had she been able to concentrate solely on that, everything would have been much simpler. But she also thought of Xavière's contorted face.

'You can't imagine,' said Pierre more calmly, 'how tender she was with me. Nothing obliged her to put on that amorous act.' His voice hardened again. 'She's nothing but undiluted coquetry, caprice, and treachery. Her sleeping with Gerbert was due solely to another wave of hatred, to make our reconciliation worthless, to fool me, and to get her revenge. She didn't fail, but it's going to cost her very dear.'

'Listen,' said Françoise, 'I can't prevent you from doing as you please, but promise me one thing. Don't tell her that I know, for in that case she couldn't bear to live near me any more.'

Pierre looked at her.

'All right,' he said. 'I'll pretend that I haven't told a soul.'

Françoise put her hand on his arm, and she was overcome with bitter grief. She loved him, and to save Xavière, with whom no love was possible, she was confronting him as a stranger; tomorrow, perhaps, he would become her enemy. He would suffer, avenge himself, hate, without her, and even in spite of her. She was casting him back into his aloneness, she who had never desired anything but to be united with him! She withdrew her hand. He was staring into space. She had already lost him.

Chapter Six

Françoise cast a final glance at Eloy and Tedesco who were in the middle of a passionate dialogue on the stage.

'I'm going,' she whispered.

'Will you speak to Xavière?' said Pierre.

'Yes, I promised I would,' said Françoise.

She looked pitifully at Pierre. Xavière stubbornly avoided him, and he insisted on having an explanation from her: his nervous tension had increased steadily during these past three days. When he wasn't finding fault with Xavière's feelings, he would fall into moods of black silence; in his company, the hours passed so slowly that Françoise had welcomed this afternoon's rehearsal with relief, as providing a kind of alibi.

'How shall I know if she accepts?' Pierre asked.

'At eight o'clock you'll see whether or not she's there.'

'But it will be unbearable to wait without knowing.'

Françoise shrugged her shoulders helplessly. She was almost certain that this step would be futile, but if she were to say that to Pierre, he would doubt her sincerity.

'Where are you meeting her?' he asked.

'At the Deux Magots.'

'Well, I'll telephone in an hour's time. You can tell me what she's decided.'

Françoise stifled a protest: she had already had too many opportunities of contradicting Pierre and now in their most minor disagreements there was something bitter and mistrustful that wrung her heart.

'Very well,' she said.

She rose and went to the centre gangway. The dress rehearsal would take place the day after tomorrow. She hardly gave it a thought – or Pierre, for that matter; eight months ago, in the same theatre, they were finishing the rehearsal of *Julius Caesar*: in the semi-darkness, the same fair and dark heads could be made out; Pierre was sitting in the same seat, his eyes fixed on the stage, lit by the same spotlights. But everything had become so different! Not so very long ago, a smile from Canzetti, a gesture from Paule, the fold of a dress, would

325

have been the inspiration or the source of a fascinating story. The inflection of a voice, the colour of a shrub, stood out with feverish sharpness against a vast horizon of hope. In the shadow of the red seats was hidden a whole future. Françoise left the theatre. Passion had drained the wealth of the past, and, in this arid present, there was nothing left to love, nothing more to think about. The streets had stolen the memories and the promises which, in the past, had protracted their existence into infinity. Beneath the over-cast sky broken by brief glimpses of blue, the streets were now nothing but measured distances to be crossed on foot.

Françoise sat down on the terrace of the café. A moist aroma of walnut cordial was hanging in the air. This was the season when, in other years, they began to think about sun-baked roads and shadowy mountain tops. Françoise called to mind Gerbert's sunburnt face, his tall body bent under a rucksack. Where did he stand with Xavière? Françoise knew that she had gone to meet him the very evening after that tragic night, and that they had made it up between them. While affecting total indifference towards Gerbert, Xavière admitted that she saw him often. How did he feel about her?

'Greetings,' said Xavière gaily. She sat down and laid a small bunch of lilies-of-the-valley in front of Françoise. 'This is for you,' she said.

'How sweet of you,' said Françoise.

'You must pin them to your dress,' said Xavière.

Françoise obeyed with a smile. She was not unaware of the fact that this trustful affection dancing in Xavière's eyes was only a mirage. Xavière hardly gave her a thought, and unhesitatingly lied to her. Remorse, perhaps, lay hid behind her smiles, certainly spellbound satisfaction in the idea that Françoise was the submissive victim of them; and Xavière was no doubt also seeking an ally against Pierre. But however false her heart, Françoise was susceptible to the seduction of her perfidious face. In her plaid blouse, with its bright colours, Xavière looked very spring-like, and a limpid gaiety enlivened her features now devoid of mystery.

'What lovely weather,' she said. 'I'm very proud of myself. I walked for two hours, just like a man, and I'm not the least bit tired.'

'It's really too bad,' said Françoise. 'I didn't take advantage of the sun, I spent the afternoon at the theatre.'

Her heart contracted. She wished she could abandon herself to the delightful illusions that Xavière was so graciously creating for her. They would tell each other stories, they would walk down to the Seine, sauntering and exchanging fond words: but she was denied even this fragile sweetness. She must at once lead up to a thorny discussion that would change Xavière's smiles and make her seethe with incalculable hidden venom.

'Are things going well?' asked Xavière eagerly.

'Pretty well. I think it'll keep up for three or four weeks – enough to finish the season.'

Françoise took a cigarette and rolled it between her fingers.

'Why don't you come to the rehearsals? Labrousse asked me again if you'd made up your mind not to see him any more.'

Xavière's face clouded over. She gave a slight shrug.

'Why should he think that? It's stupid.'

'You've been avoiding him for the last three days,' said Françoise.

'I'm not avoiding him. I cut one appointment because I was mistaken about the time.'

'And another because you were tired,' said Françoise. 'He has asked me to ask if you could meet him at the theatre at eight o'clock.'

Xavière turned away.

'At eight o'clock. I shan't be free,' she said.

Apprehensively, Françoise studied the sullen and averted profile behind the thick fair hair.

'Are you sure?' she said.

Gerbert was not going out with Xavière that night. Pierre had made sure of this before settling the time.

'Yes, I'm free,' said Xavière. 'But I'd like to go to bed early.'

'You can see Labrousse at eight o'clock and still go to bed early.'

Xavière looked up and rage flashed in her eyes.

'You know very well I won't be able to! I'll have to argue until four o'clock in the morning!'

Françoise shrugged her shoulders.

'Why don't you admit frankly that you don't want to see him again?' she said. 'But at least give him your reasons.'

'He'll scold me again,' drawled Xavière. 'I'm sure he hates me now.'

327

It was true that Pierre wanted this meeting only to break off with Xavière dramatically; but perhaps if she were to agree to see him, she might quell his anger. By evading him once again, she would completely exasperate him.

'I don't really think he feels very pleased with your behaviour,' said Françoise. 'But in any case, you're not gaining anything by going to earth. He'll be able to find you. You'd far better go and speak to him this very evening.' She looked impatiently at Xavière. 'Make an effort.'

Xavière's face fell.

'I'm afraid of him,' she said.

'Look,' said Françoise, putting her hand on Xavière's arm, 'you don't want Labrousse to stop seeing you altogether, do you?'

'Does he never want to see me again?' said Xavière.

'He certainly won't want to if you go on being obstinate.'

Xavière bent her head despondently. How many times had Françoise looked dispiritedly at that golden crown into which it was so hard to force sensible thoughts!

'He'll telephone me at any moment now,' she continued. 'Make the appointment.'

Xavière did not answer.

'If you like, I'll go and see him before you do. I'll try to explain.'

'No,' said Xavière vehemently. 'I'm fed up with all your fussing. I don't want to go.'

'You prefer a bust-up?' said Françoise. 'Do think it over, for that's what you're heading for.'

'Then it can't be helped,' said Xavière dramatically.

Françoise snapped the stalk of one of the lilies-of-the valley with her fingers. She could get nothing from Xavière. Her cowardice only enhanced her treachery; but she was deluding herself if she thought she could escape Pierre: he was capable of knocking at her door in the middle of the night.

'You're saying it can't be helped because you never think seriously of the future.'

'Oh!' said Xavière. 'At any rate, we couldn't get anywhere, Labrousse and I.'

She plunged her hands into her hair, baring her smooth temples. A wave of violent hatred and suffering swelled her face. Her mouth was partly open in a smile, like a cut on an over-ripe fruit; and this open wound exposed to the sun a

328

secret, venomous pulp. It was impossible to get anywhere. It was the whole of Pierre that Xavière coveted, and since she could not have him without sharing him, she renounced him with an infuriated bitterness which enveloped Françoise together with him.

Françoise was silent. Xavière was adding difficulties to the battle she had vowed to fight for her. Unmasked and powerless, Xavière's jealousy had lost none of its violence. She would only have granted Françoise a little real affection, if she had succeeded in taking Pierre from her, body and soul.

'Telephone for Mademoiselle Miquel!' shouted a voice.

Françoise rose to her feet. 'Say yes,' she urged.

Xavière threw her an imploring look and shook her head.

Françoise went down the stairs, stepped into the booth and picked up the receiver.

'Hullo, Françoise speaking,' she said.

'Well,' said Pierre. 'Is she coming or not?'

'It's still the same old story,' said Françoise. 'She's too afraid. I couldn't manage to convince her. She seemed frightfully upset when I told her that you'd end by breaking with her.'

'All right,' said Pierre. 'She won't miss anything.'

'I did everything I could,' said Françoise.

'I know. You're very kind,' said Pierre. His voice was sharp. He rang off.

Françoise came back and sat down beside Xavière who greeted her with a pert smile.

'You know,' said Xavière, 'no hat has ever looked so well on you as that little sailor hat.'

Françoise smiled without conviction.

'You must always choose my hats for me,' she said.

'Greta was watching you and looking thoroughly annoyed. It makes her ill to see another woman as well dressed as herself.'

'She's wearing a very pretty suit,' said Françoise.

She almost felt a sense of relief. The die had been cast. By stubbornly refusing her support and her advice, Xavière had relieved her of the heavy responsibility of ensuring her happiness. Her eyes glanced over the terrace, where light-coloured coats, summery jackets, and straw hats were making their first timid appearance. And suddenly, as in other years, she felt a keen desire for the sun, for foliage, and for strenuous mountain walks.

Xavière looked at her furtively with an insinuating smile.

'Did you notice that little girl in her first communion dress? Flat-chested girls of that age are so depressing.'

She looked as if she wanted to tear Françoise away from painful preoccupations which were not entirely concerned with her. The whole of her body exuded a carefree and good-natured serenity. Françoise glanced obediently at the family who were passing by, dressed in their Sunday best.

'Did you ever make your first communion?' she asked.

'I should say so,' said Xavière, and she laughed a little too excitedly. 'I insisted on having roses embroidered on my dress from top to bottom. My poor father finally gave in.'

She stopped short. Françoise followed the direction of her glance and saw Pierre shutting the door of a taxi. The blood rushed to her face. Had Pierre forgotten his promise? If he spoke to Xavière in her presence, he could not pretend to have kept the secret of his shameful discovery.

'Hail,' said Pierre. He pulled up a chair and nonchalantly sat down. 'I hear that you're not free again tonight,' he said to Xavière.

Xavière kept staring at him as though bewitched.

'I thought we ought to break this evil spell that's been hanging over our appointments.' Pierre wore a very friendly smile. 'Why have you been avoiding me for three days?'

Françoise rose. She did not want Pierre to humiliate Xavière in her presence and, beneath his politeness, she recognized merciless determination.

'I think it would be better if you talked things over without me,' she said.

Xavière clutched her arm.

'No, stay,' she said in a lifeless voice.

'Let me go,' said Françoise gently. 'What Pierre has to say to you does not concern me.'

'Stay, or I'll go,' said Xavière, through clenched teeth.

'Well, stay then,' said Pierre impatiently. 'You can see she's about to have a fit of hysterics.'

He turned to Xavière. There was now no trace of politeness in his face.

'I would like to know just why I terrify you so much?'

Françoise sat down again and Xavière let go of her arm. She swallowed and then seemed to regain her full composure.

'You don't terrify me,' she said.

'It certainly looks as if I do,' said Pierre. He stared into Xavière's eyes. 'What's more, I can tell you why.'

'Then don't ask me,' said Xavière.

'I wanted to learn it from your own lips,' said Pierre. He paused a little theatrically, and, without taking his eyes off her, continued: 'You're afraid that I might read into your heart and tell you out loud what I see there.'

Xavière's face contracted.

'I know that your mind is full of filthy thoughts. They're repulsive to me and I don't want to know what they are,' she said with disgust.

'It's not my fault if the thoughts you inspire are filthy,' said Pierre.

'In any case, keep them to yourself,' said Xavière.

'I'm sorry,' said Pierre. 'But I came for the express purpose of telling them to you.'

He was taking his time. Now that he held Xavière in his power he seemed calm and almost amused at the notion of directing the scene as he pleased. His voice, his smile, his pauses, everything was so carefully calculated that Françoise had a gleam of hope. His object was to put Xavière at his mercy, but if he succeeded effortlessly, perhaps he would spare her the too harsh truths, and perhaps he would let himself be persuaded not to break with her.

'You seem not to wish to see me any more,' he continued. 'You will doubtless be pleased to hear that I, too, have no desire to continue our relationship. However, I am not in the habit of dropping people without giving them my reasons.'

Abruptly, Xavière's brittle composure crumbled. Her eyes were popping, her half-open mouth now expressed nothing but an indication of incredulous surprise. It was impossible that Pierre should not be affected by the sincerity of her anguish.

'But what have I done to you?' said Xavière.

'You have done nothing to me,' said Pierre. 'What's more, you owe me nothing. I never assumed any rights over you.' His manner became crisp and detached. 'No, it's simply that I have finally discovered what you are and the whole affair has ceased to interest me.'

Xavière looked all round her, as if seeking help. Her hands were clenched. She seemed extremely anxious to fight or to defend herself, but she could clearly find no words that did not conceal traps. Françoise wanted to prompt her. She was now certain that Pierre was not bent on burning his bridges behind him: she hoped that his very severity would wrench from Xavière words that would make him relent.

'Is it because of the appointments I failed to keep?' Xavière finally said, almost in tears.

'It's because of the reasons that caused you to fail to keep them,' said Pierre. He waited a moment, for Xavière made no comment. 'You were ashamed of yourself,' he continued.

'I was not ashamed, but I was certain that you were furious with me. You're always furious when I see Gerbert, and since I got drunk with him . . .' She shrugged her shoulders disdainfully.

'But I'd thoroughly approve of your being friendly with Gerbert or even loving him,' said Pierre, 'you couldn't make a better choice.' This time the anger rumbling in his voice was not controlled. 'But you're incapable of any clean feeling. You've never seen anything in him but an instrument to soothe your pride, to appease your anger.' He checked a protest from Xavière. 'You yourself admitted that when you put on that little romantic act with him, it was out of jealousy. And it was not for nothing that you brought him home with you the other night.'

'I was sure you'd think that,' said Xavière. 'I was sure of it.' She clenched her teeth and two tears of rage ran down her cheeks.

'Because you know that it's true,' said Pierre. 'I'll tell you myself what happened. When I forced you to acknowledge your infernal jealousy, you trembled with rage. There is no limit to the vileness you allow yourself, provided that it remains concealed. You were disconcerted because all your coquetry failed to hide the depths of your puny soul from me. What you demand of people is blind admiration. And truth offends you.'

Françoise looked at him apprehensively, and she wished she could stop him. He seemed carried away by his own words, and he was losing control. The stern expression on his face was no longer play-acting.

'That's too unfair,' said Xavière. 'I stopped hating you immediately.'

'You certainly did not,' said Pierre. 'I'd have to be very innocent to believe that. You've never stopped. Only, to indulge in hate body and soul, you'd have to be less lazy than you are. Hate takes it out of you, so you took a breather. You felt quite safe, knowing that as soon as it suited you, you'd recover all your bitterness. So you set it aside for a few hours, because you felt like being kissed.'

Xavière's face became contorted.

'I had no desire to be kissed by *you*,' she said sharply.

'That's possible,' said Pierre. He had a set smile. 'But you felt like being kissed and I happened to be there.' He surveyed her up and down before adding in more vulgar tones: 'Now understand, I'm not complaining: it's very pleasant to kiss you, and I got as much out of it as you did.'

Xavière gasped. She looked at Pierre with such sheer horror that she appeared almost soothed, but silent tears belied the hysterical calm of her features.

'What you're saying is outrageous,' she whispered.

'What is outrageous,' said Pierre vehemently, 'is your behaviour. Your entire relationship with me has been nothing but jealousy, pride and treachery. You could not rest until you had me at your feet. You still have no feeling of friendship for me except in your childish exclusiveness. Out of spite, you tried to start a quarrel between Gerbert and me. In addition, you were jealous of Françoise to the point of jeopardizing your friendship with her. When I begged you to try and build a human relationship with us, unselfishly, without capriciousness, you could only hate me. And finally, with your heart full of this hatred, you threw yourself into my arms because you were in need of sensations.'

'You're lying,' said Xavière. 'You've invented everything.'

'Why did you kiss me?' said Pierre. 'It wasn't to please me. That presupposes generosity, and no one has ever seen the slightest trace of it in you. And besides, I didn't ask that much of you.'

'Oh! How I regret those kisses,' said Xavière, gritting her teeth.

'I should imagine you do,' said Pierre with a vicious smile. 'Only you couldn't resist them, because you never deny yourself anything. You wanted to hate me that night, but my love was precious to you.' He shrugged his shoulders. 'To think that I could have taken those ravings for complexity of feelings!'

'I was trying to be polite with you,' said Xavière.

She had intended to be insulting, but she no longer had

control of her voice, now shaking with sobs. Françoise wanted to stop this slaughter: it had gone far enough. Xavière could no longer raise her head in front of Pierre, but Pierre was now being stubborn: he would see the matter through to the finish.

'That's carrying politeness too far,' he said. 'The truth is that you were unscrupulously leading me on. Our relationship continued to please you, so you intended to keep it intact and you reserved the right to hate me under the surface. I know you well. You aren't even capable of following a line of your own. You are yourself betrayed by your own cunning.'

Xavière gave a short laugh.

'Your beautiful theories are very easy to construct. I wasn't at all as passionate as you say that night, and, what's more, I didn't hate you.' She looked at Pierre with a little more self-assurance: she must have begun to think that his assertions were not based on fact. 'It's you who's inventing this story of my hating you, because you always choose the worst possible interpretation.'

'I'm not talking out of the back of my neck,' said Pierre in a somewhat menacing tone. 'I know what I'm saying. You hated me without ever daring to formulate your thoughts in my presence. As soon as you'd left me, infuriated by your own weakness, you immediately looked for some means of getting your own back; but, coward that you are, you were only capable of doing so in an underhand way.'

'What do you mean?' said Xavière.

'It was very well contrived. I would have gone on adoring you unsuspectingly, and you would have accepted my devotion whilst you made a fool of me; that's just the sort of triumph you revel in. The trouble is that you're too ineffective to carry out a brilliant lie. You think you're clever, but your tricks are obvious: you can be read like a book. You don't even know how to take elementary precautions to conceal your treachery.'

Abject terror spread over Xavière's face,

'I don't understand,' she said.

'You don't understand?'

There was a silence. Françoise threw him an imploring look, but, at this moment, he was in no way friendlily disposed towards her. If he did remember his promise, he would not hesitate deliberately to cast it aside.

'Do you think you're going to make me believe that you brought Gerbert home with you by chance?' said Pierre. 'You deliberately made him get drunk, because you had decided, cold-bloodedly, to sleep with him in order to take revenge on me.'

'Ah! So that's it!' said Xavière. 'That's just the sort of calumny you're capable of imagining!'

'Don't bother to deny it,' said Pierre. 'I'm not imagining anything. I know.'

Xavière stared at him with the sly and triumphant look of a lunatic.

'Do you dare to suggest that Gerbert invented such filth?'

Again, Françoise silently made a desperate appeal to Pierre. He must not crush Xavière so cruelly! He must not betray Gerbert's naïve confidences! Pierre hesitated.

'Of course, Gerbert told me nothing,' he said finally.

'Well?' said Xavière. 'You see . . .'

'But I have eyes and ears,' said Pierre, 'and I use them whenever I have occasion. It's easy to look through a key-hole.'

'You . . .' Xavière put her hand to her throat. Her neck swelled as if she were about to choke. 'You didn't do that, did you?' she said.

'No! Should I feel shy?' said Pierre sneering. 'With someone like you, any behaviour is permissible.'

Xavière looked at Pierre, then at Françoise, in a frenzy of impotent rage. She was gasping. Françoise searched in vain for a word or a gesture. She was afraid that Xavière might begin to scream or smash glasses in front of everyone.

'I saw you,' said Pierre.

'Oh! That's enough,' said Françoise. 'Shut up.'

Xavière rose. She put her hands to her temples. Tears were pouring down her cheeks. Suddenly, she rushed blindly away.

'I'll go with her,' said Françoise.

'If you like,' said Pierre.

He leaned back affectedly, and pulled his pipe out of his pocket. Françoise ran across the road. Xavière was walking very rapidly, her body erect, her head tilted back. Françoise caught up with her, and they walked along a stretch of the rue de Rennes in silence. Xavière suddenly turned to Françoise.

'Leave me alone!' she said in a strangled voice.

'No,' said Françoise. 'I won't leave you.'

'I want to go home,' said Xavière.

'I'll go with you,' said Françoise, as she stopped a taxi. 'Get in,' she said firmly.

Xavière obeyed. She leaned her head back against the cushion and stared at the roof. Her upper lip curled back in something like a sneer.

'That man – I'll get even with him,' she said.

Françoise touched her arm.

'Xavière,' she whispered.

Xavière shuddered, and jerked away.

'Don't touch me,' she said vehemently.

She stared at Françoise with a wild look, as if a new thought had struck her.

'You knew about it,' she said. 'You knew everything.'

Françoise said nothing. The taxi stopped. She paid the driver, and hurried up the stairs after Xavière. Xavière had left the door to her room ajar. She was leaning with her back against the wash-basin, her eyes swollen, her hair dishevelled, her cheeks blotched with red. She seemed possessed by an enraged demon whose convulsions were bruising her frail body.

'So, all these days you've let me speak to you, and you knew that I was lying!' she said.

'It wasn't my fault if Pierre told me everything, and I wanted to disregard it,' said Françoise.

'How you must have laughed at me!' said Xavière.

'Xavière! The idea never entered my head,' said Françoise, taking a step towards her.

'Don't come near me,' screamed Xavière. 'I never want to see you again. I want to go away, for good.'

'Do calm down,' said Françoise. 'All this is stupid. Nothing's happened between us. I had no part in any of these goings-on with Labrousse.'

Xavière had seized a towel and was fiercely tugging at the fringe.

'I'm accepting your money,' she said. 'I'm letting you support me! Do you realize that?'

'You're raving,' said Françoise. 'I'll come back when you are yourself again.'

Xavière dropped the towel.

'Yes,' she cried. 'Go away.'

She went over to the divan, sobbing, and threw herself down on it.

Françoise hesitated. Then she walked softly out of the bedroom, closed the door, and went up to her room: she was not

336

very worried. Xavière was still more apathetic than proud, and she would not have the absurd courage to ruin her life by going back to Rouen. The trouble was that she would never forgive Françoise for the indisputable superiority she had gained over her: that would be one more grievance, in addition to so many others. Françoise took off her hat and looked at herself in the glass. At this moment she did not even have the strength to feel worn out; she no longer regretted an impossible friendship; she found no bitterness in herself towards Pierre. All she could do was to try patiently, sadly, to save the poor remains of a way of living in which she had taken so much pride. She would persuade Xavière to remain in Paris and she would try to win back Pierre's confidence. She smiled weakly at her reflection. After all these years of passionate demands, of triumphant serenity and avidity for happiness, was she, like so many others, about to become a woman resigned to her fate?

Chapter Seven

Françoise crushed the stub of her cigarette in her saucer.

'Will you have enough energy to work in this heat?' she said.

'It doesn't bother me,' said Pierre. 'What are you going to do this afternoon?'

They were sitting on the balcony outside Pierre's dressing-room where they had just had lunch. Below them, the little square in front of the theatre had the appearance of being crushed under the heavy blue sky.

'I'm going to the Ursulines, with Xavière. There's a Charlie Chaplin festival.'

Pierre's lip jutted out.

'You never leave her side nowadays,' he said.

'She's her own worst enemy,' said Françoise.

Xavière had not returned to Rouen, but although Françoise gave her a great deal of attention, and though she was seeing Gerbert frequently, she had for the past month dragged herself, like a soulless body, through the blazing summer heat.

'I'll come for you at six o'clock,' said Françoise. 'Will that be all right?'

'Fine,' said Pierre. With a forced smile, he added: 'Have a good time.'

Françoise returned his smile, but as soon as she had left the room, all her shallow cheerfulness vanished; for when she was alone, nowadays, her heart was always sad. To be sure, Pierre did not blame her, even in thought, for having kept Xavière to herself, yet nothing henceforth could prevent him from feeling that she was thoroughly impregnated with a hated presence; it was Xavière whom Pierre continually saw hovering in the background.

The clock at the Vavin crossing pointed to two-thirty. Françoise quickened her pace. She picked out Xavière in her dazzling white blouse, seated on the terrace of the Dôme; her hair was shining from a distance, and she looked radiant; but her face was lifeless and her eyes were dull.

'I'm late,' said Françoise.

338

'I've only just arrived,' said Xavière.

'How are you?'

'It's very warm,' said Xavière with a sigh.

Françoise sat down beside her: with amazement she noticed, in addition to the usual whiff of Virginia tobacco and tea peculiar to Xavière, a strange new medicinal smell.

'Did you sleep well last night?' said Françoise.

'We didn't go dancing – I was too worn out,' said Xavière, pouting, 'and Gerbert had a headache.'

She readily talked about Gerbert, but Françoise would not let herself be taken in by that. It was from no feelings of friendship that Xavière occasionally confided in her; it was to counteract any impression of solidarity with Gerbert. She must be greatly attracted to him physically, and she took an easy revenge by criticizing him harshly.

'I went for a long walk with Labrousse,' said Françoise, 'along the banks of the Seine: it was a gorgeous night.' She stopped. Xavière was not even pretending to be interested; she was staring into space with a worried expression.

'We'll have to go now, if we're really going to a cinema,' said Françoise.

'Yes,' said Xavière.

She rose and took Françoise's arm. It was a mechanical gesture; she did not appear to feel any presence at her side, as Françoise fell into step with her pace. At this moment, in the oppressive heat of his dressing-room, Pierre was busy working: Françoise herself could have stayed on peacefully in her room and done some writing. In the old days, she would never have missed the chance of throwing herself eagerly into these long unoccupied hours: the theatre was closed, she had some free time, yet she could do nothing but waste it. It was not even a case of thinking that she was already on holiday: she had totally lost her old sense of self-discipline.

'Do you still want to go to the cinema?' she asked.

'I don't know,' said Xavière. 'I think I'd much rather go for a walk.'

Françoise recoiled in fright before the lukewarm desert of boredom that was suddenly spreading out beneath her footsteps; unaided she would have to pass through this great stretch of time, alone! Xavière was in no mood to talk; but because of her presence it was impossible to enjoy a real silence which might afford a good opportunity for reflection.

'Well then, let's walk,' said Françoise.

The streets smelt of tar, and it stuck to one's feet. These first stormy heat waves had come as a complete surprise. Françoise felt like a tasteless wad of cotton-wool.

'Are you still tired today?' she asked in an affectionate tone.

'I'm always tired,' said Xavière. 'I'm growing old.' She cast a sleepy glance at Françoise. 'I'm sorry, I'm not good company.'

'How foolish you are! You know I'm always happy to be with you,' said Françoise.

Xavière did not return her smile: she had already withdrawn into herself. Françoise would never be able to make her understand that she was not expecting her to display for her either the grace of her body or the attractions of her mind, but only to allow her to participate in her life. All through the past month, she had tried persistently to become reconciled with her, but Xavière stubbornly remained a stranger whose negative presence cast a threatening shadow over Françoise. There were some moments when Françoise was absorbed in herself and others when she gave her entire self to Xavière, but she often called to mind with anguish that second personality, revealed to her one evening in a maniacal smile: the only way to destroy its abominable reality would have been to sink her own personality with Xavière's in a single friendship. During these long weeks, Françoise had felt the need of this more and more keenly; but Xavière would never sink her own personality.

A dragging, dismal chant pervaded the hot and sultry atmosphere. At a deserted street corner, a man was seated on a camp stool, holding a saw between his knees, and to the wailing of this instrument his voice matched melancholy words:

> *This evening in the r-a-i-n,*
> *My sad heart full of p-a-i-n*
> *I listen once a-g-a-i-n*
> *For the echo of your step.'*

Françoise pressed Xavière's arm. The listless music in this scorching solitude seemed to her the very reflection of her heart. The arm remained on hers, yielding but insensible: even through this beautiful tangible body it was not possible to reach Xavière. Françoise longed to sit down on the kerbstone and never to move away from it.

340

'Supposing we go to some place,' she said, 'it's too hot for walking.' She no longer had the strength to wander about aimlessly under this relentless sky.

'Oh, yes! I'd like to sit down,' said Xavière. 'But where shall we go?'

'Would you like to go back to the Moorish café where we enjoyed ourselves so much? It's quite close.'

'Well, let's go there,' said Xavière.

They turned the corner: it was already more comforting to be walking towards some definite objective.

'That was the first time that we spent a really long happy day together,' said Françoise. 'Do you remember?'

'It seems such ages ago,' said Xavière. 'How young I was then!'

'It's not even a year ago,' said Françoise.

She, too, had aged since that not so distant winter. In those days she used to live without asking herself any questions, the world all round her was wide and rich, and it belonged to her; she loved Pierre, and Pierre loved her; from time to time, she even used to indulge in the luxury of thinking her happiness monotonous. She pushed open the door and at once recognized the wool rugs, the copper trays, the multicoloured lanterns: the place had not changed. The dancing-girl and the musicians, squatting on their heels in a recess at the back, were talking among themselves.

'How sorry-looking it's become,' said Xavière.

'That's because it's still early. It will probably fill up,' said Françoise. 'Would you like to go somewhere else?'

'Oh, no. Let's stay here,' said Xavière.

They sat down on the rough cushions in the same place as before, and ordered mint tea. Again, as she sat beside Xavière, Françoise caught a breath of the unusual smell that had intrigued her at the Dôme.

'What did you wash your hair with today?' she said.

Xavière ran her fingers through a lock of silky hair.

'I didn't wash my hair,' she said with surprise.

'It smells like a chemist's shop,' said Françoise.

Xavière gave an illuminating smile, which she immediately repressed.

'I didn't touch it,' she said.

Her face darkened, and she lit a cigarette in a slightly dramatic manner. Françoise gently laid her hand on her arm.

341

'You're so depressed,' said Françoise. 'You mustn't let yourself get like this!'

'What can I do?' said Xavière. 'I'm not a happy person.'

'But you're not making the slightest effort. Why didn't you take the books which I put out for you?'

'I can't read when I'm in a gloomy mood,' said Xavière.

'Why don't you work with Gerbert? The finest cure for you would be to work out a good act.'

Xavière shrugged her shoulders.

'It's impossible to work with Gerbert! He acts for his own benefit, he's incapable of suggesting anything. I might as well work with a brick wall.' She added in a cutting tone, 'And besides, I don't like what he's doing, it's so trivial.'

'You're unfair,' said Françoise. 'He lacks depth of feeling, maybe, but he's sensitive and intelligent.'

'That's not enough,' said Xavière. Her face contracted. 'I loathe mediocrity,' she said furiously.

'He's young, and he hasn't had much experience. But I think he'll do something yet,' said Françoise.

Xavière shook her head.

'If at least he were downright bad, there'd be hope, but he's contemptible. He can just about manage to reproduce correctly what Labrousse has taught him.'

Xavière had a great many grievances against Gerbert, but one of the most bitter was certainly his admiration for Labrousse. Gerbert always said that she was never so peevish with him as when he had just seen Pierre or even Françoise.

'That's a pity,' said Françoise. 'It would change your outlook on life if you were to do a little work.'

She looked warily at Xavière. She did not really know what anyone could do for her. Suddenly she could put a name to the strange new smell she had noticed.

'Why, you smell of ether,' she said with astonishment.

Xavière turned away without answering.

'What are you doing with ether?' asked Françoise.

'Nothing,' said Xavière.

'But what are you doing?'

'I inhaled a little,' said Xavière. 'It's pleasant.'

'Is this the first time you've taken it, or have you done it before?'

'Oh! I've taken it occasionally,' said Xavière with studied rudeness.

Françoise had the impression that she was not sorry at having her secret discovered.

'Be careful,' said Françoise, 'you'll become a dope-fiend or wreck yourself completely.'

'I have nothing to lose,' said Xavière.

'Why do you do it?'

'I can't get drunk any more. It makes me ill,' said Xavière.

'You'll make yourself much more than ill,' said Françoise.

'Just think,' said Xavière, 'all you have to do is put a piece of cotton-wool to your nose, and then you are practically unconscious for hours.'

Françoise took her hand.

'Are you really unhappy?' she said. 'What's the matter? Tell me.'

She knew why Xavière was suffering, but she could not make her admit to it point-blank.

'Except for your work, are you getting along well with Gerbert?' she continued.

She watched for the reply with an interest prompted not by concern for Xavière alone.

'Oh, Gerbert! Yes,' Xavière shrugged her shoulders. 'He doesn't matter much, you know.'

'Still, you're very fond of him,' said Françoise.

'I'm always fond of what belongs to me,' said Xavière. She added with a fierce look, 'It's restful to have someone entirely to yourself.' Her voice softened. 'But after all, it's just something pleasant in my existence, nothing more.'

Françoise turned cold. She felt personally insulted by Xavière's disdainful tone.

'Then it's not because of him that you're depressed?'

'No,' said Xavière.

She had such a defenceless and pitiful look that Françoise's wave of hostility subsided.

'And it's not my fault either?' she said. 'Are you satisfied with our relationship?'

'Oh, yes,' said Xavière. She had a brief sweet smile that fell immediately. Suddenly her face brightened. 'I'm bored,' she said passionately. 'I'm disgustingly bored.'

Françoise did not answer. It was Pierre's absence which was causing such a void in Xavière's existence: he would have to be returned to her, but Françoise was very much afraid that this was impossible. She had finished her glass of tea. The café

343

had been filling up; for some time past the musicians had been playing their reedy flutes. The dancing-girl advanced to the middle of the room and a quiver ran through her body.

'What big hips she has,' said Xavière with disgust. 'She's put on weight.'

'She's always been stout,' said Françoise.

'Possibly,' said Xavière. 'I was so easily dazzled in the old days.' She let her eyes wander slowly over the wall. 'I've changed a great deal.'

'Actually,' said Françoise, 'that's plain bosh. Now you only like what's truly beautiful and there's nothing to regret in that.'

'No, no,' said Xavière. 'Nothing whatever moves me now!' She blinked a few times, and then she drawled, 'I'm worn out.'

'You like to think so,' said Françoise with annoyance. 'But they're just words. You're not worn out. You're simply moody.'

Xavière gave her an unhappy look.

'You give in to yourself,' said Françoise more gently. 'You mustn't go on in this way. Listen, first of all you're going to promise me not to take any more ether.'

'But you don't understand,' said Xavière. 'These endless days are horrible.'

'It's serious, you know. You're going to wreck yourself completely, if you don't stop.'

'That won't hurt anyone,' said Xavière.

'In any case it would hurt me,' said Françoise tenderly.

'Oh!' said Xavière incredulously.

'What do you mean?' said Françoise.

'You can't still set such great value on me,' said Xavière.

Françoise was unpleasantly surprised. Xavière did not often seem touched by her tenderness, but at least she had never seemed to question it.

'What!' said Françoise. 'You know how very much I've always valued you.'

'In the old days yes. You thought well of me then,' said Xavière.

'Why should I think less of you now?'

'It's just an idea I have,' said Xavière languidly.

'And yet, we've never seen more of each other. I've never sought greater intimacy with you,' said Françoise, disconcerted.

'Because you feel sorry for me,' said Xavière. She gave an unhappy laugh. 'That's what I've come to! I'm somebody for whom people feel sorry!'

'But you're wrong,' said Françoise. 'Whoever put that notion into your head?'

Xavière stared stubbornly at the end of her cigarette.

'Explain yourself,' said Françoise. 'People don't say things like that without good reason.'

Xavière hesitated, and again Françoise had the unpleasant feeling that, by her reticences and her silences, it was Xavière who had been responsible for the course of their conversation.

'It's only natural that you should be disgusted with me,' said Xavière. 'You have good reason to despise me.'

'It's always the same old story,' said Françoise. 'But we've thrashed all that out already! I thoroughly understood that you did not want to talk to me at once about your relations with Gerbert, and you agreed that, in my place, you would have kept silent just as I did.'

'Yes,' said Xavière.

Françoise knew that, with her, no explanation was ever final. Xavière must still wake up at night in a fury, remembering with what ease Françoise had deceived her for three days.

'You and Labrousse think so much along the same lines,' continued Xavière. 'And he holds such a wretchedly low opinion of me.'

'That's entirely his business,' said Françoise.

These words cost her an effort – in regard to Pierre, they were a kind of repudiation – and yet they only expressed the truth. She had once and for all refused to take his part.

'You think me far too easily influenced,' she said. 'Actually, he hardly ever talks to me about you.'

'He must hate me so,' said Xavière sadly.

There was a silence.

'And what about you? Do you hate him?' said Françoise.

Her heart sank. The whole of this conversation had had no other aim than to prompt this question. She began to catch a glimpse of the end towards which she was moving.

'I?' said Xavière. She cast a pleading glance at Françoise. 'I don't hate him,' she said.

'He's convinced you do,' said Françoise. Still under the influence of Xavière's desire, she continued, 'Would you agree to see him again?'

Xavière shrugged her shoulders. 'He has no great wish to see me.'

'I don't know,' said Françoise. 'If he knew that you miss

him, it would make a difference.'

'Of course I miss him,' said Xavière slowly. She added in a clumsy attempt to seem off-hand, 'You know, Labrousse is not somebody you can stop seeing without regretting it.'

She looked carefully at the pale swollen face which exhaled pharmaceutical essences. The pride that Xavière maintained in her distress was so piteous that Françoise said, almost in spite of herself, 'I could perhaps try to talk to him.'

'Oh! That wouldn't do any good,' said Xavière.

'I wouldn't be too sure,' said Françoise.

It was done. The decision was made of its own accord, and Françoise knew that she could no longer prevent herself from implementing it. Pierre would listen to her with a scowl. He would answer her discourteously, and his cutting words would reveal to himself the extent of his hostility towards her. She bent her head, crushed.

'What will you tell him?' said Xavière in an insinuating tone.

'That we talked about him,' said Françoise. 'That you showed no hatred, quite the contrary. That if only he would forget his grievances, you for your part would be happy to regain his friendship.'

She stared vaguely at the variegated wall-hanging. Pierre pretended not to be interested in Xavière, but whenever her name was mentioned, she could sense that he was all attention. He had passed her once in the rue Delambre, and Françoise had noticed a wild desire to run after her dart into his eyes. Perhaps he would agree to see her again that he might torment her at closer range; perhaps, if that happened, he would again be won over by her. But neither the appeasement of his bitterness nor the resurrection of his troubled love would reconcile him with Françoise. The only possible reconciliation would be to send Xavière back to Rouen, and start life afresh without her.

Xavière shook her head. 'It's not worth the effort,' she said with woeful resignation.

'I can always try.'

Xavière shrugged her shoulders as if declining all responsibility. 'Oh! Do as you like,' she said.

Françoise felt angry. It was Xavière who had brought her to this, with her smell of ether and her woebegone looks, and now she withdrew, as she always did, into a haughty indifference, thus sparing herself the shame of a failure or an obligation of gratitude.

'I'm going to try,' said Françoise.

She no longer had any hope of achieving with Xavière that friendship which could alone have saved her, but at least she would have done everything to deserve it.

'I'll speak to Pierre at once,' she said.

When Françoise entered Pierre's dressing-room, he was still seated at his desk, his pipe in his mouth, unshaven, and looking happy.

'How industrious you are,' she said. 'You haven't budged all this time?'

'You'll see. I think I've done a good piece of work,' said Pierre. He pivoted round on his chair.

'And what about you? Did you have a good time? Was it a good programme?'

'Oh! We didn't go to the cinema. That was to be expected. We dawdled along the streets and it was outrageously hot.' Françoise sat down on a cushion on the balcony sill. The air had cooled off a little, and the tops of the plane trees were gently quivering. 'I'm glad I'm going on this walking tour with Gerbert. I'm fed up with Paris.'

'And I'll hang on here, shaking in my shoes,' said Pierre. 'You'll be a good girl and send me a telegram every evening: "I'm still alive." '

Françoise smiled at him. Pierre was satisfied with his day's work; his face was gay and affectionate. There were moments like this when it might have seemed that nothing had changed since last summer.

'There's nothing to be afraid of,' said Françoise. 'It's much too early to do any real mountain climbing. We'll go to the Cevennes or to Cantal.'

'You're not going to spend the evening making plans!' said Pierre apprehensively.

'Don't worry, we'll spare you,' said Françoise. She smiled again, a little timidly. 'We two will also have plans of our own to make soon.'

'That's true. We'll be leaving in less than a month,' said Pierre.

'We really must make up our minds where we're going,' said Françoise.

'I think we'll stay in France, whatever happens,' said Pierre. 'We must expect a period of tension towards the middle of August, and even if nothing does happen, it wouldn't be very pleasant to find ourselves at the other end of the world.'

'We've spoken about Cordes and the Midi,' said Françoise. She added with a laugh, 'Of course there won't be many panoramas, but we'll see lots of small towns. You do like small towns, don't you?'

She looked hopefully at Pierre. When just the two of them were alone, far from Paris, perhaps he would never lose that friendly and relaxed look. How she longed to take him away with her for weeks on end.

'I'd love to wander with you round about Albi, Cordes and Toulouse,' said Pierre. 'You'll see, I'll really go for a long walk every once in a while.'

'I'll stay in cafés as much as you like without complaining,' said Françoise with a laugh.

'What will you do with Xavière?' said Pierre.

'Her family is quite willing to have her for the holidays. She'll go to Rouen. It won't do her any harm to get her health back.'

Françoise looked away. If Pierre were to become reconciled with Xavière, what would become of all these happy plans? His passion for her might return and he might revive the trio. They would have to take her with them on the tour. A lump rose in her throat. Never had she desired anything so keenly as this long period alone with him.

'Is she ill?' said Pierre coldly.

'She's in rather a bad state,' said Françoise.

She must not talk; she must let Pierre's hatred die slowly of indifference. He was already on the way to being cured. One more month, and under the sun of the Midi this feverish year would be nothing more than a memory. She need add nothing, but simply change the subject. Pierre had already opened his mouth. He was going to talk about something else, but Francoise forestalled him.

'Do you know her latest? She's begun to take ether.'

'Ingenious,' said Pierre. 'To what end?'

'She terribly unhappy,' said Françoise, 'and she couldn't do without it. She trembled at the thought of danger, but it attracted her irresistibly. She never had been able to play for safety.'

'Poor child!' Pierre carried on with heavy irony. 'What can be the matter with her?'

Françoise began to roll her handkerchief between her moist hands. 'You left a void in her life,' she said in a bantering tone, which sounded false.

Pierre's face hardened. 'I'm terribly sorry,' he said. 'And what would you like me to do about it?'

Françoise squeezed her handkerchief tighter. How raw the wound still was! No sooner had she opened her mouth than Pierre was on the defensive: she was now no longer talking to a friend. She gathered up her courage.

'You don't consider the possibility of seeing her again?'

Pierre gave her an icy look. 'Ah!' he said. 'She asked you to sound me out?'

Françoise's voice hardened in turn. 'I was the one to suggest it,' she said, 'when I understood how terribly she missed you.'

'I see,' said Pierre. 'She broke your heart with her ether-addict-act.'

Françoise blushed. She knew that there had been self-satisfaction in Xavière's tragic manner, and that she had allowed herself to be out-manœuvred, but before Pierre's cutting tone she determined to make a stand.

'That's too easy,' said Françoise. 'If you don't care a damn what happens to Xavière – all right; but the fact remains that she's down in the depths, and it's because of you!'

'Because of me!' said Pierre. 'Well, you certainly do get hold of good ones.' He got up and planted himself in front of Françoise with a sneer. 'Do you expect me to lead her by the hand every night to Gerbert's bed? Isn't that what she needs for the peace of her mingy little soul?'

Françoise kept a tight hold on herself. There was nothing to be gained by getting angry.

'You know very well that when you left her, you said such cruel things that even someone with less pride than she would never have recovered. You're the only person who can wipe those things out.'

'I beg your pardon,' said Pierre. 'I'm not preventing you from forgiving wrongs, but I don't happen to have the vocation of a sister of charity.'

Françoise felt cut to the quick by this scornful tone.

'After all, it wasn't such a crime to sleep with Gerbert. She was free, she hadn't promised you anything. It was painful to you, but you know that you could accept it, if you wanted to. She threw herself into an armchair. 'I find your bitterness towards her to be sexual and shabby. You're acting like a man who's furious with a woman he's never had. That, I think, is unworthy of you.'

She waited nervously. The blow had struck home. Hatred flashed into Pierre's eyes.

'I hate her for having been a flirt and a traitor. Why did she let me kiss her? Why all those fond smiles? Why did she pretend to love me?'

'But she was sincere. She's fond of you,' said Françoise. Harsh memories suddenly welled up in her heart. 'And besides, it was you who demanded her love,' she said. 'You know she was bowled over the first time you mentioned the word.'

'Are you insinuating that she didn't love me?' said Pierre.

Never before had he looked at Françoise with such decided hostility.

'I didn't say that,' said Françoise. 'I do say that there is something forced in that love, in the sense in which one forces the flowering of a plant. You were always demanding more and more in the way of intimacy and intensity.'

'You've certainly devised a strange reconstruction of the story,' said Pierre with a malevolent smile. 'It was she who finally proved to be so demanding that she had to be stopped, because she asked nothing less of me than to give you up.'

Françoise suddenly broke down. It was true. It was out of loyalty to her that Pierre had lost Xavière. Had he come to regret it? Did he now hold a grievance against her for what he had done on so spontaneous an impulse?

'If she could have had me all to herself, she would have been ready to love me passionately,' Pierre continued. 'She slept with Gerbert to punish me for not having kicked you overboard. You must admit that all that is rather shabby. I'm amazed that you should take her part!'

'I'm not taking her part,' said Françoise weakly. She felt her lips beginning to tremble: with one word, Pierre had awakened a burning bitterness in her. Why was she suddenly siding with Xavière? 'She's so unhappy,' she murmured.

She pressed her fingers against her eyelids. She did not want to cry, but she suddenly found herself plunged into a bottomless despair: nothing seemed clear to her any longer, and she was weary of trying to find a way out. All she knew was that she loved Pierre and him alone.

'Do you think that I'm so very happy?' said Pierre.

Françoise was so cruelly smitten that a cry rose to her lips. She clenched her teeth, but the tears sprang to her eyes. All Pierre's suffering surged back into her heart. Nothing else on earth counted but his love, and during the whole of this month, when he needed her, she had let him struggle alone. It was too late to ask his pardon. She had withdrawn too far for him still to want her help.

'Stop crying,' said Pierre a little impatiently. He was staring at her coldly. She knew that after standing up to him she had no right again to inflict her tears on him, but she was now nothing more than a chaotic mass of pain and remorse.

'Please calm yourself,' said Pierre.

She could not calm herself, because it was by her own fault that she had lost him. Her life would not be long enough to mourn her loss. She buried her face in her hands. Pierre was pacing up and down the room, but she was now not even concerned over him. She had lost all control over her body, and her thoughts kept on eluding her. She was an old, broken down machine.

Suddenly, she felt Pierre's hand on her shoulder. She looked up.

'You hate me now,' she said.

'Of course not, I don't hate you,' he said with a forced smile.

She caught hold of his hand. 'You know,' she said in a broken voice, 'I'm not so friendly with Xavière, but I feel such great responsibility. Ten months ago she was young, ardent, full of hope, and now she's a poor wreck.'

'In Rouen, too, she was to be pitied. She was always talking about committing suicide,' said Pierre.

'That was different,' said Françoise.

She sobbed again. It was tormenting. The moment she called to mind Xavière's pale face, she could no longer make up her mind to sacrifice her, even for Pierre's happiness. For an instant she remained motionless, her hand riveted to the hand resting inertly on her shoulder. Pierre was looking at her. Finally he said, 'What do you want me to do?' His face was set.

Françoise let go of his hand and wiped her eyes. 'I no longer want anything,' she said.

'What did you want a little while ago?' he said controlling his impatience with difficulty.

She rose and walked towards the balcony. She was afraid to ask anything of him. Whatever he might grant her, reluctantly, would only separate them the more. She came back to him.

'I thought, that if you were to see her, perhaps you'd regain your friendship with her. You mean so much to her.'

Pierre cut her short.

'Very good, I'll see her,' he said.

He went out and leaned on the balcony railing, and Françoise followed him. With bent head he was studying the formal garden where a few pigeons were hopping about. Françoise stared at the curved nape of his neck and again she was overcome by remorse. At the very time when he was really trying so hard to find peace, she had thrown him back into the raging torrent. She recalled the happy smile with which he had greeted her. Now she had before her a man full of bitterness, preparing himself with rebellious obedience to submit to a demand which it went against the grain to accept. She had often asked things of Pierre, but in the days when they were united, never could anything the one granted the other be felt as a sacrifice. This time she had put Pierre in the position of giving in to her with resentment. She touched her temples: her head ached and her eyes burned.

'What is she doing this evening?' said Pierre suddenly.

Françoise started.

'Nothing that I know of.'

'Well! Ring her up. While I'm about it, I'd prefer to settle this matter as soon as possible.'

Pierre nervously bit his nail. Françoise walked to the telephone.

'And what about Gerbert?'

'You'll see him without me.'

Françoise dialled the hotel number. She became aware of that hard iron band that was cutting across her stomach. All the old miseries would come back again. Pierre would never have a serene friendship with Xavière. Even now, his haste augured future storms.

'Hullo! Would you call Mademoiselle Pagès please?' she said.

'At once. Hold on.'

She heard the click of heels on the stairs, and confused

sounds. Someone shouted Xavière's name up the stair well. Françoise's heart began to race. Pierre's nervousness was catching.

'Hullo,' said Xavière's unsteady voice. Pierre picked up his earphone.

'This is Françoise. Are you free this evening?'

'Yes, why?'

'Labrousse would like to know if he may come to see you.'

There was no reply.

'Hullo!' repeated Françoise.

'To see me now?' said Xavière.

'Would that be inconvenient?'

'No, it wouldn't.'

Françoise sat for a moment not knowing what else to say.

'Well, that's settled,' she said. 'He'll come at once.'

She rang off.

'You're putting me in a false position,' said Pierre with a look of annoyance. 'She was not at all anxious for me to come and see her.'

'I think rather that she was overcome.'

They were silent for a long while.

'I'm going,' said Pierre.

'Come back and see me, and tell me how it went off,' said Françoise.

'All right. I'll see you tonight,' said Pierre. 'I think I'll be there early.'

Françoise walked to the window and watched him across the street. Then she came back and sat down in the arm-chair: she leaned back, exhausted. She felt that she had just made the final choice, and that it was calamity she had chosen. She jumped. There was a knock at the door.

'Come in,' she said.

Gerbert entered. With amazement Françoise saw the fresh face framed in black hair, as smooth as that of a Chinese woman's. Before the light of his smile, the shadows gathering in her heart were dissipated. She suddenly remembered that in this world there were other things to love that were neither Xavière nor Pierre. There were snow-capped peaks, sun-lit pines, roadside inns, people and stories. There were these laughing eyes that rested on her with friendliness.

Françoise opened her eyes and closed them again immediately.

Dawn was already breaking: she was sure she had not slept, she had heard every hour strike, and yet she felt as if she had gone to bed only a few moments ago. On her return at midnight, after having worked out with Gerbert a detailed plan of their journey, Pierre had not yet arrived. She had read for a little while, and then she had turned out the light and tried to go to sleep. It was only natural that the heart-to-heart talk with Xavière should have been protracted: she did not want to ask herself any questions about its outcome, she did not want to feel a vice grip her throat once again, she did not want to wait. She had been unable to sleep, but she had fallen into a torpor in which noises and images reverberated endlessly, as had happened during the feverish period of her illness, and the hours had seemed of unequal duration. Perhaps she would manage to get through the remainder of the night without anguish.

She shuddered. She heard footsteps on the staircase; the treads creaked too loudly for it to be Pierre, and the steps were already continuing up the next flight. She turned to the wall. If she were going to begin to listen to the murmuring of the night, to count the minutes, it would be hellish, and she wanted to remain calm. She was lucky to be lying comfortably in her bed, snug and warm. At this moment, there were tramps sleeping on the hard pavements of les Halles, and harassed travellers standing in the corridors of trains, and soldiers on guard at barracks gates.

She huddled more snugly under the sheets. During the course of these long hours, Pierre and Xavière must surely more than once have experienced mutual hate, only, in turn, to become reconciled; but how was she to know whether, in this rising dawn, love or bitterness had finally triumphed? She could see a red table in a large, all but unpeopled room, and over empty glasses two faces, now in ecstasy, now enraged. She tried to concentrate on each expression in turn, but neither of them concealed a threat; things had now reached such a state that there was nothing left to be threatened. Only she ought to have been able to determine upon one or the other. It was this uncertain vacuum that finally threw her heart into panic.

The room was growing perceptibly lighter. At almost any moment Pierre would be there, but she could not project herself into that very moment which his presence would fill: she could not even feel she was being swept towards it, for its place in time had not yet been set. Françoise had experienced periods of waiting that resembled mad gallops, but on this occasion she was marking time. Periods of waiting, moments of flight, the whole year had been spent thus. And now, what was she to begin to hope for? The happy equilibrium of their trio? Its final break-up? Neither the one nor the other would ever be possible, for there was no way of uniting with Xavière, and no way of freeing oneself from her: even exile would not obliterate this existence that refused to be annexed. Françoise remembered how she had at first denied her through her indifference; but her indifference had been conquered, yet their friendship had failed. There was no salvation. She could flee, but she would have to return, and there would be other periods of waiting and other moments of flight, endlessly.

Françoise reached for her alarm clock – seven o'clock – it was broad daylight out of doors. Her whole body was already alert, and immobility changed into anxiety. She threw back the sheets and began her toilet. She noticed with surprise that, once she was up, in broad daylight and with her head clear, she wanted to cry. She washed, applied her make-up and slowly put on her clothes. She did not feel nervous, but she did not know what to do with herself. Once dressed, she again lay down on her bed. At this moment, there was no place for her anywhere in the world. Nothing drew her out of doors, but here nothing held her back but an absence. She was no more than an empty longing, bereft of soul and body to the extent that the very walls of her room astonished her. Françoise sat bolt upright. This time, she recognized the step. She composed her features and sprang towards the door. Pierre smiled at her.

'Are you up already?' he said. 'I hope you weren't worrying.'

'No,' said Françoise. 'I knew that you had so many things to say to each other.' She looked him up and down; it was clear that he was not returning from the void. In his high colour, his lively look, his gestures, was reflected the fullness of the hours he had just lived. 'Well?' she said.

Pierre assumed an embarrassed but happy look that Françoise knew well.

'Well, everything's starting afresh,' he said. He touched Françoise's arm. 'I'll tell you all the details, but Xavière's waiting for us for breakfast. I said that we'd come back at once.'

Françoise put on her jacket. She had just lost her last chance of regaining a pure and peaceful intimacy with Pierre, but she had hardly dared to believe in this chance for even a few minutes: she was now too weary for regret or for hope. She went downstairs: the idea of being once more one of the trio was barely awaking in her more than a resigned anxiety.

'Tell me in a few words what happened,' she said.

'Well, I went to her hotel last evening,' said Pierre. 'I felt at once that she was very much moved, and that moved me. We stayed there for a while talking stupidly about the weather, and then we went to the Pôle Nord and had a gigantic discussion.' Pierre said nothing for a moment, and then he continued, in that conceited, nervous tone that had always pained Françoise, 'I have the feeling that it wouldn't take much to make her drop Gerbert.'

'Did you ask her to break it off?' said Françoise.

'I don't want to be odd man out,' said Pierre.

Gerbert had never worried about the quarrel between Pierre and Xavière. Their whole friendship had never seemed to him to rest on anything more than a whim, and he was going to be cruelly hurt when he learned the truth. Actually, Pierre would have done better to have kept him informed from the very beginning; Gerbert would willingly have given up trying to win Xavière. At the moment, he was not deeply attached to her, but it would certainly be unpleasant for him to lose her.

'When you have gone off on your trip,' said Pierre, 'I'll take Xavière in hand, and if by the end of the week the question isn't settled, I will ask her to make a choice.'

'Yes,' said Françoise. She hesitated. 'You'll have to explain the whole story to Gerbert, otherwise you'll appear a dirty dog.'

'I'll explain it to him,' said Pierre quickly. 'I'll tell him that I didn't want to use authority over him, but that I thought I had the right to compete as an equal.' He looked at Françoise without much assurance. 'You don't agree with me?'

'There's something to be said for it,' said Françoise.

In one sense, it was true that there was no reason for Pierre to sacrifice himself for Gerbert, but neither had Gerbert deserved the cruel disillusionment awaiting him. Françoise kicked along a little round pebble. Doubtless, she would have to give up the idea of finding the perfect solution to any problem. For some time it had seemed that, whatever decision she made, she must always be in the wrong. And besides, no one worried very much any more about knowing what was right or what was wrong. She herself took no interest in the question.

They walked into the Dôme. Xavière was seated at a table, her head bowed. Françoise touched her shoulder lightly.

'Good morning,' she said with a smile.

Xavière shuddered, and raised a surprised face to Françoise. Then she, too, smiled, but with restraint.

'I couldn't believe it was you so soon,' she said.

Françoise sat down beside her. Something in this greeting was painfully familiar to her.

'How fresh you look!' said Pierre.

Xavière must have taken advantage of Pierre's absence to make her face up again meticulously. Her complexion was smooth and clear, her lips brilliant, her hair glossy.

'Yet I'm tired,' said Xavière. Her eyes rested first on Françoise and then on Pierre, and she put her hand to her mouth and stifled a yawn. 'In fact, I think I'd like to go home and go to sleep,' she said with an embarrassed, affectionate look that was not directed at Françoise.

'Now?' said Pierre. 'You have the whole day.'

Xavière's face clouded over.

'I feel very uncomfortable,' she said. She shook her arms, making the wide sleeves of her blouse puff out. 'It's unpleasant to wear the same clothes for hours on end.'

'At least have a cup of coffee with us,' said Pierre disappointedly.

'If you wish,' said Xavière.

Pierre ordered three coffees. Françoise took a croissant and began to nibble at it. Her courage failed her and she made no attempt to speak a friendly word. She had already lived this scene more than twenty times. She was sickened in advance by the cheerful tone, the bright smiles she felt rising to her lips, and by the irritated disgust she felt welling within her. Xavière was sleepily staring at her fingers. For quite a while no one breathed a word.

'What did you and Gerbert do?' said Pierre.

'We had dinner at the Grille and we planned our walking tour,' said Françoise. 'I think we'll leave the day after tomorrow.'

'Are you really going to climb mountains?' said Xavière in a dismal voice.

'Yes,' said Françoise curtly. 'You think that ridiculous?'

Xavière raised her eyebrows.

'Well . . . if you enjoy it,' she said.

Again silence fell. Pierre looked uneasily from one to the other.

'You both look sleepy,' he said reproachfully.

'This isn't a very good time to look at people,' said Xavière.

'Still, I can remember a very pleasant time we spent here at this same hour,' said Pierre.

'Oh! It wasn't so pleasant,' said Xavière.

Françoise well remembered that morning and the soapy smell of the tiles. It was then, for the first time, that Xavière's jealousy was openly declared. After every effort to rid her of it, she found her today exactly as before. At this moment, it was not only Françoise's presence, it was her very existence that Xavière wanted to eradicate.

Xavière pushed away her glass.

'I'm going home,' she said firmly.

'Above all, get a good rest,' said Françoise ironically.

Xavière shook her head without answering. She smiled vaguely at Pierre and hurried out of the cafe.'

'It's a fiasco,' said Françoise.

'Yes,' said Pierre. He seemed vexed. 'Still, she looked very pleased when I asked her to wait for us.'

'Doubtless she didn't want to leave you,' said Françoise. She laughed slightly. 'But what a shock she must have had when she saw me standing in front of her.'

'It's going to be hellish again,' said Pierre. He stared dismally at the door through which Xavière had left. 'I wonder if it's worth starting again. We'll never get out of it.'

'How did she speak to you about me?' said Françoise.

Pierre hesitated.

'She seemed to be friendly towards you,' he said.

'And what else?' She looked with annoyance at Pierre's puzzled face. It was now he who felt bound to spare her. 'Hasn't she got any little grievances?'

'She seems to be slightly angry with you,' Pierre admitted. 'I think she's come to the conclusion that you have no deep love for her.'

Françoise stiffened.

'What exactly did she say?'

'She told me that I was the only person who didn't try to throw cold water on her moods,' said Pierre. Beneath the indifference in his voice there could be detected a faint satisfaction at feeling himself irreplaceable to this degree. 'And then at one point she said to me with delight: "You and I are not moral beings: we are capable of doing vile things." And when I protested, she added: "It's because of Françoise that you're so bent on appearing moral, but deep down you're as treacherous as I am and your soul is just as black." '

Françoise blushed, for she, too, was beginning to consider this legendary morality at which people laughed indulgently as a ridiculous fault. Perhaps it would not take her long to shake it off. She looked at Pierre. His hesitant expression did not reflect a very clear conscience. It was obvious that Xavière's words had flattered him in some way.

'I suppose she holds my effort at reconciliation against me, as proof of lukewarmness,' she said.

'I don't know,' said Pierre.

'What else did she say?' said Françoise. 'Let me have the full story,' she added impatiently.

'Well, she made a bitter allusion to what she calls loves of devotion.'

'What's that?'

'She explained her character to me, and she told me with feigned humility: "I know that I'm often very disagreeable with people, but what can I do? I'm not made for loves of devotion." '

Françoise was dumbfounded: this was a double-edged betrayal. Xavière blamed Pierre for remaining capable of so wretched a love, while she herself bitterly rejected him. Françoise had far from suspected the degree of this hostility, blended as it was with jealousy and disgust.

'Is that all?' she said.

'I think so,' said Pierre.

That was not all, but Françoise was suddenly tired of asking questions. She knew enough to have on her lips the treacherous taste of this night in which Xavière's triumphant rancour had wrenched from Pierre a thousand petty betrayals.

'Anyway, you know, I don't give a damn how she feels,' she said.

It was true. Suddenly, at this culminating point of misery,

nothing was of importance. Because of Xavière, she had almost lost Pierre, and in return Xavière gave her only contempt and jealousy. No sooner was Xavière reconciled with Pierre, than she tried to establish between them an underhand complicity which he only half-heartedly disclaimed. Their dual rejection of Françoise left her in such a forlorn state of desolation that there was no room either for anger or for tears. Françoise hoped for nothing more from Pierre, and his indifference no longer affected her. With respect to Xavière, she felt rising within her, with a kind of joy, something black and bitter that she did not yet know and which was almost a deliverance: powerful, free, finally bursting unhindered into bloom. It was hate.

Chapter Eight

'I think we're almost there at last,' said Gerbert.

'Yes, it's that little house we can see up there,' said Françoise.

They had covered a considerable distance during the day, and for the past two hours it had been hard uphill going. Night was falling and it was cold. Françoise looked tenderly at Gerbert, who was walking ahead of her up the steep path. They were both tramping at the same pace; they both felt the same happy fatigue; and both together were silently looking forward to the red wine, the supper, and the log fire they hoped to find up there. Whenever they arrived in these isolated villages, it was always something of an adventure. They could never be certain whether they were going to sit down at a noisy table in a peasant kitchen, have their dinner alone in an empty inn, or land up in some small middle-class hotel already filled with holidaymakers. Whichever it was, they would throw their packs down in a corner, and with their muscles relaxed and their hearts content, they would spend quiet hours side by side, talking over the day they had just lived together and making plans for tomorrow. Françoise was hurrying more towards the warmth of this intimacy, than to the rich omelette and the raw, home-made spirits. A gust of wind whipped her face. They were reaching a pass that dominated a fan of valleys lost in the hazy dusk.

'We won't be able to pitch the tent,' she said. 'The ground is very damp.'

'We'll probably find a barn,' said Gerbert.

A barn. Françoise felt a sickening emptiness within her. Three nights earlier, they had slept in a barn. They had gone to sleep at no great distance from each other, but, in his sleep, Gerbert's body had slipped towards hers and he had thrown his arms about her. With a vague regret she had thought: 'He takes me for someone else,' and she had held her breath so as not to wake him. Then she had dreamed; and in her dream she was in this same barn, and Gerbert, with his eyes wide open, had clasped her in his arms. She had yielded, her

361

heart filled with sweetness and security, till anguish had undermined this state of tender well-being. 'It's not true,' she found herself saying. Gerbert had clasped her tighter, and exclaimed: 'It is true. It would be too ridiculous if it weren't true.' Not many moments later a ray of light had struck her eyelids. She had wakened to find herself still lying in the hay, pressed close to Gerbert, and there was no truth in it at all.

'You've been tossing your hair into my face all night,' she had said with a laugh.

'Not at all, you've kept on poking your elbows into me,' Gerbert replied indignantly.

Not without distress did she think about reliving a similar awakening tomorrow. Beneath the tent, huddled in a narrow space, she felt protected by the hardness of the earth, the discomfort, and the wooden tent-pole separating her from Gerbert; but she knew that, later, she would not have the courage to make up her bed far from his. It was useless to keep on trying to under-rate the vague yearning that had been hanging over her all these days. During the two hours of silent climbing, it had been persistently in her thoughts until it had become at length choking desire. Tonight, while Gerbert was innocently sleeping, she would dream again, regret and suffer, all to no purpose.

'Do you think this place is a café?' said Gerbert.

On the wall of the house was a red sign bearing the word *BYRRH* in huge letters, and stuck above the door was a handful of dried branches.

'It looks like one,' said Françoise.

They walked up the three steps and into a large warm room that smelled of cooking and dried twigs. There were women seated on benches, peeling potatoes, and three peasants at a table, with glasses of red wine.

'Good evening,' said Gerbert.

Every eye turned towards him. He went up to the two women.

'Could we please have something to eat?'

The women looked at him with distrust.

'You've come far?' said the elder.

'We've come up from Burzet,' said Françoise.

'That's a fairish distance,' said the other woman.

'That's just why we're hungry,' said Françoise.

'But you aren't from Burzet,' said the elder woman, with

362

an accusing look.

'No, we're from Paris,' said Gerbert.

There was a silence. The women looked questioningly at each other.

'The trouble is that I haven't much to give you,' said the old woman.

'Haven't you any eggs? Or a bit of pie? Anything at all . . .' said Françoise.

The old woman shrugged her shoulders.

'Eggs, yes. We have plenty of eggs.' She rose and wiped her hands on her blue apron. 'Would you care to step inside?' she said somewhat reluctantly.

They followed her into a low-ceilinged room where a wood fire was burning: it looked like a middle-class provincial dining-room. There was a round table, a wooden chest loaded with knick-knacks, and on the arm-chairs, orange satin cushions appliquéd with black velvet.

'Would you please bring us a bottle of red wine now,' said Gerbert.

He helped Françoise take off her rucksack and put down his own.

'We're as comfortable as kings here,' said Gerbert with a look of contentment.

'Yes, it's wonderfully pleasant,' said Françoise.

She walked up to the fire. She knew only too well what was lacking in this cosy evening. If only she had been able to touch Gerbert's hand, to smile at him with affection, then the blaze, the smell of the dinner, the black velvet cats and the sparrows would have rejoiced her heart. But it all remained scattered around her, without touching her. It almost seemed absurd that she should be there.

The innkeeper returned with a bottle of cloudy, heavy wine.

'You don't by any chance happen to have a barn where we could spend the night?' asked Gerbert.

The woman was laying the places on the oilcloth. She looked up.

'You aren't going to sleep in a barn?' she said, looking shocked. She thought for a moment. 'You're out of luck. I might have had a room for you, but my son, who's got a job as a postman, has just come home.'

'We'd be very happy in the barn, if only it won't put you out,' said Françoise. 'We have blankets.' She pointed to the rucksacks. 'But it's too cold to pitch our tent.'

'It won't put me out,' said the woman. She left the room and brought back a steaming soup tureen. 'At least this will warm you up a bit,' she said in a friendly tone.

Gerbert filled the soup bowls and Françoise sat down opposite him.

'She's getting tame,' said Gerbert when they were alone again. 'Everything's turning out splendidly.'

'Splendidly,' echoed Françoise with conviction.

She looked furtively at Gerbert. The gaiety enlivening his face resembled tenderness. Was he really beyond reach? Or was it just that she had never dared to reach out her hand to him? Who was holding her back? It was neither Pierre nor Xavière. She no longer owed anything to Xavière who, moreover, was preparing to betray Gerbert. They were alone, at the top of a wind-flayed mountain pass, separated from the rest of the world, and their story concerned no one other than themselves.

'I'm going to do something that will disgust you,' said Gerbert in a threatening tone.

'What?' she said.

'I'm going to pour some wine into my soup.' As he was speaking, he suited his action to his words.

'That must be horrid,' said Françoise.

Gerbert put a spoonful of the blood-red liquid to his mouth. 'It's delicious,' he said. 'Try it.'

'Not for anything in the world,' said Françoise.

She swallowed a little wine. Her palms were moist. She had always disregarded her dreams and her desires, but this self-effacing wisdom now revolted her. Why did she not make up her mind to will what she hoped for?

'The view from the top of the pass was magnificent,' she said. 'I think we'll have good weather tomorrow.'

Gerbert scowled at her.

'Are you going to insist that we get up at dawn again?'

'Stop complaining. The real expert is on the peaks at five o'clock in the morning.'

'They're all crazy,' said Gerbert. 'I'm a cocoon before eight o'clock.'

'I know,' said Françoise. She smiled. 'You know, if you go to Greece, you'll have to be on your way before dawn.'

'Yes, but then you take a nap in the afternoon,' said Gerbert. He thought for a moment. 'I hope that plan for a tour doesn't collapse.'

'If there's another crisis,' said Françoise, 'I'm afraid it's going to fall through.'

Gerbert resolutely cut himself a huge chunk of bread.

'In any case, I'll manage to find a way out. I'm not going to stay in France next year.' His face lit up. 'It seems you can make a fortune on Mauritius.'

'Why Mauritius?'

'Ramblin told me about it. The place is full of millionaires who'll pay anything for a little amusement.'

The door opened and the innkeeper came in. She was carrying a huge potato-omelette.

'Why, this is a feast,' said Françoise. She helped herself and passed the platter to Gerbert, 'Here, I'll leave you the big piece.'

'Is that all for me?'

'All for you.'

'That's very honest of you,' said Gerbert.

She glanced at him.

'Am I not always honest with you?' she said. There was a boldness in her voice that embarrassed her.

'Yes, I can't deny the fact,' said Gerbert without turning a hair.

Françoise was kneading a tiny pellet of bread between her fingers. She would have to cling fast to the decision which had suddenly come upon her. She did not know how, but something would have to happen before tomorrow.

'Do you plan to be away for a long time?' she said.

'One or two years,' said Gerbert.

'Xavière will never forgive you,' said Françoise insincerely. She rolled the tiny grey ball on the table and said casually: 'It wouldn't upset you to leave her?'

'On the contrary,' said Gerbert with enthusiasm.

Françoise looked down. There was such a burst of light within her, that she was afraid it might be visible from without.

'Why? Is she such a burden to you? I thought you were really quite fond of her.'

She was happy to think that if, at the end of this trip,

Xavière were to break with him, Gerbert would suffer hardly at all. But that was not the reason for this immodest joy that had just blazed within her.

'She isn't a burden to me, when I think that it's soon going to end,' said Gerbert. 'But off and on, I wonder if that isn't the way people are drawn into living together. I'd loathe that.'

'Even if you were in love with the good woman?' said Françoise.

She held out her glass to him and he filled it to the brim. She was now distressed. He was there, facing her, alone, unattached, absolutely free. Owing to his youth and the respect he had always shown Pierre and herself, she could hardly expect him to take any initiative. If she wanted something to happen, Françoise could count only on herself.

'I don't think I'll ever love any woman,' said Gerbert.

'Why?' said Françoise. She was so tense that her hand was trembling. She leaned forward and drank a sip without putting her fingers to the glass.

'I don't know,' said Gerbert. 'You can't do anything with a female: you can't go walking, you can't get drunk, or anything. They can't take a joke, and then, besides, you always have to make a fuss of them or you always feel you're in the wrong.' He added with conviction: 'I prefer it when I can be just what I am with people.'

'Don't stand on any ceremony with me,' said Françoise.

Gerbert burst out laughing.

'Oh you! You're like a man!' he said warmly.

'That's right, you've never regarded me as a woman,' said Françoise.

She felt a queer smile on her lips. Gerbert looked at her inquisitively. She looked away and emptied her glass. She had made a bad start; she would be ashamed to treat Gerbert with clumsy flirtatiousness, she would have done better to proceed openly: 'Would it surprise you if I were to suggest that you sleep with me?' or something of that sort. But her lips refused to form the words. She pointed to the empty platter.

'Do you think she's going to give us something else?' she said. Her voice did not have the ring she would have liked.

'I don't suppose so,' said Gerbert.

The silence had already lasted too long. Something equivocal had slipped into the atmosphere.

'Well, we can always ask for more wine,' she said.

Again Gerbert looked at her a little uneasily,

'A half bottle,' he said.

She smiled. He loved simple situations. Had he guessed why she needed the help of intoxication?

'Madame, would you mind?' Gerbert called.

The old woman entered and placed a dish of boiled beef and vegetables on the table.

'What would you like after that? Some cheese? Some preserves?'

'I don't think we'll be hungry any more,' said Gerbert. 'But please get us a little more wine.'

'Why did that old lunatic start off by telling us there was nothing to eat?' said Françoise.

'Most of the people round about here are like that,' said Gerbert. 'I don't think they're very anxious to make twenty francs and they think that people are apt to be a nuisance.'

'It must be something like that,' said Françoise.

The woman returned with a bottle. After thinking it over, Françoise decided to drink no more than a glass or two. She did not want Gerbert to attribute her behaviour to the instability of the moment.

'On the whole,' she said, 'what you hold against love, is that you can't feel at ease. But don't you think that you seriously impoverish your life if you reject any close relationship with people?'

'But there are close relationships other than love,' said Gerbert quickly. 'I put friendship far above it. I'd be very well satisfied with a life in which there are nothing but friendships.'

He looked at Françoise a little persistently. Was he, too, trying to make her understand something? That he had a true friendship for her, or that she was precious to him? He rarely talked at such length about himself. Tonight, there was a kind of receptiveness about him.

'As it happens, I can never love someone for whom I have not first a feeling of friendship,' said Françoise.

She had put the sentence in the present, but she had used an off-hand and matter-of-fact tone. She wished she could have added something, but she could utter none of the words that rose to her lips. Finally, she said: 'I think just a simple friendship is barren.'

'I don't think so,' said Gerbert.

He was bristling a little. He was thinking of Pierre. He was thinking that it was impossible to be fonder of anyone than he was of Pierre.

'Yes, basically, you're right,' said Françoise.

She put down her fork and went to sit by the fire. Gerbert rose, too, and picked up a big round log lying near the fireplace and skilfully laid it on the andirons.

'Now you can smoke your pipe,' said Françoise. She added, without repressing a burst of affection: 'I like to see you smoke a pipe.'

She stretched out her hands to the fire. She felt content: tonight, there was almost an avowed affection between Gerbert and herself. And why need she ask for more? His head was slightly bent. He was studiously drawing on his pipe, and the fire gilded his face. She broke off a piece of dry wood and threw it on the hearth. Nothing could quell her desire to hold his head between her hands.

'What are we going to do tomorrow?' said Gerbert.

'We'll go up to Gerbier des Joncs, then to Mézanc.' She rose and rummaged in her rucksack. 'I don't know exactly what would be the best way to go down.' She spread out a map, opened the guide-book and lay flat on the floor.

'Do you want to look?'

'No, I trust you,' said Gerbert.

She absently studied the network of tiny roads edged in green and dotted with blue marks which indicated the best views. What would tomorrow bring? The answer was not on the map. She did not want this trip to end in regrets that would soon turn into remorse and into self-hatred. She was about to speak. But did she even know whether Gerbert would find pleasure in kissing her? He had probably never thought about it. She could not bear that he should give in to her out of kindness. The blood rushed to her face; she remembered Elisabeth – a woman who takes – and she loathed the thought. She looked up at Gerbert and felt somewhat reassured: he had too much affection and too much esteem for her to mock her in secret. What she had to do was to give him an opportunity for a frank refusal. But how was she to go about it?

She started. The younger of the two women was standing in front of her, a big stable-lamp swinging in her hand.

'If you want to go to bed, I'll show you the way.'

'Yes, thank you very much,' said Françoise.

Gerbert took the two rucksacks, and they went out of the house. It was a pitch-black night and a gale was blowing. The round vaccillating spot of light illuminated the muddy ground ahead of them.

'I don't know if you'll be very comfortable,' said the woman. 'One of the windows is broken, and, besides, the cows make a noise in the stable alongside.'

'Oh! That won't bother us,' said Françoise.

The woman stopped and pushed open a heavy wooden door. Françoise happily inhaled the smell of hay. It was a huge barn, and in among the piles of hay she caught a glimpse of stacks of logs, crates, and a wheelbarrow.

'You aren't using matches, are you?' said the woman.

'No, I've got a torch,' said Gerbert.

'Well, good night,' she said.

Gerbert closed the door and bolted it.

'Where shall we settle down?' said Françoise.

Gerbert played a thin beam of light over the floor and the walls.

'In the corner at the back, don't you think? The hay is nice and deep and we'll be far away from the door.'

They walked forward warily. Françoise's mouth was dry. The time was now or never. She had only some ten minutes, for Gerbert always fell into a sound sleep almost immediately. And she had absolutely no idea how to approach the question indirectly.

'Listen to that wind,' said Gerbert. 'We'll be much better off here than under a tent.' The walls of the barn were shaken by the squalls. Next door, a cow kicked at her stall and rattled her chains.

'You'll see what a fine set-up we'll have,' said Gerbert.

He put the torch on a board on which he carefully laid out his pipe, his watch, and his wallet. Françoise took out her sleeping-bag and a pair of flannel pyjamas from her rucksack. She walked a few paces away and began to undress in the shadow. She now had not a thought in her head, only the gripping constriction in her stomach. She had no time to invent a way out, but she did not give up. If the torch went out before she had spoken, she would call: 'Gerbert,' and she would say in one breath: 'Has it never occurred to you that we might sleep together?' What happened afterwards would be of no importance. She now had but one desire and that was to free herself from this obsession.

'How industrious you are,' she said, coming back into the light.

Gerbert had laid the sleeping-bags side by side, and had fashioned pillows by stuffing two sweaters with hay. He walked away and Françoise slipped half-way into her sleeping-bag. Her heart was pounding fit to burst. For a moment she wanted to give it all up and escape into sleep.

'How comfortable the hay is,' said Gerbert as he lay down alongside her. He had put the torch on a beam behind them. Françoise looked at him and again she felt a violent desire to feel his lips against hers.

'We've had a wonderful day,' he continued. 'This is great country.'

He was now lying on his back, smiling. He seemed in no hurry to go to sleep.

'Yes, I enjoyed that dinner and sitting in front of the wood fire talking like two old folk.'

'Why like old folk?' said Gerbert.

'We were talking about love and friendship, as if we were dried up and out of the game.'

In her voice there was a resentful irony that did not escape Gerbert. He looked at her in embarrassment.

'Have you made some good plans for tomorrow?' he asked after a brief silence.

'Yes, that was easy,' said Françoise.

She let the conversation drop. She felt pleased that the atmosphere was growing oppressive. Gerbert made another effort.

'This lake you were talking about, it would be nice if we could go and bathe in it.'

'We probably can,' said Françoise.

She withdrew into a stubborn silence. Usually, conversation between them did not flag. Surely Gerbert would finally sense something.

'Look what I can do,' he said suddenly.

He raised his hands above his head and moved his fingers, and the torch light cast a vague animal silhouette on the opposite wall.

'How clever you are!' said Françoise.

'I can also make a judge,' said Gerbert,

She was now sure that he was trying to put a bold face on the situation. She felt a lump in her throat. She watched him intently forming shadows of a rabbit, a camel, a giraffe. When he had exhausted his repertoire he lowered his hands.

'Shadow silhouettes are fun,' he began glibly, 'they are almost as good as marionettes. Didn't you ever see the silhouettes Begramian designed? Only we didn't have a script. Next year we'll have to try it again.'

He stopped short. He could no longer pretend not to see that Françoise was not listening. She had rolled over on to her stomach, and was staring at the torch which was getting weaker.

'The battery is dying,' he said. 'It's going out.'

Françoise did not reply. Despite the cold draught coming through the broken pane, she was perspiring. She felt as if she had come to a halt above an abyss, without being able to advance or withdraw. She was without thought, without desire, and suddenly the situation seemed plainly absurd. She smiled nervously.

'Why are you smiling?' said Gerbert.

'For no reason at all,' said Françoise.

Her lips began to tremble. With all her soul she had invited this question, and now she was afraid.

'Were you thinking about something?' said Gerbert.

'No,' she said, 'It was nothing.'

Suddenly, tears rose to her eyes. She was at her nerves' end: now she had gone too far. It was Gerbert himself who would force her to speak, and perhaps this delightful friendship between them would be ruined for ever.

'Well, I know what you were thinking,' said Gerbert challengingly.

'What?' said Françoise.

Gerbert waved his hand proudly.

'I won't tell you.'

'Say it,' said Françoise, 'and I'll tell you if you're right.'

'No, you tell me first,' said Gerbert.

For a moment they surveyed each other like two enemies. Françoise became completely negative, but the words finally crossed her lips.

'I was smiling because I was wondering how you would look – you who loathe complications – if I suggested that you should sleep with me.'

'I thought you were thinking that I wanted to kiss you and didn't dare,' said Gerbert.

'It never occurred to me that *you* wanted to kiss me,' said Françoise, stiffly. There was a silence. Her ears were singing. Now it was done. She had spoken. 'Well, answer me. How would you take it?' she said.

Gerbert shrivelled. He did not take his eyes off Françoise, but his whole face was on the defensive.

'It isn't that I wouldn't like to,' he said. 'I'd be too frightened.'

Françoise caught her breath and managed to smile benignly.

'That's a clever answer,' she said. She finally steadied her voice. 'You're right. It would be artificial and embarrassing.'

She reached for the torch: she must switch it off quickly and take refuge in the night; she would have a good cry, but at least she would no longer drag this obsession about with her. The only thing she feared was that their waking in the morning might be awkward.

'Good night,' she said.

Gerbert continued to stare at her obstinately with a fierce, uncertain look.

'I was convinced, before going on this trip, that you had bet Labrousse that I'd try to kiss you.'

Françoise pulled back her hand.

'I'm not as conceited as all that,' she said. 'I know you think of me as a man.'

'That's not true,' said Gerbert. His outburst stopped short, and once again a mistrustful shadow passed over his face. 'I'd loathe to be in your life what people like Canzetti are for Labrousse.'

Françoise hesitated.

'You mean, to have an affaire with me that I wouldn't take seriously?'

'Yes,' said Gerbert.

'But I never take anything lightly,' said Françoise.

Gerbert looked at her hesitatingly.

'I thought you had noticed it and that it amused you,' he said.

'Saw what?'

'That I wanted to kiss you the other night in the barn and yesterday on the bank of the stream.' He shrank back even more and said somewhat angrily: 'I'd made up my mind that

372

when we got back to Paris, I'd kiss you on the platform. Only I thought you'd laugh in my face.'

'I!' said Françoise. Joy had now put fire into her cheeks.

'Otherwise, there would have been dozens of times I'd have wanted to. I'd love to kiss you.'

He lay huddled up in his sleeping-bag, motionless, like a trapped animal. Françoise gauged the distance separating him from her, and took the plunge.

'Well, kiss me, you silly little Gerbert,' she said offering him her mouth.

A few moments later, Françoise incredulously ran her hand over this young, smooth, firm body that for so long had seemed beyond reach. This time she was not dreaming. She was actually holding him, wide awake, clasped to her. Gerbert's hand caressed her back, the nape of her neck: it rested on her head and stayed there.

'I love the shape of your head,' whispered Gerbert. He added in a voice unfamiliar to her: 'It seems strange that I should be kissing you.'

The light went out. The wind was raging and a cold blast came in through the broken pane. Françoise rested her cheek against Gerbert's shoulder, and with her body surrendered against him, relaxed, she felt no further embarrassment in talking to him.

'You know,' she said, 'it wasn't just sensuality that made me want to be in your arms; it was above all affection.'

'Is that true?' said Gerbert joyfully.

'Of course it's true. Have you never felt how fond I am of you?'

Gerbert's fingers tightened on her shoulder.

'That makes me happy,' he said. 'Really very, very happy.'

'But wasn't it obvious?' said Françoise.

'Not at all,' said Gerbert. 'You were always as stiff as a poker. It even hurt me when I saw you give Labrousse or Xavière a certain look. I thought you'd never have a look like that for me.'

'It was you who were always so matter-of-fact with me,' said Françoise.

Gerbert cuddled up against her.

'Still, I was always extremely fond of you,' he said. 'In fact, very, very fond of you.'

'You kept it well hidden,' said Françoise. Her lips touched

373

his long-lashed eyelids. 'The first time that I wanted to hold your head in my hands was in my office the night before Pierre returned. Do you remember? You were sleeping on my shoulder. You weren't paying any attention to me, but all the same, I was happy to know you were there.'

'Oh! I wasn't fast asleep,' said Gerbert. 'And I did like, too, to feel you against me, but I thought you were giving me your shoulder the way you might have given me a pillow,' he added with an astonished look.

'You were wrong,' said Françoise. She ran her hands through his soft black hair. 'And you know that dream I told you about the other day, in the barn, when you said to me: "No, it's not a dream. It would be too ridiculous if it weren't true . . ." I was lying to you. It wasn't because we were wandering about in New York that I was afraid of waking up. It was because I was in your arms, just as I am now.'

'Really?' said Gerbert. He lowered his voice. 'The next morning I was so afraid you suspected me of not really having been asleep. I was only making believe so that I could hold you close to me. That was dishonest, but I did so want to do it.'

'Well! I certainly never suspected that,' said Françoise. She laughed. 'We might have played hide-and-seek for a long time. It was a good thing I vulgarly threw myself at you.'

'You?' said Gerbert. 'You didn't throw yourself at me. You didn't want to say anything.'

'Do you maintain that it's thanks to you that we've reached this point?' said Françoise.

'I helped just as much as you. I left the light on, and I kept the conversation going to prevent you from going to sleep.'

'How bold of you!' said Françoise. 'If you knew how you were looking at me during dinner, when I tried a few feeble advances.'

'I thought you were beginning to get drunk,' said Gerbert. Françoise pressed her cheek against his.

'I'm so glad I didn't get discouraged,' she said.

'So am I,' said Gerbert.

He put his warm lips to her mouth and she felt his body cleave tightly to hers.

The taxi whisked along between the lines of chestnut trees on the boulevard Arago. Above the tall houses, the blue sky was as pure as the sky up in the mountains. With a timid smile, Gerbert put his arm round Françoise's shoulder. She leant against him.

'Are you still happy?' she said.

'Yes, I'm happy,' said Gerbert. He looked at her trustfully. 'What delights me, is that I feel you're really fond of me. So it almost doesn't matter not to be able to see you for a long time. That may not seem like a very nice thing to say, but it really is.'

'I understand,' said Françoise.

A little wave of emotion rose in her breast. She recalled their breakfast at the inn after their first night; they had looked laughingly at each other with delighted, slightly embarrassed surprise; they had gone on their way with fingers intertwined like Swiss sweethearts; in a meadow, at the foot of Gerbier des Joncs, Gerbert had picked a small dark-blue flower and given it to Françoise.

'It's foolish,' she said. 'It oughtn't to be so, but I don't like to think that tonight someone else will be sleeping beside you.'

'I don't like it either,' said Gerbert in a low voice. He added with a kind of distress: 'I wish you were the only person who loved me.'

'I love you very much,' said Françoise.

'I've never loved any woman in the way I love you,' said Gerbert. 'I love you far, far beyond.'

Françoise's eyes became dim. Gerbert would never take root anywhere: he would never belong to anyone. But he was unreservedly giving her all that he could give of himself.

'Dear, darling Gerbert,' she said kissing him.

The taxi stopped. She sat facing him for a moment, her eyes blurred, incapable of bringing herself to let go of his fingers. She felt a physical anguish, as if she were being forced to jump into deep water.

'Goodbye,' she said suddenly. 'I'll see you tomorrow.'

'See you tomorrow,' said Gerbert.

She went through the small door of the theatre.

'Is Monsieur Labrousse upstairs?'

'Yes he is. He hasn't even rung yet,' said the concierge.

'Would you please bring up two cafés-au-lait,' said Françoise, 'and some toast.'

375

She crossed the courtyard. Her heart was pounding with incredulous hope. The letter had been sent three days ago. Pierre might have changed his mind, but it was just like him, when once he had given up something, to feel completely detached from it. She knocked.

'Come in,' said a sleepy voice.

She turned on the light. Pierre opened two sleepy eyes. He was tightly wrapped in the bedclothes. He had the blissful, lazy look of a huge cocoon.

'You certainly look as if you've been sleeping,' she said gaily.

She sat down on the edge of the bed and kissed him.

'How warm you are. You make me feel like going to bed myself.'

She had slept well, stretched out full length on a seat, but these white sheets looked so inviting.

'Oh! I'm so glad you're here!' said Pierre. He rubbed his eyes. 'Wait. I'll get up.'

She walked to the window and pulled back the curtains, while he put on a beautiful red velvet dressing-gown made from an old costume.

'How well you look,' said Pierre.

'I've had a good rest,' said Françoise. She smiled. 'Did you get my letter?'

'Yes,' said Pierre. He too smiled. 'You know, I wasn't very surprised.'

'It wasn't so much sleeping with Gerbert that surprised me,' said Françoise. 'It's the kind of fondness he has for me.'

'And what about you?' said Pierre tenderly.

'Me, too!' said Françoise. 'I'm very fond of him. And what really delights me, is that our relationship has become so close without losing its light-heartedness.'

'Yes, that's a good job,' said Pierre. 'He's as lucky as you are.'

He smiled, but there was a shade of reticence in his voice.

'You don't see anything wrong in it?' said Françoise.

'Of course not,' said Pierre.

There was a knock.

'Here's your breakfast,' said the concierge.

She put the tray on the table. Françoise seized a piece of toast, it was all crisp on the surface and soft inside; she spread it with butter and poured coffee into the cups.

'Real café-au-lait,' she said, 'and real toast. This is wonderful. I wish you could have seen the black treacle Gerbert used to concoct for us.'

'God forbid,' said Pierre. He looked preoccupied.

'What are you thinking about?' said Françoise a little uneasily.

'Oh! Nothing,' said Pierre. He hesitated. 'If I look a little perplexed it's because of Xavière. All this is going to be the devil for her!'

Françoise's heart stopped.

'Xavière,' she said. 'I wouldn't allow myself to make one more sacrifice for her.'

'Oh! Don't think I'd reproach you for anything,' said Pierre quickly. 'But what dismays me a little, is that I've just convinced her that she must build a stable and decent relationship with Gerbert.'

'Well, obviously, it's inopportune,' said Françoise with a slight laugh. She looked him up and down. 'Just where do you stand with her? How did things turn out?'

'Oh! It's very simple,' said Pierre. He hesitated a second. 'You remember when I left you, I wanted to force her to break off. Well, as soon as we spoke about Gerbert, I was aware of a far stronger resistance than I had expected. She's tremendously fond of him, whatever she may say, and that made me hesitate. Had I insisted, I think I would have won; but I wondered if I really wanted to.'

'Yes?' said Françoise. She did not yet dare believe the promises of this reasonable voice and this trusting face.

'The first time I saw her again, I was shaken.' Pierre shrugged his shoulders. 'And then, when I had her at my disposal from night till morning, repentant, full of good-will, almost loving, she suddenly lost all importance for me.'

'Well really, you are perverse,' said Françoise cheerfully.

'No,' said Pierre. 'You see, if she had thrown herself into my arms without reserve, I would almost certainly have been touched, and perhaps, at the same time, I would have been on my mettle if she had remained on the defensive. But I saw that she was both extremely eager to win me back, and so anxious not to sacrifice anything for me, that it simply gave me a feeling of pity and disgust.'

'Well?' said Françoise.

'Once I was, all the same, tempted to persist,' said Pierre. 'But I felt so alienated from her, that it seemed dishonest,

377

with respect to her, to you, and to Gerbert.' He stopped for a moment. 'And besides, when an affaire is over, it is over. There's nothing to be done. The fact that she slept with Gerbert, the scene we had, what I thought about her and about myself, all that is irreparable. The first morning at the Dôme, when she had another fit of jealousy, I was sick at the thought that everything was about to begin all over again.'

Unashamedly, Françoise welcomed the evil joy pouring into her heart. Not so very long ago, it had cost her dearly to try to keep her soul pure.

'But do you still see her?' she asked.

'Of course,' said Pierre. 'We've even agreed that there's now an irreplaceable friendship between us.'

'She wasn't angry with you when she knew that you weren't passionately fond of her any longer?'

'Oh! I was clever about it,' said Pierre. 'I made believe I was reluctant to withdraw, but at the same time, I convinced her that since she was disinclined to give up Gerbert, she should give herself fully to this love.' He looked at Françoise. 'I don't wish her any harm, you know. As you once said, it's not up to me to play the judge. If she was at fault, I was too.'

'We all were,' said Françoise.

'You and I have to come out of this experience unharmed,' said Pierre. 'I'd like her to get out of it as well.' Thoughtfully, he began biting his nails. 'You've rather upset my plans.'

'You're out of luck,' said Françoise with indifference. 'After all she needn't have affected such contempt for Gerbert.'

'Would that have stopped you?' said Pierre fondly.

'He would have been fonder of her if she'd been more sincere,' said Françoise. 'That would have made all the difference . . .'

'Well, what's done is done,' said Pierre. 'Only we'll have to be careful not to let her suspect anything. You do see that? All she'd have left would be to drown herself.'

'She won't suspect anything,' said Françoise.

She had no desire to throw Xavière into despair, and she could certainly be allotted a daily ration of soothing lies. Scorned, duped, she would no longer dispute Françoise's place in the world.

Françoise gazed at herself in the looking-glass. In the long run, capriciousness, intransigence, arrogant selfishness, all these artificial values had revealed their weakness, and it was the old disdained virtues which had triumphed.

'I've won,' thought Françoise triumphantly.

Once again she existed alone, with no obstacle at the heart of her own destiny. Confined within her illusory and empty world, Xavière was now but a futile, living pulsation.

Chapter Nine

Elisabeth walked through the deserted hotel, and out into the garden. There they were, both of them, seated near the rockwork grotto, enveloped in its shade. Pierre was writing, Françoise was lying in a deck-chair; neither stirred: they looked like a *tableau vivant*. Elisabeth stood rooted to the spot: as soon as they caught sight of her, their expressions would change, and she must not let them see her until she had deciphered their secret. Pierre looked up, and smilingly spoke a few words to Françoise. What had he said? She was getting no further by studying his white sports shirt, and his bronzed skin. Beyond their gestures and their faces, the truth about their happiness remained concealed. This week of daily intimacy had been as deceptive from Elisabeth's point of view as her furtive glimpses in Paris.

'Are your suitcases packed?' she said.

'Yes, I've reserved two seats on the bus,' said Pierre. 'We still have an hour.'

Elisabeth put a finger on the sheets of paper displayed in front of him.

'What's this opus? Are you starting a novel?'

'It's a letter to Xavière,' said Françoise with a smile.

'Well, she can't feel that she's been forgotten,' said Elisabeth. She failed to understand how it was that Gerbert's presence had in no way altered the harmony of the trio. 'Are you bringing her back to Paris this year?'

'Certainly,' said Françoise. 'Unless there's some real bombing.'

Elisabeth looked all about her. The garden spread out in the form of a terrace above a vast green and rose plain. It was quite small. Round each flower-bed, a whimsical hand had planted sea-shells and large mis-shapen stones; stuffed birds were nesting in the rock structures, and in among the flowers glittered metal balls, glass reflectors and glossy paper figures. War seemed far away. One almost had to make an effort not to forget it.

'Your train is going to be packed,' she said,

'Yes, everyone's clearing out,' said Pierre. 'We're the only customers left.'

'Oh dear,' said Françoise. 'I do so love our little hotel.'

Pierre laid his hand on hers.

'We'll come back. Even if war does break out, even if it does last for a long time, it must end some day.'

'How will it end?' said Elisabeth thoughtfully.

The day was drawing to a close. There they were, three French intellectuals, who were meditating and chatting in the uneasy peacefulness of a French village, with war hanging over them. Beneath its deceptive simplicity, this moment had the grandeur of a page of history.

'Ah! Here's something to eat,' said Françoise.

A maid had come out, carrying a tray loaded with beer, cordials, jams and biscuits.

'Would you like jam or honey?' said Françoise cheerfully.

'I don't mind,' said Elisabeth grumpily.

They seemed purposely to be avoiding serious conversation. In the long run, this kind of elegance became aggravating. She looked at Françoise. In her linen dress, with her shoulder-length hair, she looked very young. Elisabeth suddenly wondered if the serenity for which she was admired was not partly due to thoughtlessness.

'We're going to have a funny sort of life,' she continued.

'What I'm really afraid of is that we're going to be bored to death,' said Françoise.

'Oh no, on the contrary, it will be thrilling,' said Elisabeth.

She did not know exactly what she would do: the German-Soviet pact had been a heavy blow; but she was sure that her energy would not be wasted.

Pierre bit into a slice of bread spread with honey and smiled at Françoise.

'It's funny to think that tomorrow we'll be in Paris,' he said.

'I wonder if many people have gone back,' said Françoise.

'In any case, Gerbert will be there.' Pierre's face lit up. 'Tomorrow night we simply must go to a movie. There are a lot of new American films on now.'

Paris. On the café terraces of Saint-Germain-des-Prés, women in summer frocks were drinking iced orangeade; huge, alluring posters were displayed all the way up the Champs-Elysées to the Etoile. Soon all this happy-go-lucky, pleasant life was going to disappear. Elisabeth's heart was sad: she had not known how to enjoy it. It was Pierre who had made her loathe frivolity; yet, in the conduct of his own life, he was not so severe. She had been thinking along these lines, with annoyance, all the week; whilst she had been living, and gazing on them as on a pair of exacting paragons, they were calmly yielding to their whims.

'I ought to go and pay the bill,' said Françoise.

'I'll go,' said Pierre. He rose. 'Ouch,' he said. 'Damn those pebbles.' He picked up his sandals.

'Why are you always barefoot?' said Elisabeth.

'He says that his blisters haven't healed yet,' said Françoise.

'They haven't,' said Pierre. 'You made me do too much walking.'

'Oh, we've had such a wonderful trip,' said Françoise with a sigh.

Pierre went off. In a few days they would be separated. In his army clothes Pierre would be only an anonymous, lonely soldier. Françoise would see the theatre close and her friends scatter. And meanwhile, Claude would vegetate at Limoges, out of range of Suzanne. Elisabeth stared at the blue horizon where the pinks and the greens of the plain finally merged. In the tragic light of history people were stripped of their disquieting mystery. Everything was calm. The whole world was in suspense, and in this period of universal waiting, Elisabeth felt that she was attuned, fearless yet with no desire, to the stillness of the evening. She felt that she had at least been granted a long respite wherein nothing more was required of her.

'Everything's ready,' said Pierre. 'The suitcases are in the bus.' He sat down.

He, too, with his cheeks bronzed by the sun, and his white sports shirt, looked years younger. Suddenly, something unknown, something forgotten, swelled Elisabeth's heart. He was going away. Soon he would be far away, deep in an inaccessible, dangerous zone, and she was not going to see him again for a long time to come. Why had she been unable to profit by his presence?

'Have some biscuits,' said Françoise. 'They're very good.'

'No, thanks,' said Elisabeth. 'I'm not hungry.'

The pang that shot through her was unlike any she had known and it was something merciless, it was something irremediable. 'What if I never see him again,' she thought. She felt herself growing pale. 'You have to report at Nancy?' she asked.

'Yes, that's not a very dangerous place,' said Pierre.

'But you won't stay there for ever. You're not going to try any heroics, I hope?'

'You can trust me,' said Pierre with a laugh.

Elisabeth looked at him with anguish. He might die. Pierre, my brother. I'm not going to let him leave without telling him . . . What can I tell him? . . . This ironical man sitting opposite her had no need of her affection.

'I'll send you lovely parcels,' she said.

'That's true, I'll be getting parcels,' said Pierre. 'That's really delightful.'

He smiled with an affectionate look in which she could read no ulterior meaning. He had often looked like that during this past week. Why was she so mistrustful? Why had she for ever lost all the joys of friendship? What had she been seeking? What was the use of all these struggles and these hatreds? Pierre was going away.

'You know,' said Françoise, 'we ought to be going.'

'Let's go,' said Pierre.

They rose. Elisabeth followed them, with a lump in her throat. 'I don't want him to be killed,' she thought in despair. She was walking beside him without even daring to take his arm. Why had she made all sincere words and gestures impossible? Now the spontaneous feelings in her heart seemed out of place, and yet she would have given her life for him.

'What a mob!' said Françoise.

There was a crowd around the gaudy little bus. The conductor was standing on the roof surrounded by suitcases, trunks and boxes; a man perched on a ladder at the back of the bus was handing him up a bicycle. Françoise pressed her nose against the window.

'We've got our seats,' she said with satisfaction.

'I'm afraid you'll have to stand in the corridor when you're in the train,' said Elisabeth.

'We've got some sleep in hand,' said Pierre.

They started to walk round the little bus. Only a few minutes left. No more than a word, a gesture. Let him know . . . I don't dare. Elisabeth looked at Pierre with despair. Could everything not have been different? Could she not have lived close to them all these years, in confidence and joy, instead of being on the defensive against an imaginary danger?

'All aboard,' shouted the driver.

'It's too late,' thought Elisabeth in a frenzy. She would have had to annihilate her whole past, her whole personality, to be able to rush to Pierre and fall into his arms. Too late. She was no longer mistress of the present moment. Even her face did not obey her.

'See you soon,' said Françoise.

She kissed Elisabeth and went back to her seat.

'Goodbye,' said Pierre.

He hastily shook his sister's hand and smiled at her. She felt the tears rising to her eyes. She seized him by the shoulders and put her lips to his cheek.

'You'll be very careful,' she said.

'Don't worry,' said Pierre.

He gave her a quick kiss and climbed into the bus. For a moment more his face was framed in the open window. The bus started off. He waved his hand. Elisabeth waved her handkerchief, and when the bus disappeared behind the wall she turned on her heels.

'For nothing,' she murmured. 'All that for nothing.'

She pressed her handkerchief to her lips and ran back to the hotel.

With eyes wide open, Françoise was staring at the ceiling. Beside her, Pierre was sleeping, half-dressed. Françoise had dozed a little, but down in the street a loud scream had pierced the night and she had woken up: she was so afraid of nightmares that she did not close her eyes again. The curtains were not drawn and moonlight streamed into the room: she was not suffering; she was not thinking about anything: she was only astonished at the ease with which the cataclysm was entering into the natural course of their lives. She leaned towards Pierre.

Pierre groaned and stretched. She turned on the lights. Open suitcases, half-filled haversacks, tins of food, socks, were strewn in confusion all over the floor. Françoise stared at the full-blown red chrysanthemums on the wallpaper and anguish came upon her – tomorrow, they would still be in exactly the same place with the same inert obstinacy. The scene in which she would live during Pierre's absence was already set. Until now the expected separation had remained an empty threat, but this room was the future materialized. It was here, fully present, in its unalterable desolation.

'Are you sure you have everything you'll need?' she said.

'I think so,' said Pierre. He had put on his oldest suit and stuffed his wallet, his fountain pen, and his tobacco pouch into his pockets.

'When you think of it, it was stupid of me not to have bought you any walking shoes. I know what I'll do. I'll give you my ski-shoes. You were very comfortable in them.'

'I don't want to take your shoes,' said Pierre.

'You can buy me a new pair when we can go to winter sports again,' she said sadly.

She took them from the back of a cupboard and handed them to him. Then she packed the underwear and food in a haversack.

'Aren't you taking your meerschaum pipe?'

'No, I'm saving that for my leaves,' said Pierre. 'Take good care of it.'

'Don't worry,' said Françoise.

The fine primrose-coloured unsmoked pipe was lying in its case as if in a midget coffin. Françoise snapped down the lid and put it in a drawer. She turned to Pierre. He had put on her shoes. He was sitting on the edge of the bed, biting one of his nails. His eyes were bleary and his face had the idiotic expression that he used to assume in some of his games with Xavière. Françoise was standing in front of him without knowing what to do with herself. They had talked all day long, but now there was nothing more to say. He was nibbling at his nail and she was watching him, tense, resigned and empty.

'Shall we be going?' she said at last.

'Let's go,' said Pierre.

He slung his two haversacks over his shoulder and walked out of the room. Françoise closed the door behind them, the door that he was not to pass through for months, and her legs felt like giving way under her as she went down the stairs.

'We have time for a drink at the Dôme,' said Pierre. 'But we'll have to be careful, because it won't be easy to find a taxi.'

They walked out of the hotel and for the last time set out on the way they had so often followed. The moon was down and it was dark. For several nights now the sky over Paris had been dimmer: in the streets, there were only a few weak yellow lights whose gleam hugged the ground, and the pink glow which used to announce the carrefour Montparnasse from afar had vanished. Nevertheless, the café terraces still glimmered weakly.

'After tomorrow, everything closes at eleven o'clock,' said Françoise. 'This is the last pre-war night.'

They sat down on the terrace. The café was filled with people, noise and smoke. One group of youths was singing: a host of uniformed officers had sprung up overnight and they could be seen scattered in groups around the tables. Women were harassing them with echoless laughter. The last night, the last hours. The nervous snatches of conversation contrasted strangely with the apathetic faces.

'Life will be strange here,' said Pierre.

'Yes,' said Françoise. 'I'll write and tell you all about everything.'

'I hope Xavière isn't going to be too much of a burden on you. Perhaps we shouldn't have made her come back so soon.'

'No, it's better for you to see her again,' said Françoise. 'It really wouldn't have been worth the effort to write all those long letters and then destroy their effect with one blow. And besides, she must be near Gerbert these last days. She couldn't stay in Rouen.'

Xavière. This name was hardly more than a memory, an address on an envelope, an insignificant fragment of the future. She could hardly believe that in a few hours she would see her in the flesh.

'As long as Gerbert is at Versailles, you're bound to get a glimpse of him from time to time,' said Pierre.

'Don't worry about me,' said Françoise. 'I'll always manage.'

She laid her hand on his. He was about to leave. Nothing else counted. They sat there for some time without saying a word, watching peace die.

'I wonder if there'll be a crowd there,' said Françoise, rising.

'I don't think so. Three-quarters of the men have already been called up,' said Pierre.

They strolled a short distance along the boulevard, till Pierre hailed a taxi.

'Gare de la Villette,' he said to the driver.

They crossed Paris in silence. The last stars were growing

pale. Pierre had a faint smile on his lips. He was not tense, rather he had the intent look of a child. Françoise felt a feverish calm within her.

'Are we there?' she said in surprise.

The taxi stopped at a small, round, deserted open space. Two gendarmes wearing silver-braided képis were leaning against an upright in the middle of the central parking place. Pierre paid the taxi and walked up to them.

'Is this the mobilization depot?' he said, handing them his military pay-book.

One of the gendarmes pointed to a small piece of paper tacked to the pole.

'You must go to the Gare de l'Est,' he said.

Pierre seemed taken aback. Then he turned to the gendarme with one of his simple expressions, of which the unpredictable ingenuousness always moved Françoise.

'Have I time to walk it?'

The gendarme laughed.

'They're certainly not going to put on a special train for you. Don't be in such a hurry.'

Pierre walked back to Françoise. He looked very small and ridiculous in this deserted place with his two haversacks and her ski-shoes on his feet. Françoise felt that these ten years had not been enough to let him know how much she loved him.

'We still have a little time,' he said, and she saw by his smile that he knew everything there was to know.

They set off along the narrow streets as dawn was breaking. It was mild; the clouds were already roseate. It was just such a walk as they had so often taken after a night's hard work. They stopped at the top of the steps leading down into the station: the shining rails, submissively hedged in between asphalt platforms at their starting point, suddenly escaped, became interlaced in their courses, and fled on out towards infinity. For a moment they looked at the long flat roofs of the trains lined up along the platforms, where ten black dials with white hands each indicated five-thirty.

'This is where there's going to be a crowd,' said Françoise a little apprehensively. She pictured gendarmes, officers, and all the civilian mob she'd seen in the newspapers. But the station entrance-hall was almost empty: there wasn't a uniform in sight. There were a few families seated amongst piles of bundles, and single figures carrying haversacks over their shoulders.

Pierre walked up to the ticket-office, and then came back to Françoise.

'The first train leaves at six-nineteen. I'll get on at six o'clock to be sure of getting a seat.' He took her arm. 'We can still take a little walk,' he said.

'This is a funny departure,' said Françoise. 'I didn't think that it would be like this. Everything seems so free and easy.'

'Yes,' said Pierre, 'there seems to be no signs of regimentation anywhere; I didn't even receive a mobilization order. No one came to fetch me; I ask what time my train leaves, just like a civilian; I almost feel I'm leaving on my own initiative.'

'And yet we know you can't stay behind; it seems almost as if an inner fate were compelling you,' said Françoise.

They went a few steps outside the station. The sky was cloudless and soft above the deserted avenues.

'There isn't a taxi to be seen,' said Pierre, 'and the métro isn't running. How are you going to get home?'

'I'll walk,' said Françoise. 'I'll go and see Xavière and then I'll tidy up your office.' Her voice died away. 'You'll be sure to write to me at once?'

'From the train,' said Pierre. 'But letters certainly won't reach you for some time. You'll be patient?'

'Oh! I think I have patience enough and to spare,' she said.

They went a little way along the boulevard. In the early morning, the calm of the streets seemed completely normal: there were no indications of war, only those posters, with one huge beribboned tricolor, stuck on the walls – an appeal to the French people and one small, modest poster with black and white flags on a white background – the order for general mobilization.

'I'll go now,' said Pierre.

They went back into the station. Above the barrier was a placard stating that travellers alone were admitted to the platforms. Near the barrier a few couples were clasped in each other's arms, and suddenly, when she looked at them, tears rose to Françoise's eyes. Once generalized, the experience she was now living became comprehensible. On these strangers' faces, in their trembling smiles, all the tragedy of separation was apparent. She turned to Pierre; she did not want to break down; she found herself once more plunged into a blurred moment whose bitter and fleeting taste was not even painful.

'Goodbye,' said Pierre. He pressed her gently to him, looked at her for one last time and turned away.

He walked past the barrier. She watched him disappear with a rapid and too determined step which bespoke the tenseness in his face. She, too, turned away. Two women turned away at the same time; of a sudden, their faces fell and one of them began to cry. Françoise straightened her back and walked towards the exit. Sob as she might for hours on end, she would still have as many tears to shed. She walked off with a long, even-paced stride – her travelling stride – across the unwonted calm of Paris. Calamity was as yet nowhere in evidence, neither in the warmth of the air, nor in the gilded foliage of the trees, nor in the fresh smell of vegetables emanating from les Halles. So long as she kept walking, calamity would not become tangible; but she felt that, were she ever to stop, this insidious presence which she sensed all round her would surge back into her heart and break it.

She crossed the place du Châtelet and retraced her steps up the boulevard Saint Michel. The Luxembourg fountain had been drained; its now-visible bed was corroded by a slimy leprosy. In the rue Vavin, Françoise bought a newspaper. She would have to wait some time before she could knock at Xavière's door, and she decided to go and sit down in the Dôme. She hardly gave Xavière a thought, but she was glad to have something definite to do with her morning.

She entered the café and suddenly the blood rushed to her cheeks. At a table near the window, she caught sight of a fair head and a dark head. She hesitated, but it was too late to retreat: Gerbert and Xavière had already seen her. She was so limp and exhausted that a nervous shiver ran through her as she drew near their table.

'How are you?' she said to Xavière, holding her hand.

'I'm well enough,' said Xavière in an intimate tone. She surveyed Françoise. 'But you look tired.'

'I've just taken Labrousse to the train,' said Françoise. 'I've had very little sleep.'

Her heart was pounding. For weeks Xavière had been no more than a vague image drawn from within herself. And here she was, suddenly resurrected, in an unknown blue print dress with tiny flowers on it, her hair far fairer than any memory;

her lips, with their forgotten line, opened in a completely new smile: she had not changed into a docile phantom. It was her presence in the flesh that had again to be faced.

'I was out walking all night,' said Xavière. 'Those black streets were really beautiful. It was like the end of the world.'

She had spent all these hours with Gerbert. For him, too, she had again become a tangible presence: how had he welcomed her in his heart? His face gave no clue.

'It will be still worse when the cafés are closed,' said Françoise.

'Yes, that's dismal,' said Xavière. Her eyes lit up. 'Do you think we'll really be bombed?'

'Perhaps,' said Françoise.

'It must be terrific to hear the sirens at night and see people come running from all sides like rats.'

Françoise smiled stiffly. Xavière's deliberate childishness aggravated her.

'You'll have to go down into the cellar,' she said.

'Oh! I won't go down,' said Xavière.

There was a brief silence.

'I'll see you later,' said Françoise. 'You can meet me here. I'm going to sit down at the back.'

'See you later,' said Xavière.

Françoise sat down at a table and took out a cigarette. Her hand was trembling, she was astonished to find how violently upset she was. It was undoubtedly the tension of these last hours that, when it snapped, left her so defenceless. She felt herself thrown forward towards the unknown; uprooted, buffeted, with no recourse to her inner self. She had calmly accepted the idea of a denuded and uneasy life. But Xavière's existence had always threatened her, even beyond the very limits of her life, and it was this old anguish that she recognized with terror.

Chapter Ten

'What a pity, I've no more oil,' said Xavière.

She looked with dismay at the window, with the panes of its lower half covered with a coat of blue paint.

'You've made a very nice job of it,' said Françoise.

'Well, I'm sure Inès will never be able to see through her windows again.'

Inès had fled from Paris the day after the first false alert, and Françoise had sub-leased her flat. In her room at the Hotel Bayard the memory of Pierre was too present, and during these tragic nights when Paris offered neither light nor escape, she felt the need for a home of her own.

'I must have some oil,' said Xavière.

'There's none to be had anywhere,' said Françoise.

She was in the middle of addressing, in capital letters, a parcel of books and tobacco that she was sending to Pierre.

'You can't get anything nowadays,' said Xavière savagely. She threw herself into an arm-chair. 'Really, I might just as well have done nothing,' she said in a sullen voice.

She was wrapped in a long, frieze dressing-gown, tied round her waist by a twisted cord; she buried her hands in the wide sleeves; with her hair neatly cut and falling perfectly straight round her face, she looked like a little monk.

Françoise put down her pen. The electric light bulb, muffled by a silk scarf, disseminated a feeble violet light over the room.

'I ought to go and work,' thought Françoise, but she lacked the will to do so. Her life had lost all consistency of late, it had become a flaccid substance into which she expected to sink at every step, and then she would bob back just sufficiently to sink in a little further along, with the hope of a final engulfment at one moment, and, at the next, the hope of suddenly finding solid ground. There was no longer any future. The past alone retained reality, and it was in Xavière that the past was incarnate.

'Have you had any news from Gerbert?' said Françoise. 'How's he getting along in barrack life?'

She had seen Gerbert again one Sunday afternoon ten days

391

ago, but it would have been unnatural had she never asked about him.

'He doesn't seem bored,' said Xavière. She had a faint, inward smile. 'Especially since he loves grumbling.'

Her face reflected the fond certainty of complete possession.

'He must have plenty of opportunities,' said Françoise.

'What's worrying him,' said Xavière, with a self-satisfied and pleased air, 'is to know whether he'll be afraid.'

'It's difficult to imagine what things will be like.'

'Oh! he's like me,' said Xavière, 'he gets impressions.'

There was a silence.

'Did you know that they put Bergmann into a concentration camp?' said Françoise. 'Political exiles are getting a rotten deal.'

'Bah!' said Xavière. 'They're all spies.'

'Not all,' said Françoise. 'A great many genuine anti-fascists are being imprisoned in the name of an anti-fascist war.'

Xavière pouted scornfully.

'Considering how interesting people are,' said Xavière, 'it's not so tragic that someone should tread on their corns.'

With a feeling of revulsion, Françoise looked at this young, cruel face.

'If you're not interested in people, I wonder what is left,' she said.

'Oh! but we're not made the same way,' said Xavière, enveloping her in a scornful and malicious look.

Françoise said no more. Conversations with Xavière always degenerated into hate-ridden comparisons at once. What appeared in Xavière's tone, in her shifty smiles, was something far more than a childish and capricious hostility: a true female hatred. She would never forgive Françoise for having kept Pierre's love.

'How about playing a record?' said Françoise.

'As you wish,' said Xavière.

Françoise placed the first record of *Petrouchka* on the turntable.

'It's always the same thing,' said Xavière heatedly.

'There's no choice,' said Françoise.

Xavière tapped her foot.

'Is it going to last long?' she said through clenched teeth.

'What?' said Françoise.

'The black streets, the empty shops, the cafés closing at

eleven o'clock. The whole business,' she added in a tremor of rage.

'It may last a long time,' said Françoise.

Xavière buried her hands in her hair.

'But I'll go mad,' she said.

'People don't go mad so easily,' said Françoise.

'I'm not the long-suffering kind,' said Xavière in a tone of despairing hate. 'I'm not content to contemplate events from the bottom of a tomb! It's not enough for me to tell myself that people on the other side of the world are still in existence, if I have no contact with them.'

Françoise flushed. She should never have said anything to Xavière. Whatever you said to her, she immediately turned it against you. Xavière looked at Françoise.

'You're lucky to be so sensible,' she said with equivocal humility.

'All that is necessary, is *not* to take oneself too tragically,' said Françoise curtly.

'Oh! some people can manage that, some can't,' said Xavière.

Françoise looked at the bare walls, the blue panes that seemed to screen the interior of a tomb. 'I oughtn't to mind,' she thought unhappily. Still, to do herself justice, she had hardly left Xavière during these three weeks; she was going to continue to live with her till the war was over; she could no longer deny this alien presence which cast a pernicious shadow over her and over the whole world.

A ring of the door-bell shattered the silence. Françoise went down the long passage.

'What is it?'

The concierge handed her an unstamped envelope addressed in a strange hand.

'A gentleman just left this.'

'Thanks,' said Françoise.

She tore open the letter. It was Gerbert's handwriting: 'I'm in Paris. I'm waiting for you at the Café Rey. I have the whole evening.'

Françoise hid the paper in her bag. She went into her room, took her coat and her gloves. Her heart blazed with pleasure. She tried to assume the appropriate expression, and returned to Xavière's room.

'My mother's asked me to make up a bridge-four,' she said.

'Oh! You're going out,' said Xavière reproachfully.

'I'll be back about midnight. Aren't you going to budge from here?'

'Where would I be going?' said Xavière.

'Well, see you later,' said Françoise.

She walked down the unlighted staircase and ran down the street. Women were strolling up and down the pavements of the boulevard Montparnasse, the grey cases containing their gas-masks slung over their shoulders. An owl hooted behind the cemetery wall. Françoise stopped, out of breath, at the corner of the rue de la Gaieté. A huge red sombre brazier was shining out of the avenue du Maine: it was the Café Rey. Their curtains drawn, their lights extinguished, all the public places had assumed the tantalizing appearance of houses of ill repute. Françoise drew aside the hangings over the door. Gerbert was sitting near the mechanical piano with a glass of marc in front of him. He had put his forage cap on the table. His hair was cut short, and he looked ridiculously young in his khaki uniform.

'How marvellous that you were able to come!' said Françoise. She took his hand and their fingers intertwined. 'That scheme finally worked?'

'Yes,' said Gerbert. 'But I couldn't let you know in advance. I didn't know beforehand whether I'd manage to get away.' He smiled. 'I'm so pleased. It's very easy. I'll be able to do it again off and on.'

'Then I can look forward to Sundays,' said Françoise. 'There are so few Sundays in a month.' She looked at him regretfully. 'Especially since you'll have to see Xavière.'

'Yes, I'll have to,' said Gerbert unenthusiastically.

'You know, I've got red-hot news from Labrousse,' said Françoise. 'A long letter. He's living a completely bucolic life. He's rusticating in Lorraine in the home of a priest who stuffs him with plum tarts and creamed chicken.'

'What a bore!' said Gerbert. 'I'll be far away when he gets his first leave. We won't see each other for ages.'

'Yes. If it would only go on without any fighting,' said Françoise.

She looked at the scarlet banquettes on which she had so often sat beside Pierre. The bar and the tables were crowded, but the heavy blue cloth concealing the windows lent this swarming café something intimate and clandestine.

'I've no objection to going into action,' said Gerbert. 'That oughtn't to be as boring as rotting away in barracks.'

'Are you bored stiff, my poor lamb?' said Françoise.

'It's unbelievable how browned-off you can get,' said Gerbert. He began to laugh. 'Day before yesterday the captain sent for me. He wanted to know why I wasn't applying for a commission. He found out that I used to guzzle every night at the Brasserie Chanteclerc. He just about told me: "You have money; your place is among the officers."'

'What did you answer?'

'I said I didn't like officers,' said Gerbert with a dignified air.

'You must have had a poor reception.'

'And how!' said Gerbert. 'When I left, the captain was purple. I mustn't tell that to Xavière,' he said shaking his head.

'Does she want you to be an officer?'

'Yes, she thinks we'd see more of each other. Women are enough to drive you mad,' said Gerbert in heartfelt tones. 'They seem to think that love affairs are the only things that count.'

'You're now the only one Xavière has,' said Françoise.

'I know,' said Gerbert. 'It's just that that's getting me down.' He smiled. 'I was cut out to be a bachelor.'

'Well, you've certainly got off to a bad start,' said Françoise gaily.

'Idiot,' said Gerbert, digging her in the ribs. 'That doesn't apply to you.' He looked at her lovingly. 'What's wonderful about us is that there's such a friendship between us. I'm never uncomfortable with you. I can tell you anything and I feel perfectly free.'

'Yes, it's wonderful to love each other so much and still remain free,' said Françoise.

She squeezed his hand. She held even more dear than the sweetness of seeing and touching him, his passionate confidence in her.

'I can't go to any swank places in this rig-out,' said Gerbert.

'No. But what would you think of walking down to les Halles, having a steak at Benjamin's, and then coming back to the Dôme?'

'Fine,' said Gerbert. 'We'll have a Pernod on the way. It's amazing how I can take Pernod now.' He rose and pulled aside the blue curtains to let Françoise pass. 'Gosh! How you drink in the army! I come home soused every night.'

The moon had risen, and its light bathed the trees and the rooftops: a real country moonlight. A motor sped down the long deserted avenue, its blue headlights looking like enormous sapphires.

'This is magnificent,' said Gerbert, looking at the night.

'Yes, the moonlit nights are magnificent,' said Françoise. 'But when it's pitch black it isn't very pleasant. The best thing you can do is to stay dug in at home.' She nudged Gerbert. 'Did you notice the policemen's beautiful new helmets?' she asked

'They look very martial,' said Gerbert. He took Françoise's arm. 'You poor thing, this life can't be very cheerful,' he said. 'Isn't there anyone in Paris nowadays?'

'There's Elisabeth. She'd gladly lend me her shoulder to cry on, but I avoid her as much as possible,' said Françoise. 'It's funny, but she's never looked more prosperous. Claude is in Bordeaux. But the minute he's alone, away from Suzanne, I think she gets along very well without him.'

'What do you do all day long?' said Gerbert. 'Have you started working again?'

'Not yet. No. I trail around with Xavière from morning to night. We do some cooking, fuss with our hair, listen to old records. We've never been so intimate.' Françoise shrugged her shoulders. 'And I'm sure that she's never hated me more.'

'Do you think so?' said Gerbert.

'I'm sure of it,' said Françoise. 'Doesn't she ever talk to you about our being together?'

'Not often,' said Gerbert. 'She's on her guard. She thinks I'm on your side.'

'Why?' said Françoise. 'Because you defend me when she attacks me?'

'Yes,' said Gerbert. 'We always start to quarrel when she talks to me about you.'

Françoise felt a twinge in her heart. What on earth could Xavière have said about her?

'Well, what does she say?' said Françoise.

'Oh! any old thing,' said Gerbert.

'You can tell me, you know,' said Françoise. 'The way we are together, there's nothing to hide between us.'

'I was speaking in general,' said Gerbert.

They walked a few steps in silence. A sharp whistle made

them jump. A bearded air-raid warden directed his torch-beam at a window showing a thin ray of light.

'These old boys are in their element,' said Gerbert.

'I know,' said Françoise. 'The first few days they threatened to fire their revolvers at our windows. We covered over all the lights, and now Xavière is painting the windows blue.'

Xavière . . . Naturally . . . She talked about Françoise . . . And perhaps about Pierre . . . It was irritating to think of her complacently preening herself at the heart of her little well-ordered universe.

'Has Xavière talked to you about Labrousse?' said Françoise.

'She's spoken about him,' said Gerbert in a noncommittal tone.

'She told you the whole story!' said Françoise emphatically.

'Yes,' said Gerbert.

The blood rushed to Françoise's cheeks. My story. Under that fair crown, Françoise's thoughts had assumed an unalterable and unknown form, and it was in this alien form that Gerbert had had them confided to him.

'Then you know that Labrousse was fond of her?' said Françoise.

Gerbert did not answer.

'I'm so sorry,' he said finally. 'Why didn't Labrousse tell me?'

'His pride wouldn't let him,' said Françoise. She squeezed Gerbert's arm. 'I didn't tell you just because I was afraid you'd imagine things,' she said. 'But don't worry. Labrousse was never angry with you, and in the end, he was even quite happy that the affair ended as it did.'

Gerbert looked at her mistrustfully.

'He was happy?'

'Of course,' said Françoise. 'She doesn't mean anything to him any more, you know.'

'Really?' said Gerbert.

He seemed incredulous. What did he believe? Françoise looked with anguish at the Saint-Germain-des-Prés bell-tower standing out against a metallic sky, as pure and calm as a village belfry.

'What is her version?' she asked. 'That Labrousse is still passionately in love with her?'

'Just about,' said Gerbert, puzzled.

'Well, she's making a big mistake,' said Françoise.

Her voice was trembling. Had Pierre been there she would have laughed disdainfully, but he was far away from her, and she could only say to herself, 'He loves only me.' It was intolerable that a contrary certainty should exist somewhere in the world.

'I wish you could see how he talks about her in his letters,' continued Françoise. 'She'd be edified. It's out of pity that he's been keeping up an outward show of friendship.' She looked at Gerbert challengingly. 'How does she explain his giving her up?'

'She said that it was she who no longer wanted this relationship.'

'Ah! I see,' said Françoise. 'And why?' Gerbert looked at her with embarrassment. 'She maintains that she didn't love him?' said Françoise. She squeezed her handkerchief in her clammy hands.

'No,' said Gerbert,

'Well?'

'She said that it displeased you,' he said hesitantly.

'She said that?' said Françoise. Emotion prevented her from saying more. Tears of rage rose in her eyes. 'The little bitch!'

Gerbert did not answer. He seemed overwhelmed with embarrassment.

Françoise laughed derisively. 'In short, Pierre loves her to distraction, and she rejects this love out of consideration for me, because I am consumed with jealousy?'

'Well, I was pretty certain she was arranging things to suit her own ends,' said Gerbert in a conciliatory tone.

They were crossing the Seine. Françoise leaned over the balustrade and looked into the shining black water in which the disc of the moon was reflected. 'I won't stand for it,' she thought in despair. There, in the sepulchral light of her room, Xavière was sitting wrapped in her brown dressing-gown, sullen and maleficent; Pierre's grieved love was humbly caressing her feet; and Françoise was wandering about the streets, scorned, content with the old remains of a jaded devotion. She wanted to hide her face,

'She lied,' she said.

Gerbert hugged her to him.

'Well, I'd certainly think so,' he said.

He seemed disturbed. She pressed her lips together. She could talk to him, tell him the truth; he would believe her,

398

but it would be futile. There, the young heroine, the sweet sacrificial face, would continue to feel in her flesh the noble and intoxicating taste of her life.

'I shall speak to her, too,' thought Françoise. 'She shall know the truth.'

'I shall speak to her.'

Françoise crossed the place de Rennes. The moon was brightly illuminating the deserted street and the blind houses, shining, too, on naked plains and on forests where helmeted men were keeping watch. In the impersonal and tragic night, the anger, which was overwhelming Françoise's heart, was her sole preoccupation. The black pearl, the precious one, the sorceress, the generous one. 'A bitch,' she thought, enraged. She climbed the stairs. She was there, crouching behind the door, in her nest of lies; once again she was going to batten on Françoise and force her to become part of her story. This cast-off woman, armed with a bitter patience, will be me. Françoise walked in and knocked at Xavière's door.

'Come in.'

An insipid syrupy smell permeated the room. Xavière was perched on a step-ladder, daubing blue paint on a window pane. She came down from her perch.

'Look what I've found,' she said. In her hand she was holding a bottle of golden liquid. With a theatrical gesture she handed it to Françoise. The label bore the title, *Ambre Solaire*.

'It was in the dressing-room. Sun-tan lotion is a good substitute for oil,' she said. She looked dubiously at the window. 'You don't think I should put on another coat?'

'Oh! It'll be like a hearse. It's good enough as it is,' said Françoise.

She took off her coat. She must speak, but what would she say? She could not make use of Gerbert's confidences, and yet, she could not live in this poisonous atmosphere. Beneath the smooth blue windows, in this oppressive smell of *Ambre Solaire*, there was ample evidence of Pierre's rejected passion, and Françoise's base jealousy. They must be eradicated. Xavière alone could eradicate them.

'I'll make some tea,' said Xavière.

There was a gas-ring in her room. She set a saucepan full of water on it, and then sat down opposite Françoise.

'Did you have fun playing your bridge?' she said scornfully.

'I didn't go for fun,' said Françoise.

There was a silence. Xavière's eyes fell on the parcel Françoise had made up for Pierre.

'You have made up a very good parcel,' she said with a thin smile.

'I think it will make Labrousse very happy to get some books,' said Françoise.

Xavière's smile spread inanely over her lips as she rolled the string between her fingers.

'Do you think that he *can* read?' she said.

'He works. He reads. Why not?'

'Yes, you told me he is being very brave, that he's even doing physical exercises.' Xavière raised her eyebrows. 'I was beginning to see him in a different light.'

'Still, that's what he says in his letter,' said Françoise.

'Yes, of course,' said Xavière.

She drew up a length of the string and then let it go with a faint snap. She thought for a moment, then looked candidly at Françoise.

'Don't you think that in their letters people never tell one things as they are? Even if they don't intend to lie?' she added politely. 'Just because they're telling them to someone?'

Françoise felt anger closing her throat.

'I think Pierre says exactly what he means to say,' she said sharply.

'Oh! I should certainly not expect him to be off in a corner crying like a baby,' said Xavière. She laid her hand on the parcel of books. 'Perhaps I'm made wrong,' she said thoughtfully, 'but when people are away, it seems to me to be so futile to try to keep up any relationship with them. You can think of them. But writing letters and sending parcels . . .' She pouted. 'I'd much prefer table-turning.'

Françoise looked at her with impotent rage. Was there no way of annihilating this insolent pride? In Xavière's mind, Martha and Mary were brought face to face over the memory of Pierre. Martha played the part of a war-time god-mother, and in return, won a respectful gratitude; but it was of Mary whom he thought when, from the depths of his aloneness, the man at the front nostalgically lifted a grave, pale face to the autumn sky. Had Xavière passionately clasped Pierre's living body in her arms, it would have hurt Françoise less than this mysterious caress with which she enveloped his image.

'You'd have to know whether the people in question share this point of view,' said Françoise.

Xavière gave a slight smile.

'Yes, naturally,' she said.

'You mean that other people's points of view are a matter of indifference to you?' said Françoise.

'They don't all attach such great importance to letter writing,' said Xavière. She rose. 'Would you like some tea?' she said.

She filled two cups. Françoise raised the cup to her lips. Her hand was trembling She recalled Pierre's back, bent under his two haversacks, as he disappeared along the platform at the Gare de l'Est. She recalled his face when he had looked at her a moment earlier. She wanted to keep this pure image within her, but it was an image that received its vitality only from the beating of her heart, and it was not sufficient in the face of this woman of flesh and blood. Reflected in these living eyes were Françoise's weary face and her stern profile. A voice whispered, 'He doesn't love her any more, he cannot love her any more.'

'I think you have a very romantic conception of Labrousse,' said Françoise suddenly. 'You know he bears things only as long as he chooses to do so. He cares for them only as long as he sees fit.'

Xavière pouted.

'That's what you think.'

Her tone carried more insolence than a savage denial.

'I know,' said Françoise. 'I know Labrousse well.'

'You can never know people,' said Xavière.

Françoise looked at her with rage. Was it impossible to make any impression on this stubborn mind?

'But, with him and me, things are different,' she said. 'We've always shared everything. Absolutely everything.'

'Why are you telling me this?' said Xavière arrogantly.

'You think you're the only person who understands Labrousse,' said Françoise. Her face was burning. 'You think I've got a clumsy unsophisticated conception of him.'

Xavière looked at her transfixed. Never had Françoise spoken to her in this tone.

'You have your conception of him and I have mine,' she said curtly.

'You choose the conception that suits you,' said Françoise.

She had spoken with such assurance that Xavière was taken aback.

'What do you mean?' she said.

Françoise's lips were set. How she wanted to tell her to her face, 'You think he loves you, but he has nothing but pity for you.' Xavière's insolent smile had already faded. Only a few words and her eyes would fill with tears. This beautiful, proud body would be bowed. Xavière stared at her transfixed; she was afraid.

'I don't mean anything in particular,' said Françoise wearily. 'But, in general, you believe what you find it convenient to believe.'

'Give me an instance,' said Xavière.

'Well, for instance,' said Françoise more calmly, 'Labrousse said in his letter to you that he had no need to receive letters from people to think about them; that was a polite way of excusing your silence. But you've convinced yourself that he believes in communion of souls over and above words.'

Xavière's lip curled back over her white teeth.

'How did you know what he'd written to me?'

'He told me in a letter,' said Françoise.

Xavière's eyes rested on Françoise's hand-bag.

'Ah! he speaks about me in his letters to you?' she said.

'Occasionally,' said Françoise. Her hand tightened on her black leather hand-bag. Should she throw the letters in Xavière's lap? In disgust and rage Xavière herself would cry her defeat; there could be no possible victory without her confession. Françoise would once more find herself alone, sovereign, and freed for ever.

Xavière ensconced herself more deeply in her chair, and shuddered slightly. She was all huddled up, and her face was haggard.

'I loathe to think that someone's talking about me,' she said.

Françoise suddenly felt very tired. The arrogant heroine she had so passionately hoped to vanquish, was there no longer; there remained a poor, hunted victim, from whom no vengeance could be exacted. She rose.

'I'm going to bed,' she said. 'See you tomorrow. Don't forget to turn off the gas.'

'Good night,' said Xavière without looking up.

Françoise went back to her room. She opened her desk, took Pierre's letters out of her bag, and laid them in a drawer beside those of Gerbert. There would be no victory. There would be no deliverance. She locked her desk and put the key back in her bag.

'Waiter,' called Françoise.

It was a beautiful sunny day. Lunch had lasted longer than usual and, early in the afternoon, Françoise had come with a book to sit on the terrace of the Dôme. Now it was growing cooler.

'Eight francs,' said the waiter.

Françoise opened her purse and took out a note. She looked with surprise at the bottom of her hand-bag. It was in this bag that she had put the key of her desk the night before.

Nervously, she emptied her pocket-book – compact – lipstick – comb. The key must be somewhere. She had not set down her bag for a minute. She turned it upside down, shook it out. Her heart was beating violently. One minute. The time it had taken to carry the breakfast tray from the kitchen to Xavière's room. And Xavière was in the kitchen.

With the back of her hand she swept pell-mell back into her bag all the various articles scattered over the table and hurriedly made off. Six o'clock. If Xavière had the key, there was no hope.

'It's impossible!'

She was running. Her whole body was throbbing. She began to feel her heart between her ribs, behind her eyes, in her finger-tips. She rushed up the stairs. The house was silent and the entrance door looked perfectly normal. In the passage the scent of *Ambre Solaire* was still noticeable. Françoise took a deep breath. She must have lost the key without noticing it. If anything had happened, there would have been some indication of it in the atmosphere. She pushed open the door of her room. The desk was open. Some of Pierre's and Gerbert's letters were lying scattered over the carpet.

'Xavière knows.' The walls of the room began to whirl. A bitter burning night had descended on the world. Françoise dropped into a chair, crushed by a deadly weight. Her love for Gerbert was there before her, black as treason.

'She knows.' She had come into the room to read Pierre's letters. She had expected to slip the key back into the bag or hide it under the bed. And then she had seen Gerbert's writing.

'Dear, dear Françoise.' She had run through to the bottom

of the last page. 'I love you.' Line after line, she had read it.

Françoise rose, and went down the long passage. Her mind was not working. Before her and within her, this coal-black night. She walked up to Xavière's door and knocked. There was no answer. The key was in the lock, on the inside. Xavière had not gone out. Françoise knocked again. There was the same dead silence. 'She has killed herself,' she thought. She leant against the wall. Xavière might have swallowed some sleeping tablets; she might have turned on the gas. She listened. She still heard nothing. Françoise pressed her ear to the door. Some inkling of hope broke through her terror. There was one solution, the only solution imaginable. But no, Xavière used only harmless soporifics; any smell of gas would have been apparent. In any case, she would not yet have gone to sleep. Françoise banged on the door.

'Go away,' said a muffled voice.

Françoise wiped the perspiration from her forehead. Xavière was alive. Françoise's treason lived.

'Open the door to me,' shouted Françoise.

She did not know what she would say, but she wanted to see Xavière immediately. 'Open it,' she repeated, shaking the door.

The door opened. Xavière was wrapped in her dressing-gown. Her eyes were hard.

'What do you want of me?' she said.

Françoise walked past her and sat down near the table. Nothing had changed since lunch time. Yet, behind each familiar piece of furniture something horrible was lying in wait.

'I want to have a word with you,' said Françoise.

'I want nothing from you,' said Xavière.

She was staring at Françoise with burning eyes, her cheeks were on fire, she was beautiful.

'Listen to me, I beg of you,' said Françoise.

Xavière's lips began to tremble.

'Why have you come to torture me again? Aren't you satisfied with things as they are? Haven't you done me enough harm?'

She threw herself on the bed and buried her face in her hands.

'Ah! how well you've tricked me,' she said.

'Xavière,' murmured Françoise.

She looked about her with anguish. Would nothing come to her rescue?

'Xavière!' she repeated in a pleading voice. 'When this affair began I was not aware that you were in love with Gerbert, and he didn't suspect it either.'

Xavière lowered her hands. A sneer distorted her mouth.

'That little swine,' she said slowly. 'This doesn't surprise me in him. He's nothing but a filthy little beast.'

She looked Françoise straight in the eye.

'But you!' she said. 'You! How you must have laughed at me.'

An unbearable smile revealed her white teeth.

'I did not laugh at you,' said Françoise. 'I only thought more of myself than of you. But you left me very little reason to love you.'

'I know,' said Xavière. 'You were jealous of me because Labrousse was in love with me. You made him loathe me, and to get better revenge, you took Gerbert from me. Keep him, he's yours. I won't deprive you of that little treasure.'

The words poured from her mouth with such vehemence that they seemed to choke her. Françoise contemplated with horror this woman at whom Xavière's flashing eyes were gazing: this woman was herself.

'That's not true,' she said.

She took a deep breath. It was hopeless to attempt to defend herself. Now, nothing could save her.

'Gerbert loves you,' she said in a steadier voice. 'He did you a wrong. But at that time he had so many grievances against you! It would have been difficult to talk to you afterwards; he hadn't yet had time to establish a real relationship with you.' She leaned towards Xavière and said in a pressing tone, 'Try to forgive him. You'll never again find me in your way.'

She clasped her hands. A little silent prayer rose within her: 'Let everything be wiped out, and I will give up Gerbert! I no longer love Gerbert, I never loved him, there was no betrayal.'

Xavière's eyes flashed.

'Keep your gifts,' she said vehemently. 'And get out of here, get out immediately.'

Françoise hesitated.

'For God's sake, get out,' said Xavière.

'I'm going,' said Françoise.

She crossed the passage, staggering as though blind, and tears burned her eyes. 'I was jealous of her. I took Gerbert from her.' The tears, the words, scorched like a hot iron. She sat down on the edge of the couch, dazed, and repeated, 'I did that. It was I.' In the shadows, a black fire flickered round Gerbert's face, and the letters scattered on the carpet were as black as an infernal pact. She put her handkerchief to her lips. A black, torrid lava was coursing in her veins. She wanted to die.

'This is what I am for ever.' There would be a dawn. There would be a tomorrow. Xavière would return to Rouen, and each morning she would wake up in a bleak provincial house with this despair in her heart. Each morning this abhorred woman, who was henceforth Françoise, would be reborn. She recalled Xavière's face, contorted with pain. 'My crime.' It was going to exist for ever.

She closed her eyes. Her tears flowed, and the burning lava flowed on and consumed her heart. A long time passed. Far away, in another world, she suddenly saw a bright, tender smile. 'Well, kiss me, you silly little Gerbert.' The wind was blowing, the cows were rattling their chains in the stable, a young, trusting head was leaning on her shoulder and a voice was saying, 'I'm happy, I'm so happy.' He had given her a small flower. She opened her eyes. This story, too, was true. Light and tender as the morning wind on the dewy plains. How had that innocent love become this sordid betrayal?

'No,' she said. 'No.' She rose and walked to the window. The globe of the street-lamp had been disguised with a black metal shield scolloped like a Venetian mask. Its yellow light resembled a glance. She turned away, and switched on the light. Her image suddenly sprang from the depth of her looking-glass. She faced herself. 'No,' she repeated, 'I am not that woman.'

It was a long story. She stared at her reflection. There had been a long enduring attempt to rob her of it. Inexorable as a duty. Austere and pure as a block of ice. Self-sacrificing, scorned, clinging obstinately to hollow morality. She had said, 'No.' But she had whispered it, she had secretly embraced Gerbert. 'Isn't that I?' She had often hesitated, spellbound. And now, she had fallen into the trap, she was at the mercy of this voracious conscience that had been waiting in the shadow for the moment to swallow her up. Jealous, traitorous, guilty. She could not defend herself with timid words and furtive deeds. Xavière existed; the betrayal existed. 'My guilty face exists in flesh and bone.'

It would exist no more.

Suddenly, a great calm enveloped Françoise. Time had stopped. Françoise was alone in an icy firmament. It was an aloneness so awful and so final that it resembled death.

It is she or I. It shall be I.

There was a sound of steps in the passage. Water was running in the bathroom. Xavière returned to her room. Françoise walked to the kitchen and turned off the gas meter. She knocked. Perhaps there was still a way of escaping . . .

'Why have you come back again?' said Xavière.

She was in bed, propped up against her pillows. Only her bedside lamp was switched on. A glass of water beside a bottle of atropine tablets stood on the night-table.

'I'd like to have a talk with you,' said Françoise. She took a step and stood with her back against the chest of drawers on which the gas-ring stood.

'What do you intend to do now?' she said.

'Is that any of your concern?' said Xavière.

'I have done you a wrong,' said Françoise. 'I don't ask you to forgive me. But listen to me; don't make it impossible for me to atone for my sin.' Her voice was trembling with emotion. If only she could convince Xavière . . . 'For a long, long time I thought only of your happiness. You never thought of mine. You know that I do not altogether lack justification. Make an effort, in the name of our past. Give me a chance not to feel odiously guilty.'

Xavière stared at her blankly.

'Stay in Paris,' continued Françoise. 'Resume your work at the theatre. Live wherever you wish: you will never see me again . . .'

'Should I accept your money?' said Xavière. 'I'd rather drop dead. Here and now.'

Her voice, her face, left no hope.

'Be generous. Accept,' said Françoise. 'Spare me this remorse of having ruined your future.'

'I would rather drop dead,' repeated Xavière vehemently.

'At least see Gerbert again,' said Françoise. 'Don't condemn him without having spoken to him.'

'Do you presume to give me advice?' said Xavière,

407

Françoise put her hand on the gas-ring and turned on the tap.

'I'm not advising you; I'm imploring you,' she said.

'Imploring!' Xavière laughed. 'I'm not a noble soul.'

'Very well,' said Françoise. 'Goodbye.'

She took a step towards the door and silently looked at this livid, childlike face that she would never again see alive.

'Goodbye,' she repeated.

'And don't come back,' said Xavière with fury.

Françoise heard her leap from her bed and bolt the door. The ray of light filtering beneath it went out.

'And now?' Françoise thought.

She stood staring at Xavière's door: alone; unaided; relying now entirely on herself. She waited for some time. Then she walked into the kitchen and put her hand on the lever of the gas meter. Her hand tightened – it seemed impossible. Face to face with her aloneness, beyond space, beyond time, stood this alien presence that had for so long overwhelmed her by its blind shadow: Xavière was there, existing only for herself, entirely self-centred, reducing to nothingness everything for which she had no use; she encompassed the whole world within her own triumphant aloneness, boundlessly extending her influence, infinite and unique, everything that she was, she drew from within herself, she barred all dominance over her, she was absolute separateness. And yet it was only necessary to pull down this lever to annihilate her. 'Annihilate a conscience! How can I?' Françoise thought. But how was a conscience not her own capable of existing? If it were so, then it was she who was not existing. She repeated 'She or I.' She pulled down the lever.

She went back to her room, gathered up the letters strewn on the floor and then threw them into the fireplace. She struck a match and watched the letters burn. Xavière's door was locked on the inside. They would think it was an accident or suicide. 'In any case, there will be no proof,' she thought.

She undressed and put on her pyjamas. 'Tomorrow morning she will be dead.' She sat down, facing the darkened passage. Xavière was sleeping. With each minute her sleep was deepening. On the bed there still remained a living form, but it was already no one. There was no longer anyone. Françoise was alone.

Alone. She had acted alone: as alone as in death. One day

Pierre would know. But even his cognizance of this deed would be merely external. No one could condemn or absolve her. Her act was her very own. 'It is I who will it.' It was her own will which was being accomplished, now nothing at all separated her from herself. She had at last made a choice. She had chosen herself.

P.S.

Ideas,
insights
& features...

About the author

About the book

Read on

Finding a Voice

by Louise Tucker

'The unfortunate episode of the trio did much more than supply me with a subject for a novel; it enabled me to deal with it.'

The Prime of Life, Simone de Beauvoir

Students the world over have relied on biography as an easy, and lazy, way to interpret fiction ever since studying literature became an exam subject. But de Beauvoir herself claimed that writing *She Came to Stay* helped her 'deal with' the trauma of Sartre's affair: just as Françoise finishes off Xavière in order to prove that she is second to no one, so by finishing the book de Beauvoir finished off any notion of herself as second to her philosopher boyfriend.

Françoise decides not to have an affair with Gerbert at the beginning of the book, even though she is attracted to him. She thinks about telling him she loves him but then stops herself: 'She could not say: "I love you." . . . She loved Pierre. There was no room in her life for another love.' Even though Pierre has affairs, she does not want to: she and Pierre are one, indivisible from each other, united by love and work. However, it is obvious to the reader, if not to Françoise, that she is always second to him, not equal. Pierre's work dominates their lives, whilst her novel is only worked on when he doesn't need her at the theatre; whereas she decides not to play the field, he does so consistently, defending himself by saying, '"I no longer enjoy these affaires"'. When she is jealous and he asks her if she minds, she doesn't tell him the truth, because it compromises the image of their 'free' relationship, thus compromising herself. In existentialist terms she is 'inauthentic'.

Pierre and Françoise's relationship is similar to de Beauvoir and Sartre's – freedom and openness is prized above all else; the woman places his work and desire for other women above her own wishes, in de Beauvoir's case forgoing the man that she considered her 'American husband' Nelson Algren because she couldn't leave Sartre – and the novel was based on the trio formed by the writers when Sartre began seeing Olga Kosakievicz. Much to the frustration of later critics who see her as one of the mothers of feminism on paper but a traitor in her life, de Beauvoir always considered herself as less important than Sartre. She, like the Sex she later wrote about, was always second. Perhaps de Beauvoir saw herself as secondary to Sartre because of their relative placings in the extremely competitive agrégation exam when they were students. He came first, she second. However, he was three years older than her, had failed the year before and had a privileged education in the most competitive and exclusive of establishments, the ENS, Ecole Normale Supérieure, whereas she had been to the Sorbonne, which despite its romanticized view outside France, is a free-access, non-entrance-exam university. She was also, and remains, the youngest ever *agrégée* in philosophy. So why did she consistently put him and his work first? Did she, like Françoise, convince herself that her contribution to his philosophy was equal ▶

Interviewer:
'And how do you rank yourself among contemporary writers?'

Simone de Beauvoir:
'I don't know. What is it that one evaluates? The noise, the silence, posterity, the number of readers, the absence of readers, the importance at a given time? I think that readers will read me for some time. At least, that's what my readers tell me. I've contributed something to the discussion of women's problems. I know I have from the letters I receive. As for the literary quality of my work, in the strict sense of the word, I haven't the slightest idea.'

Interview, 'The Art of Fiction' 35, *The Paris Review*, 1965

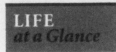
BORN
....
Paris 1908

EDUCATED
....
At the Sorbonne, Paris.
She was the youngest
person ever to pass the
agrégation, a high-level
graduate exam, in
philosophy.

CAREER
....
Teacher, writer, founder
of *Les temps modernes*
(with Jean-Paul Sartre,
Raymond Aron and
Maurice Merleau-Ponty)

BOOKS
....
Novels include *The
Mandarins* (winner of the
Prix Goncourt in 1954,
even though de Beauvoir
was, at 46, not eligible for a
prize awarded to authors
under 35), *The Blood of
Others* and *Les Belles
Images*. Non-fiction
includes *The Second Sex*,
four volumes of memoir
and *A Very Easy Death*, the
story of her mother's
death from cancer.

RELATIONSHIPS
....
Simone de Beauvoir was
Jean-Paul Sartre's friend,
companion, editor and
lover from their time
together at the Sorbonne
until his death in 1980. ▶

Finding a Voice *(continued)*

◀ to his, if not headlining: 'Pierre was on the stage, she was in the audience, and yet for both of them it was the same play being performed in the same theatre. Their life was the same.'? Could she only write the theory, not live it? Or, as *She Came to Stay* suggests, did the mere fact of having a choice – in her case to devote herself to his work in a country which was one of the last in the world to give women the vote – matter more than what she chose?

Françoise and her creator most resemble each other by choosing and acting, thus being 'authentic' in terms of themselves. Françoise finally chooses not to come second and murders her opponent. If she had chosen second place and had accepted Xavière, as she pretends to do throughout the narrative, that choice would also have been 'authentic' because she made it. Neither choice is judged better, but without one the protagonist/ writer doesn't exist: 'Her act was her very own ... She had at last made a choice. She had chosen herself.' Similarly de Beauvoir, in finishing her first novel, chooses to be a writer, separate from Sartre, no longer just his 'audience' and starts her journey to modern iconhood: 'Before writing *She Came to Stay* I spent years fumbling around for a subject. From the moment I began that book I never stopped writing' (*The Prime of Life*). As Françoise recognizes the need to act alone, to take responsibility for what she wants by murdering Xavière, so de Beauvoir recognizes that by completing her first novel she will become a writer independent of her relationship with Sartre: 'By releasing

Françoise, through the agency of a crime, from the dependent position in which her love for Pierre kept her, I regained my own personal autonomy ... writing remains an act for which the responsibility cannot be shared with any other person' (*The Prime of Life*).

De Beauvoir needed to finish this novel in order to find her voice – 'From now on I always had something to say' – and *She Came to Stay* starts her process of intellectual thought for the next half-century: a woman who allows a man to take responsibility for her choices, for her life, as Françoise does with Pierre until the last pages, deprives herself of independence and language. De Beauvoir, now known as much for her writing as for her relationships, may have placed herself as less important than Sartre but history and criticism have considered them as equals, as performers both. ∎

* For a more detailed psychoanalytic discussion of Françoise's murder of Xavière, see Chapter 4 in Toril Moi's *Simone de Beauvoir: The Making of an Intellectual Woman*.

LIFE *at a Glance*
(continued)

◄ She is buried with him in Montparnasse, where they both lived for most of their lives. She also had a long love affair with the American writer Nelson Algren (on which *The Mandarins* is said to be based) which ended when she would not give up Sartre for him.

DIED

Paris 1986

The Pain of Freedom

by Fay Weldon

It is understandable that my editors should ask me to write this piece about *She Came to Stay*, inasmuch as I have just published a novel called *She May Not Leave*. And there are similarities. It is about what happens when you invite a young woman into your life. It does not work out as planned. They do tend to stay. They do tend not to leave. And that can be very, very painful.

I read de Beauvoir's novel when I was a student – I remember to this day the shock of recognition: this is what life for a clever woman in a man's world is like. Youthful appeal and looks are valued above all other qualities. What use is intelligence when there's a pretty girl about? Eyes, male and female both, shift at once from Germaine Greer to Kate Moss.

Then, of course, I identified with the girl: now I identify with the woman. Otherwise not so much has changed in sixty years as one might hope. Except these days we are more strapped for time and money: Paris may not be collapsing around our ears, but few of us, alas, have time to sit around in bars contemplating the minutiae of our feelings and the nature of existentialism; we have to get back to the e-mail or the babysitter. But at least we have novels – we can read *She Came to Stay* if only on the train on the way to work, and immerse ourselves in these other, distant, still compelling lives.

When you come to read this, you will either have finished *She Came to Stay* and want to share your reaction to it with someone, anyone, or you will be leafing through the volume wondering if it is worth your while reading it or not. (It is, of course. It quite takes your breath away with its particular mixture of pain, excitement and description, and affects the way you think, feel and act. Classics do not become classics for nothing.)

Should you come into the second category of casual, page-hopping reader, best not to read on. Turn back to the beginning, or where you left off. There is a shock at the end of *She Came to Stay* it is better not to know in advance. And since it is the end which both makes and breaks the novel, be content to read this in its proper place, as a postscript.

But for those of you who have read it, probably, like me, you felt outraged by the ending. Novels need some other outcome, some other more subtle conclusion, than the murder of one of the protagonists on the last page. It's cheating: it's gross. Sure, Françoise was driven to the deed by her own confusions and Pierre's particular pattern of self-justification and self-indulgence, and Xavière deserved no better for having such a bottomless fund of undeserved self-esteem – but it is still no way for anyone, let alone a feminist, to end a novel. There must be, there is, some other conclusion to sexual jealousy than murder.

It's as if Simone de Beauvoir is using the pages (and us) to say to her real life lover, the existentialist philosopher Jean-Paul Sartre, *'Now see what you made me do!'* The novel is thinly disguised autobiography – ▶

She Came to Stay quite takes your breath away with its particular mixture of pain, excitement and description, and affects the way you think, feel and act. *

The Pain of Freedom *(continued)*

◄ it charts de Beauvoir's three-way relationship with Sartre, who appears in the book as Pierre, his young protégée Olga Kosakievicz (Xavière), and Simone herself (Françoise). And the ending she gives the novel seems almost like an attempt to win Sartre's approval, in this as in so much else. A deed done for the sake of the deed, an existentialist act! It is literature bent into the service of a theory, of a philosophy, and this is why it jars. It is a product of love, not art.

In real life of course de Beauvoir didn't do it: she didn't take a life because 'her act was her very own': no, she lived to be 78, at one with Sartre to the end. Olga, left to her own devices, drifted off soon enough. Simone continued with Sartre – the 'essential love' intact, surviving his many affairs and her own few, writing, thinking, obsessing, her wonderful powers of expression and persuasion never quiet. She went on to win the Prix Goncourt with *The Mandarins*, much public favour worldwide with the feminist classic *The Second Sex*, to lose reputation temporarily with the pro-communist tract *La Marche Longue* – remaining to the end wrong-headed, deluded, passionate in her integrity, drinking too much, and changing the world.

Existentialism is all very well – a life in which the values are to do with exactitude of thought and the minute examination of emotion and action – but is all too easily interpreted as an elaborate excuse for predatory male behaviour in which women collude. Françoise and Pierre's relationship with Xavière is monstrous – exploitative, voyeuristic and sadistic – when seen through the eyes of the twenty-first century. But what a novel!

'Women, you owe her everything,' was said upon de Beauvoir's death in 1986. If not everything, certainly a great deal. Others worked for political and practical equality for women – her concern was for their emotional and intellectual dignity. If women could only reason their way out of their emotional dependency on men, all would yet be well between the genders.

Throughout the novel Françoise struggles to subdue jealousy, seen as the most despicable of emotions, almost to the point of denying its existence – let alone as a justification for thought or deed. If women need no longer be rivals for male affection, the theory went, and settle for the higher good of intimacy and a close companionship of thought, then women could surely be set free.

True enough: but how this freedom hurts in practice! So much so that since those days female pride has taken a different route: rather than claim sexual freedom for themselves, they claim a right to a faithful man. Infidelity, taken seriously, ends in divorce, upset children, the breakdown of the old society – and, alas, it seems we are not born to be monogamous.

But how they live, Pierre, Françoise and Xavière, in a Paris on the brink of war. Taut, extreme, nervy, watchful. They work in the theatre, sleep in rented rooms in cheap hotels, live in cafés, worry about the ▶

❝ Françoise and Pierre's relationship with Xavière is monstrous – exploitative, voyeuristic and sadistic – when seen through the eyes of the twenty-first century. ❞

The Pain of Freedom (continued)

◄ approaching cataclysm, gossip, tear one another to bits, investigate their own feelings immoderately, find themselves in the wrong bed, on the wrong side of a too-thin wall – and how I long for Françoise to say to Pierre, *oh get lost*, because she's worth ten of him, but of course she won't. She loves him. ■

Have You Read?

Other books by or about Simone de Beauvoir

The Woman Destroyed
Three stories of three women at different
stages of their lives. In the first, 'The Age of
Discretion', a successful academic must find a
way to face the dwindling of her career and
her life as old age approaches. In the second,
'Monologue', a young mother alone on New
Year's Eve rails against her husband who has
left her, taking their son with him. Finally,
in the title piece, middle-aged Monique
discovers the cost of investing her whole self
in her marriage when her husband starts an
affair with a younger woman.

The Mandarins
The Second World War has ended and a
group of French intellectuals must re-
examine their loves and lives. Said to be
based on de Beauvoir's own relationships
with Camus, Sartre and Nelson Algren, it
offers both a love story and philosophical
debate.

Simone de Beauvoir: Memoirs
(various volumes)
Although de Beauvoir is perhaps best known
for *The Second Sex* and *The Mandarins*, in
the latter part of her career she produced
many extraordinary volumes of memoir.
These give a fascinating insight into such
subjects as her upbringing (*Memoirs of a
Dutiful Daughter*), her experience of the
ageing process (*Old Age*), and her time
with Jean-Paul Sartre (*Adieux: A Farewell
to Sartre*). ▶

Have You Read? *(continued)*

The Second Sex

De Beauvoir's landmark feminist text weaves
together contemporary interviews, facts and
myths to create a hugely comprehensive
overview of what it meant, in post-war
France and America, to have been born a
woman. Centred around de Beauvoir's
theory of 'otherness', whereby women have
only ever been defined in relation to men,
The Second Sex uses a breathtaking range
of examples from anthropology, literature,
mythology and politics to explore the
changing role of the female gender
throughout history.

Simone de Beauvoir: a biography
Deirdre Bair

The definitive official biography of de
Beauvoir, drawn from extensive interviews
towards the end of her life, as well as
previously unseen (and still unpublished)
private correspondence with both Jean-Paul
Sartre and Nelson Algren. A superb overview
of de Beauvoir's fiction, her philosophy, and
the buzz of intellectual life in Paris before,
during and after the Second World War.

Simone de Beauvoir
(Lives of Modern Women)
Lisa Appignanesi

A short, compelling and accessible biography.

Simone de Beauvoir: The Making of an
Intellectual Woman
Toril Moi

An academic approach to de Beauvoir's life
and works, from a leading feminist critic. ∎

If You Loved This,
You Might Like...

The Golden Notebook
Doris Lessing
A classic of feminist and political history,
this is the story of a young divorced novelist,
Anna Wulf, who, faced with writer's block
and fed up with failed relationships, fights
her fears about descending into madness by
writing down her feelings and experiences in
four coloured notebooks: black for writing,
red for politics, yellow for relationships and
blue for diarizing the everyday. Eventually a
fifth, the golden notebook, supersedes the
others and helps Anna find her identity.

A Room of One's Own
Virginia Woolf
First published in 1928, Woolf's feminist
treatise remains, sadly, still pertinent in many
respects. Like de Beauvoir's work, this is a
landmark of women's writing but, unlike *The
Second Sex*, it is very short and witty, a great
introduction to twentieth-century feminist
writing.

Gigi and *Chéri*
Colette
Another great French writer, who put
women's experience, often scandalously, at
the heart of her books. These two novels
show two different aspects of a courtesan's
life in early twentieth-century France: that
of the young woman training for such a life
but resisting it, and that of the older woman,
eking out the last days of her relationship
with a younger man whom she has been
training in the art of love. ▶

If You Loved This . . . *(continued)*

◄ *The Outsider*
Albert Camus

A classic work of existentialism, by a writer who claimed he wasn't an existentialist. Meursault lives his life nonchalantly and with little engagement with anything, not even the death of his mother, until an act of violence changes his life for ever. A book that is easy to read but difficult to forget.

The Plague
Albert Camus

One of the most readable of all existentialist novels, *The Plague* is the story of Oran, a city in Algeria that is taken over by a plague. It is also an allegory for the occupation of France in the Second World War. The novel's narrator is Dr Bernard Rieux who must battle the authorities' indifference in order to save the city and its citizens.

Being and Nothingness
Jean-Paul Sartre

It is almost impossible to talk about the life of Simone de Beauvoir without acknowledging the influence upon her of Jean-Paul Sartre, her constant companion, both intellectually and emotionally, for some fifty years. *Being and Nothingness*, which Sartre wrote largely while in a prisoner-of-war camp during the early part of the Second World War, is widely seen as being the 'Bible' of existentialism, a hugely influential work of philosophy which challenges the reader to confront the fundamental dilemmas of human freedom, responsibility and action. Although Sartre increasingly distanced himself from *Being and Nothingness* towards the end of his life, for de Beauvoir it remained the defining model of her own beliefs, the basis of everything that she wrote, both fiction and memoir.

The Words
Jean-Paul Sartre
Sartre's autobiography of his childhood is funny as well as thought-provoking. ■

Find Out More

To experience de Beauvoir's world, visit the Left Bank of Paris, especially the cafés and bars. Notable locations include the Café de Flore, 172 boulevard Saint-Germain, 75006 Paris (http://www.cafe-de-flore.com) and Les Deux Magots, 170 boulevard Saint-Germain, 75006.

Cimetière de Montparnasse, 3 boulevard Edgar Quinet, 75014 Paris

De Beauvoir was buried in the same grave as Sartre. It can be visited at the Cimetière de Montparnasse, along with those of Samuel Beckett, Man Ray, Jean Seberg and Guy de Maupassant.

Stanford Encyclopedia of Philosophy

A dynamic online reference with information about de Beauvoir as well as Sartre, Camus and existentialism. See http://plato.stanford.edu/archives/fall2004/entries/beauvoir/.

The Blood of Others

Directed by Claude Chabrol, this adaptation of *Le sang des autres* starred Jodie Foster and Sam Neill.

www.theparisreview.com/media/4444_DEBEAUVOIR.pdf

A long and detailed interview with the author, which took place in 1965. Fascinating.